A: *A world-class intelligence organization run by women who really* know *their foundation.*

WHEN NIKKI LANIER signs up as a cosmetics rep at Carrie Mae, it's hardly her idea of a dream job. With a degree in linguistics and a hard-core workout regimen, the twenty-six-year-old redhead once had hopes for a real career. But unemployed and desperate to escape life at home with her nagging mother, she'll try anything—even selling makeup to housewives. Soon, Nikki learns that the powder and lipstick are simply cover-up for the Carrie Mae Foundation: a secret organization of international espionage and high-tech mascara founded for the purpose of "helping women everywhere."

Whisked off to Thailand with the legendary Carrie Mae agent Val Robinson, Nikki is soon in over her head. Between investigating the abduction of a human rights activist, tracking down a murderous arms dealer, keeping up with her wildly dangerous new partner, and occasionally trying to date a hunk who may or may not be CIA, Nikki has to use all the courage and cosmetic technology she's got to bring down the bad guys and get out alive.

With the support of the colorful Carrie Mae crew, Nikki will overcome even the most harrowing obstacles—including incessant phone calls from her mother—or die trying.

BULLETPROOF
MASCARA

a novel
BETHANY MAINES

ATRIA PAPERBACK
NEW YORK LONDON TORONTO SYDNEY

ATRIA PAPERBACK

A Division of Simon & Schuster, Inc.
1230 Avenue of the Americas
New York, NY 10020

First Atria Paperback edition March 2010

ATRIA PAPERBACK and colophon are trademarks of Simon & Schuster, Inc.

For information about special discounts for bulk purchases, please contact Simon & Schuster Special Sales at 1-866-506-1949 or business@simonandschuster.com.

The Simon & Schuster Speakers Bureau can bring authors to your live event. For more information or to book an event, contact the Simon & Schuster Speakers Bureau at 1-866-248-3049 or visit our website at www.simonspeakers.com.

Manufactured in the United States of America

10 9 8 7 6 5 4 3 2 1

Library of Congress Cataloging-in-Publication Data

Maines, Bethany.
  Bulletproof mascara / Bethany Maines.—1st Atria paperback ed.
    p.   cm.
  1. Women spies—Fiction. 2. Cosmetics industry—Fiction.
  3. Undercover operations—Fiction. I. Title.
  PS3613.A34964B85 2010
  813'.6—dc22   2009014250

ISBN 978-0-7432-9277-1
ISBN 978-1-4165-4635-1 (ebook)

To Jennae

After the Interview

"Excuse me, Nicole?" asked the man next to her at the bar in a voice like Jack Daniel's whiskey. "Would you care to be my wife?"

Nicole Lanier looked up from the depths of her vodka martini–drenched misery. The man was holding her passport, plucked from the debris scattered by her purse when she'd flung it down in fury on the hotel bar. She had noticed him earlier, despite her headlong rush to become an alcoholic. He had been speaking into a cell phone, his back to her—a solid wall of well-tailored gray suit—his voice set at pissed-off growl. He flipped her passport closed and held it out to her with a friendly smile.

"It's Nikki," she corrected, dazedly smiling back at him.

"Nikki," he said, with a nod. His eyes were a warm dark brown, sleepy yet observant. She tried to guess his ethnicity. Not quite black or Italian or Hispanic or white. Not quite anything in particular, but maybe a lot of everything.

"The question stands. Would you care to be my wife?" The

question didn't make any more sense the second time around, but it sounded good coming from him.

"Sorry?" asked Nikki, uncertain if she had heard him correctly or if the vodka was just now hitting bottom.

"Just over my left shoulder there's a man out on the terrace talking to a man in golf clothes."

Nikki wondered if he had escaped from the group home. Brushing an errant red curl back behind her ear, she leaned to her right and looked through the tall windows of the hotel bar. There was indeed a pair of men on the terrace, one in a navy suit, the other covered in an obscene amount of plaid. She returned her gaze to the stranger with a questioning look.

"Yes?" she prodded, one of her eyebrows raised in a way that made her strongly resemble her father when he was being sarcastic: it was a look her mother hated.

"His name is Jirair Sarkassian. He's a very big man in shipping and a very important asset to my company. When he's done talking to the man in golf clothes he's going to come in here, shake my hand, and ask to meet my wife."

"So why don't you introduce him to your wife?" asked Nikki.

"I haven't got a wife."

"But he thinks you do?"

"I told him I did."

"Then I can see why he would think you do. But why would you tell him that you're married if you're not?"

"Because he has a sister and I have a boss who believes in customer service."

"Lots of men have sisters; that doesn't mean you have to get married. She can't be *that* bad," Nikki objected reasonably.

"You wouldn't say that if you'd met his sister. She's . . . difficult."

"Oh." Nikki tried to imagine what kind of woman would be so

intolerable. "Is she horse-faced or something?" For guys, *difficult* was usually code for either ugly or smart.

"Ha. I wish she were horse-faced. Horse-faced I wouldn't mind. Look," he said, running his fingers over the closely cropped stubble of his brown hair, "I had a friend who was going to help me with this, but she's stuck in traffic. All you have to do is shake his hand, say, 'Nice to meet you,' and then make a graceful exit."

"What if he wants me to have lunch with you or something?" Nikki asked, taking a sip of her martini.

"Tell him you have plans and can't possibly join us."

For a moment, Nikki was tempted. What was five minutes of her time, anyway? She reached for her drink again, and as she leaned forward she saw the dark silhouette of a shoulder holster peeking from the man's suit jacket, and in her mind the headline "Canadian Gangster Kills Girl in Bar" splashed across the top of a newspaper. Then she shook her head; she couldn't imagine anything that sounded less Canadian than *gangster*. He was probably just an overvigilant businessman, but getting involved with a guy who packed concealed weapons was not on her list of things to do that day, no matter how good-looking he was. Pretending she hadn't noticed the gun, Nikki picked up her martini and finished it in one long swallow. Setting it down firmly, so that it made a solid sound on the bar, she slid it into place next to her other empty glasses.

"Sorry, buddy," she said, counting out cash for the bill and tip, then shoveling the contents of her purse back into her bag. "I'll give you an A-plus for bravado, but a C-minus for believability. I mean, come on, I wouldn't even buy that from a romance novel."

The bartender came back, and Nikki started to push the pile of money across the bar, but the stranger put his hand firmly over hers.

The shock of physical contact ran from his fingers and through her arm like an electrical current, holding Nikki paralyzed. She found herself staring at their hands where they overlapped on top of the pink Canadian money.

"Put it on my room tab," the man told the bartender, moving his hand away. Nikki wanted to grab it back and hold on—it had felt safe and comfortable. She felt an irrational twinge of anger at herself for wanting to hold a stranger's hand.

"No, really," she said, transferring her irritation to the man. "I don't need you to pay for me." Buying drinks was a way to buy leverage, and Nikki wasn't going to fall for it. The brown-eyed man gave a nod to the bartender, who shrugged and walked off without her money. Nikki felt a surge of exasperation as she stuffed her cash back into her purse, stubbornly leaving the tip. Why did guys always stick together?

She shut her purse with a fierce snap and stepped off the barstool. The ground took an odd lurch as she stepped on it, but she still had one hand on the bar for stability, so she didn't think it showed. Maybe finishing that martini hadn't been the best idea.

"I'm sorry, Nikki," the man said, perhaps sensing he had offended her somehow, "but I'm really in a bind here. Come on. It'll only take a minute, and you'll be saving my bacon." And then he smiled. Nikki found herself smiling back.

"Please," he said, sensing her hesitation, and touching her lightly on the arm. It wasn't a touch as much as a suggestion of contact. His fingers barely brushed the fabric of her sleeve, and inside her stylish yet businesslike jacket, Nikki felt the hairs on her arm stand upright. "No risk, no fun," the man said, with an expression that suggested he was both of those things.

Nikki felt herself waver. She shook her head, trying to clear it and firm up her resolve. Everything seemed a little fuzzy. She didn't want to do this, did she?

Burbank

The problem with Burbank, Nikki decided, was that it wasn't in black-and-white. The low-slung airport was perfect for some tragic forties drama; they even wheeled the stairs up to the doors of the airplane. All she needed now was a man in a trench coat.

She ignored that train of thought and exited the plane, swinging her backpack up onto her shoulders; she staggered a little as it connected firmly with her back. Her feet followed the arrows on the baggage claim signs while her head swiveled around, taking in the scene. Nobody was wearing a trench coat; flip-flops and micro jean skirts seemed to be the order of the day, hardly the Bogart-esque style Nikki had been picturing.

Since she was already carrying all of her belongings on her back, she avoided the mob of people who were lining up for the baggage carousel and looked around for someone holding a card with her name on it. But no one in the crowd seemed to be looking for her. Nikki found a bench near the double sliding doors and checked her watch. She was a little bit early.

Sitting down, she took out her cell phone and turned the power back on. It cycled through the On sequence and then declared that she had three new messages. Nikki dialed voice mail and then dutifully listened to each message from her mother. It was raining in Tacoma, where had she put the remote, and hadn't Nikki landed yet? Nikki hit Erase following each message and flipped her phone closed, determined not to return any of the calls. Her resolution was rendered obsolete when the phone rang. Nikki picked it up with a sigh.

"I thought you only packed that ridiculous backpack," said Nell without preamble.

"I did," Nikki agreed, knowing exactly what her mother was leading up to.

"I was just in your room, and the closet is empty. Where are all your clothes?"

"Most of them were old," Nikki said, stalling for time. "I had stuff in there from high school."

"There were some expensive clothes in there! What did you do with them?"

"Took them to the Goodwill," Nikki mumbled.

"What?!" The screech echoed across the airwaves, and Nikki held the phone away from her ear as Nell continued at full volume. "I paid for those clothes! You had no right . . ." Nikki held the phone out even farther until the words were just a high-pitched jumble. When the pitch dropped, she put the phone back to her ear.

"I am very disappointed in you," Nell said.

"Sorry, Mom," Nikki said, paying more attention to the passing crowd than to the conversation. She knew the script by heart.

"Hmph," Nell snorted, not placated by Nikki's rote apology. "I suppose you took the remote to the Goodwill, too?"

"No. Did you look under the couch cushions?"

"Yes!" she snapped. "And in the drawer and under the couch. I may not have gone to college like some people, but I'm not an idiot."

"How about under the newspaper? Sometimes it gets lost under the newspaper." Nikki ignored the jab about college; it was barely a two on the Nell scale of snide. There was a silence on the other end of the line, and Nikki knew her mother hadn't looked under the newspaper.

"That's a stupid place to put the remote. I don't know why it would be there."

"I agree, but sometimes the paper just gets spread out over it on accident." Nikki kept her tone soothing. She heard rustling in the background, followed by a click and the theme song from *Jeopardy*.

"Are you sure about this job?" asked Nell, changing subjects. "I thought you wanted something in your field. Selling cosmetics clearly isn't something you're trained for."

"Linguistics jobs weren't exactly hopping out of the woodwork, and besides, I won't be selling cosmetics. The Carrie Mae charity foundation is different, and it's a really good opportunity."

"Do you even know what you're going to be doing?"

"Well, no," said Nikki, squirming, "but that's why I'm going to do training."

"I just think it's weird, is all. I mean, why you? Why did Mrs. Merrivel offer you a job?" Nikki didn't know why Mrs. Merrivel, the Carrie Mae recruiter, had offered her the job, but she wasn't about to admit that to her mother.

"OK, well, I'm at the airport now, and I have to look for my ride. Gotta go."

"Well, you could call me next time. I'm only up here worrying myself to death about your safety." She could hear Alex Trebek introducing the contestants.

"Yeah, I'll call. Bye, Mom."

"Bye, sweetie."

Nikki hung up the phone and ran her fingers through her hair. Worse than simply irritating her, Nell always managed to plant the seed of doubt that Nikki had spent careful time weeding out. Today was no exception.

She checked her watch again and scanned the room: still no one. She was starting to sweat.

Another unbearable minute ticked past, and then an older man in a rumpled green Tommy Bahama shirt and navy slacks entered through the doors opposite her. He was tall and fit and, but for the wrinkled shirt, managed to look distinguished. Pausing by Nikki, he placed his foot on a bench and used his bent leg as a steady writing surface for a yellow legal pad. He paused with pen poised over the paper and then flipped over his left hand to consult something written on the palm. From where she was sitting Nikki could see that it was "Nikki Lanier."

"Excuse me," Nikki said.

"Just a sec," the man said without looking up. "Got to get this spelled correctly."

"It's *i*, then *e*," corrected Nikki.

"Thanks," the man said, and then held the sign out at arm's length to view the results. "Now, then," he said, tucking the pad under his arm and putting the cap on the pen. "What can I do for you, young lady?" Nikki smiled. She liked this man; he had an absent-minded professor sort of aura.

"I think I'm who you're supposed to meet."

"You are?" asked the man with surprise. He flipped his hand over and read it again. "You're Nikki Lanier?"

"Yes," said Nikki, smiling again. "That's me."

"Oh," the man said, and pulled out the pad with her name on it. "Well, I guess I don't need this." He seemed a little disappointed.

"No, I guess not."

"Oh, well," said the man, shrugging it off. "Should we get your luggage?" he asked, looking around as if expecting suitcases to appear.

"Nope, this is it," Nikki said, grabbing her pack and standing up.

"Good heavens," the man said. "Are you sure you're with Carrie Mae?"

"Sort of," said Nikki. "I've never actually sold anything."

"Ah, well," the man said kindly, "some people aren't meant for sales." He smiled, and Nikki felt a sudden relief. It was true; she wasn't meant for sales, and that was just that.

"Well, this way," said the man, and walked back toward the doors.

Nikki followed him out into the blinding California sunshine and toward the parking garage. His car was a large black Mercedes and spotless—a power car. Nikki glanced at her escort. His lanky figure was set off by a head full of white hair, and he carried himself with confidence; he was obviously not a mere chauffeur.

"Just shove those clubs over and put your pack in the trunk," said the man, popping the trunk with his key fob as they reached the car. "It's why I'm late," he said, unlocking the car. "I was playing a few holes with the fellas, and the game ran long." Nikki moved the golf clubs as instructed and went to sit in the passenger seat.

"Say," the man said as she closed the door. "I guess I know your name, but you probably haven't a clue who I am."

"Well, no," confessed Nikki.

"John Merrivel," said the man, and they shook hands. "And you should be more careful about wandering off with strange men." Nikki grimaced unhappily and sighed. He was absolutely right, and after her conversation with Mrs. Merrivel, she'd promised herself that she would be less trusting and more vigilant.

"Mrs. Merrivel said that, too. Apparently, I wasn't listening very carefully."

Mr. Merrivel laughed. "Well, some things take practice," he said. "But what I want to know is why *not* wandering off with strange men is something you need to practice?" he asked quizzically.

"There was this thing . . . in Canada . . ." Nikki stumbled around, looking for words to describe the fiasco that had been her most recent trip to Canada. "It was kind of a mess," she finished lamely. "It's where I met Mrs. Merrivel."

"Ah," Mr. Merrivel said, as if she really had explained everything. "Well, as long as it worked out all right in the end."

"It did!" affirmed Nikki. She ran over the events in her mind; it had worked out . . . mostly. "I'm here, anyway," she said with a shrug. "It was nice of Mrs. Merrivel to send you to pick me up." A change of topic was probably for the best; he was the boss's husband after all.

"To tell the truth," he said, easing the car out of the airport parking garage, "I wasn't supposed to pick you up today, but there seems to have been a bit of a dustup at the ranch over your arrival, so Mrs. M sent me to bring you round to our house while she gets it all straightened out."

"I'm staying with you?" Nikki asked, nervous at the prospect of being Mrs. Merrivel's houseguest. "I thought I was going to some sort of training center."

"Well, you will eventually, I expect." Nikki looked doubtful. "It'll probably only be a night or two," said Mr. Merrivel cheerfully. "And we're perfectly good hosts, I assure you. None of our guests have died since that time in '92." He waggled his eyebrows comically, and Nikki couldn't help but laugh.

"Wait," Nikki said, catching up to the rest of Mr. Merrivel's comment. "Dustup? Over me?" Nikki was worried that her potential job was in peril.

"Not to worry," said Mr. Merrivel. "Just that Connie's got a bee in her bonnet about you starting late."

"Late? How late am I?" Nikki was confused. Mrs. Merrivel hadn't said anything about starting late.

"A couple of weeks, I think. Not really my department, you understand. More the wife's thingie. Connie doesn't like to bend the rules so much, but I expect Mrs. M will get her way. She usually does, my little Miranda."

"That was my impression of her," agreed Nikki, trying to keep her tone diplomatic.

"She's a bit of a bulldog," Mr. Merrivel said, smiling fondly. Nikki thought Mrs. Merrivel was probably more of a Rottweiler in poodle's clothing, but didn't mention it.

They passed through smoggy Burbank, and Nikki noticed with a comforting feeling of familiarity that they were on I-5 going north. If they stayed on this little ribbon of concrete, in another seventeen hours she would be standing on her mother's doorstep. Nikki laughed at herself a little; it was ridiculous to feel comforted by an interstate. Especially since she didn't want to go home at all. At least, most of her didn't. There was a little voice in the back of her head that was insisting that this entire escapade was doomed to failure. The voice sounded suspiciously like her mother's.

Mr. M turned on the radio. He flipped channels for a while before settling on an oldies station. They caught the last half of

"Last Train to Clarksville" before it ended and the DJ began to talk. After a moment of chatter, the DJ stated that they were listening to K-Earth 101 and this was the Mamas and the Papas with "California Dreamin'."

"And the skyyy is grayyyy," harmonized Nikki, unintentionally singing out loud. She stopped moments later, blushing, but Mr. M picked up the next line as if singing with strangers were perfectly natural.

"Say," he said as the song ended, "we sound pretty good."

The DJ began to talk again, and Mr. M snorted with irritation. "Let's see what we've got in the old CD player. Maybe we can find something else to sing to." He flipped through several CDs, listening to the beginning of each before punching up the next one.

"Mr. M?" Nikki said, distractedly feeling through her own thoughts. His finger was still hovering over the Fast Forward button.

"Did you just call me Mr. M?" Mr. Merrivel asked. Nikki paused guiltily, and hesitantly she nodded. "Ha. I like it! I always call Miranda Mrs. M, but she just thinks I'm strange. What's up?"

She smiled, relieved that her habit of shortening names hadn't offended him.

"Well, frankly, I'm a little nervous."

"About the job?" he asked, nodding sympathetically.

"Well, I'm not really sure what I'm expected to do. And I didn't realize I'd be behind in the training. And I don't know if I'll be able to catch up, because I don't really know what kind of training it is. And I really want this job. Well, *a job* anyway. And . . . I'm just nervous." Nikki stopped herself before she devolved into a blubbering fountain of uncertainty. She hadn't meant to spill that much; she'd meant to ask for a few useful hints about the new job, not reveal her quaking Jell-O center. Mr. M's cheerful face wore an expression of seriousness for a moment.

"They didn't tell you what you'd be doing?"

"Mrs. M just said she'd tell me all about it when I got here," Nikki said.

"Hmm." He scratched his forehead. "Well, I'm sure it will be fine."

"What will be fine?" asked Nikki, wondering if one more time she'd gotten herself in over her head.

Mr. M shook his head as if to dismiss her question and his thoughts at the same time. "Not my place. But trust me, everything will be fine. If you want this job, it's yours. And since you seem to be a very bright, in-shape person, I see no reason why you shouldn't be able to excel."

His calm statement of confidence in her abilities momentarily relaxed Nikki. And then she began to worry about being "in shape." What had he meant by that? What kind of charity foundation required people to be in shape? Her ribbon of thoughts was snipped short by the musical jangling of Mr. M's cell phone.

"Sounds like the wife," said Mr. M, reaching for the phone. "Hello, sweet pea!" he proclaimed. "Yes, mission complete, got her right here!" He was silent for a moment, listening.

"Hmm," he said. "Well, yes, but I'm not sure . . ." He trailed off, listening to Mrs. M. "Nope, it's not a problem." He glanced at Nikki. "Yup, love you, too. Bye."

"Everything OK?" Nikki asked.

"Just fine, but Connie's being a stick-in-the-mud, so until Mrs. M can get all your paperwork signed off at headquarters you'll have to stay with us."

"How long will that take?" asked Nikki, worry lines furrowing into her forehead.

"A couple of days. A week at most. Not to worry. We'll think of something to do. I don't suppose you play golf?" Nikki shook her head, still worried. "Want to learn?" he asked with a cheerful grin.

Permanent Record

"Well, it's very clear that a bunch of women live here," Nikki said.

"Yes," Connie agreed. "And in line with our company philosophy."

The week with the Merrivels had flown by, but eventually Mrs. Merrivel announced that Nikki would be meeting Connie for a tour of the facilities on the following day at 8:00 A.M. sharp. Mr. M had gotten up early to drive her over the winding Santa Clarita roads and up to a wide plantation-style property that encompassed several acres and was surrounded by a rock wall and arching iron gates.

"The company philosophy?" Nikki was trying to ignore the alarm buzzing in her brain.

"Making the lives of women everywhere a little better!" Connie looked at Nikki as if she'd asked what color the sky was. Connie Hinton was tall and broad-shouldered with a wide, flat bottom. She reminded Nikki of a basketball player she had known in college.

"I haven't been with the company very long," Nikki said, by way of explanation. Connie sniffed with disapproval.

The alarm was flashing purple now. The tour really hadn't gone as she had expected. First there had been the nondisclosure form with the clause on death and dismemberment, and then there had been the guns. Nikki was pretty sure that most charity foundations didn't have their own gun range. Not to mention an obstacle course and scenario training ground. The computer lab and the dorms had seemed reasonable. Connie had been very keen on the dorms: they all had en suite bathrooms. And now they were standing in one of the bathrooms and admiring the multiple outlets, dual sinks, marble tile, and built-in gun safe. It was a very pretty gun safe—Carrie Mae purple.

"Um," said Nikki, sensing that she had better ask something before her brain melted. "So this, er, training center"—she wasn't sure what else to call the place—"how does it fit in with that philosophy?"

"Ah," said Connie, smiling as though Nikki had finally done something worthwhile. "We here at the Carrie Mae West Coast Training Facility train operatives to carry out the Carrie Mae philosophy in many ways. Whether it's navigating the international red tape to allow women to work with Carrie Mae or through the use of more clandestine methods to ensure that they have the opportunity to live peaceful lives."

Nikki wondered if there was a brochure somewhere that Connie had memorized, and if so, why hadn't Nikki seen it? Mrs. Merrivel hadn't said anything about things like this, had she? She remembered Mrs. M using the word *clandestine*, but at the time she had thought it meant things like bribing border guards. Now she was beginning to think it involved things that needed a gun safe.

"So the Carrie Mae charity foundation is actually some sort of SWAT team for women?" Nikki asked slowly.

"No," Connie said icily. "We are not about police action."

"Oh," Nikki said, laughing with embarrassment and relief. "I thought . . . my mistake. It just sounded like you were some sort of international espionage organization. Really, I must have misunderstood. So silly of me." She knew she was babbling.

"The Carrie Mae Foundation is *also* an international espionage organization," Connie interrupted. "Our public face remains very committed to bringing help to women worldwide in the form of medicine, education, and financial assistance."

"But your not-public face . . ." Nikki noticed that the vocabulary portion of her brain had developed an unsettling disconnect with her speech center; she had no words to wrap around her thoughts.

"The confidential side of the foundation works toward the same goals, improving the lives of women, but we use slightly different methods—different parts of the same machine. Let's go back up to the house; Mrs. Merrivel will be waiting."

Connie walked past Nikki, giving her no time to ask further questions. Nikki couldn't decide if that was a good thing or not. She rode back to the main house with her face frozen into a polite half-smile of disbelief.

Mrs. Merrivel was waiting for them in an office with a long oval table ringed with chairs. A thick manila folder sat neatly at one end. But it was Mrs. Merrivel who commanded Nikki's attention: she was petite, over sixty, and scary. From the moment Nikki had laid eyes on her at the Carrie Mae recruiting meeting she had found the older woman's energy, efficiency, and perfect appearance intimidating. And a week spent living in her house had not done much to diminish that impression.

"Nikki!" exclaimed Mrs. Merrivel, coming forward to give a hug. Her beautifully tinted brown hair brushed against Nikki's nose, and Nikki returned the gesture gingerly. She wasn't practiced in the art of the hug as greeting. "How was your tour? I hope you found the facilities to your liking."

"Well, yes, but . . ." said Nikki.

"But what?" Mrs. Merrivel asked, taking her seat at the head of the table.

"You're running a spy farm in the middle of California!" Nikki exclaimed, unable to hold it in any longer.

"I know," Mrs. Merrivel said cheerfully. "It's great, isn't it? So convenient to be able to do our training inside the States."

"But . . ." said Nikki again.

"But what?" repeated Mrs. Merrivel, a single wrinkle forming between her brows.

"You're makeup ladies! Carrie Mae sells makeup. Ding dong, I'm with Carrie Mae. Try my blusher. You're just makeup ladies. I mean . . ." Nikki became aware of an overwhelming silence filling up the room as she spoke. Mrs. Merrivel had pursed her lips as if she smelled something distasteful. Nikki knew she should shut up, but couldn't.

"I was at the recruiting meeting in Canada. You said the Carrie Mae Foundation helped with education and medical needs in the third world. You didn't say anything about guns and . . ." Nikki waved her hands, trying capture in gesture what she couldn't in words. "You didn't say anything about spies. I think I would have remembered."

"Well, we can't, of course," said Mrs. Merrivel, smiling sweetly again. "But I had hoped that by now you would have gathered that Carrie Mae is not just about makeup. And, by the way, I resent our other team members being described as 'just makeup ladies.'

Our sales consultants provide needed income for their families and affordable, quality cosmetics for women everywhere. Our sales consultants are the backbone of Carrie Mae and the heart of America. Please do not take them for granted or belittle their status simply because they have chosen not to pursue corporate jobs." Mrs. Merrivel's rebuke was delivered in a quiet tone of gentle disappointment.

Nikki hung her head. "Sorry, Mrs. Merrivel," she said meekly.

"That's quite all right. Did you enjoy the tour of the ranch?"

"Yes, it was very nice," said Nikki dutifully.

"I'm glad you thought so. Now what do you think about joining us?"

Nikki stared. Of all the unbelievable parts about this place this was the one that required the largest suspension of disbelief. There was no way that they could want her.

"Why me?" she asked at last, unable to think of anything better.

"Why wouldn't we want you, Nikki?" asked Mrs. Merrivel, looking shocked.

"Well, Connie told me about the other girls, and they're all, you know, super soldiers or whatever. I don't think I'm . . . I don't think I'm what you're looking for." In response, Mrs. Merrivel flipped open the folder in front of her.

"Nikki," she said, leafing through the pages, "I have been over your entire record. You got your bachelor's degree in linguistics, with minors in classical literature—where you learned Italian and Latin—and physical education."

"I took a lot of aerobics classes," mumbled Nikki.

"And a lot of judo and martial arts classes," Mrs. Merrivel added, flipping a few more pages. "By high school you had acquired full command of French and Spanish."

"My father is Quebecois," Nikki said. "We always spoke French at home."

"Yes, I notice here in your grade-school record that you attended Catholic school in Quebec through third grade. Then you moved to Washington after your parents divorced. So you hold dual citizenship with Canada, is that correct?"

"What do you mean 'in my grade-school record'?" asked Nikki, ignoring Mrs. M's question. "Where did you get all that information?"

"I looked up your permanent record," Mrs. Merrivel said, flipping a page.

"That's a myth," Nikki said in disbelief. "There's no such thing as a 'permanent record.' That's just something adults make up to scare kids, like the bogeyman."

"My point is, Nikki," Mrs. Merrivel said, ignoring Nikki's interjection, "you hold dual citizenship, speak five languages, have a firm grounding in martial arts and a sharp mind. You're exactly what Carrie Mae is looking for. So, what do you think?"

"I think I'm seriously reconsidering my position on the bogeyman," Nikki said, focusing on details because she couldn't take in the big picture. They weren't seriously measuring her for a pair of James Bond pumps, were they? She knew very well that James Bond did not wear pumps. Spies were boys, or really hot chicks who had a more active sex life than she did.

"What do you think about working at Carrie Mae?" Mrs. Merrivel asked, ignoring Nikki's comment.

Nikki chewed her lip. She had said she would do anything for a job, but this wasn't what she'd had in mind. But her mother would have a field day if she returned home still trailing the stench of unemployment. Or worse yet, what if she tried it and they found out Mrs. Merrivel was wrong? What if she couldn't do the job?

"What if I fail?" she asked, blushing as she unintentionally spoke out loud.

"Give us your best, and we won't let you," said Mrs. Merrivel.

It was a big decision. Not safe. The road less traveled. Different. Her mother wouldn't approve.

"Yes," Nikki said. "I'll do it. Where do I sign?"

Tactics

"That was terrible! Your strategy was stupid, your formations sloppy! You couldn't hit the broad side of a barn with a Howitzer if you were standing next to it. And you!" Mrs. Boyer, the physical training instructor, pointed an accusing finger at Dina, two spots down from Nikki. "You are wearing blue eyeliner!"

Nikki smothered a laugh, but not before her shoulders gave a revealing twitch. With two quick strides, Mrs. Boyer was bellowing in Nikki's ear.

"Don't think I didn't notice that your socks don't match, Miss Lanier!"

"There was a mix-up in the laundry!" protested Nikki weakly.

Mrs. Boyer threw her hands up in disgust and turned back to the rest of the squad. "We are Carrie Mae, ladies! We do not have mix-ups in the laundry! We are always impeccably dressed, and we always achieve our objective. If I tell you to take that hill, then I expect you to take that hill, and I expect you to take it in style. I do not want excuses. I want success!"

Mrs. Boyer's vicious glance raked the line of assembled women, but little by little, Nikki watched her reel her anger back in.

"Give me three laps of the compound before you turn in," Mrs. Boyer said with a dismissive sniff. Dejectedly, the squad began their jog with leaden feet.

"I hate this!" Ellen gasped as they rounded the corner. Ellen's comfortable figure, short gray hair, and pleasant round face gave the impression that she ought to have been hovering over her grandchildren, not playing war games in the high deserts of California.

"Maybe you shouldn't have sucked, then!" said Dina, bounding by like a gazelle.

"We didn't suck," Nikki muttered. "Dina's the one who gave the orders."

"What do you expect from a woman who wears blue eyeliner?" Jenny said, jogging up beside them and eyeing Dina's back in disgust. "I mean, has she not seen a *Cosmo* since 1984?" Jenny's accent was Southern—Georgian, maybe—and just as manicured as her bright pink nails. She had long blond hair, long tan legs, and a perfect beauty queen figure that Nikki envied.

"She did follow all the rules," Ellen said, her tone split between pragmatic and gasping for air.

Nikki thought that following the rules was the problem with Dina's leadership, but she didn't say anything. She had been in the Carrie Mae training facility for only a week; she wasn't sure she was allowed to have opinions on things at this point.

"You know, I have to say," said Ellen, and Jenny and Nikki waited for the rest of the sentence. "I never really thought when I started selling Carrie Mae cosmetics . . ." Nikki and Jenny waited three more steps. "That it would involve this much running."

"I'd rather run than sell cosmetics," Nikki said, trying not to remember her single, disastrous sales attempt.

"That's easy for you to say," said Ellen. "You can run."

It was true. Nikki could run. When an extended period of post-college unemployment had forced her to move back in with her mother, she had taken up working out just to get out of the house. After seeing her for the fifth day in a row, one of the personal trainers at her gym had joked that they were going to give Nikki her own permanent locker. She had smiled the expected smile, but Nikki knew that working out was just the latest in a long line of carefully honed avoidance techniques.

"I just like to jog occasionally," she muttered. An inability to deal with her mother was not something to brag about, even if it had given her buns of steel.

"Well, occasionally I'd just like to kick Dina's ass," said Jenny; her genteel accent made the comment funny, but Nikki knew she meant it. "Seriously y'all, what are we going to do about her?"

"I'm too tired to think of solutions; these late-night study sessions are killing me," Nikki said, and Ellen tsked sympathetically.

They ran in silence for the rest of the distance. The sun was past its zenith and the shadows were starting to lengthen when they finally dropped to a walk.

"Are we going to go shooting tonight after dinner?" Jenny asked suddenly, and Nikki groaned. She was already tired, and trekking down to the firing range didn't have nearly the appeal of a really great after-dinner doze in front of the TV.

"I think maybe we ought to," Jenny continued, "because, no offense or anything, Nikki, but I think that Howitzer-barn comment was kinda about you."

"Yes," Nikki agreed with a sigh. "Thanks," she added after a moment, knowing the extra practice and instruction was a favor. Jenny made a waving motion and dismissed the matter entirely.

"I'll go with you," volunteered Ellen, and Nikki felt a surge of appreciation. It didn't seem possible that she had known Jenny and Ellen only a week; they were already better friends than anyone she had known in high school.

"But first," said Ellen, "I'm going to beat you to the shower."

"Hey," Nikki said, laughing as Ellen made a spirited effort to sprint for their room.

"Are you going to put up with that?" Jenny asked in mock seriousness.

"Yes," Nikki said, and Jenny laughed. "I'll see you at dinner." She waved goodbye to Jenny and followed Ellen to their room.

The shower was already running as she pulled the rubber band out of her hair and stripped off her sweat-soaked shirt. Catching sight of herself in the mirror, she groaned. Her red hair was standing out from her head in the kind of whimsical mess that a hairstylist would have taken two hours to complete, but would take Nikki hours and a ton of detangler to undo. In the mirror, her gray eyes stared wearily back at her, and she waved at her reflection to cheer it up, but it didn't work. She sank down onto the bed and considered skipping dinner to take a nap.

The leisurely week spent golfing and singing swing standards with Mr. Merrivel had left her with a lazy feeling of a summer vacation. But once she had made the decision to join Carrie Mae, events had moved swiftly, leaving Nikki no time to unpack. As a consequence, her side of the room looked as if her backpack had exploded, and to make matters worse, she had somehow managed to lose essential items—her hairbrush and workout gear—in transit.

Ellen's side was almost unbearably tidy. Everything was placed with extreme precision, and Nikki could tell that she had even dusted. There was a picture of a cheerfully smiling man of about Ellen's age beside her roommate's bed. Nikki wondered if he was Ellen's husband and what he thought about his wife's new job.

Nikki flopped full length onto the bed. The constant working out was OK. The weird subjects were fine—except for target shooting, and what was Cocktails class anyway? And even having to play catch-up on all the classes she'd missed and the resulting lack of sleep were all right, but she was surrounded by fifteen women, all of whom were smarter, prettier, and more confident than she was. Or at least that's what it seemed like. As usual, Nikki felt like the odd girl out, a circumstance that made her all the more grateful for Ellen and Jenny's friendship.

She kicked off her shoes, hearing them smack against the wall and rebound to the floor. Slowly, she tried to peel off her socks by pinching at them with her toes. After a moment of futile effort, she flung a hand down and shoved off one sock, then she used the toes of her naked foot to peel the sock off the other. Ellen came in, humming.

"Shower's all yours," she said, pulling on sweats.

"Yeah," Nikki said, not moving.

"I'm going to head down. Sarah said she'd let me look at her notes on hot-wiring."

"Cool," said Nikki.

"So you'll be down in a bit, right?" Ellen asked, hovering, but trying not to.

"Yeah," said Nikki, smiling at her. "As soon as I work up the energy to sit up."

"OK," said Ellen, laughing. "See you down there."

The door closed behind Ellen, and after a moment Nikki rolled herself off the bed and stumbled into the shower. As the water poured over her, she leaned against the wall and considered whether or not she was crazy. It wasn't too late; she could still become a teacher, get a job at Starbucks, go back to school, go be a fill-in-the-blank.

She'd been waiting to be a fill-in-the-blank for four years. After college she had wandered from one stupid job to another. She kept waiting to discover what she wanted to be when she grew up. Only she was twenty-five now, which was supposed to be grown-up. She was supposed to know something, be something, have something by now. But she didn't. She sighed and wrapped a towel around herself as she stepped out of the shower. Carrie Mae. It might be crazy, but at least it was something.

Borrowing Ellen's brush, she bullied her hair into a ponytail and went downstairs determined to hold Jenny to her promise of shooting practice. She wasn't going to screw up her opportunity in Carrie Mae through lack of effort.

Downstairs, in the common room, most of the girls were on the couches chatting. The cook opened the sliding window between the kitchen and the dining area and began to place dishes on the counter.

"Anytime," the cook yelled, and the girls went to stand in line.

"So, after dinner," said Nikki, pulling Jenny into line ahead of her, "we'll go over to the armory and check out guns and go down to the range?"

"Sure," agreed Jenny easily.

"I really do appreciate your helping me," Nikki said earnestly.

"Well, you can't shoot for shit, and I like shooting shit, so it works out well," Jenny said cheerfully.

"I never shot a gun before I came here," said Nikki. Jenny stared. Her pale blue eyes were the perfect complement to her French-braided strawberry blond hair.

"I'd never shot a gun before my fortieth birthday," Ellen said, lining up behind Nikki. Nikki smiled at her gratefully. "And I was pretty bad my first time. You can improve; you just need to get your muscles in shape, and practice."

Nikki had witnessed Ellen's improvement firsthand, at shooting practice earlier in the week. Most of the stalls at the gun range had high counters for resting equipment, but the last two stalls were empty except for a mound of dirt. Over one of these mounds, Ellen had aimed a very long rifle at some distant wavering balloons tethered in the far field. She had seemed oblivious to the wind, the popping of the smaller firearms, and the hot glare of the sunshine. She simply lay on the ground looking through the scope, her gray hair fluttering in the wind. Then the rifle gave a small hiccup, and out in the field the balloon burst silently. Connie had proudly announced that Ellen was an Olympic-qualifying shooter and that they could all learn from her, and Nikki had noticed that despite Ellen's soft appearance, her forearms carried muscles like steel cords. When it came to shooting, she had obviously taken her own advice on training.

"Yeah, you need a lot of practice," said Jenny, but instead of finishing her commentary on Nikki's shooting skills, she groaned as the cook scooped a heaping spoonful of broccoli onto her plate. "Why do they give us broccoli? I hate broccoli."

"It's good for you," answered Ellen.

"I'll take it," said Nikki. "I like broccoli." That earned another stare of disbelief from Jenny, who willingly scooped the offending broccoli onto Nikki's plate. Dina walked by and jogged Jenny's elbow, scattering broccoli onto the floor.

"Well, I guess you want your pee to smell," Dina said, staring at Nikki's heaping pile of broccoli and snickering. Nikki stared back at her, and then at her broccoli, puzzled by the comment.

"I think you're thinking of asparagus," said Nikki at last. Dina shut her mouth with a click like a mousetrap slamming shut and stalked away without another word.

"You know," Jenny said, picking up the broccoli and shooting it into the wastebin, "you'd think she could at least get her insults right. I'm starting to think that girl is a few bricks shy of a load."

"I wish we could get rid of her somehow," Ellen agreed. "I can't think why Mrs. Boyer picked her to be team leader."

"I think they just draw the names out of a hat," Jenny said, heading for a table.

As if on cue, Mrs. Boyer bustled into the room. "Lanier!" she barked, scanning the room.

"What'd you do?" Jenny joked; at least, Nikki thought it was a joke. Hesitantly, she waved her hand and caught Mrs. Boyer's attention.

"You have a visitor up at the main house," Mrs. Boyer said, and left before Nikki could ask anything further.

"That's exciting," said Ellen. "Who's visiting you?"

"I don't know," Nikki said, shaking her head. "I don't know anyone around here. Save my plate for me?" Jenny nodded, and Nikki hurried to the exit.

The main house was set on a gently sloping hill. From the front, the main level was even with the ground, but from the rear, as the hill dropped in elevation, it exposed the second level of the house. The path from the dorms took the most direct route and passed quite close to the house, under the windows in the rear, through the rock garden, and to the side door. The setting sun illuminated the paved trail like a ribbon on the green grass. Nikki stretched her stride to cover the ground quickly, intent on reaching her destination.

As she passed under the windows at the rear of the house, she heard the sound of voices. One of the voices was Mrs. Merrivel's. Without thinking, Nikki slowed her steps, trying to catch the words.

Another voice said, "It's a disaster! I do not approve of this course. Mrs. Boyer doesn't, either." The other speaker was Connie Hinton.

"I appreciate your feelings," Mrs. Merrivel said. "What do you think?"

"What do I think?" a new voice spoke, sounding bored. "I think they're sloppy, unimaginative, and totally useless." Nikki noticed that the speaker bit down hard on her consonants, giving her voice a sharp, clipped quality. Sort of East Coast, but no Boston drawl. Maybe New York.

"I *told* you," said Connie. "This is not what Carrie Mae does. We're not about strike teams and SWAT action." There was the edge of a whine in Connie's voice, and for the first time Nikki wondered if Mrs. Boyer's anger at the trainees during war games was more about the war games than about them.

"The world changes, Connie, and Carrie Mae needs to change with it." The voice was Mrs. Merrivel's again. "That's why headquarters sent me out here. They wanted a fresh eye to make sure that West Coast Carrie Mae was evolving into the twenty-first century. I want to maintain Carrie Mae's core values, but let's face it, the need for our ladies to deal with these kinds of emergencies is crucial. And, as the military and other agencies field rapid-response teams, we have to be able to deal with, understand, and respond to these kinds of tactics."

Mrs. Merrivel managed to blend just the right amount of soothing and command into her voice. Once again, Nikki was impressed by her ability to manage people.

"I know, but—" Connie began.

"But they suck," the third voice interjected. "They should have gone around to the south, ambushed the other team, and then worried about the objective. Instead, most of the teams wandered around like they were lost the whole afternoon until one team finally tripped over the objective and everyone else just gave up."

"That's interesting, Valerie," Mrs. Merrivel said, and Nikki couldn't tell whether or not she was being sarcastic. "And I agree —the results have not been what we hoped for, but that is exactly why I asked you up here."

"I could have told you on the phone that they sucked," said the Valerie voice.

"Yes, but then you couldn't have shared your insights with the girls."

"Oh, no. No, no, no, no," Valerie said. "I'm not giving a SWAT team pep talk to your baby spies. I am not instructor material. Not here, not now, not ever."

Non hic, non nunc. Nikki's mind gratuitously translated Valerie's words into Latin, and she quickly blocked a memory of her disastrous visit to Canada that threatened to spring up.

"But Val," said Mrs. Merrivel sweetly. "It's just a two-day seminar. You'll get to judge, and we'll even let you give out grades."

"I'd get to grade them?" Valerie sounded tempted.

The grading system, as far as Nikki could tell, was totally arbitrary, but everyone said it counted toward the final grade and a trainee's job placement.

"Absolutely," Mrs. Merrivel said.

"Just one day, one class?"

"Two days, a seminar and a practical," said Connie.

"OK," Valerie said after a long moment of consideration. "I'll do it as long as I get to flunk people."

"I don't know," Connie protested, but Mrs. Merrivel overrode her objection.

"Very well, but just the class. You can't flunk them from the program."

"Fine, whatever," Val agreed.

Nikki frowned. She wasn't sure this Val person sounded like someone she wanted grading her. There was a knock on the office door and the low murmur of voices.

"Excuse us a minute, won't you, Val," Connie said. Nikki heard the clack of shoes and the office door close. She frowned again, pondering everything she'd just heard. A puff of cigarette smoke drifted past her face.

"Didn't your mother ever tell you not to eavesdrop?" said a smooth voice.

Nikki looked up to find a woman sitting on the edge of the window frame. She was dangling one leg outside the window. Her boots were black and shiny with a pointy toe, of the variety Nikki's mother referred to as "Hey, sailor" boots. Nikki's gaze followed the boot up the leg covered in black slacks, to a trim torso in a white shirt, and then farther up to a head of sleek black hair and brown eyes under perfectly arched brows. It was difficult to tell how old she was—late thirties to mid-forties was Nikki's best guess.

"I wasn't eavesdropping. I was . . ." Nikki coughed.

"Yes?" said the older woman, clearly amused.

"I was information gathering."

"Oh, really? Gather anything interesting?"

"Yes, I learned that my team leader sucks and we should have done it my way."

"Get a new team leader," Valerie said with a laugh.

"Can't. They're chosen every couple of weeks, and the time isn't up yet."

"Well, it looks like you can kiss your SWAT grade goodbye

then, doesn't it?" Val said, taking another drag of her cigarette.

Nikki frowned. She didn't like her choices. "There has to be another way," she said.

"There is," Val assured her, and Nikki wrinkled her nose trying to see what Valerie saw. "Don't strain your brain, kid. I wouldn't want you to hurt yourself."

"I guess if I could get Dina to resign," said Nikki tentatively.

"Now you're thinking, but better yet, why don't you just trip her on the obstacle course and 'accidentally' bust her ankle?"

"I couldn't do that!" Nikki exclaimed, shocked.

"I'm just teasing! Relax. Jeez," said Valerie, exhaling another puff of smoke.

She hadn't sounded like she'd been teasing, but Nikki decided not to argue.

"There really isn't a way to get rid of her," said Nikki dejectedly.

"Sure, there is. Slip her a mickey. Just give her a little something to send her to the infirmary for the day, and you'll be golden."

"Well, as tempting as the idea of making Dina puke her guts out is, I'm pretty sure it's against the rules," said Nikki, trying to repress a smile.

"I don't think it's specified," disagreed Valerie.

"Because they didn't think anyone would do it," Nikki answered tartly.

"Well, you can just wait for me to flunk you if you want." The woman shrugged and tossed her cigarette butt into the flowerbed. "Up to you." She smirked and pulled the window closed. Walking slowly, Nikki entered the house. She was about to approach the receptionist when she saw Mr. M waving at her from the front hall.

"Mr. M!" Nikki exclaimed, hugging him. "I'm so glad to see you! How are you? Did you manage to get par on that hole?"

"Below par!" he said happily, and Nikki grinned, throwing up her hands triumphantly. "I know!" he said, agreeing with her unspoken congratulations.

"Not that I'm not happy to see you, but what are you doing here?" she asked. "Aside from bringing me the victorious news, of course."

"Ah," he said, and reached into a paper grocery bag he was carrying. He pulled out her hairbrush. "And it looks like I didn't get here a moment too soon," he said, tugging at her messy ponytail.

She laughed. "I knew I lost it somewhere," she said, batting his hand away and taking the brush.

"Left it at our house with some T-shirts. Housekeeper found 'em," he said, holding out the bag for her to take.

"You didn't have to bring them yourself!" she said, touched by his thoughtfulness. "You could have sent them with Mrs. M."

"Yes, but I wanted to see how you were getting on. Are you having a good time? Are you making friends? Did you get to ride the ponies?" Nikki laughed as he dropped his voice into an overly cute grandfatherly tone.

"I met some nice girls," Nikki said, pitching her voice a bit higher to go with the joke. "I really like Jenny and Ellen." She really did feel like she was talking about summer camp. *And after arts and crafts we rode the ponies, but the mean girl put bugs in our shoes.*

"And some not so nice people?" he asked perceptively, dropping the cute voice.

"Yes, our team leader, Dina," Nikki confided, flopping down on one of the chairs. Mr. M followed suit. "We're afraid she'll make us flunk." Discouragement colored her tone. "She's really terrible. Everyone thinks so. I think she's actually pretty smart, book smart anyway. She doesn't seem very good with the everyday stuff like broccoli." Mr. M made a puzzled expression, but

Nikki continued. "She won't listen to suggestions because she thinks she has everything all figured out, and if she weren't so freaking cocky I'd think she had low self-esteem or something."

"Fire her," he suggested.

"I don't think you can fire the team leader," Nikki said.

"Sure, you can. Just calmly tell her that you are unhappy with her leadership and that you have decided to take the team in another direction."

"I couldn't do that!" exclaimed Nikki, almost as shocked as if he'd suggested breaking Dina's ankle. "I can't be boss."

"Being boss is just being the first person willing to do something. And being a good boss is being open to suggestions. You can do that." Nikki looked doubtful, but he grinned broadly and nodded encouragingly.

"I'll think about it," she said, wondering if she could tell Ellen to be the boss.

"Hello, Nikki," Mrs. Merrivel said, coming out of a back office.

"Hello, Mrs. Merrivel." Nikki stood up with a slight guilty twitch.

"Hey, sweet pea," Mr. M said, leaning down to kiss his wife on the cheek. Mrs. M gracefully inclined her cheek upward and slipped her arm around his waist.

"Did you give Nikki her letter?"

"Letter?" asked Nikki, looking at the pair of them.

"Letter!" he exclaimed, smacking his forehead with his palm. "Clean forgot about it. It's in the bag. Your mother forwarded it to us."

"Oh," Nikki said, reaching into the brown paper grocery bag with her clothes in it. The letter had been placed on top of her neatly folded and laundered shirts, along with her brush. The letter now smelled faintly of fabric softener.

The envelope had been forwarded from their Canadian P.O. box to the house in Tacoma, where her mother, always the penny pincher and still irritated about Nikki's abrupt departure, had crossed out the Washington address and written, "No longer at this address," in a tight, cramped script. Beneath that she had written in the Merrivels' address. Nikki squinted at the smudged return address and felt her heart skip a beat as she saw the name Z'EV CORALLES written in bold, block letters, along with a Canadian postmark.

"I didn't have time to tell my friends where I was going or where to write me," Nikki lied, trying not to breathe hard, and hoping that the Merrivels wouldn't question her any further.

"They can write to a P.O. box here at the ranch," Mrs. Merrivel said helpfully. "They usually distribute the mail once a week. Ask the girl at the desk on the way out; she can give you the address."

"I'll do that," promised Nikki. "And thanks for bringing me my stuff, Mr. M. I really appreciate it."

"Of course!" he said cheerfully.

There was an awkward moment as she hugged Mr. M goodbye and wasn't sure whether to hug Mrs. M or not, but Mrs. Merrivel solved the problem by stepping in and enfolding her briefly in a light lavender-scented embrace before letting Nikki escape. As she hurried down the path to the dorms at a pace approaching a trot, Nikki's only thought was to get to the privacy of her room as soon as possible and open that letter.

Shooting Script

Nikki rushed inside and up the stairs to her room. Sitting on the bed, she took out the envelope again. It was too big for a regular letter, and thicker besides; it had to be some sort of card. Slitting the envelope with her nail file, she pulled out a pale blue greeting card. There was a drawing of two pairs of shoes on the cover: a girl's pair of dancing slippers and men's lace-up business dress shoes. Between them was a pair of interlocking gold rings. Nikki laughed; it was an anniversary card.

Inside, the message read, "We make a pretty great pair! Happy Anniversary!" Under the preprinted words, Z'ev had written in the same strong block letters from the envelope: TO MY FAVORITE WIFE: THANKS! LOVE ALWAYS, Z'EV.

"Jackass," murmured Nikki softly, falling back onto her bed and staring up at the ceiling. What was the matter with him? He could find her address but not her phone number?

"Nikki?" Ellen asked, appearing in the doorway. She was carrying Nikki's dinner plate. "Is everything all right? Did you want your dinner?"

"Oh," said Nikki, sitting up. "Uh, yes, thanks."

"I brought you a Co-Cola," said Jenny, shortening the name Southern style and holding up a can of Coke.

"Thanks," Nikki said, shoving the card under her mattress and reaching for the dinner plate. She knew Jenny and Ellen had noticed the maneuver, but she didn't want to explain the complicated set of circumstances that had led to an anniversary card being delivered to an unmarried woman.

"So, are we still up for shooting?" she asked, hoping to divert their attention.

"Yeah, absolutely," Jenny agreed, nodding.

"Cool," Nikki said, shoving her remaining piece of chicken into her roll and reaching for the soda pop. "Let's go."

With the sun sinking lower behind them, Jenny, Nikki, and Ellen trooped out to the gun range. Jenny and Ellen carried several handguns apiece. Nikki munched on her makeshift sandwich.

"So, is there a reason you guys brought ten guns?" Nikki asked as they walked.

"We didn't bring ten. We brought . . ." Jenny paused to count. "Six."

"OK, so why did we bring six?" Nikki said absentmindedly, still pondering Z'ev's note.

"Because it's important to know the basics of how guns function. And once you know that, you can apply that knowledge and fire accurately with any gun. Are you ever going to tell us who came to visit you?" demanded Jenny, abruptly switching topics.

"Hush!" Ellen said. "Maybe it's bad news and she doesn't want to talk about it."

"If she doesn't talk about it, we can't help her fix it!"

They both turned to Nikki, their eyes filled with speculative curiosity.

"It's not a big secret," Nikki said, feeling awkward. "I just . . . I stayed with the Merrivels before I came here, and Mr. M brought me stuff I forgot."

"You stayed with Mrs. Merrivel? What's her house like?" Ellen asked.

"Plush," Nikki said. "Really tasteful, and the kitchen is fantastic."

"Never mind that," said Jenny. "What about the card?"

Nikki blushed, and Jenny grinned.

"It's from a boy, isn't it? I knew it! Boy letters always go under the mattress. Who is he? Is he your boyfriend? How'd you meet?"

"I'm not really sure who he is," Nikki said cautiously. "It's kind of complicated. I think . . . no, I don't know what I think." She shook her head trying to clear up the confusion that always came up when she thought about Z'ev.

"You're no good at gossip at all," said Jenny disgustedly. "You're not supposed to know what to think! You're supposed to tell us, and then we talk about it and decide what you're supposed to think."

"You don't have to tell us if you don't want to," Ellen said, looking amused. "But sometimes it is good to sort of hear another opinion on things."

"Well," said Nikki uncomfortably. "It's complicated. I didn't mean to meet him at all. I just wanted to go to Canada."

"What's in Canada?" asked Jenny.

"Canadians mostly," Nikki answered without pausing. She was trying to pinpoint precisely where the story started. "But I wanted to go to Vancouver. I had a job interview. Only, I couldn't afford to go."

Sitting at the kitchen table, sunlight blazing in a sharp arc across the white paper of the "request for interview" letter, Nikki had seen that Fate was clearly taking a hand. She was supposed to go back to Canada.

"Have you ever thought that something was destiny?" she asked, coming back to the present. "I mean, believed in something so much that you had absolutely no doubt it would happen?"

"Yes," Jenny said. "I absolutely knew that Marky Mark was going to marry me."

"I don't mean like a junior-high crush," Nikki said with a laugh. "I mean, like, believed it so hard it seemed more like a memory of what happened, rather than what might happen."

"Yeah, I know. Mark Wahlberg was going to come to Peachtree, Georgia, and marry me."

"I'm incredibly disturbed by that," said Ellen. "Let's pretend she didn't say it."

"I'm fine with that," agreed Nikki.

"So, back to this job interview in Vancouver," said Ellen, restarting the conversation.

"Well, it was for a company that did glorified market research, but I would have been using my degree. I was very excited, and I don't know . . . it just all seemed so right that I believed it. I knew what I was going to wear, what I was going to say, and how much they were going to love me. The only thing I didn't know was how I was going to get there. I had like forty-two dollars in my bank account."

"What'd you do?" Jenny asked.

"I broke down and asked my mom to lend me the money. And she said she could get me a free hotel room. All I had to do was go to an informative seminar on a 'lucrative and fun new business opportunity.'"

"Carrie Mae," said Ellen, recognizing the tag line.

"Right," Nikki said, "so I said yes, because I was going to get the job and Carrie Mae wouldn't matter."

"But you didn't get the job?" Jenny asked sympathetically.

"I think you could safely say that," said Nikki disgustedly.

"What happened?" Ellen said, laughing.

"Well." Nikki hesitated. "It just didn't go well," she finished lamely. Some things were just too embarrassing. Particularly when she'd known Jenny and Ellen only a week. Z'ev's knowing was one thing. He was different. "It was just really obvious that I didn't get the job."

"So where does the boy come into it?" asked Ellen.

"At the bar in the hotel after the interview."

"Ah," Jenny said. "It was beer obvious you didn't get the job."

"Martini obvious," Nikki agreed. "And I was on my second martini, and he was sitting next to me at the bar, and then he turned around and asked me to marry him."

"What?" Ellen asked, startled.

"I know! That's what *I* said!" exclaimed Nikki. "He had some story about some business associate thinking he was married, but he really wasn't, but now he was meeting the guy and the guy expected to meet a wife."

"That's retarded," Jenny said, bluntly. "That doesn't even make sense."

"It made sense at the time," Nikki said, blushing.

"That's because y'all were drunk. What happened?"

"I went to lunch with them," Nikki said, suddenly feeling self-conscious. It hadn't sounded so ridiculous until she'd said it out loud. "And he sent me a thank-you card, that's all." They had reached the shooting range and Nikki quickly took the gun cases from Jenny and spread them out on the counter.

"So tell me about guns," she said, grateful for the opportunity to switch topics.

"Actually," Jenny said, "you're going to tell me. Yesterday Connie explained single-action, double-action, semiauto, and full automatic to you, right?"

"Right," said Nikki, knowing that the statement was true even if her absorption of the information wasn't.

"Good. Now explain it to me."

"Uh," Nikki said, floundering, trying to focus on the moment at hand. "Well, anything that isn't a revolver is an automatic."

"A revolver is defined as . . . ?"

"A handgun with a revolving cylinder into which bullets are placed. Cowboy guns," babbled Nikki, beginning to sweat.

"Not just for cowboys, but moving on. Tell me about automatics."

"Most handguns are semiautomatics because you have to squeeze the trigger each time you want a bullet to come out."

"Which makes it different from a fully automatic weapon how?" Her blue eyes fixed intently on Nikki. Jenny pushed a piece of flyaway blond hair behind her ear.

"Uh." Nikki stared back at Jenny and wished the information would stop loitering and exit her mouth promptly. "When you squeeze and hold the trigger, lots of bullets come out. Automatically."

"Good," Jenny said. "Now, back to the revolvers. Tell me about single versus double action."

Nikki licked her lips; she was a little less clear on this bit. "Double action means that you can either cock the hammer or simply pull the trigger. Soooo . . ." She paused, trying to find the words. "Single action means that you have to cock the hammer each time?"

"Exactly," Jenny said, smiling. "Now, find the safety catch on each of these guns."

Nikki quickly found the little lever on two guns that would prevent a trigger from being pulled completely and discharging the weapon, but she was stumped by the third. She turned the gun over in her hand and finally looked at Jenny in capitulation.

"I give up," she said. "Where is it?"

"Uh-huh," Jenny said, shaking her head. Ellen laughed.

"Stop being mean, Jenny. The poor girl has been doing so well."

Nikki looked at each woman with a questioning expression.

"It's a trick question, sweetie," explained Ellen. "Not all hand-guns have safeties. Rifles almost always do, and revolvers almost always don't. Just the way it is."

"Why not?" asked Nikki.

"Ask the gun companies," Ellen answered, earning a dirty look from Jenny.

"It's because they don't need them," said Jenny. "Most revolvers have an extremely hard first pull, and besides, you have to cock the hammer; it can't cock itself. *You* are the safety."

Nikki realized that like politics or religion, gun safety was a don't-bring-up-at-dinner-parties topic. Ellen shrugged, and Jenny let the subject drop. After that Jenny made Nikki unload and load all of the handguns.

"So, why'd you start late?" asked Jenny, loading her own gun. Nikki looked up from the clip of an automatic handgun. Her thumbs were already sore from pressing bullets into the small space.

"I don't know," she answered truthfully. "Mrs. Merrivel offered me the job, and I flew down, and then she said she wanted me to start in this session. Connie didn't seem that happy about it."

"Don't worry about it." Ellen said. "Connie never seems happy about anything," Jenny nodded her agreement and pressed bright orange earplugs into her ears.

Nikki continued to load her guns while Jenny fired off a clip into a distant target. The hot shells were ejected from her gun in a steady stream, and Nikki looked at the rapidly cooling brass with a groan. She had just spent ten minutes loading that gun, and Jenny had emptied it in less than two.

"Why'd you guys join?" Nikki asked, finishing the last gun.

"Because I look like crap in a cop uniform," said Jenny. Nikki could see that all of Jenny's bullets had entered the target in the head or chest.

"How 'bout you, Ellen?" asked Jenny. "It's the shooting, isn't it? That's how they got you."

"Not really," answered Ellen. "I think they wanted me for my shooting, but really I joined because I wanted something useful to do with myself. My husband has passed on and my girls don't need me, and it seems like all I ever do is putter around the house and eat too much."

"I'm familiar with that," Nikki agreed. "I've been, well, not unemployed, exactly, but underemployed since I graduated. There's only so much daytime TV you can watch before you go crazy."

Ellen laughed. "Exactly," she confirmed, her hazel eyes twinkling behind dark lashes. "I just couldn't take any more *Matlock*. And since my daughters are either in college or graduated and moved away, I just felt useless. I started selling a bit of makeup and spending a lot of time at the gun range, and then one of the ladies in my sales group invited me out for tea. Next thing you know, she's pitching what she called a 'training camp' that would allow me to help women on a global scale. I liked the idea of helping other women, so here I am."

"It's better to have a purpose," Nikki said, realizing the truth of the words as she spoke them. Ellen nodded; her round face, young-looking under the gray hair, carried such an understanding and sympathetic expression that Nikki felt embarrassed and looked away.

"All right," Jenny said, finishing her inspection of the guns Nikki had loaded. "Now we can shoot. Pick a gun."

Nikki picked a revolver because she knew it would be easier for her to reload.

"I like that one," Jenny said, smiling. "Now, point it out there at the target." Nikki did so. "Now, see at the tip," Jenny continued, "there is a little thingie with an orange dot on it?" Nikki looked, and sure enough there was. "OK now, back where the handle meets the barrel is a little notch." Nikki nodded. "Now, try and line up the orange dot in the notch."

Nikki adjusted her hands, raising her wrists and lowering the barrel until the orange dot was between the two little thingies. Moments later they were all trooping out to the target to examine the hole Nikki had put in the target's left hip. After a brief celebration, they returned to their shooting position to try again.

"How'd you learn to shoot?" Nikki asked Jenny, aiming the gun again.

"From my mama. She was a Miss Georgia," Jenny answered proudly. "I did some pageants, too, but they weren't really my thing."

"A former Miss Georgia taught you to shoot?" Ellen seemed slightly skeptical.

"Well, I don't know what it's like at y'all's high schools, but at mine, if you wanted a date on Saturday night, you'd better have your huntin' license. My brothers got me into the handguns. But really it was Mama who taught me how to put the bullet where I wanted it."

"I guess I'll be a little nicer to the next beauty queen I meet," Ellen said with a laugh.

They continued shooting, and by sunset Nikki could reasonably expect her bullet to be somewhere in the black, but she was still uncertain about her actual skills.

"What if I forget everything tomorrow?" she asked as they walked back.

"Nah," Jenny said confidently. "You'll do OK. Wait till they see you—" She stopped talking abruptly. Dina had come out of the house and was walking toward them, her arms pumping angrily.

"If you were going to go shooting, you should have informed me!" Dina said. "I'm the team leader. I'm the one who sets all the practice sessions."

"I'm sorry, Dina," Ellen said sweetly. "We thought you'd be bored. You said just this morning how good your target scores were." Dina looked torn between the two horrible fates of admitting that she needed practice and agreeing with Ellen.

"That isn't the point," she said at last. "I should have been there."

"Maybe next time," said Ellen, and she walked around her. Dina made a peculiar snorting noise of irritation, and Nikki heard Jenny smother a laugh.

The next morning, after classes, the women walked out to the range, each carrying her weapon in a hard plastic case. Nikki set up between Jenny and Ellen and squished the neon earplugs into her ears. The girls began to let off a steady pop of gunfire. Connie and Mrs. Boyer were stalking along the shooting line, offering tips and disparagement. Nikki nervously loaded her gun. It was the same revolver from the night before. She pointed the gun at the target, lining up the orange dot with the notch. Connie was behind Ellen now—only a few steps away. Nikki exhaled, pulled the trigger, and put a new white belly button in the target.

"You're overcompensating for the recoil," said Connie, making Nikki jump. "Aim more truly at the heart." Nikki nodded and tried again. A second white hole appeared only an inch or so above the first. "Keep trying," Connie said with a sniff, and stalked on down the line.

"Dina!" snapped Mrs. Boyer. "Stop waving your gun around like an idiot. If you can't follow basic gun safety, then get the hell off my shooting range."

After Connie had passed by, Jenny put her head around the partition and gave Nikki a thumbs-up and a grin. Nikki smiled back; she couldn't pretend the moment wasn't sweet.

Phone Call Day

Nikki followed the girls up to the main house. It was phone call day, and they were all excited.

"I can't wait to tell Mom about . . ." said Heidi, but Nikki lost track of the rest of the sentence as Carmella talked over her, raving about her boyfriend.

"I think you're making this guy up," protested Jenny. "He sounds too good to be true."

"Well, he has his faults," acknowledged Carmella.

"They're just harder to see from six hundred miles away," said Ellen, with a twinkle in her eye, but an understanding smile.

"My dad is going to be so proud that I learned how to pick a lock," Sarah said.

"It took you twenty minutes," said Dina sourly.

"You can't tell him about it," Carmella protested, ignoring Dina. "You're not supposed to talk about training."

"He's a locksmith," said Sarah. "He's been after me to learn the family business for years. How can I not tell him?"

"But you can't," reiterated Carmella.

"Just tell him you had to help one of the girls get into her locker or something," Ellen said helpfully. "Just make it sound informal, and then . . ."

"That's not . . ."

"My mom said . . ."

"I think my brother might have gotten engaged . . ."

"My sister totally lost it . . ."

"Can't wait to tell . . ."

"Need to ask . . ."

The sound of multiple *moms* and *dads* echoed across the field as they walked up to the main house. Phone calls were only allowed once a week, and Nikki had initially found the sabbatical from daily phone calls with her mother a little frightening. She kept reaching for a cell phone she knew wasn't there and listening for the ring she knew wouldn't come. Then she had become used to it and discovered that silence really was golden. She was starting to remember what it was like to make decisions on her own. She could almost envision a time when she wouldn't have the looming specter of an unmade call lurking in the back of her mind.

But as they walked up the hill in gathering gloom of evening, the cheerful anticipation of the girls began to rub off on her. And as she took her turn in the phone booth, she found that she was actually looking forward to hearing her mother's voice. The phone began to ring, and Nikki slid down on the seat, pulling her feet up and bracing them against the opposite panel.

"Hello?" her mother said in the fake, breathy voice that she thought made her sound like an underage babysitter. It was a clever ploy to throw off phone solicitors. Nikki thought that either the ploy was too clever or perhaps the telemarketers didn't actually care, but she'd never been able to convince her mother of that.

"Hey, Mom," she said, consciously keeping her voice from rising to match her mother's.

"Oh, it's you," said her mother, dropping into a normal tone.

"Don't sound so thrilled," Nikki said.

"I didn't mean it like that," said Nell briskly. "I've just been ducking your grandmother's calls all week."

"Why won't you talk to Grandma?"

"I left the womb for a reason," said Nell tartly. "I wanted to get away."

Nikki laughed, and Nell joined in.

"No, she's just been pestering me to go back for a visit, and I just don't have time. We're super busy at work. I really can't afford to take a week off. And you know I love your grandmother, but she drives me nuts. You wouldn't understand, but I think that woman does stuff just to drive me insane. It's enough to make me start smoking again."

"I can't imagine," Nikki murmured.

"You have no idea what that's like," reiterated Nell, perhaps sensing Nikki's incredulity.

"Well, maybe this fall we can both go back," Nikki suggested, trying to redirect the conversation before it went down a path that neither of them wanted to tread.

"Yeah, maybe. So what's up with you? How is that training school of yours going? I can't believe that they don't allow cell phones! It's the most ridiculous thing!"

"They can be kind of disruptive," Nikki said defensively.

"What if there's an emergency?"

"The instructors have phones; they would take care of it."

"You know," Nell said, switching topics and throwing Nikki

off-balance, "this school of yours sounds overly intensive. My friend worked for the Gates Foundation, and they didn't make her go through months and months of training. Just what are they teaching you?"

"We might be expected to travel later, so they need the trainees to be up on all of their projects and know all about international regulations and everything," extemporized Nikki.

"Really?"

Nikki could hear the discontent and disinterest in Nell's voice and knew that it was because she had mentioned the *T* word. Travel wasn't a concept that Nell had ever taken to.

"They do really interesting work, Mom," said Nikki, trying to reengage her mother in the conversation before it went completely south and they ended up talking about Nell's crazy colleagues. "There were these nuns in India—"

"I don't approve of Catholics," Nell said.

"The schools for girls in Afghanistan—" Nikki tried.

"I don't want to talk about Arabs," said Nell. "They make me angry."

"The political activist in Thailand," Nikki began, remembering the day they'd watched the video. Nikki hadn't immediately connected to the women in the film; it had seemed a bit like the instructors had needed the afternoon off and just popped in a video—it was the traditional method, after all. It had all seemed so very far away. And then like a burst of color in a black-and-white film, Nikki had been introduced to Lawan Chinnawat.

"What's he do?" Nell asked.

"She," corrected Nikki. "Lawan Chinnawat. She was born into a rural hill tribe, but she was kidnapped at age eight and sold to a brothel. But when she was fifteen she escaped, and ever since then she's been working to end human trafficking and the sex trade. She runs her own foundation, which Carrie Mae contributes to."

"Huh," said Nell, sounding totally disinterested, but Nikki wasn't listening, she was remembering the overpowering emotion with which Lawan had talked about ending the suffering of the women forced to live in slavery and prostitution under a haze of drug addiction. Lawan didn't give dry speeches about laws and policy—she made impassioned arguments against the cruelty of human nature and held out promises for the triumph of peace. She had made Nikki believe. None of the other girls had seemed quite as impressed as Nikki, but she couldn't help wishing that she were more like Lawan.

"She was amazing, Mom," Nikki said. "She got an education, and instead of leaving Thailand or going to work at a nice cushy job, she began a grass-roots campaign to get tougher inspections on cargo ships, harsher sentences for slave traders, and a national database for missing persons. And she started a free health clinic in Bangkok. That's the part that Carrie Mae helps with. They showed us a video of her picketing outside a brothel, and the bouncer came out and shoved her, but she just got up and stared him down. It was really cool."

"I hope they're not sending you there!" said Nell, sounding annoyed.

"I'm sure they're not," Nikki said. She meant to add that she couldn't possibly be that lucky, but decided to keep that bit to herself. She would have given an arm to meet someone like Lawan, but she suspected that only the really good agents got to handle the high-profile cases.

"Well, what else are they teaching you?" asked Nell, in a tone that sounded as if she were about as interested in the answer as a dog was interested in going to the vet.

"Uh, you know, international survival skills," said Nikki, searching for an appropriate answer, trying to remember something innocuous in the curriculum. "I think driving is next."

"Driving? You know how to drive. Why on earth would they need to teach you that?"

"You know, in case I go to England. I'll need to know how to drive on the left."

"I guess that makes sense," Nell said, and Nikki looked at the phone in disbelief. She hadn't thought her lying had improved that much. There was a tap on the glass of the phone booth, and Nikki looked up to see Heidi holding her watch up and pointing at it significantly.

"OK, Mom, one of the other girls wants to use the phone, so I'd better go."

"She can wait," said Nell firmly. "I want to tell you about work. You remember that old coot George Pembroke? Well, I had to go over to his office for . . ."

Nikki looked up apologetically at Heidi, who rolled her eyes and walked out of view. With a sigh, Nikki settled in to listen to the ongoing tale of the crazy old coot, but realized that after tonight, she had a whole seven days before she would have to hear from her mother again. Yes, she was starting to like Carrie Mae very much.

First Gear, It's All Right

As their group walked across the parking lot toward the bus, Nikki's face was plastered into an immovable grin. Behind her the Saugus Speedway, a recent Carrie Mae purchase, hung as a backdrop to her delight.

"Do we get to do this again, Jorge?" asked Nikki, as the driving instructor bounded up, clipboard tucked under one arm, multiple sets of car keys jangling from his fingers.

"All next week," he said, grinning back. "And motorcycles are the week after." There was a groan from the group in general. Nikki looked around, surprised. She had to admit she felt a little on the tired and grimy side, but the exhilaration of learning how to drive backward at speed, forward through cones, slide the car, do 180s and burnouts, and just generally drive way too fast more than compensated for tired arms and a face full of track dust and exhaust fumes.

Nikki looked back at Jorge, and he shrugged. "Some people don't like speed," he said. Nikki chuckled, and he smiled at her artless enthusiasm. "Then again, some people do."

The first question of the morning had been "How many of you know how to drive a stick?" Nikki had raised her hand and then glanced around, surprised to see Jenny intently studying the ground at her feet, hands firmly in her pockets. Four other girls had claimed ignorance, and the non-stick-shifters had been sent away with Mrs. Boyer and the guest instructor, Erica Elleson. Erica had her foot in a flexible cast, but was peg-legging it cheerfully along with a cane.

Nikki was dying to ask Jenny how her driving lesson had gone, but she wasn't sure how she would react. They filed onto the bus, and Nikki slid into her seat and dangled over the back to look at Jenny, who was stretched out on the vinyl-covered seat.

"How was it working with Erica?" she asked, striving to bring up the subject tactfully.

"Good," said Jenny. "She's got the patience of Job. Mrs. Boyer was freaking out by the end of the first five minutes, but Erica was as just as calm as anything. Even when Heidi nearly ran into a light pole. Mrs. Boyer yelled, of course, and Heidi started to cry, and then she had mascara running down her face. Which is when Mrs. Boyer really hit the roof and started screaming about water-proof mascara. It was scary."

"Mrs. Boyer is wound a little tight," agreed Nikki.

"Truer words were never spoken. Although, she's got a point about the mascara. I may have to invest in some: I know it'll be my turn to cry soon enough. I'm just terrible at shifting, Nikki. I don't get it at all!"

"I'm sure you'll get it tomorrow," said Nikki confidently. "How did Erica hurt her foot?" she continued, hoping a change of subject would lighten Jenny's mood.

"She said she 'dropped in on a bar fight,' but I think she might have been making a joke. Or maybe not. It was hard to tell, and Mrs. Boyer told us not to be impertinent."

"How do you hurt your foot in a bar fight?" asked Nikki, trying to visualize the scenario, picturing Erica John Wayne-ing up to a bar, all fists and swagger.

"Kick somebody wrong, I suppose," answered Jenny.

"Yeah, I guess," replied Nikki, revising her scenario to include Erica Jackie Chan-ing up to a bar, all flying feet and acrobatics.

"Hey," Jenny said, interrupting Nikki in the midst of her fight choreography. "I took a peek at Jorge's clipboard. You had the fastest times of anyone in your group."

"Really?" Nikki had never been the fastest at anything before.

"Yup. I don't suppose you want do a little bit of homework with me and help me with the whole shifting thing?" Jenny picked at the seam of the bus seat.

"I'd love to," Nikki replied instantly. "Maybe tomorrow, after the War Games seminar, we can get a car from the motor pool."

"Thanks. You'd think I would have learned before now, but none of my brothers wanted to teach me on their trucks, and Mama said hardly anybody drives a stick anymore and not to worry about it, so I never did learn."

"That's OK," Nikki said. "I never learned to shoot. So now we'll be even."

"Deal," Jenny said, reaching up from her supine position to shake Nikki's hand.

"I don't like all this mechanical nonsense," Ellen said, dropping down next to Nikki as the bus trundled into motion. "First it was engines and hot-wiring, and now it's driving."

"It's not nonsense," disagreed Nikki.

"I can see how this would be useful knowledge, but honestly, if I want to change my oil, I will hire a man," Ellen said.

Jenny snorted in disgust. "And your generation claims that ours isn't feminist enough," she said, sitting up. "Do you even know how to change a tire?"

"Yes, you call Triple-A," Ellen said firmly.

"What if you're somewhere that doesn't have Triple-A?" Jenny demanded.

"You know, call me crazy, but I'm just willing to bet that in whatever foreign country I go to, there will be a man who knows how to change a tire."

"That's terrible. Y'all might just as well have not burned your bras," said Jenny, shaking her head.

"Don't be silly," said Ellen. "We burned our bras so that your generation could learn how to change things. I'm not obligated to know."

Nikki laughed. "What are we doing after we get back to the ranch? More shooting?" she asked.

Jenny chuckled again, sliding down in the seat until her butt was off the bench and her knees could be felt through the padding of Nikki's seat. "Give the girl a gun and all she wants do is shoot things."

"I don't know," Ellen said, answering Nikki's question, and smacking at Jenny's knees through the seat. "I think the schedule said 'Specialty Items.'"

"What on earth are Specialty Items?" asked Jenny, still slumped in the seat, her shoulder blades nearly touching the bend of the bench.

"Search me," said Ellen as the bus pulled up to the ranch.

"All right, ladies," shouted Mrs. Boyer as the girls shuffled off the bus. "Forty minutes to shower and change, and then we're meeting in Classroom B for our next class." There was another collective groan from the group.

"Don't be late," snapped Mrs. Boyer, and she headed into the main house.

Nikki happily raced for the shower and, thirty minutes later, came down the stairs to an empty dining hall. Shrugging, she jogged toward the lecture building.

The doorway to Classroom B was open, and Nikki could hear someone inside whistling off-key. Pausing in the doorway, she saw a woman in a rumpled lab coat standing over a desk jotting down something on a piece of paper. As Nikki watched, the woman ran her hands through her blond curls, but at opposite angles, so her hair frizzed out in all directions. She had a slightly uncertain expression, as if she had just put her glasses down and couldn't quite remember where. Nikki cleared her throat, and the woman looked up. A worried furrow began to form on her forehead.

"The atomic weight of cobalt," she said. "Shoot! I had it just a minute ago!"

"Fifty-eight point ninety-three," Dina supplied, stepping into the classroom after Nikki, practically pushing her out of the way.

"Oh, thank you," the blond woman said with relief, and went back to scribbling on her piece of paper. "Yes," she said, stepping back to admire her chicken scratch, "I think that just might work." Then she looked back at the two students, her frown creeping back in.

"Can I help you with something?"

"We're here for the class," said Nikki with a smile.

"Oh! Right. Class. Right." She looked around the classroom as if surprised to find herself there.

"I'm Dina Kirk. I majored in chemistry." Dina shook the blond woman's unresisting hand. "I had the highest GPA in the class. If you'd like a student assistant, I'd be more than happy to help."

Carmella and Sarah entered the room laughing, but stopped when they saw Dina and the woman in the lab coat.

"Nice of you to offer, but why don't you all just take a seat," said the woman. "I'll be with you in a moment."

Dina tried not to look disappointed and sat at a front table. The other girls walked past her, refusing to sit next to her.

"Did she just pull the 'majored in chemistry' bit?" Carmella whispered as they walked to seats nearer the back of the room. Nikki nodded.

"Let me guess. She followed it up with the 'highest GPA in the school' bit?" Sarah asked, rolling her eyes. Nikki covered her mouth, trying not to hide a smile.

"It's easy to get good grades when you never leave your dorm room. Sucks to be a dork," Carmella said.

Nikki took a seat somewhere toward the middle of the room and waited for Jenny and Ellen. She felt bad about Dina. She'd spent her share of time feeling friendless and dorky, and she sympathized with Dina. On the other hand, even in her full-blown dork stage, she'd never been as big a bitch as Dina. It was hard to befriend someone who had all the warmth, kindness, and social understanding of a cement block.

There were eight long tables in the room. They had been covered with what appeared to be various pieces of the Carrie Mae product line. Nikki was seated in front of a bottle of Lilac Mist Body Spray and two tubes of Apricot Spring Lipstick. Carmella and Sarah's table held compacts in various sizes. More girls began to file in. Jenny sat down next to Nikki and picked up one of the lipsticks. Ellen sat in front of them, examining a pair of red stilettos.

"What's all this stuff?" Jenny asked.

"Specialty items, I guess," answered Nikki with a shrug, as the blond woman walked to the front of the room.

"Good afternoon, everybody. I'm Rachel White and I'm head of Research and Development for the Carrie Mae Foundation. In front of you, you'll find examples of our work. You'll note that each item looks very much like a standard Carrie Mae product."

"Uh, Ms. White." Heidi raised her hand. "Is mine supposed to be beeping?" Heidi held up a tube of lipstick. Its top flashed neon purple and emitted a whining beep.

Rachel White snatched the lipstick from Heidi's hand with a speed that was the antithesis of her laid-back attitude. She twisted the lipstick case a few times and set it gently back down on the table. The flashing and beeping stopped promptly.

"However," continued Rachel, as if she had not been interrupted, "these are not ordinary products, so please don't touch anything until you've been given permission."

Everyone in the class leaned away from the items on the tables in front of them, as Rachel began a highly informative lecture on pepper spray perfume, flash grenade lipsticks, mini-scanner compacts, knockout breath mints, acid nail polish, plastic explosive foundation, and stiletto stilettos. Many of the compacts had Lego-like qualities. They could be pulled apart to create bugs, tracking devices, or stun guns. Many of the liquids and powders could be combined to create various serums, gases, or a highly irritating itching powder. Nikki couldn't quite figure out why someone might need an itching powder, but it was still a pretty cool invention. From there, Rachel moved on to items that only looked like Carrie Mae compacts to the casual observer. She proudly displayed a holographic projector, a satellite uplink, and a fingerprint falsifier.

Rachel eventually ended the lecture and divided the trainees into groups, giving them instructions to rotate throughout the classroom examining each device. Nikki was holding a blusher brush and trying to decipher its alternative usage when she caught a whiff of smoke.

"Do you even have any idea what that thing does?" asked Valerie, leaning in the window frame from the outside. She was wearing a motorcycle-style leather jacket and her black hair was tucked back behind her ears.

"No," said Nikki, honestly. "We're supposed to figure it out and write it down on the questionnaire. But I haven't got a clue as to how."

"It's in the UPC code."

Nikki flipped the brush over and looked at the sticker on the bottom. A string of letters and numbers ran around the edge of the sticker.

"KNI001," Nikki read. She stared thoughtfully at the blusher brush for another moment and then turned it clockwise gingerly.

"Twist harder," advised Valerie. Nikki did as instructed until, suddenly, a sharp double-edged knife blade slid out of the brush end.

"I get it!" exclaimed Nikki. "*KNI* for *knife*?"

"Very good!" Rachel said from the front of the classroom. "That's right, everyone. The weapons identification is in the UPC code."

"That's not fair," said Dina loudly. "She had help."

"There's nothing wrong with help, Dina," Rachel said. "The whole point of Carrie Mae is women working together to better themselves."

Valerie blew smoke in Dina's direction and stared at her until Dina turned her head away and pretended to fill out her questionnaire.

"Well, Valerie Robinson," said Rachel, coming over to the window. "What are you doing here?"

"I'm teaching a war games seminar tomorrow," she said, boosting herself into the room and sitting on the window ledge. "I thought I'd see how the ducklings were doing."

"They seem to be doing well," Rachel said. There was something slightly refrigerated in her demeanor toward Val that Nikki couldn't quite put her finger on. "If you're going to smoke, will you go outside, please?" Valerie chucked her butt out the window, but showed no inclination to leave.

"So, they're doing well? That sounds unlikely." Valerie pushed herself away from the window and began to walk between the tables, examining the students and their papers. She walked with deceptive casualness over to Dina and peered at her paper.

"Dina Kirk," purred Val. "You're a team leader, aren't you?"

"Well, yes," Dina said, pulling herself up straight.

"Going to lead your team to victory, are you?"

"Assuming my team follows directions adequately," answered Dina stiffly.

"Well, yes, you are only as good as your team, it's true."

Nervously, Nikki put down the pepper spray deodorant she was examining and went to the next station. There was a gleam in Valerie's eye that she didn't trust. Dina seemed oblivious and beamed as if Val had complimented her. Val wandered some more, ignoring Nikki entirely.

"All right, class," said Rachel, checking her watch. "That's all for today. Please stack your papers on the desk and remember to check the website for your homework."

As the class began to file out, Val walked toward the front of the classroom.

"Oops, sorry," she said, bumping into Nikki and knocking her notebook and pens across the floor. "Let me help you with that."

Val quickly gathered up Nikki's scattered items and put them into her hands, but at the bottom of the pile Nikki could feel a strange metallic object—it felt like one of Rachel's specialty items. Nikki frowned in puzzlement, and with a wink, Val glanced in Dina's direction. Nikki shook her head, but Val nodded and shoved everything into Nikki's arms.

"See you all tomorrow," she said, and waved at the trainees.

Nikki walked out last, looking at Valerie Robinson over her shoulder. What had Val given her?

You Make Me Sick

"Breath spray?" Nikki muttered, holding up the object Val had given her. Turning the slender tube upside down, she checked the label. "ILL-zero-zero-one," she read. "What weapon is I-L-L?"

"Ill," translated Jenny without looking up from her notes. "It's for making people sick."

"Oh," Nikki said, and nervously stashed the breath spray in her pocket. "What's on the agenda for tonight?" she asked, changing the subject.

"Fight night!" exclaimed Jenny, squashing her notes together and ramming them into her bag.

"Facials," Ellen said.

"Facials and XFC," Jenny said happily. "Tito's team is gonna whup ass!"

"Oh," said Nikki doubtfully. "The girl's are really going to go for that?"

"I know it's a little odd," Ellen said, "but once you know a little something about fighting, you do kind of get into it."

Nikki nodded but found it hard to believe that the entire group of women was really going to be happy about tuning in for the *Extreme Fighting Challenge*. But after dinner, the common room was packed, and the smell of popcorn and mint pedicure lotion filled the air, along with the sound of a dozen conversations. Nikki was having a hard time concentrating.

"You know, it's that sound?" asked Jenny. "When you get hit really hard? Sort of a squeak and a ting at the same time, only silent?"

Nikki stared blankly at Jenny, who was sitting on the couch across from her eating popcorn. She hadn't really been paying attention—she'd been thinking about how to offer Dina ILL001 and not seem suspicious.

"Don't bother," Sarah said. She leaped over the back of the couch and landed with a jarring impact on the cushions next to Jenny, bouncing the bowl and throwing popcorn into the air. Jenny threw Sarah a dirty look and grabbed the bowl before it upended entirely. It was hard to take Jenny seriously when she was wearing a Strawberry Shortcake T-shirt, two ponytails, and a face covered in green goo.

"She has a hard head," Sarah continued. "She's probably never heard the sound."

"What sound? You guys are making this up," said Nikki irritably.

"No, it's when you get hit so hard that your senses sort of separate. You hear, but you can't see," Jenny assured her, her blond hair bouncing.

"That makes no sense," Nikki said.

"Told you," Sarah said. "She has a hard head. I hit her so hard in sparring the other day I thought I was going to cause some sort of permanent damage, but she just walked through it."

"It wasn't that hard," protested Nikki, remembering Sarah's reaction rather than the actual punch. "Well, I mean, I'm sure you punched hard, but it didn't connect hard. I kind of ducked a little. It probably looked worse than it was."

"No, I'm pretty sure you just have a hard head," Sarah said, grabbing a handful of Jenny's popcorn.

"Shhh," commanded Carmella from across the room. "The fight's starting."

"I've got more face mask!" Ellen said, coming out of the kitchen with a blender full of green stuff. "Or possibly veggie dip." She dipped a finger in and sucked off the liquid.

Something about Carrie Mae training still seemed unbelievable. The other women walked through days filled with classes and physical training and never seemed to notice, but Nikki was still experiencing profound moments of incredulity.

She glanced down at the pile of flash cards she was supposed to be studying during the commercial breaks. The chemical compounds in Specialty Items were way beyond the basic chemistry she had taken, and she didn't want to fall behind. She idly flipped through the cards, with one eye on the blender full of face mask as it was passed around. She didn't want to miss this batch.

Ellen had taken over the seat next to Jenny's, and Nikki looked at the pair curiously. They were her friends now, but sometimes Nikki wondered if it was real friendship or the kind that only existed because everyone had to be friends with someone. Nikki scrutinized the two. Ellen had the clean accent of a newscaster and occasionally used the fragmented and overwrought language of someone "encultured" in higher education—a holdover from her days as a professor's wife. Her darling Dale, an astronomy professor, had passed away two years ago of a heart attack. Jenny, Southern and proud, but still class-conscious, yin-yanged from sweet to crass in a matter of moments, her linguistic choices clearly displaying her own uncertainty about where she belonged.

Nikki felt a similar doubt and tried to watch her own language for signifiers. The trick was to be consistent and not to deviate from the average language choices too much.

She wondered if anyone else felt as if they were only here through some strange coincidence of fate, in no way connected to actual ability or merit. She definitely wasn't here on merit. She remembered a face full of lipstick and shuddered.

Nikki's hand jerked, trying to push the memory away, and scattered her flash cards on the floor, drawing strange looks from the others. She smiled in embarrassment and knelt to pick up the cards. She was not thinking about that particular evening. She was not thinking about handcuffs or anything related to that night.

The program cut to a commercial for a dental hygienist program at a local community college.

"I was going to do that," Carmella said, pointing to the TV. "If I hadn't come here, that's what I was going to do."

"I was on the waiting list for the nursing program," said Sarah.

"I just graduated from college. I was supposed to go work with my dad," Heidi said gloomily. "He was kind of pissed that I came here instead."

"I'd be twenty pounds heavier," volunteered Ellen, "and I'd be up to date on *Days of Our Lives*."

"I'd probably have gotten engaged to Ben Mitchell," Jenny said. "He was a lawyer. Mama really liked that I'd never have to work again. My family didn't really understand why I wanted to leave."

"Mine, neither," agreed Heidi. "And I couldn't say it was because I wanted something better, because Dad doesn't think there's anything better than his business."

"I was in the army for a while," Sarah said. "Good benefits and everything, but my mom kept freaking out that I was going to go die while I was in Iraq. She doesn't understand why I'm wasting a slot in the nursing program to come here."

"How about you, Nikki? Where'd you be, if you weren't here?" asked Jenny.

"Jail," said Nikki, unintentionally answering honestly. Everyone stared. "Joke." she said, hastily gathering the last flash card and resuming her seat. The girls exchanged glances, and Ellen shook her head.

"I don't think so," said Cheryl.

"There was a slight incident when I tried to sell makeup," Nikki said. Jenny and Ellen exchanged glances.

"I see," Carmella said.

"And did this incident involve some sort of police action?" asked Heidi, leaning forward with a grin.

Nikki shifted uncomfortably; she did not want to talk about this.

"Fight's back on!" Ellen said, rescuing Nikki.

"We're coming back to this," threatened Sarah.

"Later," said Jenny, around a mouthful of popcorn. "During the commercials."

But commercials came and Jenny immediately launched into a story about throwing up during a beauty pageant. By the time the contestants were diving for the tiara, the fight was back on.

"Thanks," Nikki whispered, as they walked upstairs to their rooms.

"I could see you didn't want to talk about it," Jenny whispered back.

"But you realize that now you have to tell us," put in Ellen.

"It's embarrassing," Nikki protested.

"More embarrassing than throwing up in front of the entire judging panel and my high-school crush?" Jenny demanded, and Nikki paused, trying to balance out the relative weights of their shame.

"Good point," she said, opening the door to their room.

"Hold on," Ellen said, digging through one of her dresser drawers. "I want to hear more about the boy from Canada. You never finished your story about him."

"What brought that up?" asked Nikki, amazed by Ellen's elephantine memory.

"I'm not getting my daily soap opera, so I've got to fill it in with something, and you girls are it. Besides, I've been thinking about that guy; he doesn't sound very trustworthy. I want to know what happened."

"She's right," said Jenny, laughing. "That is kind of sketchy behavior, but I want to hear about getting arrested first."

"So, what happened?" pursued Ellen.

"I told you. We went to lunch. And besides, he's not at all related to the getting arrested thing." Or was he? Canada and Carrie Mae were all sort of bundled together in her memory, and it was hard to say that they weren't related.

"Right," said Jenny. "And there is no way that lunch is going to be more interesting than getting arrested. So I want to hear about that. You can finish up the Canada story after the 'getting arrested' story."

"I think I bought some Girl Scout cookies last time we went to the store," Ellen muttered, still rummaging. "OK, jail it is then. Like sand through the hourglass, these are the days of Nikki's life." She pulled out the box and offered the opened end to the other two girls. Nikki accepted her cookie and thought about where to start her story.

The Lipstick Incident

Nikki looked at her hands. The handcuffs were very shiny, just like the remains of her nail polish. She regarded her three torn nails with sorrow—now she would have to clip all the nails to make them even. She looked up and caught sight of herself in the presumably two-way mirror. Her hair was in complete disarray and had grass and a twig sticking out of it. She reached up and removed the twig and grass with her left hand; the handcuffs dragged her right hand across her face in a tangled display of uncoordination. She laid the grass and twig neatly on the table in front of her. She made an ineffectual pat at her hair, but gave up in indifference. She sighed and studied the blade of grass. It was green with a slight vein down the middle. The police detective came back into the room, and Nikki straightened up in her chair.

"So, Miss Lanier," he said, pronouncing it like LANE-e-er.

"Lanier," she corrected automatically, and then regretted it instantly.

"What?" he said.

"Lan-yay," she said miserably. "It's pronounced Lan-yay."

"It would be," he responded enigmatically. Nikki tried a smile, but knew it was a miserable attempt. "I don't suppose you would care to explain this whole affair?" He flipped open a manila file folder and looked over the contents.

"Temporary insanity?" Nikki suggested with another half-smile.

"Well, yes, that does seem likely," said the detective, clearly examining her disheveled appearance. "But I assume you didn't go to that house intending to assault anyone."

"Well, no," said Nikki hesitantly. "I think maybe I . . . I just sort of snapped."

The house had been all red brick and white paint. Four structurally useless "Grecian" pillars had adorned the front porch and lent an impressive air to the semicircular drive that took up most of the front lawn. Nikki had a sinking feeling when she had seen that house, but Toni, her mother's friend, had exclaimed in admiration, "Isn't that cute?" Toni thought a lot of things were cute. Toni sold candles and knickknacks that Nikki wouldn't have kept in her closet. Nikki had sighed and agreed. Toni was being nice. Toni was doing Nikki—well, really Nikki's mother—a favor by bringing her along.

"Now, remember, Nikki, just let them try everything and agree with whatever they say and you'll sell a bundle. These women like personal treatment."

"I went to sell Carrie Mae with Toni," Nikki told the detective. The words were not coming readily to her tongue. "My mother won a starter kit," she explained. She didn't want the detective to think she sold Carrie Mae for *real*. "And I haven't been able to find a job, and my mother kept saying I could make money with it, and her friend Toni said she'd take me along on one of her trips. She said it would be easy."

"I see," said the detective in a bored tone. "So you went to the house to sell makeup with Toni?"

"They were everywhere!" said Nikki, her voice coming out in a whisper.

"They?" asked the detective.

Nikki swayed a little in her seat, remembering.

The white double doors had swung open. The two women were ushered into the foyer by a woman with an expensive-looking blond bob and Nordstrom slacks. Nikki thought the woman was exactly what Nikki's mother wanted to be, from her perfectly streaked hair to her "sensible" $250 shoes. Nikki and Toni followed "Mrs. Doctor" across the foyer and into the living room. Blondes in a variety of ages and tints covered the room, and not one of them, Nikki realized as she surveyed the spectrum of dye jobs, could claim it was natural.

The Exquisite Cook lady was there already, ensconced at a table next to the door to the kitchen and handing out samples fresh from the oven. Toni had set up in one corner and had gestured Nikki to another. Nikki had arranged her table into a neat array of sample cards and nail polish colors. She looked around the room. No one was looking in her direction. Toni was laughing heartily, as if she were everyone's old friend. Someone came by with a glass of wine, which Nikki accepted with gratitude. There were reasons alcohol was a legal drug.

"So there were a lot of blondes and they gave you wine?" The detective wasn't really appreciating the horror of the story.

"Yes," Nikki said. "But just a little bit. I was trying to be careful. I do dumb things when I drink."

The detective made a grunting noise that Nikki took to be a

form of agreement. She ran her fingers over the scarred laminate top of the table in front of her. Someone had carved COPS SUCK ASS into the lower lefthand corner.

"What happened next?" the detective asked.

His harsh tone yanked Nikki from her Zen-like contemplation of the carving. She stared at him, trying to remember what they had been talking about.

"I did makeovers," she said, forcing her mind back to the horror.

The blondes had passed before her in some sort of predetermined order that Nikki had never been able to fathom. They clucked and ogled and tested her samples. Cornstalk blondes had torn the packets open, bleach blondes had passed the lipsticks around. Blush powder was everywhere—the debris of twenty makeovers strewn at her feet. She had tried to steer a few people toward certain products, but the women seemed so set on particular colors, and Toni had said to just agree with them, so she had.

And the women had been nice. At least, they'd *said* nice things. Although, perhaps there was an undertone of insult in that comment about her hair. And the way they called her "honey," it was as if they couldn't remember her name.

"So, they tried your samples and called you honey?" The detective just wasn't getting it.

"They didn't just *try* my samples. They tried all of them. They used *all* the samples. If I want more, I have to buy them from the company."

"I see," said the detective, and he made a note. "OK. Then what happened?"

"Well, then it was ordering time."

"So, they ordered your makeup."

Nikki shook her head. Unbidden tears welled up in her eyes at the mere thought of her humiliation.

"No-oo," she said tremulously. "They didn't. They all ordered Exquisite Cook or Star Lite Candles. And this woman came up and said . . ." Nikki sniffed ferociously, and the detective handed her a tissue from a pack in his pocket. "Thank you. She said if I'd been more *agreeable* they would have ordered from me. *Agreeable!* I complimented her hair! I said that she looked good in green! I said that no one could see those lines! I, I . . ." Nikki trailed off, gasping in outrage.

"Is that when you tackled her?"

"I didn't tackle her," Nikki denied hotly. "I merely suggested that she keep one of the mascara brushes she had used."

The detective flipped a few pages in the file. "I believe your exact words were: 'It will make a nice change for the stick up your ass.'" Nikki blushed, color flooding her face, making her cheeks burn. "And then you tackled her?"

"She slapped me!" she answered hotly, remembering the stinging impact of the woman's ringed fingers against her cheek. "And then I . . . helped her apply the eye shadow she had admired so much," Nikki finished lamely.

"You tackled her," translated the detective.

Nikki nodded dumbly.

"And the other three women? You helped them with their makeup as well?"

Nikki remembered Mrs. Doctor running across the drive and onto the front lawn. She remembered screaming "agreeable" like a battle cry. Mrs. Doctor had gone down like Nancy Kerrigan—skating across the grass on her butt, wailing.

There was a knock on the door. It opened a crack, and a policewoman jerked her head at the detective. The detective left the room, but returned a few minutes later. He walked over to Nikki and unlocked her handcuffs.

"You're free to go, Miss Lan-yair." There was a slight mocking in his voice as he pronounced her name.

"I don't understand," said Nikki.

"The charges have been dropped. Your lawyer is waiting for you out front."

"I don't have a lawyer," Nikki said in a daze.

"Well, you do now, so up you get." He jerked a thumb in an upward direction. Nikki stood numbly and stumbled toward the door.

"I have just one more question," the detective said as Nikki's hand touched the doorknob. "Did you really make that woman eat a lipstick?"

Nikki looked at him. He displayed only a kind of bored curiosity. Nikki nodded solemnly.

"She opened a tube without asking and tried it. And once someone tries it, you can't sell it to anyone else, and she practically promised to buy it. And then she didn't."

"You'd better get going," he said, shaking his head, but kind of laughing. "The policewoman outside will show you the way."

The lawyer had pronounced her name correctly on the first try, and that was worrying Nikki. She was a heavyset woman in an impeccable cream linen suit. She had a silk scarf draped just so and pinned in place with a gold butterfly brooch. Her earrings were gold, and her hair was cut close to her head and done in an expensive finger wave. Her makeup was a perfectly golden hue that no white woman could have gotten away with, and her skin glowed with an even chocolate tone. Nikki knew that she was looking her most splotchy and trailer park at the moment, and she found herself envying the other woman's cool poise. She watched as the lawyer traded jokes with the cops, collected paperwork, and ignored Nikki entirely.

Nikki looked at the business card that had been thrust into her hands. AISHA LEWIS, ATTORNEY AT LAW was printed on very heavy cream paper in green and gold. The letters had been pressed into the paper so that Nikki could feel a slightly raised version of the letters on the back of the card. It was a very expensive card, and Nikki knew that neither she nor her mother could afford a lawyer who could afford expensive cards.

The lawyer placed a stack of paperwork in front of Nikki and spread the pages out with a practiced hand so that each page beneath the first showed only the signature section. Nikki fumbled gracelessly for a pen, and the lawyer produced one like a magic trick and handed it to her with a motherly "There you go." Nikki took the pen and signed on the lines without reading any of it. Aisha swept up the papers and handed them to one of the cops. Nikki rose to her feet, sensing that signed paperwork meant that things were coming to a close. Aisha nodded generally to everyone and then took Nikki by the elbow and began to shepherd her through the series of doors that led to the outside.

"Are you my lawyer? I mean—" Nikki fumbled for words, knowing that the woman hadn't asked what she meant—"did someone call you for me?" That still wasn't quite right, but it would have to do.

"Those are two separate questions. To answer your second question, someone did engage me to represent you in this matter. In answer to the first, no, I'm not your lawyer. I do not represent what is in your best interest. I am looking out for the best interest of the hiring body. Fortunately for you, their interests and yours appear to coincide. For the moment." Nikki turned a bewildered face to the lawyer as they stepped through the front doors of the police station.

"I'm sorry," Nikki said. "I suppose I'm being slow, but it's been a very long night. I don't understand."

"I'm sure it will all be explained," Aisha said soothingly. "Now, if you will excuse me, I really have got somewhere else I'd rather be." The lawyer lifted her wrist and checked her watch with a businesslike eye, then glanced out into the street. "Ah, right on time."

Nikki followed the lawyer's gaze to the street, where a modest-size limousine was pulling up. The limo parked. The driver got out and walked around briskly to Nikki's side of the car. He opened the door and then looked significantly in Nikki's direction.

"A word of advice, Miss Lanier," said Aisha with a smile. "Don't sign anything without reading it, and always ask for more than is being offered."

"Just on principle?" asked Nikki with a small laugh, uncertain if the lawyer was making a joke.

"Just on principle," Aisha affirmed with a wink, and she turned on her heel, walking toward the parking lot.

With nothing else to do, Nikki walked slowly toward the limo. The chauffeur seemed to be trying to hurry her along with his eyes, and Nikki had the uncomfortable feeling that she was holding up his schedule.

Nikki leaned down and looked through the door. Miranda Merrivel, National Sales Director for Carrie Mae Cosmetics, sat with one ear to a cell phone and one hand on a champagne glass. The grandmotherly aura that Mrs. Merrivel had worn when they first met had completely disappeared. Instead, she had resumed her "sleek scion of sales" persona that Nikki found indefinably irritating, and intimidating. When she saw Nikki, Mrs. Merrivel set the glass down and beckoned her to enter. Nikki did as she was asked, and the chauffeur shut the door behind her with a brisk thump. A few seconds later the engine started and the limo oozed back onto the roadway.

Mrs. Merrivel was dressed in sage green slacks and a lavender blouse. A matching suit jacket was tossed on the opposite seat, and twinkling from the lapel was a gold butterfly pin. A pin that was nearly identical to the one Aisha had been wearing on her scarf. Nikki frowned as she considered what this meant. The Carrie Mae logo was a butterfly, but why would Carrie Mae have sent a lawyer for her?

Mrs. Merrivel was making "get on with it" gestures at her phone, but her voice was calm and understanding.

"Yes, of course, we can take care of that. I understand perfectly. Now, I'm afraid I have to go." She listened for a few more minutes. "No, I don't want to cut you off, but I have a consultation in a few minutes and my guest has just arrived." That seemed to satisfy the person at the other end of the line, because the conversation was wrapped up very shortly. Mrs. Merrivel sighed as she hung up the phone.

"It's a small lie," she said to Nikki, "but Connie does tend to ramble on a bit if you don't cut her off." Mrs. Merrivel smiled suddenly. "But you know, in a way you are here for a consultation. Not the ordinary kind, I suppose. We won't be trying on makeup, but we will be trying on ideas." Mrs. Merrivel smiled a shiny, plasticine smile, and Nikki became aware that she was in the presence of Carrie Mae. Not the actual person, but Carrie Mae—the company.

"Mrs. Merrivel," Nikki said, trying to forestall whatever speech was coming, "why are you here?"

"I was doing a recruiting speech down at the La Quinta Inn. I was just finishing up when I heard about your predicament." Mrs. Merrivel wore her smile like armor, and Nikki envied that invulnerability.

"But, I mean, you don't do this for everyone, do you? How did you even know where I was? I mean . . ." Nikki trailed off. She wanted to ask how Mrs. Merrivel even remembered her, but she was too embarrassed.

Mrs. Merrivel laughed, and with some hesitancy Nikki smiled back.

"No, of course not. But I told you in Vancouver that I'd be keeping an eye on your progress." She patted Nikki's knee. "Why don't you just sit back and let me tell you about things?"

Nikki gave in and sat back against the limo cushions, feeling immensely tired. She wondered how long this would take.

The conversation meandered. Mrs. Merrivel talked about the need for an organization that put women first. She used words such as *clandestine* and *skill set*. Nikki wondered if Mrs. Merrivel's skills were color coordinated and came in a matching box. It was all leading up to something. Was she being offered a job? Nikki was too tired to believe that.

"Would you be interested in a job like that, Nikki?" Mrs. Merrivel asked directly. There was something formidable about her, as if whatever goal she sank her teeth into would be accomplished or demolished like a dog's chew toy.

"Uh, I'm not sure. What would it involve?" Nikki started to worry that Mrs. Merrivel was looking at her as if she were a really good bone.

"Travel, research, a little bit of adventure."

"Sounds like the Marines," said Nikki, and Mrs. Merrivel laughed.

"We have better clothes."

Nikki looked at Mrs. Merrivel, and somewhere under the layers of dirt, fatigue, and lint there stirred a small flame of rebellion. The embers of that fire had been burning since the day she moved back in with her mother.

"How much would it pay?" asked Nikki, trying to focus.

"Thirty-six thousand a year to start, plus training and living quarters while you're training. Of course, the training is down in California."

Nikki considered the idea. Her mother would hate it. She said charities were like working for the government, all responsibility and no compensation. And it was in California, another thought that was bound to irritate her mother. But it was thirty-six thousand more dollars than she was getting right now, and it was better than working at Starbucks, which was where she had picked up an application earlier this morning. Was it really only this morning? And besides, she'd already done it. She'd snapped. She'd been in jail. How much madder could her mother get after that?

"I'll understand if you need time to consider it," Mrs. Merrivel said.

"No. I don't need any time to consider," Nikki said. A flash of surprise and, perhaps, disappointment appeared on Mrs. Merrivel's face and then was gone as quickly as it had come. "I'll do it," Nikki said.

"Great!" Mrs. Merrivel smiled triumphantly, like Patton upon seeing the Rhine.

The words of Aisha Lewis seemed to echo in Nikki's ear. Nikki swallowed hard. She had already been figuring out how much she'd make a month. She opened her mouth to demand forty a year, medical benefits, and travel expenses to and from California, but her mother's voice seemed to be shouting in her ear to keep what she had and not reach for anything more.

"What if I don't like it when I get there?" Nikki asked cautiously, trying to ignore her mother's voice. "And will I have to pay my own way to and from California?" It took all of her courage to ask for that much.

Mrs. Merrivel's eyes narrowed slightly, but her lips retained their smile.

"I'll send you a round-trip plane ticket and arrange all your travel to and from the airport." Nikki exhaled, and only then realized she'd been holding her breath.

The limo began to slow down. Looking out the window, Nikki saw that they had arrived at the airport.

"Now, then," Mrs. Merrivel said, draining her glass and setting it in the cup holder. "I'll send you a plane ticket this week. I'll try to get you on a flight to L.A. by Saturday at the latest. Will that be enough time to get your things in order?" Nikki tried not to gape. "Just bring some clothes. If you need anything else you can always send for it later."

"Of course," said Nikki.

The limo had stopped. Nikki could hear the trunk being opened and the luggage unloaded. Mrs. Merrivel picked up her jacket from the seat beside her and slipped it on. She tidied her spread of documents and cell phone into her briefcase and closed it with a click.

"I'll ask the driver to take you home."

"Oh, thanks." Saying thank you reminded Nikki that she had a great deal more to be thankful for than a simple ride home from the airport. "About the jail," Nikki began hesitantly.

Mrs. Merrivel shook her head. "Don't worry about it."

"Yes, but, I mean . . ." Nikki didn't know what she meant. "Those women were pretty upset." Mrs. Merrivel smiled again. It was beginning to seem to Nikki that Mrs. Merrivel had only two expressions: smiling and not.

"I imagine they were, but I believe Ms. Lewis took care of everything," Mrs. Merrivel said somewhat distractedly; she was peering out the window. Nikki opened her mouth to protest, but the limo door opened just then.

"I have just one question," asked Mrs. Merrivel, sliding forward in her seat, preparing to leave. "Did you really make a woman eat lipstick?"

"I . . ." Nikki wanted to explain, but suddenly felt too tired even to make the attempt. "Yes," she said, and nodded sadly.

"Good," Mrs. Merrivel said firmly. "I'm sure she deserved it." She smiled again and exited the limousine. The door closed firmly behind her and Nikki sank further into her seat, wondering, not for the first time that night, what on earth she had just done.

Skills

"Well, that was supremely unhelpful," said Dina as they came out of the lecture. Carmella and Sarah were playing keep-away with Cheryl's stuffed animal key chain and Dina was shouting over the noise of Cheryl's protests and the rattle of the keychain.

"I thought it was interesting," Ellen said.

"Ignore everything we taught you? Improvise?" snapped Dina. "Yeah, that's helpful. I don't think she knows what she's talking about."

"That's Mrs. Robinson, dude," said Sarah. "Her name is on the Consultants of Note plaque. They say she pulled five women doctors out of Afghanistan, *by herself*."

"That doesn't mean she knows how to teach tactics." Dina sniffed.

"I don't know, she seemed to know what she was saying when she called your strategy stupid, ill conceived, and dangerous," said Heidi.

"Shut up, Heidi," Dina said.

"Ooh, clever comeback," said Carmella. "Really stretching your intellect there."

Nikki looked back to the classroom doorway where Val lounged, cigarette dangling from her hand. When she caught Nikki's eye, she mimed using the breath spray, then gave a thumbs-up. Nikki frowned and shook her head, but of its own accord her hand tightened around the small canister in her pocket and began to pull it out.

Dina was only a few steps away. She could put on a fake, cheerful smile, walk over, and offer her the breath spray, and then everything would be OK. Nikki wavered, then decided. Poisoning a teammate was not the Carrie Mae way. She just couldn't do it, no matter how obnoxious Dina was.

"Incoming," yelled Carmella as Cheryl cannoned into Nikki. Nikki staggered and tripped, her notebook and bag scattering in front of her. The breath spray bounced twice and rolled to a stop at Dina's feet.

"Hey, that's mine," said Dina, scooping up the breath spray.

"No, it's mine," Nikki said breathlessly, scrambling to her feet.

"I lost mine in the common room yesterday," Dina said, pocketing the ILL001. "You must have taken it. By mistake, I'm sure." She added a snide smile and walked away.

"Sorry, Nikki," Cheryl said, clutching the jingling mess of her keys with their stuffed dog key chain in one hand and helping to gather Nikki's belongings with the other.

"That's OK," said Nikki, forcing a smile.

"Sorry, Nikki," echoed Carmella and Heidi as they ran by. Cheryl took off after them.

"Did Dina just steal your breath spray?" Ellen asked, shaking the dirt off Nikki's notebook.

"Yes, and I need to get it back," said Nikki, following Dina toward the dorms at a quick trot.

"Don't worry. I'll pinch it off her during Cocktails," volunteered Jenny. "I've been practicing my pickpocketing skills."

"I didn't realize that you had pickpocketing skills." Ellen sounded skeptical. "If I remember correctly, in class you pretty much just flashed your boobs at people and dug around in their pockets."

"Like I said . . . skills."

"I don't think that's going to work on Dina."

"Girls! You don't understand! I have to get that breath spray back!"

Jenny and Ellen looked at her with twin expressions of curiosity.

"It's not really breath spray. It's ILL001."

Ellen's mouth stretched into an oval *O* of disbelief, while Jenny grinned and did an impromptu happy dance.

"You stole product from Specialty Items?" whispered Ellen, shocked.

"No," Nikki said. "Not exactly."

"We should let her use it," interjected Jenny.

"We don't do that," Ellen said. "We are the good guys."

"And she's the bad guy. I hope she pukes all day," said Jenny cheerfully.

"No, Ellen's right," Nikki said. "We can't poison someone who's on our side. But I sure as hell am not going to confess to Dina, so I've got to get it back."

"I still say we should let her use it," said Jenny, "but you can count on me."

"You don't have to help," Nikki protested, looking at the pair. "It's my goof-up."

"And you're our friend. You can count on us." Jenny and Ellen nodded.

"Meanwhile, we'd better keep an eye on her and make sure she doesn't use it," Ellen said.

"A good time to get it would be after she changes for Cocktails, don't you think?" Nikki said, linking arms with her friends. "Those dresses she wears don't have pockets, so she can't bring it with her. I can sneak in her room and get it then."

"That sounds good," Jenny agreed. "Her room's across the hall from mine. I'll keep an eye on her until then and give you the signal when it's safe to go in."

With the plan in place, there was little left to do but return to their rooms. Nikki looked nervously after Jenny, but Ellen pulled her firmly into their room. "No sense in worrying about it now," she said. "Just hurry and get changed, so you're ready when Jenny gives you the sign."

Mere minutes later, Nikki was standing in front of the mirror tugging with irritation at the strap of her new dress. She and Ellen had gone shopping over the weekend and Nikki had used $19.99 of her pitiful cash hoard to purchase it. She had been looking for something to wear to Cocktails class. Preferably something classy with pockets, which was apparently like getting Paris Hilton to wear underwear: entirely implausible.

When she found the little clearance rack dress with pockets, it had seemed absolutely perfect. Standing in the dressing room wearing the flirty Marilyn Monroe dress with her favorite flip-flops, Nikki wished that she'd been wearing something like it when she had met Z'ev. At the thought of Z'ev, she took a moment to savor the memory of his delicious smile, before moving on to more productive thoughts. She still hadn't come to any conclusions about Canada, despite her constant replaying of the incident, but in the dressing room it had seemed very clear that Z'ev would have liked her in the dress.

Ellen was trying on a skirt suit in front of the mirror as Nikki stepped out, but turned around as Nikki came into view.

"That is absolutely perfect!" Ellen exclaimed. "It makes you look about this big around. Well, you are this big around, but the dress just emphasizes that fact."

Nikki had beamed and pulled on her shoes before turning to look in the mirror. Then she frowned. In the store, the dress had been perfect, but now, in the privacy of her own room, with her black high heels on, the short, flowing skirt that allowed for pockets seemed too short and the top, which had been perfect in the store, seemed too tight. The other girls were going to think she looked like a tart. Maybe she could put a sweater over it.

She didn't have a sweater.

In desperation Nikki tried the dress with her zip-up sweatshirt; the effect was ridiculous. It was the shoes, Nikki decided; they just didn't match. She sighed in frustration and decided that she would just have to brave it out; she could not wear her old dress one more time.

Nikki slipped a golf pencil that she'd worn down to a nub and a small folded piece of paper into one of her pockets and surveyed herself in the mirror. Turning this way and that, she decided that the pencil and paper were invisible to a cursory glance and nodded in satisfaction.

Ellen came out of the bathroom and looked Nikki over, pausing on the shoes.

"You don't have any other color shoes?"

"If I did, I'd be wearing them," said Nikki sourly.

"Well, shoot. We should have gone shoe shopping when we were at the store."

"I didn't think about it at the time," said Nikki with a sigh.

"Neither did I. Oh well, nothing you can do about it now. You still look nice. We'll make a quick trip next weekend."

Ellen had purchased an elegant dress-and-jacket combo that was figure-flattering and left room for an unseen wire. Nikki found herself admiring Ellen's confident, graceful style and wishing that Nell could be a little more like Ellen. Ellen picked up the wire and adjusted it on her lapel, pinning it in place with a large Carrie Mae butterfly pin. She spoke quietly into it, and sounds came out of the recorder on the bed.

"We don't have to wear those tonight, do we?" Nikki asked, worried that she'd mixed up her deadlines.

"No, that's Friday. I just wanted to test this with my new outfit before then. Sort of a dress rehearsal for the dress, if you know what I mean."

Ellen looked at herself in the mirror and did a quick spin to make sure no wires were dangling. She took a quick pat at her hair and then leaned forward, her nose just inches from the glass.

"Do you think I should dye my hair?" she asked suddenly. "I let it go after Dale died. It seemed so pointless. Well," she amended, "everything seemed pointless; dyeing my hair didn't even make it near the list of things to do. But now I'm thinking maybe I should start again. It's getting so gray and it makes me feel old. I'm not that old! I'm only forty-seven. What do you think?"

She turned to Nikki with a questioning expression. Nikki paused, wondering how best to answer the question. She was never comfortable advising people on their looks.

"Well, if you're unhappy with it, then maybe just put in a little bit of color and just brighten it up a bit," she suggested. "It looks nice now, but color could be good."

"I think so, too," said Ellen, turning back to the mirror. "I'd love to go red like you, but I don't think I could pull it off."

Nikki burst out laughing. "You don't want to go red," she said firmly. "It's not a good color."

"What are you talking about? I love your hair! It's beautiful. So many colors all in one—copper and carrot and blonde. You just can't get that out of a bottle."

"I get it from my dad," Nikki said, startled by the unexpected compliment.

"I'll go check on Jenny," Ellen said, settling the microphone a little more firmly into her pin and turning on the recording device.

Nikki took a moment to adjust the strap of her dress again in the mirror and, with a pleased pat at her hair, followed Ellen into the hall. It was a pretty dress, even if the shoes were wrong, and she looked good in it.

"Dina just went down," said Ellen breathlessly. I'll go wait by the stairs and make sure she doesn't come back up."

"Right," Nikki said, hurrying toward Dina's room. Her heart was beating fast. Jenny was waiting for her by Dina's door.

"You keep lookout while I search," said Nikki, and Jenny nodded as Nikki slid into Dina's room.

The room was a mess, and Nikki suddenly felt better about her own clutter and bulging laundry basket. At least she used the laundry basket, unlike Dina, who apparently used the floor. Nikki searched quickly, trying not to leave any telltale disturbance in the strata of mess.

"Hurry!" Jenny hissed from the hall. Nikki wanted to yell something back, but she bit her tongue and lifted a bit of the pile on a chair in the corner. Heaving a sigh of relief, she pulled out the jeans Dina had been wearing earlier in the day. And there in the pocket was the tube of breath spray.

"Got it," she said, gently closing the door and slipping the tube into her pocket. Jenny grinned and led the way down to Cocktails class.

Cocktails

As this was a dinner event, the class was being held in the common room. Many of the girls were already downstairs mingling, or practicing mingling. The easy camaraderie of the day had been replaced with forced small talk as everyone pretended they didn't know each other. Mr. Bamoko, the Cocktails instructor, was waiting at the foot of the stairs. He frowned heavily at Nikki's shoes. Nikki waited as Jenny received her assignment and then stepped forward. She could see Jenny and Ellen holding a brief conversation just inside the common room.

"You know your shoes are the wrong color?" Mr. Bamoko asked, recapturing Nikki's attention. He was dressed in a pinstripe suit, matching vest, and tie. The crisp white collar of the shirt fit his neck to perfection, with no gaps or airway-blocking snugness. The high shine on his beautifully molded Italian leather shoes reflected a world not half as perfect as their owner.

"Yeah, I know, but I don't have any other dress shoes," Nikki said weakly. Mr. Bamoko raised his eyes from his clipboard and stared as if Nikki had just announced that the Pope would be converting to Buddhism. Nikki tried to smile back.

"Please dismiss the word *yeah* from your vocabulary," Mr. Bamoko said, just after the point at which his stare had became unbearable. "It is a deplorable piece of slang that has crept into our national speech. Slang is careless speech and a detriment to the language."

"Slang is a generational marker and denotes in-crowd status. Many people feel it broadens the language, adding depth and character, and is a necessary innovation for language growth."

Too late, Nikki's internal editor ran in, waving his hands, and yelling, "Shut up, shut up, shut up, you stupid cow!"

Mr. Bamoko blinked. Twice.

"I am not one of those people," he said repressively. "Furthermore, if slang denotes in-crowd status, then I can truly state that it is not a crowd I wish to be in. And since none of the said 'in-crowd' will be grading your performance in class tonight, I would suggest that you not use the word *yeah*. Have we reached an understanding in this matter?"

Her internal editor held up a cue card with her recommended dialogue, and Nikki read it carefully, word for word.

"Yes, Mr. Bamoko."

"Excellent. Here is your assignment," he said, handing her a three-by-five index card.

Nikki read the card. It said: "Discover where the ambassador will be going tomorrow and any pertinent information about her security staff."

Nikki handed the card back, and Mr. Bamoko handed her a nametag. Nikki pasted TRIXIE, TEACHER'S WIFE over her heart and hoped that the sticker's adhesive material wouldn't mess up her new dress.

Giving Ellen a subtle wink as she entered, Nikki began to introduce her teacher's wife persona around. Each time she picked up any information on the ambassador's security measures, she surreptitiously jotted down a note on the paper hidden in her pocket. She met several "journalists," two "teachers," and a "marine" before spotting the "ambassador." Erica, Jorge's assistant instructor, was taking her role as ambassador seriously, expounding to a journalist about the leading export of Carrie Mae-land and the importance of mascara in international politics. Nikki smothered a laugh and checked to make sure none of the instructors had caught her slipup.

Mrs. Boyer, Connie, and Mr. Bamoko stalked around the perimeter of the room like judges at a dog show, jotting down notes and eyeing each trainee with deep concentration. Nikki wormed her way closer to Erica and chatted with Cheryl about the unusual customs of Carrie Mae-land. Cheryl was playing a diplomatic attaché, and Nikki took a perverse sort of pleasure in pressing her for details on an "obscure eyelash curling ritual," knowing that Cheryl would have to make it up on the spot.

"Really?" said Nikki with genuine respect for Cheryl's imagination. "How do you secure an event like that? With so many people running around it must be hard to protect the ambassador." Cheryl nodded, but Nikki could see that she was suspicious of the question. Nikki smiled and feigned innocent curiosity.

She knew that Cheryl would have to obey the rules of Cocktails: she had to answer questions; she couldn't simply turn around and walk away. And although she could misrepresent information, she could not lie outright. Points were given for clever questioning, clever evasions, story consistency, and etiquette. Points were deducted for dropping character, lying, and behaving in a "less than Carrie Mae-like way." Whatever that meant. At the end of the evening each girl made her report, and the judges critiqued her technique. If Nikki didn't discover where the ambassador was going tomorrow, her mission would be stamped with a big red FAILED and she would have to do a remedial Cocktails classes on top of her already full schedule.

"Well, generally we like to keep such events invitation-only, so of course we check IDs against the guest list and try to control the access points."

"Interesting," Nikki said, fiddling with one of her earrings, a dangling crystal at the end of a thin silver chain. She had liked the chandelier effect and the sparkle it added to her hair, but she was now finding that if she twisted the crystal toward the light she could reflect a rainbow on Cheryl's cheek.

"Not really," Cheryl said, trying to change the subject.

Nikki angled the rainbow up toward the eye and Cheryl brushed her cheek distractedly with her hand as if trying to shoo away a fly. The sound of overlapping conversations filled the room as Nikki twirled the crystal again.

"Does the ambassador attend many of these rituals?" Nikki asked, continuing her small rainbow torture.

"I suppose," said Cheryl distractedly.

"Oh! That must be what all the fuss is about tomorrow!" said Nikki cheerfully.

"Tomorrow, what?" Cheryl said, squinting one eye and tilting her head slightly. Nikki switched to the other eye and watched as Cheryl tilted her head the other way.

"Oh, I heard that the ambassador's got some big thing tomorrow," said Nikki carelessly.

"No, no big thing," Cheryl said. "Just a family party."

"Oh," said Nikki, dropping her earring and letting it swing against her neck. "They must have gotten it wrong. Oh well." She smiled sweetly and then pretended to notice for the first time that her drink was empty. She noticed that Cheryl's drink was a different color. The color difference could mean that the kitchen had simply switched to grape Kool-Aid, but there might have been another reason.

"I'd better go get a refill. Nice to have met you"—Nikki paused to read Cheryl's nametag—"Terry."

Nikki strolled over to the drink table and got a refill on her Hawaiian fruit punch, noticing that all the drinks were still red.

"Thirty more minutes," Ellen said, sidling up and picking up a drink.

"What?" Nikki asked, noticing that Ellen was THERESA, A JOURNALIST this evening.

"Thirty more minutes, and then I can get out of these panty hose."

Nikki opened her mouth to remind Ellen that she was recording herself, but then closed it abruptly. Ellen's mission might be to uncover a spy.

"These events do seem to go on forever," Nikki responded, opting for a noncommittal reply.

"Unfortunately, so do my panty hose," said Ellen. Caught off-guard, Nikki laughed louder than she had intended, and saw Mr. Bamoko frown in her direction.

"I sympathize," Nikki said. "Do you come to many of these state functions?"

"That's your banter? Your cocktail chatter? Let's see something with a little more wit," Mr. Bamoko said sternly.

"Oh sure," Ellen said, ignoring Mr. Bamoko's intrusion, but Nikki could see she was starting to sweat. "I've been around the world twice reporting for the Associated Press. The food is terrible and the party really only gets good once everyone starts drinking. Last year I was at an embassy dinner in Colombia and a fist fight broke out over the oysters."

"Hmm," Mr. Bamoko said, making a note on his clipboard.

"I don't think that's likely with this crowd," said Nikki, wondering what Ellen was angling at and trying to ignore Mr. Bamoko, who was now glaring at her.

"Too bad." Ellen was playing the hard-boiled reporter for all it was worth. "I could use a drink."

"They don't allow alcohol in Carrie Mae-land," volunteered Nikki, as Mr. Bamoko sniffed disapprovingly.

"What! None?" asked Ellen in apparent shock.

"Well, sometimes you can get some illegal stuff imported, but you have to have a connection." Nikki suspected that Ellen was on the hunt for a smuggler. But whether her mission was to smuggle something or arrest a smuggler, Nikki couldn't tell. She didn't know if she was going to get downgraded for helping Ellen or not.

"I don't suppose you happen to know such a connection?" asked Ellen, managing to look conspiratorial and trustworthy at the same time.

"I don't drink, myself," Nikki said, covering all her bases. "But I have noticed that Terry over there"—she pointed to Cheryl— "can usually find something stiffer to drink than fruit punch if she wants to." Mr. Bamoko nodded and made a note as he moved on to the next set of girls.

"Thanks," said Ellen with a smile and a wink. "You're a real pal." She slid off into the crowd, aiming for Cheryl.

It was fun to watch everyone interact on several different levels at once. Nikki wondered if she would be able to do the same thing at a real cocktail party with strangers. But then again what was a real cocktail party but an effort to discover new facts about strangers? Dating was like that, too. Nikki reached up to adjust her earring again and stopped, frowning. It occurred to her that all of this felt strangely similar to her lunch with Z'ev. "You know," said Jenny, who had sidled up to her and was looking both ways for an eavesdropping instructor, "I've been thinking about your boyfriend, the one with the funny name."

"He's not my boyfriend," Nikki said, and gulped her fruit punch.

"Whatever. But I was thinking about that crazy story he told you."

"What do you mean?" asked Nikki, frowning, and wishing she hadn't told Jenny and Ellen all the details about Canada.

"Oh, come on. 'I need a fake wife'? I think he was doing this." Jenny waved at the cocktail party, as if that explained everything. "But for real. Did he say anything else during the lunch?"

"That's very interesting, Susan," said Nikki, seeing Mrs. Boyer approaching them behind Jenny. "I can't say I disagree, but I'm not convinced."

"Well, Carrie Mae politics are very complex," said Jenny, covering quickly.

"Dinner is starting, ladies," Mrs. Boyer said, marking notes on her clipboard. Nikki and Jenny quickly fled into the dining room.

They had barely seated themselves when Dina began to hiccup loudly. Nikki exchanged a horrified look with Ellen across the table as Dina's hiccups increased in volume and violence. Dina pushed herself away from the table and ran toward the downstairs bathroom, but they all heard the splat as she missed the toilet and threw up on the hard tile floor.

Mrs. Boyer ran toward the restroom, but the rest of the girls remained seated, staring at one another with expressions of mingled horror and amusement.

"Well," said Ellen, folding her hands neatly. "I suggest we start dinner with a prayer for the health of our friend Dina." There was a wave of snickers around the table.

"We will delay dinner for a few moments while we assess the situation," Mr. Bamoko said sternly, trying to squash the rebellion.

Moments turned into thirty minutes, while Dina was helped to the infirmary, the bathroom was cleaned, and Cocktails class was declared finished for the evening. Dinner was reheated and served again, while the girls discussed Dina's sudden illness. Nikki cringed at the sound of "food poisoning" and made a break for her room as soon as possible, with Jenny and Ellen in tow. Jenny had taken off her shoes, and they thumped against every rung in the banister.

"That was freaking hilarious," she said around a yawn.

"Not for Dina," said Nikki.

"Well, it was unfortunate, but it's probably for the best anyway. At least we don't have to deal with her during war games tomorrow," Ellen said realistically.

"I still feel bad," Nikki said. "I didn't want to sabotage her."

"She sabotaged herself," said Jenny coldly. "Serves her right for being a bitch."

"Well," Nikki said, assessing the situation, "karmically speaking, she may have had it coming, but I'm not sure my karma isn't dented for helping."

"As long as Dina doesn't know we helped, then karma is perfectly welcome to have my car stereo stolen at some later point in time," Ellen said.

"Practical, as usual," Jenny said, laughing.

The next morning the teams lined up for war games, with Nikki's team conspicuously short one person. Mrs. Boyer and Connie were still discussing this when Valerie Robinson arrived.

"Tell them to suck it up," she said, lighting up a cigarette, as Mrs. Boyer told her of the situation.

"It's an unfair advantage for the other teams," protested Mrs. Boyer. "Dina was their team leader."

"Poor babies," Val said dryly. "You"—she pointed at Nikki— "you're the new team leader. See, problem solved."

"I'm not sure that's a real solution," Mrs. Boyer began, but Val was walking away from her.

"OK, everyone, you all know the rules," said Val, picking up a starter pistol from Mrs. Boyer's gear. There was a general murmur of agreement from the girls, and Val nodded.

"Great," she said, "then get the hell out of here," and she fired the pistol.

There was a mad scramble as the teams gathered gear and rushed to get under cover. Nikki looked doubtfully at Ellen and Jenny. Ellen smiled, and Jenny gave her a thumbs-up. With a sigh, Nikki picked a direction and marched out.

It was much later in the evening when Nikki returned to campus. On a whim, she headed up to the infirmary.

Dina looked horrible. Her skin was pasty white, and she had dark circles under eyes. Her usually well-ordered brown hair was one frizz away from total disaster, and Nikki was pretty sure that the dried flaky substance on her shirt was old puke.

"The war games went really well," said Nikki, plastering a smile on her still-camouflage-painted face. "We won!" She held up the small gold golf trophy as proof. There was a glitter in Dina's brown eyes that was making Nikki nervous. "Mrs. Robinson gave us an A."

Nikki didn't mention that Val had winked as she had said, "A-plus for handling the situation correctly."

"I made sure that the grade applied to you, too," said Nikki, still forcing her smile. "Because you trained with us the whole time, so it seemed only fair. So, uh, not to worry, you'll be right on track when you get out of here. And I'll just go now and let you rest." Nikki reached out to pat Dina's hand, but the other girl seized her by the wrist.

"I know what you did, Lanier. And when I get out of here I'm going to tell everyone that you poisoned me with breath spray from Specialty Items."

Nikki yanked her hand back.

"You're going to be kicked out of here so fast that you won't even know what hit you. You and your little friends, Jenny and Ellen. I know you were all in on it and I'm going to make you pay."

"I don't know what you're talking about," Nikki said coldly. "But if something like that were said, I'd have to tell everyone about the fifth of tequila you've got hidden under your bed."

Dina's eyes glittered angrily, but she didn't say anything.

"You got your A in War Games, so I suggest you just shut up and stay the hell away from my friends."

Dina looked as though she might say something, but then slumped back on the pillow as the nurse bustled in.

"Visiting hours are over, I'm afraid," she said kindly.

"That's all right, I was just leaving," Nikki said, without taking her eyes off Dina. "I think we said everything that needed to be said. Didn't we, Dina?"

Dina nodded reluctantly, and Nikki felt the cold thrill of triumph followed by a sharp twist of guilt.

In the Boys' Room

Taking a deep breath, Nikki was about to say no and walk away when the man in the navy suit entered briskly, smiling from ear to ear, his hand extended. He was a handsome man, somewhere in his forties, with a slender build, olive skin, black hair, and deep-set eyes.

"Jim, you look good." His intonation was more British than American, but Nikki could tell that English was not his native tongue, although she couldn't quite place his accent. "And this must be your wife. You never told me how pretty she was." The compliment was accompanied by a smile that didn't quite reach his eyes.

"Mr. Sarkassian, this is my wife, Kim," said her new husband, and gave Nikki a reckless look, daring her to deny him.

Nikki shook hands, noticing that besides the designer suit, Mr. Sarkassian also sported a watch that ran well into the thousands, and a pair of ostentatious ruby cufflinks that she estimated to cost more than a month's rent on a very nice place. She also noticed that despite the manicure, Sarkassian's hands were callused and his knuckles were flattened from long years of punching something hard.

"Kim and Jim. Charming. You're a matched set." Mr. Sarkassian's amusement carried an undertone of mocking that sparked a current of dislike in Nikki. "Come along, children," he said, turning on his heel, assuming that they would follow, "my car's double parked."

"Where shall we go to lunch?" asked Mr. Sarkassian as they entered the lobby.

"Actually . . ." Nikki said, glancing significantly at her watch and preparing to make her graceful, if resentful, exit.

Then she saw her mother, Nell, emerge from the elevator. Nell was dressed in a pair of tight black slacks and her usual cleavage-baring top.

Nikki realized that she was unprepared to explain her sudden marriage to her mother, and there was no way she was ready to introduce her mother to her new husband, or his sardonic business acquaintance. And then there was the interview. Nikki shook at the idea of telling anyone about the interview, but telling her mother seemed the very definition of hell. Nikki was not nearly drunk enough for that kind of lunch.

"Kim can't join us," said "Jim," filling in when her pause had gone on too long. "You've got plans, don't you, honey?"

She glanced at her new husband; he seemed big enough to hide behind. There was a possibility that she was just drunk enough for *this* lunch. Maybe she hadn't really seen that shoulder holster. Maybe it was just the strap on some strange set of suspenders. Yeah, that was it.

"Well, I do have theater tickets, but as long as you promise to get me back here by five, I think I've got plenty of time," Nikki said, crossing her fingers and thinking of her mother's stupid Carrie Mae meeting. Missing lunch would be one thing, but missing the speech would send her mother absolutely bananas.

"I'd love to go," she added, "as long as you don't talk too much business," she said coquettishly to Sarkassian, with a sidelong look at "Jim." His face had frozen into position as if he'd been dipped in carbonite. Nikki stepped forward to take Mr. Sarkassians's arm and smiled her best "charm the boss" smile.

Thirty minutes later Nikki was pushing a piece of lettuce around her plate and pondering the idea that she had lost her mind. What happened to Stranger Danger? Had she learned nothing from McGruff the Crime Dog? For all she knew, these two men could be serial killers who took innocent women to expensive restaurants and made small talk before brutally stabbing their victims to death with a salad fork.

Or possibly they just ignored them to death.

Sarkassian was on his third phone call. This time, at least, he had been courteous enough to excuse himself from the table. As far as Nikki could tell, Sarkassian had something to do with shipping, but just how "Jim" was involved Nikki couldn't tell. He had his head turned in the direction that Mr. Sarkassian had gone.

Nikki looked around the restaurant. There was a clearly involved couple by the windows, and a few tables away a petite woman in an electric blue suit dined alone. Her face was mostly hidden behind a bouffant brown, vaguely Jackie O cut. The woman seemed comfortable dining alone, and Nikki wished she had half her composure and elegance. As she watched, the woman put down her fork and asked the waiter something. He pointed toward the lobby, and the woman rose gracefully and exited in that direction. Nikki watched her walk away and admired the clear definition on her calves and the way she maneuvered gracefully in such high heels.

Nikki looked back at her dinner companion, but he was still ignoring her. Unhappily, Nikki pulled the lettuce back across her plate. She knew she wasn't exactly Tyra Banks, but getting a boy's attention had never been a problem before.

"What's our name again?" she asked, studying his profile. He just didn't look like a Jim to her.

"Jim and Kim Webster," he answered. Nikki chuckled.

"I've always liked dictionaries," said Nikki. When he raised an eyebrow, she added, "Webster. Like the dictionary."

"I was thinking of Emmanuel Lewis," he said, leaning back in his chair and running his hand over his face and then up over his scalp.

"And what do you do again?"

"I'm a lawyer."

"You don't look like a lawyer."

"What does a lawyer look like?" he asked, and Nikki shrugged; even she wasn't sure what she meant.

"Meaner?" she suggested, with a teasing smile.

"I think I'll take that as a compliment," he said.

"What do you want with Mr. Sarkassian?" she asked.

"I specialize in international law; he's in shipping, needs meeting, blah, blah, blah." The topic of his career seemed to bore him, and he turned his head again, looking for Sarkassian.

"I'm going to the restroom," Nikki announced. She stood up, draping her napkin over the back of her seat.

"I'm not sure . . ." he said, half rising. Nikki couldn't quite tell if it was a movement of old-fashioned courtesy or a gesture of protest.

"Not sure that I can make it to the bathroom on my own? Pretty sure I can," she said, tossing her head slightly, and strode past him, before he could say anything else. She walked into the lobby following the signs pointing toward the restroom, considering that she might have just lied—especially in light of earlier events that day.

The restaurant was as expensive as Sarkassian's clothes; the lobby was a marble-and-tile affair, flanked by long tanks of tropical fish floating like suspended flowers in an aquamarine sky. Nikki saw her reflection behind the fish and realized that the tank was not as deep as it looked, a mere six inches perhaps. Someone was speaking an odd Indo-European language, and she looked around, trying to spot the speaker. Sarkassian was standing near the door, his back to her, nearly hidden by a large potted palm. Occasionally, he tapped a few things into his SideKick, but otherwise, he seemed engrossed in the conversation being piped through the earpiece glued to his head. Nikki sidled closer, trying to identify the language. It had sounded like Greek for a moment, and then like Persian, but then neither. He started to turn, and Nikki quickly stopped eavesdropping and went toward the bathroom doors.

But she still paused to carefully examine her bathroom options and equally carefully chose the door marked WOMEN in a curling, ostentatious font. Some things she didn't want to repeat in a day. Once inside, she paused. The restroom was lit with a curious wavering blue-green light and she realized that it came from fish tanks. The tanks in the lobby had been backed with a two-way mirror and from inside the restrooms, patrons could see into the lobby through the long window of glass and water.

She watched curiously as Sarkassian walked toward her and then sat down on the cushioned bench beneath the fish tank. If she leaned forward she could see the words he typed into his Sidekick.

His fingers obscured the tiny buttons, but she could see the letters appear on the screen, and Nikki realized suddenly that he was typing in his password. Suppressing a slight twinge of guilt for her nosiness, she cranked her head to the left, trying to see the words and wishing the water wouldn't blur her view so much.

"H-i-c-e-t-n-u-n . . ." Nikki muttered each letter under her breath as it was typed in.

A toilet flushed, startling her. She jumped.

"These fish tanks are such an interesting feature," said the woman in the blue suit coming out of a stall. "Don't you think?"

There was something knowing in the way the woman smiled, and Nikki knew she'd been caught. The woman was older than Nikki had guessed—north of middle age, but by how much, Nikki couldn't say. She had an oval face, perfect makeup, and twinkling blue eyes. Nikki noted that she had the round, even tones of a Californian; she certainly wasn't Canadian, at any rate.

"Um, yes, fascinating," said Nikki, and hurried into a stall, avoiding eye contact. When she came out again, the woman had gone and Sarkassian had wandered back to the embrace of the potted palm. Nikki stared at his back, pondering his password. The HICE letter combo wasn't common in English, and starting a word with TN was equally unlikely. Mentally, she tried parsing the letters in different ways. "Here and now," said Nikki triumphantly, as another woman came in. Nikki blushed and hurried out, trying not to make any noise with her heels on the marble floor before gaining the safety of the carpeted dining area. *Hic et nunc,* translated from Latin, meant "here and now." Extremely pleased with her translation, she dropped into her seat, hoping that her face wasn't carrying a revealing flush, and prepared to make small talk.

But "Jim" wasn't focused on her. Instead, he sagged into his chair, his expression fading from intense to blank. To Nikki he looked very tired, and for a moment she had to fight the urge to wrap her arms around him and tell him it, whatever it was, would be OK.

"Jim?" she said quietly, meaning to ask about Sarkassian.

"It's not really my name, you know," he said. Nikki stared at him, uncertain of what to say or what to make of his change in tone. He slumped back in his chair as though very tired; his right hand extended past the arm of his chair and he dangled a steak knife from the table between his fingers. He twirled the knife in an idle manner, catching light from the large windows overlooking the bay and reflecting it in thin slices onto the walls, the table, Nikki. She found herself holding her breath, as if she had fallen into some sunlit aquarium.

"What *is* your name?" she asked softly, trying not to break the mood.

"Z'ev," he answered, still fixated on the knife and the light.

"Z'ev," she repeated, sifting the name around in her head for a moment. "That's a Jewish name, isn't it?"

"Yeah. I guess. I was named after my granddad; he was Jewish." He was staring at her now, the reflected light from the knife resting on her cheek. Nikki started to feel a little warm, but tried to return his gaze calmly.

"Mostly I'm a bit of a mutt. Mixed heritage—all that."

"My father is Quebecois," said Nikki, nodding.

He laughed. "Meaning what?"

"Mixed heritage."

"Ah, yes, the mixing of different kinds of white people can be tricky." It was Nikki's turn to laugh.

"It *is* tricky," she objected. "He had a whole different background from my mother. Different kind of family, different holiday traditions, different language. Just . . . different," she concluded with a shrug.

"Mixed heritage," he agreed,

"Why don't you use your name?" asked Nikki.

He was hard to read, but Nikki found herself looking for the flitting shadows of emotion that crossed his face faster than clouds across the sun. He frowned slightly now, as if he regretted sharing that piece of information.

"Z'ev is a little too memorable for my taste," he responded after a long moment. His gaze was fixed on her again, and Nikki felt a blush beginning to start somewhere below her collarbone and head upward.

"Huh," she said. "You're just a big old liar, aren't you?" She made a quick head toss, flipping her hair over her shoulder while trying to look as flirty and teasing as possible. It was a move that had been working for her since junior high.

"What? No!" He was smiling, but she felt she had startled him.

"Oh, come on," she said, laughing at his surprised expression and feeling in control of the conversation again. "You lie about your wife, your name, and I don't think you really like rugby. Just what are you trying to sell Mr. Sarkassian?"

"What makes you think I'm trying to sell Sarkassian anything?"

"Well, if you're not, you're going to an awful lot of trouble for lunch. And you complimented his cufflinks."

"I said they were interesting," said Z'ev, shifting in his chair, but there was a smile lurking behind his rough tone.

"Yes, but when you say 'interesting' with a smile it nearly always sounds like a compliment."

"Really? How interesting." He gave a smile of perfect bland surprise.

"Really," retorted Nikki with marked sarcasm. "And you still haven't answered my question."

"I'm sorry, I've forgotten the question."

"What do you want from Sarkassian?" she asked with an exasperated sigh.

"I'll tell you what," he said, still smiling. "You tell me why *you* came along with us today and I'll tell you why I'm here."

Nikki hesitated, not really wanting to share her humiliation with a stranger.

"That's the deal," he said, "take it or leave it."

"I graduated in linguistics," she said, trying to explain, but starting in the wrong place as usual. "I've had five jobs in the last three years, and none of them has been close to my degree. And it's not like I haven't been looking. But I need experience to get a job, and I need a job to get experience."

"Real life is hard to do," he said with impassive calm. His tone should have given the impression of disinterest, but instead it was somehow reassuring. As if everyone had trouble with reality and it was nothing to get excited about.

"It's not like I thought it would be easy to grow up and get a real life," protested Nikki. "I just didn't think it was going to be this hard. I feel like I'm just stumbling around blindfolded, looking for the piñata while everyone else in the crowd laughs and shouts totally useless directions."

"Hit 'em with the stick," he advised in the same stolid tone, but there was a slight twinkle in his eye.

Nikki laughed. "I'll try that. Anyway, two weeks ago I saw an ad for someone with my background. I was pretty excited. I got the interview, and my mom paid for the hotel." Nikki decided to gloss over the part about Carrie Mae cosmetics. Some things were just too embarrassing. "And things were going really well until I actually got to the interview."

"Why, what happened?" Z'ev picked at his salad, and Nikki frowned, uncertain that she really wanted to tell anyone. Then he caught her eye and smiled.

The world seemed entirely still when he smiled. It was possible that he had the most perfect mouth she had ever seen on a man.

"I accidentally went into the men's bathroom," said Nikki in a rush. She hadn't been planning to mention the bathroom thing, but she had been distracted by his lips.

He tried to laugh and then coughed, choking on a carrot.

"I wasn't expecting that. How'd you manage that?" he asked, reaching for his water.

"I somehow misread the signs and walked in on one of the interviewers." Nikki paused, while Z'ev let out a booming chuckle. "Which would have been bad enough," she said over his laughter, "except that later in the interview, they asked me about Ebonics. Which is when I knew I wasn't going to get the job."

"Ebonics?" Z'ev repeated quizzically.

"Do you really want to know?"

"Yeah," he said, obviously enjoying her misery.

"I tried to explain that languages aren't really permanent structures," Nikki said with a sigh. "They can't really be corrupted. It's more of an evolutionary model. Among linguists, African American English Vernacular, or AAEV, has been an accepted English dialect for many years. It has its own grammatical structure, consistent word usage, everything that makes a dialect. AAEV or Ebonics or street slang or whatever you want to call it is just the ongoing process of language growth. You can't really freeze a language in place except on paper, and then, of course, it's dead. What I failed to realize was that Mrs. Densley, the head interviewer, was an English freak."

"The language of Shakespeare is hardly dead," Mrs. Densley had said acidly, her small piggy eyes widening to their fullest.

"I already knew I wasn't getting the job; I was just praying to get out of there with some last shred of dignity, when the guy from the bathroom, who up until then had been totally OCD'ing on the ceiling tiles and avoiding all eye contact, looked directly at me."

Nikki looked at the smooth white tablecloth and her chipped nail polish. This had been the worst part.

"What'd he ask?" Z'ev tilted his head slightly to the right, catching Nikki's downturned gaze. Nikki looked into his eyes and forgot what she was going to say. She forgot her embarrassment—forgot everything. His dark, coffee-colored eyes were full of sympathy, and suddenly it was easy to tell this last humiliating memory.

"I have one," Bathroom Man had said, taking his eyes off the ceiling to look directly at Nikki. "How are you special?" Nikki had stared at him, dumbstruck.

"How are you special?" Z'ev repeated skeptically.

"I realize that it was embarrassing to be literally caught with his pants down, but the way he asked the question was vindictive. I'd just spent the last three hours justifying my entire existence to these people, and he wanted me to feel like . . ." She searched for the right words. "He wanted me to feel like nothing. I couldn't think of anything to say to him. I couldn't think of anything that I could do that they couldn't hire five monkeys to do." Z'ev's lips twitched. He was trying not to smile, and Nikki appreciated the effort.

"I was just sitting there staring at him, probably gaping like a fish, and, really, I felt like giving them all the finger and walking out. Which I should have done, but I ended up just saying some nonsense and waiting for the interview to end."

"What'd you say?" persisted Z'ev.

Nikki blushed, but held her head a little higher, remembering her last stubborn flare of pride in the interview.

"How much I really enjoy Ebonics."

"Good for you," he said, grinning.

"Now it's your turn," said Nikki. "Tell me what you want from Sarkassian."

"Nuh-uh," he said, and shook his head.

"I told my story. Now you have to tell me about Sarkassian. We had a deal, buster."

"Not Buster. Z'evvvv." He drew out the v sound, for emphasis, and Nikki rolled her eyes. "Come on, you can say it."

"Z'evvvv," mimicked Nikki, and threw a crouton at him, which he caught and ate. "I'm out of croutons, but I will throw silverware if I have to," she threatened.

"No, please, not the spoon." His calm expression rendered the statement into sarcasm, and Nikki couldn't help but laugh.

"Come on, spill, Z'evvv. It's your turn."

"Nuh-uh. You're not finished yet."

"What do you mean? I told them to f'shizel my nizel, came back to the hotel, and drank like a fish. End of my story, start of yours."

"No, that's why you were in the bar," Z'ev began, but then stopped. Whatever he had been about to say was cut short as Sarkassian returned to the table, closely followed by a waiter carrying their steaks.

"Sorry to be so long," Sarkassian said, folding into his chair, his long legs kicking out under the table, taking up space and forcing Nikki to tuck her feet under her own chair. "You wouldn't think getting cargo to the correct destination would require so much effort. But for every new port there's a new special interest to deal with: the longshoremen hate the boat crews, the crews hate the captains, I hate their unions. It just seems never ending."

"That's why you need me," said Z'ev, bluntly.

"We'll see," said Sarkassian with a shrug, reaching for his drink. "Fortunately, you two seem to be able to entertain yourselves without me. I could hear you laughing out in the lobby, Jim." He briskly sawed at his steak while he spoke and, at the last word, popped a piece into his mouth. If he saw Z'ev's slight frown, he ignored it.

"Mmmm," Sarkassian said around his mouthful. "I'm telling you, brilliant steak."

"So you own those big container ships?" asked Nikki, cutting up her own steak. "You make sure the cargo all gets where it's going?" Z'ev eyed her suspiciously, and Nikki smiled sweetly.

"That is the general idea of shipping," Sarkassian said. "We're just like FedEx with much, much bigger packages. I would have thought Jim would have explained that to you. You should try to educate her more, Jim."

Nikki gritted her teeth and smiled.

"Oh, I hear all about international waters and injunctions and things like that," she said, trying to remember some factoid from her one International Politics and Policies class. "But I don't get to hear much about the people actually doing the work."

Sarkassian smiled, pleased with her slight massaging of his ego.

"Shipping is a complicated business, I won't go into it at the dinner table. But needless to say, it gets more complicated all the time. All the increased security and cargo searches—it just slows down business."

"People want to feel secure," protested Z'ev mildly. "You can't really blame them after 9-11."

Sarkassian's eyes were narrowed, and he chewed his steak with quick, decisive movements of his jaw.

"They want to feel more secure, but trust me, they don't want to pay for what it's going to take to be secure. Besides, it's not like they actually catch the professional smugglers. And aren't you supposed to be on my side?"

"I'm a lawyer," said Z'ev, calmly sectioning off a forkful of mashed potatoes. "I'm on the side of my client."

"Meaning you're on the side of whoever pays you. You don't mind being married to a hired gun, do you?" asked Sarkassian, switching his focus back to Nikki.

Nikki smiled awkwardly. She felt like Sarkassian was poking at her with the same kind of sadistic pleasure that a small boy might get from burning ants with a magnifying glass.

"Well," she said, trying to think of something clever and in character to say, "I think the basic assumption is that, having married him, he's my hired gun."

"Good point," said Sarkassian, nodding. "How's that steak, love?"

"Good. Really good," Nikki said, swallowing hard and forcing a smile, and Sarkassian matched it, enjoying the way she squirmed when he used condescending pet names.

Nikki felt as if she were standing in a kitchen between a freezer and an oven. Sarkassian was warmly expansive about his latest project. To her left, Z'ev nodded and smiled a bit, all the while giving off an aura of deep freeze that made Nikki shiver. She wished she hadn't given in to the impulse to go along with this ridiculous charade.

"Armenian!" said Nikki suddenly, and Sarkassian paused, pinning her with an unwavering cold stare. "You're Armenian," she said, feeling silly for having spoken out loud. "I couldn't place your accent, but I finally realized that you're Armenian and that must be interesting . . ." She fell into silence under his heavy stare.

"Interesting. Yes," he said, smiling his shark smile again. "I suppose you could call it interesting. When I was born we were the whipping boy of the Soviet pigs, and then of course there was the earthquake that killed my parents, the Catholic orphanage, and then the war with Azerbaijan. Good times, really interesting. Thanks for bringing that up."

Nikki smiled weakly and kept her mouth shut as the rest of lunch dragged by. She was beginning to find Jirair Sarkassian's *loves* and *honeys* harder and harder to take. She knew he was doing it on purpose, and he knew she wasn't going to say anything about it.

Nikki subtly checked her watch and felt a spasm of panic. It was 4:45. She glanced at Z'ev. The conversation had returned to sports, and both men appeared cheerful.

"Uh, gentlemen," she said softly, not wishing to interrupt. "I don't mean to rush either of you, but I do have . . ." She paused, trying to remember what she had told them as an excuse for her five o'clock deadline.

"Oh, yes, of course," said Z'ev. "Those theater tickets. Mary Ann is meeting you back at the hotel?"

"Yes," Nikki agreed, "and I think she might be bringing Mrs. Howell, so I don't want to be late." Z'ev choked back a laugh, but Sarkassian didn't appear to notice.

"Well, we'd better get going, then," said Sarkassian, waving at a waiter.

It still took fifteen minutes to settle the bill. Nikki tried to keep herself from looking at her watch or tapping her foot, but she could feel the number of minutes she was late piling up on each other like vehicles in a traffic jam. Finally they were in their car and weaving with all appropriate speed back to the hotel.

"There you go, honey," Sarkassian said as they pulled up in front of the hotel. "You don't mind, do you, if I steal Jim for a couple more hours?"

"No, of course not," said Nikki, smiling graciously and opening the door, suppressing her desire to withhold her permission just to see his reaction. She just wanted to get out of the car. She was going to be late for that ridiculous speech. Her mother would be furious as it was.

"Just give me a minute," Z'ev said from the backseat as she was about to close the door. "I'll walk her to the door."

"Really, Jim," Nikki started to say, "you don't have to." But he was already taking her arm and walking her up the wide cement steps to the gilded front door.

"You know," Nikki said with some asperity, "if I'd known I was going to be 'honeyed' all afternoon I don't think I'd have come along."

"You invited yourself along," he replied. "You can't complain now."

"Watch me," she snapped.

Z'ev gave a small chuckle. "Look," he said, tugging her to a stop at the top of the stairs, a few feet from the door. "Why did you come with us?"

"I told you about the interview," Nikki answered in confusion.

"No, you weren't going to go with us until you got to the lobby."

"I do dumb things when I drink?" suggested Nikki. He shook his head, and Nikki sighed. She really didn't want to discuss her mother.

"I'm traveling with my mother and I saw her coming out of the elevator and, well, I didn't really want to see her."

"You were ducking your own mother by running off with two perfect strangers?" He seemed incredulous. "You must really not get along with your mom."

"No, I do usually, but . . ." She glanced up at him with an abashed squint. "I just really didn't want to explain that interview to her. She wouldn't have gotten it; she would have just told me what I should have done. As if that helps me now."

"Not exactly the supportive type?" he asked, not looking at her, but turning to give a wave to Sarkassian waiting in the car.

"Not really, no." She looked up at his profile; he was still looking at the car. Nikki followed his gaze down to the street, where a taxi was depositing a woman in an electric blue suit. She looked like the same one from the restaurant. Nikki noted the coincidence, but noted also that Z'ev was still fixated on Sarkassian.

"Not that you care, I suppose," she said, realizing as she said the words that it was probably true. He *was* a complete stranger; why would he care about her?

"You're my wife," he said, eyes still on the car. "Of course I care." He finally looked back at her, and Nikki could see the twinkle in his eyes.

"Of course, what was I thinking?" she asked sarcastically, trying to cover up her sudden urge to go wobbly.

"I have no idea," answered Z'ev. "But I'll tell you one thing, Bathroom Man should go back to counting ceiling tiles. Anyone can see you're special." Then, leaning forward, he kissed her.

If she was surprised by the compliment, she was thunderstruck by his kiss. His lips were just the right mixture of firm and soft and carried a faint taste of the breath mints they'd eaten in the car.

Nikki ran the fingertips of one hand along the curve of his brow and into the tightly curled stubble of his hair. She knew she should have felt outraged, but all she felt was safe. Just as she recovered enough to become a more active participant in the kiss, he released her and walked down the stairs to the street.

"See you later, honey," he said over his shoulder with a malicious grin.

At the Tone, the Time Will Be . . .

The final week of training arrived, and the girls breathlessly tried to cram last-minute studying into an already hectic schedule, the final test looming over their heads. At last, there was no more time for practice, and the girls were divided into groups. They were rotated through a schedule of written tests, but eventually they all had to take what was termed "the practical." The group that had the practical the first night didn't return to the dorms, and that very fact set up a twitter of nervousness in the remaining women. Nikki tried to brush off the whispers of fear that were beginning to cling to her, but she had to take a deep breath as she reported to the main house.

The front lawn was being set up for graduation, and even in the gloom of evening she could see the ghostly tent spires being raised on the far side of the cactus garden. She hoped she would be among those sitting in the folding chairs and walking up the aisle to shake hands with the faculty.

As she walked up the drive toward the rock garden, she noticed a florist's van parked near the front gate.

"Well, I don't know," said the van driver, walking into Nikki's view from behind the van. "I can't make heads or tails of your chicken scratch." He was talking on his cell phone and his exasperation came through clearly. "No, there's no one I can ask." The driver glanced up and spotted Nikki. "No, wait, here comes someone. I'll ask her. Call you back." The driver took the cell away from his ear and smiled at Nikki as she approached.

"Excuse me, miss," he said. "I'm supposed to make a delivery, but when I knock on the door, no one answers. Can you help me?"

Nikki nodded, as she checked her watch with a frown. There had to be someone in the house; the final was at 8:30. She started to worry that she had misread her appointment notice.

"I just need to find Mrs . . ." The van driver patted his pockets. "Left my paperwork in the van," he said sheepishly. "It's written on the box. Maybe you can read it better than I can." He walked toward the van, and Nikki followed a step or so behind.

The driver reached out to the big double doors at the back of the van and swiftly yanked one open, stepping behind it so that Nikki was fully exposed to the interior. Before she had time to register that, instead of boxes, the van was filled with several black-clad people, there was a sudden burst of mist, and she inhaled a lung full of pepper spray.

Her eyes streamed, and she doubled over as she began to cough. The van driver picked her up and shoved her into the van. Before she knew what was happening, she was tied up and blindfolded like a Christmas turkey going to the guillotine.

"OK, Nikki."

She heard the scratching sound of a pen on a clipboard and recognized Mrs. Boyer's voice.

"Welcome to the final test." Mrs. Boyer's voice was smug. Nikki hated that, but right now she was concentrating on not coughing up a lung.

There was silence in the van, and in between coughs she heard the rushing sound of tires over pavement. She thought about asking for an explanation, but then decided against it. Asking anything was probably a waste of oxygen. Mrs. Boyer wasn't famous for answering questions.

Nikki felt the van turn, but realized that in her present condition this information did her absolutely no good. She hadn't been paying attention to anything previous to that turn, and as far as she knew, they could have circled the block twice and be heading back to the ranch.

"The final test," said Mrs. Boyer, deciding that the time for explanations had arrived, "is a timed, practical test. I'm attaching an emergency beacon to your collar. If at any point during this test you wish to quit or need assistance, press the button and you will be picked up." Nikki felt a hard plastic tag like the ones used as theft deterrents in clothing stores being attached to her collar. "You will be dropped at a location some distance from the ranch. You will have exactly three hours from your starting time to make it back to the entrance hall of the office building at the ranch. If you use your emergency beacon, or arrive after your allowed time, you will fail. You may use any means necessary to cross the distance, but remember, you will be downgraded for excessive force or extensive property damage. There will be Carrie Mae consultants on the course. They can detain you if they catch you. They will carry no identifying badges; they will only verbally identify themselves. You may encounter other trainees. You may not join forces or interfere with them in any way."

The van lurched off pavement and onto a gravel road. Nikki heard the crunch of tiny pebbles and an occasional thud as a rock hurled itself against the body of the van. They drove farther and Nikki felt the texture of the road change from gravel to outright dirt. Her hands were starting to fall asleep from being tied behind her back, and a small bubble of panic had begun to form in her stomach, but she calmed herself with the thought that at least half the class had been through this already. If they could survive it, so could she. Couldn't she?

She heard the shrill, metallic squeal of the van doors swinging open. The panic bubble expanded and lodged in her throat.

"The time is now 9:02," announced Mrs. Boyer.

The van slowed and coasted almost to a standstill as Mrs. Boyer pushed Nikki out of the van. Nikki hit the dirt and rolled to a painful stop.

"Good luck, Lady!" yelled Mrs. Boyer, and Nikki heard the van doors slam shut and the van pull away. She lay on the ground and thought about life and the fact that her bladder was sending up serious distress flares. 9:02. She had three hours to get back to the ranch, she was blindfolded, her hands were tied behind her back, and all she was really concerned with was the fact that she hadn't gone to the bathroom before leaving. The panic bubble popped. Nikki rolled onto her back and then, hoping no one was around to laugh at her, rolled back even farther onto her shoulder blades. Heaving her butt into the air, she wiggled her hands around her hips, then pulled her legs between her arms until her arms passed around her sneakers. Rolling up into a sitting position, she pulled off the blindfold with a flourish.

"Oh yeah! Cheerleading pays off!" she exclaimed, and then slapped her hands over her mouth. She looked around carefully, hoping that there weren't any agents around to hear her inadvertent celebratory crowing. The ground was covered in waving wild grass and sloped at a downward angle from where she sat; there didn't appear to be any Carrie Mae consultants lying in wait for her. In the distance she heard the excited yipping of a coyote.

"I ought to be more frightened than this," Nikki said, looking up. Somehow the small weight dragging at her collar and the familiar constellations above made everything seem more cheerful than it was.

She began to attack the rope around her hands with her teeth. Finding the end of the rope, she backtracked to the point where it entered the knot and then followed it around until it looped out around a wrist. She tugged and pulled and eventually loosened the rope enough to slip one hand free and then the other. Her wrists were a bit scraped, but she was free.

Spitting out the rope, she shook it from her wrists and, standing up, made as if to throw it into the brush, but paused, weighing the rope in her hands. General principles of the universe stated that if she threw it away, she was sure to need it later. Deciding quickly, she knotted the lengths of rope together and then looped it around her waist.

She stepped onto the road and considered which direction to go. The North Star was at her back, which meant that south was downhill and west was to her right. She thought about the drive up. There had been a paved road in the direction they had come from. If there was pavement, there were people, and she could get directions. She jogged a few steps along the road and then stepped off again, stopping behind some bushes. When she stepped out again her bladder declared itself ready to jog.

She ran at a steady pace, keeping light on her toes to avoid twisting an ankle. She had just reached the top of a hill when she saw her first sign of civilization. From the crest of the hill she saw a blur of light. Putting on speed, she ran downhill and out onto a flatter stretch of road. The texture of the road under her feet changed from dirt to gravel. She was sweating now and unzipped her sweatshirt. She climbed another hill, but she could tell that overall the altitude was dropping. From the top of this hill she saw that the smear of light was made up of a string of RVs and trailers. She even heard engines roaring and the bass of someone's thudding radio. She ran a bit closer and saw that each RV had a row of dirt bikes and four-wheelers parked near it.

Pausing outside the circle of light, she considered what to do next. Asking one of these people for help might be risky; it might be better to simply borrow one of their extra vehicles. But which, dirt bike or four-wheeler? Nikki remembered the motorcycle portion of the driving instruction class. She had fallen down twice and gone around limping for a week. On the other hand, a motorcycle would be faster.

Throwing caution to the wind, she ran forward and got on the nearest dirt bike. It didn't look quite like the others; it had more of a street appearance, which suited her purposes fine. She was about to hot-wire it when she realized that the key was in the ignition. She grinned at her good fortune and turned the bike on. She headed away from the camp and back to the road. She was about halfway to the road when she heard someone yell. She didn't look back, but put on speed.

Hitting the road in a spray of gravel, she risked a glance back and saw three headlights heading after her. She twisted the throttle and felt the bike jerk forward. She didn't think she could outrun an experienced dirt biker and hoped that it was only four-wheelers on her trail. Cutting around a hill, she saw where the road detoured around the scenery. She pointed herself straight and ignored the road. When she took another look over her shoulder, one rider had stuck with the road; the two remaining bikers were still on her tail and gaining.

The dirt was grainy now and the hills more like dunes, a perfect dirt biking course. She wove in and out between the hills and listened for the chasing engines. Her hair stung her face in a thousand tiny whips, and at one point she thought she'd swallowed a bug. She giggled. She was going to die. This was fun.

A short dropoff and the following skid and moment of panic convinced her that the fun was less and the dying more likely. She aimed for the relative safety of the road, where the gravel was white and glowed in the moonlight. The knobbly tires of the dirt bike dug reassuringly into the small rocks. She hit a pothole and felt her foot slip off the pedal. She slowed, steadying the bike and her nerves, and heard a gunning of engines from behind her.

She left the road again, heading steadily downhill, dodging her pursuers. As she exited a grove of Joshua trees, she saw a streak of light that indicated a street or freeway. She couldn't hear anyone chasing and slowed to a crawl to listen for the sound of engines, preparing to make her dash for that bright section of light. She looked back and saw no headlights.

As she was turning back, the bike hit a hidden ditch. The motorcycle high-sided, sending her flying end over end. She tucked herself and rolled as she hit the ground and then skidded a fair distance before being stopped by a dirt mound. She lay where she had fallen and thought about life and breathing.

After what seemed like forever, she gingerly got to her feet and tested all her limbs. Everything seemed to be functional. Her left side was going to be one lovely bruise, but fortunately she hadn't been going very fast when she'd crashed. She took a deep breath and felt her hands shaking.

She limped over to the dirt bike and righted it. The motor had quit running and one of the tires was flat. There was a smell of gasoline. She kicked the bike in disgust. There was nothing to be done for it. She tried to jog toward the road she had seen, but found she couldn't. The crash had left her shaky, and her stomach tumbled around on itself.

"You're never going to make it back before midnight at this rate," she muttered.

She concentrated some more on breathing and walking, and by the time her hands had stopped shaking, she saw a gas station on the horizon. She jogged toward it, but just as at the RV camp, she stopped outside the reach of the light and studied the scene. It was a truck stop. Three big rigs and a few cars were parked in the lot, and two trucks had pulled up to the gas pumps. There was something vaguely familiar about the truck stop, and after a few minutes pondering, she decided that she had seen it on the drive with Mr. M from the airport. Which meant she was south of the ranch by a twenty-minute car ride, give or take.

She considered her options. She could go in and ask for a ride, but truckers had to make time and probably wouldn't be willing to make a detour for a dusty stranger with no cash. One of the car drivers might be persuaded, but then again, they were more likely to be Carrie Mae agents. She could hot-wire one of the cars parked in the lot, but that was likely to bring the police down on her head. Even if she did make it back to the ranch, getting arrested would probably score her negative points on the test. As she watched, one of the fueling truckers took some bills out of his wallet and then tossed it back into the cab. The trucker left the truck and went into the restaurant.

She seized her opportunity and walked casually forward. When she reached the truck she opened the door and jumped inside, closing the door behind her. She expected, at any second, to hear an angry voice demanding an explanation. She felt around the cab for the wallet, keeping her head ducked to avoid being seen from the outside. She found the wallet and opened it; there were three fifty-dollar bills. She took one and exited the far side of the truck, where she was less likely to be seen. Nikki snuck past the trucks and then doubled back and went into the restaurant. Before going in, she tore off the emergency beacon and stuffed it into her pocket.

The waitress greeted her with a disbelieving stare, and Nikki knew that she must look a mess. She gave the waitress a relieved smile and walked up to the counter.

"Hi," she said brightly. "Boy, am I glad to see you guys."

"Uh-huh," the waitress said.

"I was camping with my boyfriend. Drove down here on a dirt bike, but it crashed." She gave an embarrassed laugh and gestured to her dirty sweats. "I guess you can tell."

"Uh-huh," the waitress said.

"I'm fine, but I really need change for the phone and the name of a close taxi service that can take me to Santa Clarita." She laid the fifty dollars on the counter.

"They won't drive you back to your campsite," the waitress said, not reaching for the bill.

"Well, that's just fine with me. If I never see that man or that campsite again, it'll be too soon." Nikki knew she had put just the right amount of anger in her voice when the waitress smiled.

"Got in a fight, did you?" the waitress asked, taking the money over to the till.

"Calling it a fight would be polite. That jackass said I was just like my mother."

The waitress winced sympathetically and shook her head. "You're better off without him." She gave Nikki a handful of change and a wad of bills. "The phone's back there. There's a corkboard full of business cards next to it. I think SCV Taxi is up there. They should be here pretty fast."

"Thanks," Nikki said. "Hey, what time is it?"

"10:38," the waitress answered, glancing at her watch.

Nikki grinned in delight and headed for the phone. With any luck she would be pulling up at the ranch by 11:30.

The taxi service promised to have a car at the truck stop no later than eleven, and Nikki went to the bathroom to clean herself up.

The restroom was a standard truck stop affair: covered in tile and generally grungy and next to the kitchen. Someone had obviously been in the middle of cleaning because the wheeled mop bucket was out and a cleaning supply closet stood open. Nikki filched a work rag from the closet, washed her face, and tried to scrub the worst dirt off of her sweats. She was just finishing up when Dina burst into the bathroom. Dusty, but hardly as disheveled as Nikki, Dina seemed irritated. For a long moment they stared at each other in surprise.

"You are not getting there before me," Dina snarled, and swung a punch. Nikki side-stepped the punch, and charged at her. Using both hands, she shoved Dina into the broom closet, slammed the door, and leaned breathlessly against it. Dina pounded against the door in shuddering thuds, forcing Nikki to readjust her hold on the door every few moments. Reaching out with her toe she pulled the mop bucket toward her inch by inch. When the mop was in reach, she jammed it through the broom closet door.

"Nicole, you let me out of here right this second!"

Startled, Nikki looked at the wooden door. Dina had somehow managed to copy her mother's exact phrasing. Involuntarily, she reached for the broom handle.

"Oh, come on, Nikki," Dina said, changing her tone to Nutra-Sweet stickiness. "Let me out."

The hand drier quit and in the silence Nikki thought she heard a car pull up outside.

"I'm not letting you out. You tried to punch me!"

"I didn't mean it," Dina protested from inside the closet. Nikki thought about believing her. Wanted to believe her. Couldn't quite do it.

"Yes, you did. You meant it. I don't know why you don't like me, but I'm tired of it. You want to be mad at me, then fine, you can be mad at me for locking you in a closet, because that's what I'm about to do."

Nikki pushed the broom handle in more securely and ran to the window, hoping that the vehicle she'd heard was her cab. She scanned the parking lot and saw a yellow SCV cab park by the front entrance. Her heart leapt. The end was in sight. But as she watched, the cab driver pulled out a walkie-talkie, spoke briefly into it, and then hid the walkie-talkie under his sweater. Didn't cabs come with CBs already in them? Nikki frowned as the cab driver walked into the restaurant. Was there something overly cabbie-ish about his clothes? The newsboy cap and cigarette were perhaps a little too cliché? Glancing back at the rattling broom closet, Nikki decided she couldn't take the chance.

She slipped out of the bathroom and into the kitchen.

"Back door?" she demanded of a bemused busboy, who simply pointed past the large refrigerators. She dashed through the door and around the corner into the parking lot. Diving into the front seat of the cab, she fumbled with the wires under the dash, hoping desperately that she was remembering the class on hot-wiring correctly. The engine turned over, and she sat up, jammed the cab into Drive, and hit the gas. Roaring past the restaurant, she saw the cabbie throw his cap on the ground and yell into his walkie-talkie.

Driving through the darkened streets, Nikki watched the LED clock on the dash click the minutes off. When the numbers passed 11:15, she began to get nervous. At 11:33 she pulled the cab into the gate at the front of the Carrie Mae Ranch.

She left the door swinging open and ran to the gate. She wanted to finish before anything else happened. Her finger was on the buzzer and she was about to push it and ask for a triumphal entry when she paused. Mrs. Boyer had been specific in her instructions. She had said the entry hall of the office building. Mrs. Boyer was not known for wasting words or saying things she didn't mean. Nikki carefully pulled her finger away from the buzzer.

Running along the wall, she tried to find a spot where she could climb over, but the smooth concrete wall offered no fingerholds, and the drainage ditch below the wall left no good surface for a running jump. Stopping below one of the posts that segmented the wall, Nikki had an idea. Unslinging the rope from around her waist, she searched the ground for a rock. Finding a fist-size stone, she tied it to one end of the rope and flung the rope and rock in a looping arc at the post. On her third attempt, the rock went around the top of the post, and Nikki grabbed it. Looping one end of the rope around her right hand and holding onto the rock with her left, she walked her feet up the wall. Every few feet she looped the rope around her hands again, shortening the rope until there was no more rope and she was at the top of the wall.

She threw her legs over the wall, extended her arms, and dropped down into darkness. She hovered in the dark pool of shrubbery and examined the grounds.

The paths were lit as usual, with ground-level lights glimmering from the bordering flowerbeds. Everything looked as it always did. Nikki began to doubt her instincts, but then shook her head.

Her instincts hadn't failed her yet; it was better to trust them now. Keeping to the shadows, she worked her way up to the house.

Her circumspection was rewarded when she saw two women dressed in black move in the bushes ahead of her. The women in front of her were working their way quietly across the grounds, and Nikki assumed they were looking for girls returning from the obstacle course. Nikki smiled and followed them, trying to move at the same time so that any sounds of her movement were camouflaged. When they reached a covered point close to the main house, Nikki let them proceed in front of her. After an eternity of waiting, she ran across the exposed lawn and threw herself into the meager cover of the flowerbeds beneath the side windows. She stood up and peeked into the window, horribly aware that she made a very dark silhouette against the white stucco. Mrs. Boyer and Connie were in the main hall poring over a large map laid out on the table.

There was a piercing whistle and Nikki knew she'd been spotted. She took off at a dead run, rounding the corner of the building and heading for the front door. One of the black-clad women was racing across the lawn, hoping to cut her off. Nikki put on speed. The woman gave a flying tackle, but Nikki dodged. The woman rolled and was up again in a flash, diving at Nikki. As the woman made her last lunge, Nikki slammed through the front door. She and the woman crashed into the room, stumbling a little as they struggled. Momentum was against them, and they slipped as the entry rug gave way and sent them both sprawling across the floor to end up at Connie's feet.

"I am stopping your clock now," said Mrs. Boyer, looking down at Nikki. "The time is 11:47. Well done."

Coo Coo Ca Choo

Nikki graduated with the rest of her class under the bright California sunshine, walking, albeit stiffly, across the stage to shake hands with Connie Hinton and the rest of the faculty. Jenny and Ellen were both assigned to an advanced training facility in Mexico, and Dina, much to everyone's delight, was assigned to a Specialty Items quality control office in northern Idaho. But instead of receiving an assignment like the rest of the class, Nikki returned to stay at the Merrivels. Mrs. M had requested she stay until things were ready. Further questioning had not revealed what the "things" were or when "ready" was going to be, and Nikki had eventually given up and gone golfing with Mr. M.

Entering the kitchen on the afternoon of the fourth day after graduation, Nikki found Mr. M enjoying an afternoon snack and the paper. He merrily waved at her, his mouth full of rice crackers. Nikki brought a plate of melon wedges from the fridge to the table. Mr. M was engrossed in the Sports section, so she took the front page without fear of repercussion.

After a few minutes of companionable silence, Mr. M looked down at the crumbs on his plate. "I'm still hungry. Do you want a sandwich? Not even grilled cheese?" he asked, as Nikki shook her head. He shrugged and bustled around the kitchen getting out deli meat and cheese.

"You look worried about something," he said, scrutinizing her from the stove.

"Mrs. M said she'd be assigning me soon, and I hate not knowing what I'm expected to do. I just wish I could prepare myself better. I feel like I need more intel."

"Yeah, new jobs can be very stressful," he agreed, laughing a little at her choice of words. "But I expect they'll give you more 'intel' at some point."

"But what if it's not enough?" Nikki asked. "I mean, there's the job and then there's the other stuff."

"Other stuff?" he asked, looking over his shoulder at her.

"Like in college, I turned in a perfectly decent paper, and my professor gave it a C-minus because he'd 'expected more' from me. What if something like that happens? What if I'm supposed to do more, but I don't know it?"

"Mmm," he said, concentrating on buttering the bread and laying out the cheese. The blue flame on the gas burner caressed the cast iron pan as he slid the sandwich onto a slick of melted butter. There was a sizzle as the bread began to cook.

"One of the first things I learned in law school, or possibly from *Perry Mason*, was not to draw conclusions from facts that are not in evidence."

"Meaning what?" asked Nikki, filching a piece of bread and putting it into the toaster, before returning to the table.

"Meaning, worry about Mrs. M's expectations when she tells you what they are."

"Stop borrowing tomorrow's troubles for today?"

"Exactly!" he said, smiling. "I understand your concern, but the only thing you can do is do the job to the best of your ability. And I suspect that the perfectly good paper you turned in was not to the best of your ability."

"Mm," said Nikki guiltily. The kitchen was silent for a moment, filled only with the wafting smell of grilled cheese. She tidied the table and brought the condiments from the fridge. When the toast popped, Mr. M hustled the slices to the table between two burning fingers.

"Hot toast," he stated, dropping the toast onto the melon plate.

"I thought you were supposed to be watching your cholesterol?" Nikki asked, eyeing the sandwich as he flipped it out onto a plate.

"What Mrs. M doesn't know won't hurt her," he said firmly.

"But it might hurt you," said Mrs. Merrivel, coming into the kitchen and planting a kiss on the top of her husband's head. She was demurely dressed in a light blue blouse and navy skirt. She looked tiny and sweet standing next to Mr. M, and Nikki wondered how many people she had fooled with that look.

"Nikki, when you're done with your toast, I'll see you in my office."

Nikki swallowed her suddenly too dry toast and nodded. The phone rang just then, and Mrs. M answered it. There were a few polite comments, but Nikki could tell that she was irritated by the call.

"Go on ahead," said Mrs. M, covering the mouthpiece. "I'll be there in a minute."

Nikki walked slowly along the hallway, her shoes making no noise on the thick carpet. The only sound was the rustling of paper from inside the office. The door was open a crack, and Nikki pushed it open and entered unannounced.

Inside, Valerie Robinson was elbow deep in Mrs. Merrivel's desk drawer.

"Jeez," said Valerie, withdrawing her hand. "What is this? Carrot Top investigates?"

"I prefer to think of myself as more of a Nancy Drew," Nikki said, raising a defensive hand to pat her hair. During the war games seminar she had been given plenty of time to examine Mrs. Valerie Robinson, but once again she was struck by the woman's boundless confidence, careless élan, and perfect physique.

"Nancy Drew was a blonde," said Val, returning to the interrupted task of rifling through Mrs. Merrivel's desk.

"In the original books she was Titian haired. *Titian* meaning red."

"Well, I suppose only Ned Nickerson knows for sure," Valerie said.

Nikki almost gasped out loud. Slandering the sainted Nancy Drew was like eating potato chips in church: the crunch really echoed, everyone noticed, and it was somehow deeply satisfying.

Val had just completed her search of the desk and was in the process of lighting a cigarette when Mrs. Merrivel entered. Val clicked the lighter a few times before the flame ignited, pretending not to see Mrs. Merrivel in the doorway.

"Really, Val!" Mrs. Merrivel exclaimed, standing on the threshold, one hand on the knob. "Do you have to smoke in my office?"

"I'll open a window," replied Val around her cigarette. She opened one of the large bay windows and flicked her ash onto the neatly trimmed hedge below. With a wordless frown, Mrs. M handed Valerie an ashtray.

"So what's new, Miranda?" Valerie asked, sitting on the sill and bracing one foot against the window frame. Nikki had never heard anyone but Mr. M use Mrs. Merrivel's first name.

"Many things, and don't put your feet on my white wood-work," said Mrs. Merrivel sourly, taking her place at the desk. Valerie shrugged and swung her foot out the window. She took a last drag of the cigarette and stubbed it out in the ashtray with a neat twist, so that the cigarette butt collapsed into a neat spiral of filth.

"So, Nikki," said Mrs. Merrivel, and Nikki snapped her attention back to Mrs. M. "You must have met our always charming Mrs. Robinson at the War Games seminar. You won that, didn't you? I hope you've been getting reacquainted."

"Um, yes?" Nikki guessed, feeling that some response was expected of her.

"I'm glad. It's so much better when partners get along," Mrs. M said without turning around, and Val froze mid-drag on a cigarette and then began to cough.

"You know, Valerie, I don't think you would cough so much if you didn't smoke." Mrs. Merrivel's tone was saccharine sweet, but Nikki was starting to wonder how well she and Valerie Robinson actually got along.

"I don't need a partner," Val said. "You've said yourself that I work better without one."

"No, I said it was better that you work without a partner than lose any more consultants." Mrs. M beamed at Nikki, and Nikki started to feel very nervous. She didn't want to be the dead meat partner to anyone's Dirty Harry, no matter how cool they were. "But now," Mrs. M continued, "I think I've found someone who's up to the challenge."

"Who? Little Nancy Drew over here?" Valerie gave Nikki a once-over and a skeptical shake of the head. "Just because she won the War Games?" She didn't do it, but Nikki sensed the finger quotes around "won." They both knew Nikki wouldn't have won without Val's interference.

"She also beat your time on the final test," said Mrs. Merrivel, as if she were commenting on the weather.

"She did not!" Valerie looked outraged.

"By three minutes and three point two seconds," Mrs. Merrivel said, opening her Day-Timer. Valerie examined Nikki again, this time with narrowed eyes. Nikki flinched a little under the examination.

"It doesn't mean anything," said Val. "I've always said I could beat that time."

"You've also been saying for years that you wouldn't mind working with someone if she didn't slow you down." Mrs. Merrivel was jotting a few things down in her planner, apparently divorced from the entire argument, except for the fact that she was a main participant.

"So she can jump through a few hoops. It doesn't mean she can do the work."

"She's passed all of her tests, Valerie. I believe that it is the general purpose of those tests to prove that she *can* do the work."

Valerie made a snorting noise of disbelief and left the sanctuary of the windowsill long enough to scoop up her pack of cigarettes from the desk, before retreating to the window to renew the complex rite of lighting a cigarette. By the time she exhaled the first lungful of smoke, she had apparently reached a decision.

"All right, I'll give her a try."

"Well, that's all settled, then," said Mrs. M, smiling. "I believe Lillian has some new details for you on the smuggling case you've been working on. You should give her a call when we're done here. She's expecting Nikki as well, so don't worry about that. You won't mind having her stay with you until she finds a place, will you?" Mrs. M didn't wait for Val to reply, but turned her full attention to Nikki. "Val will take you into town and get you geared up. They will fill you in on everything at the office. I look forward to seeing your progress." Mrs. Merrivel stood up and extended her hand to Nikki. Nikki shook it, but was at a loss for what to do next. Val walked to the door.

"Um, thank you," said Nikki, barely avoiding making it into a question, and Mrs. M smiled and added a quick hug.

"Good luck," she said. "To the both of you," she added, almost as an afterthought.

Already walking down the hall, Val gave a half wave without turning around. Nikki gave a last smile to Mrs. M and then followed Val out of the office.

CALIFORNIA XII
Killer Queen

Nikki lugged her backpack downstairs and hugged Mr. M goodbye. Valerie was standing on the porch silhouetted by the sunshine streaming through the open front door.

"Don't mind Val," Mr. M whispered to Nikki. "She's stubborn, but stick to your guns and she'll respect you." Nikki nodded and trudged toward her future.

She stopped next to Val and heaved her backpack up onto one shoulder. Six months of training had only added to its contents, and now it seemed to bulge at the seams. Staring out at the immaculate green vista of the Merrivels' lawn, Val stood ritually smacking her soft pack of cigarettes against the palm of one hand. Eventually, she gave the pack a shake, ejecting one cigarette from the hole at the top, and lit up.

"Sorry if it sounded like I didn't want you in there," she said, blowing out a steady stream of smoke. "But you have to argue. If you don't argue they think they can always have everything their own way. And we don't want that." Val fixed Nikki with a keen eye and added a ghost of a smile.

Nikki smiled tentatively back.

"Come on," Val said. "We've got places to be."

She led the way to a sky blue Chevy Impala convertible. Nikki stared at the car in surprise. It wasn't the car she would have imagined for Valerie. Although, now that she'd seen them together, she really couldn't imagine anything else that would fit.

"Nice car," she said, offering a sincere compliment.

"1967 Chevy Impala. It's a piece of shit, but it attracts guys. I'm thinking of trading it in."

"Oh," said Nikki, not sure what to do with any of that information. She looked at the car again. She had never really thought of a vehicle in terms of attracting men.

"You coming?" asked Valerie, the door open, one foot in the car.

"Yeah, coming," said Nikki, breaking from her contemplation of the car. "I've been wanting to ask you," she said, gathering her courage as the car crunched down the gravel drive. "Is your name really Mrs. Robinson?"

Valerie laughed, throwing her head back and releasing the sound from her gut. "I got two things out of that marriage, Red," she said. "A really excellent name and a cat that pisses in my shoes. But you might as well call me Val. I've never really understood the Carrie Mae obsession with proper titles."

"It does seem anachronistic," said Nikki, and then she remembered the rest of Val's statement. "So a cat that pees in your shoes . . . I take it we're going shoe shopping then?"

The wind whipped Val's hair into her face and she gave a slightly surprised smile.

"You got a problem with that?"

"Nope," said Nikki. "But my sponsor in Shoe Shoppers Anonymous might."

Valerie drove downhill, passing neighborhood parks and cul-de-sac turnoffs. Every yard was green, displaying the owner's ability to pay a ludicrous water bill. The houses got smaller as they drove down, though not any less nice. The stucco was pristine, and the tile roofs were all in an orderly gentleman-rancher red.

"How'd you beat my time on the final?" Val asked abruptly.

"I got lucky."

"Huh," Val said, giving Nikki a narrow-eyed stare. She lapsed into silence and they drove on farther, finally approaching the mall on Magic Mountain Parkway.

"It's hard to take a street named after an amusement park seriously," said Nikki, staring at the street sign.

Val chuckled. "That's California for you. If it makes money, it must be important. They aren't very original about things like names. This is Town Center Mall. See what I mean?"

The mall had been laid out in an architect's rendition of a small-town center. One of the roads was even called Town Center Drive. The architect hadn't wanted anyone to miss his vision. Like the streets, it was very clean. Nikki couldn't help feeling it was a little too clean.

"Is it just me or are the Stepford Wives going to come and get us?" she asked, as Valerie pulled the car into an angled parking slot.

"Yeah, I know," Valerie said, getting out and feeding quarters into the meter. "It's kind of like it ought to have a sign that says, DECORATING BY THE GAP, with all their built-in bits of 'flair' and 'ethnic character.' But they do have a Nordstrom's, and that means shoes. I mean it's not Rodeo Drive and they don't sell any Manolos, but shoes are shoes, even in the boonies."

Valerie led the way into the obviously new Nordstrom's building, and Nikki was glad she was wearing her "nice" outfit. Nordstrom's clerks were notoriously snobby to the poorly dressed. Nikki had once asked a perfume lady about a particular scent and had been answered with "We don't sell that perfume. Maybe you should try Kmart." Since then, Nikki had been slightly paranoid about shopping there.

"So," Valerie said, modeling a pair of beige snakeskin stilettos in a foot mirror, "how'd you get to be Mrs. Merrivel's pet?"

"What?" Nikki exclaimed, stopping with a foot halfway into a pair of brown patchwork leather boots. The boots had a thick, nearly platform sole, and Nikki had been considering what she would wear them with before Val had made her egregiously incorrect statement about Nikki's status.

"Oh come on, Red," Val said with acerbity. "Never kid a kidder. You are staying at her house and you started training late. Someone did some serious sucking up."

"I did not!" Nikki protested.

"And hey," continued Val, "you got partnered with me. And trust me, that's not normal."

"That doesn't mean she likes me," Nikki said.

Val laughed. "OK, you've got a point. In that case, what'd you do to piss her off?"

"That's not what I meant," Nikki mumbled, blushing scarlet.

The sales clerk arrived, carrying a stack of boxes. "I want these in a size smaller," Valerie said, handing him the stilettos. The clerk disappeared again.

"I don't know why I'm here," Nikki said when the clerk was out of hearing range.

"She's not your godmother or anything? Not childhood chums with your mum? You didn't graduate from the same finishing school or something?"

"I went to public school," said Nikki. "I never met Mrs. Merrivel before . . ."

"Before what?" asked Val, stopping to stare at a woman who was browsing too close for her comfort. After a few agonizing moments of scrutiny, the shopper hurried out of the shoe department.

"Before the Carrie Mae recruiting speech," Nikki said, happily skipping the entire Canada issue.

"Huh," Val said, pulling on a pair of boots similar to the ones Nikki had discarded. Nikki thought they looked better on Val. "What about her friend?"

"What friend?" Nikki looked up and found Val watching her through skeptical eyes. Nikki returned the look with the ease of the completely uninformed.

"She's up to something," Val said.

"Mrs. Merrivel's friend?" Nikki was lost.

Val rolled her eyes. "Mrs. Merrivel, you dope. The woman makes Machiavelli look like a used car salesman when it comes to scheming. I know she's up to something. I just don't know what. She didn't tell you anything?"

"I don't think she's up to anything," protested Nikki. "She didn't say anything to me."

"Well, I wouldn't say anything to you if I were her, either," Val said, flopping down into a chair and unzipping the boots.

Nikki pulled on a pair of white espadrille sandals with a wedge heel and lace-up straps that wrapped around her ankle and considered how to respond.

"Personally," Val said, leaning back and flexing her perfectly pedicured toes, "I think she's angling for Lillian's job."

"Who's Lillian?" asked Nikki.

"Dr. Lillian Hastings, director of the West Coast branch. She and Miranda have been enemies for longer than you've been alive probably, but it wasn't a problem until Miranda got assigned to overhaul the training program on the West Coast. Lillian was not amused."

"And you think Mrs. M wants to be the West Coast Director? I don't see how I could help with that." Nikki frowned thoughtfully at the espadrilles, pleased at how thin they made her ankles look.

"Neither do I," Val agreed. "You should get those," she said, pointing at the espadrilles. "They look really cute on you."

"I already have a pair of wedges," said Nikki sadly. "What I really need are some stylish sneakers or some sort of flat. I don't really like flats. I'm so short, I think they make me look like I'm going to visit Snow White, but if we're going out on a mission, then I need some sort of shoe I can run in."

"Mission shoes," Val said, nodding. "Here, try these." She held a pair of black sneakerish-looking things. Black, mesh, and low to the ground, the shoes were exactly what Nikki had had in mind, and she eagerly pulled them on before she caught sight of the price tag.

"Haven't got the cash," she said, reluctantly putting them back in the box.

Val tossed the boots into their box as the clerk returned with another stack of shoes. "We're done," she announced, as the clerk put down the load of shoes. "We want these." She pointed to the stilettos. "And these." She pointed to the sneakers.

"No, no, I can't . . ." Nikki began, but Val cut her off.

"Sure, you can. My treat. Call it my good deed for the decade."

The sun was setting outside the mall, painting everything in dusty California gold. Even the Town Center Plaza and the "happy" mother and dancing children statues managed to look good in that light.

"Are you going to tell Dr. Hastings?" Nikki asked.

"Tell her what?"

"That you think I'm part of some sort of plot to take over her job," said Nikki meekly.

"Why would I do that?" Val retorted. "It's none of my business. Lillian can look after her own job without me. Besides, unless you're holding out on some information, then there really isn't any proof, is there?"

Nikki shook her head, and they walked in silence toward the parking garage. Just as Nikki was formulating some sort of lame small talk, Val's phone erupted into "Another One Bites the Dust."

Nikki hummed along as Val pulled out her phone and checked out the Caller ID. She grimaced, but flipped open the phone.

"Ain't no sound but the sound of his feet, machine guns ready to go," Nikki sang under her breath.

"Yeah?" barked Val, walking away. Nikki dropped her shopping bag into the backseat of the convertible and leaned against the side of the car, still humming the tune.

A few moments later, Val slapped the phone shut, frowning thoughtfully. "Looks like Mrs. Merrivel's serious about this," she said, returning to the car.

Are you ready, hey, are you ready for this?

"Serious about what?" asked Nikki, getting in.

Are you hanging on the edge of your seat?

"We are going on a mission," Val said with a grin. "It's time to go to work."

Nikki gulped and clicked her seat belt shut as Val revved the engine and threw the Impala into Drive.

Wonderland: Red Square

The trip to the office was accomplished in silence, except for an occasional burst of road rage from Val. They finally screeched to a stop in front of a glass-faced office building. Light shone out into the darkening evening with a warm, sparkling glow.

They entered the gracious indoor plaza through a revolving door. Nikki stared around in wonder. It was a movie set version of a perfect office: Lights poured through the sparkling clean glass onto a green area, a tinkling water feature, and sculptures. People bustled everywhere, looking well-dressed and important.

"What is this place?"

"Well, officially," said Val, "it's listed as the West Coast headquarters of the Carrie Mae Foundation."

"What is it unofficially?"

"Oh, well, unofficially it's the West Coast headquarters of the Carrie Mae Foundation. The first three floors belong to the foundation's official functions—fund-raising, relief organization, et cetera. But the upper floors and the basement are all ours. It's a new building. We just moved in about six months ago."

Valerie headed for the elevators and Nikki trotted after her, trying not to stare at people. Val went to the end elevator, and pressed the Up arrow, holding her thumb on the button longer than Nikki thought she had to.

"Fingerprint scanner," Val said. "The elevator won't open if you're not in the system." The doors slid apart. Val stepped inside with Nikki close behind and punched the button for the eighth floor. The elevator rose eight floors and stopped, but didn't open. Val appeared unperturbed by this and opened up the emergency phone panel. She lifted the red phone to her ear and said, "All mimsy were the borogoves, and the mome raths outgrabe."

Nikki was about to comment on the poetry when the elevator opened onto a charmingly decorated waiting room.

"Good morning, Mrs. Robinson, Dr. Hastings will be out in a moment," said the girl at the desk. "Will you and your guest please sign in?"

Valerie walked to the desk and signed in. Nikki had just signed the clipboard when a woman came out to meet them. She was a tall woman with perfectly coifed auburn hair and a dancer's aristocratic posture. A brilliant russet scarf was draped elegantly across her shoulders, and she wore her Anne Klein suit with an easy grace.

"Valerie, good afternoon," the woman said, walking forward and embracing Val. "And you must be Nikki. I'm Lillian Hastings. I'm sure we're all pleased to welcome you to the team." Dr. Hastings's cool smile, coupled with Val's previous assessment of the politics of the situation, gave Nikki the impression that the woman was less than pleased with her presence. Nikki smiled back, trying to look innocuous. She wished she had Val's ability to stand around looking like the whole point of a setting was to display her, but she knew she'd be more comfortable blending into the background.

"Jane's team has been setting up the conference call," said Dr. Hastings. "I believe they're set up in room six, if you're ready?" Without waiting for any assenting comments, Dr. Hastings turned and led the way into the maze of Carrie Mae. Eventually they were led into a well-lit conference room, where another of Carrie Mae's seemingly endless supply of bright, competent Ladies was putting file folders on the table next to empty chairs.

"Good evening," said the girl, focusing on the women as they entered. Nikki noticed that she was wearing an earpiece that wrapped around her ear so that she looked like some sort of cyborg. "The video conference call will begin as soon as we make contact. Background information is available in the folders on the table." Her gaze stopped focusing and her hand traveled up to her earpiece. "That's affirmative. Go ahead with the two-forty-two."

"What am I looking at, Jane?" Val asked, ignoring the interjection of numbers into the conversation and taking a chair. She pulled the file folder toward her, and Nikki followed suit, but was distracted by Jane's shirt and never made it to the contents of the folder.

Jane wore a T-shirt that bore the words THE MORE YOU DISAPPROVE, THE MORE FUN IT IS FOR ME. She had officed-up her ensemble with a black blazer over a short plaid skirt and tights in a kind of classy punk look that Nikki had always envied but had never been able to pull off.

"Jane, why don't you start at the beginning, for Nikki's sake?" asked Lillian, interrupting Nikki's train of thought. "Unless you've already been briefed on all of this, Nikki?" There was an icy vindictiveness underlying the older woman's tone, and Nikki smiled nervously.

"No, I haven't covered anything," she said.

"Very well, Jane, proceed," responded Lillian, but she didn't seem any happier.

Jane's eyes tilted up, fixing Dr. Hastings with a bright-eyed stare. Then she nodded, her full Bettie Page bangs bouncing slightly. Nikki felt a swell of envy for such well-behaved hair. She watched as Dr. Hastings read Jane's T-shirt and tightened the muscles around her mouth so that her lips flattened out in a disapproving straight line.

"OK," Jane said, either ignoring or not seeing Dr. Hastings's disapproval as she hit a button on her laptop. The lights dimmed and a screen dropped from the ceiling. "This is Laura Daniels, the wife of the U.S. ambassador to Thailand, and a childhood friend of Mrs. Merrivel."

Jane displayed a picture of a woman about Mrs. Merrivel's age. Her hair was an unrealistic blond and she wore a news anchor's professional smile.

"Mrs. Daniels has made a lifelong commitment to charitable works, particularly focusing on women's health and education. Our charity foundation has worked with her on several occasions, and she is currently planning the first annual South East Asian Women's Health Conference, to be held next week in Bangkok."

"Give the woman a gold star," Val said.

"This is Lawan Chinnawat," Jane said, ignoring Val. "Based out of Thailand, Lawan has been one of the loudest voices protesting the sex trade that flourishes throughout Asia. She's also funded her own free health clinic in the red light district, and she works with the scholarship fund started by Laura Daniels to place the children of prostitutes in boarding schools. The hope being that with an education or a skill, these children will break the cycle of prostitution, violence, and drug abuse."

"Give her two gold stars," Val said, and this time Jane shot her a dirty look. "I mean, great, they're wonderful people," Val continued. "But why are we here? I assume there's a problem? Cut to the chase, Jane."

"Lawan is missing," said Jane.

"What do you mean 'missing'?" Val asked. "I mean there's 'stepped out for a romantic getaway without telling anyone' missing, and then there's 'blood all over the kitchen floor' missing. Which is it?"

"That is what we are here to ascertain," said Dr. Hastings. "I believe we will have Laura Daniels on the line shortly"—she looked at Jane, who nodded—"and then we can ask her. Personally, I wouldn't have bothered to call you in on this matter, but Miranda was most insistent."

Nikki hadn't grown up with Nell's backhanded compliments and veiled insults without learning a thing or two about barbed comments. At the very least, she knew when one was aimed at her.

"Connection has been made. Video feed commencing now," Jane said.

The screen flickered, and then a slightly off-color version of Laura Daniels appeared.

"Oh," she said, and the picture stabilized into more lifelike colors. "Oh," said the woman again. "Oh, there you are. Am I doing this right? I'm not sure I'm doing this right."

"You're coming through loud and clear, Mrs. Daniels," said Jane reassuringly. "You're speaking to Dr. Hastings, Valerie Robinson, and Nikki Lanier."

"And of course you must be Jane. Call me Laura," the woman said, smiling warmly. "And thank you all so much for taking the time to talk to me."

Laura was clearly practiced at the social niceties of making gracious speeches, but she also very clearly meant it. Nikki was with-holding final judgment, but upon her first impression, she liked Laura Daniels.

"We are always gratified to help a friend of Mrs. Merrivel's," Dr. Hastings said with a wintery smile, "but perhaps in the inter-ests of time we should proceed expeditiously."

Nikki glanced at Jane, wondering if anyone else had noticed the expensive vocabulary being thrown around. Jane dropped the tiniest wink, and Nikki covered her mouth with her hand to hide a smile.

"Oh, of course," said Laura. "I understand that you're very busy, but honestly, I wouldn't have contacted you if I didn't think it was an absolute necessity."

"Please tell us your problem," said Dr. Hastings.

"My friend Lawan Chinnawat, you may have heard of her . . ."

"We've seen her profile," said Dr. Hastings, cutting her off.

"Oh. Yes, well, she has a lot of political enemies, you know. It's practically not safe for her and her daughter—Lindawati, so precious; she's at boarding school now—to walk by themselves." Nikki was amused by Laura's grandmotherly interjection about Lawan's daughter, but she could see that Dr. Hastings wasn't.

"She's always getting threats and things," continued Laura, "but ordinarily she just takes her precautions and things are fine. But lately things have been . . . tense. Tenser than usual. Since the coup in 2006, speech isn't as free as it used to be. Activists like Lawan are targets. Not that Lawan takes any notice of that—although, really, I wish she would. Recently, I asked her to be the keynote speaker at my conference. I wish I hadn't; it probably put her too much in the limelight, but no one else is as well versed in the difficulties facing women in Thailand and Asia right now."

"Mrs. Daniels," interrupted Dr. Hastings again, "is there a point to any of this?"

"I'm getting there," said Laura, looking slightly irritated. "I'm just trying to explain what Lawan has been working on, and that things have been tense for the last few months."

"Noted," said Dr. Hastings. "When did Lawan actually disappear?"

"Ten days ago. I went to her house, and she was on the phone arguing in Thai, and she looked upset, like she had been crying. Lawan said everything was fine, but the next day she was gone. The house is empty. She won't answer her phone. I don't even know if she's alive!" Laura dabbed at her eyes with a tissue. "I'm so worried! And the conference is next week. What am I supposed to do?"

"Don't worry," said Nikki impulsively, wanting to stop Laura's tears. "I promise we will do everything we can to find her."

Laura lifted her face out of the tissue with a glowing smile. Across the table, Dr. Hastings tapped her fingernails on the lacquered surface of the conference table in a steady cadence.

"Oh, thank you!" beamed Laura. "I'm at my wit's end! Miranda was right, you Carrie Mae ladies are the best!"

"We're just the tops," Val said, giving Nikki a disgusted look.

"Give us a gold star?" asked Nikki, with a weak smile.

"Mmph," snorted Dr. Hastings, sounding irritated. "I'll tell you what, Mrs. Daniels, Val and Nikki will fly to Thailand and meet with you. Hopefully, they will be able to turn up something, but, really, I'm afraid I can only allocate one week for this kind of investigation."

"Oh, of course," Laura agreed eagerly. "I totally understand. Anything you can do to help will be very much appreciated. I'm just glad to have professionals on the case!"

"Of course," said Dr. Hastings. "Thank you for calling. We'll be in touch." She nodded at Jane, who shut off the feed and began to mutter instructions into her headset.

"Nicole," said Dr. Hastings, "perhaps we should clarify the chain of command and the decision-making process. We do not simply promise people that we will solve everything for them! This is clearly a matter for the Thai police. Flying one of my top agents to Thailand for a week is a waste of resources."

"I thought we were already committed to helping her," Nikki said, sinking in her chair.

"You are a novice. We're not paying you to think," said Dr. Hastings. "Valerie, I'm sorry to be sending you on a wild goose chase, but it appears that others have spoken for us."

"Don't they always?" Val said, stacking her papers into the folder and giving it a sharp thwack on the table. "I'm used to it." She smiled at Dr. Hastings, stretching her lips to the fullest, and Nikki thought that Val probably had a double meaning in her statement, but Dr. Hastings didn't appear to notice.

Thank you for coming in, ladies." Dr. Hastings stood up and nodded her dismissal at them. "As usual, please be careful."

"I'm always careful," said Val dryly, standing herself and stretching.

"If I were that careful with my birth control, I'd be pregnant," Jane mumbled from behind the computer.

"Jane!" snapped Dr. Hastings. "That is not appropriate for a meeting."

"Yes, Dr. Hastings," Jane said meekly, stepping back into her place.

Wonderland: White Square

"You and your big mouth," Val said bitterly as they entered the elevator. "Do you know how hot it is in Thailand right now?"

"No," said Nikki, still smarting from Dr. Hastings's tongue lashing.

"It's hot," Val said, jabbing the button for B2. "Damn hot. Really, really hot. Baboon ass sweat hot."

"I'm really sorry," said Nikki. "I thought, since she was calling, that we already going to help." What she really meant was that she hadn't realized that an organization committed to "helping women everywhere" might possibly turn down someone like Laura Daniels.

"Yeah, probably," Val said with a shrug. "But it's always better to let the boss think she's making the decisions, ya know?"

"Got it," said Nikki glumly.

Val laughed. "Don't worry so much. Lillian wasn't going to like you anyway."

"That's supposed to make me feel better?"

"It's very liberating," Val said. "It's not like she can like you any less. Now you can be as big of a bitch as you want."

"I guess," said Nikki, unconvinced. "What's in the basement?" she asked, hoping to change the subject.

"Fun stuff," said Val.

The elevator sank ten floors and stopped, but didn't open. As before, Val appeared unperturbed by this and opened up the emergency phone panel. She lifted the red phone to her ear and said, "'Twas brillig, and the slithy toves, did gyre and gimble in the wabe."

"'Beware the Jabberwock, my son!'" said Nikki, and Val gave her a blank stare.

"Oh. Yeah, the poetry," she said, just when Nikki had reached the point of crawling under a rock. "One of the techies said that coming down here was a little like falling down the rabbit hole in *Alice in Wonderland*: nothing is what it appears to be. So some joker makes all the passwords poems from *Alice in Wonderland*."

"*Through the Looking Glass*," Nikki corrected.

"What?" asked Val, stepping off the elevator and into a long cement hallway. The cement had been painted a cheerful shade of lavender on the bottom half of the hallway, but it didn't particularly cheer things up.

"*Through the Looking Glass,*" said Nikki, her mind mostly preoccupied by wishing the lavender weren't so bright. "It's the second Alice book and it's the one 'The Jabberwocky' comes out of. She falls down the rabbit hole in the first book."

"True," said Rachel White, as she walked down the hallway

toward them. Her kinky blond curls fluffed away from her head in a profuse tangle as dense as her thoughts seemed to be. Given the setting, Nikki was reminded of Alice's White Queen. "But we feel *Wonderland* encompasses both books, and we therefore need not limit ourselves to one."

"Show-off," Val muttered at Nikki, but with a twinkle in her eye.

"Sorry," answered Nikki with a self-deprecating smile. "It's just that the poem is an excellent example of the way our brains can comprehend correct grammar without understanding the words. One of my classes used it as an example all the time. I guess I'm a little overly familiar with it."

"What do you mean?" asked Rachel, and she beckoned them to follow her, moving down the hallway at an amble.

Another woman in a lab coat passed by carrying something under a sheet, and Rachel stopped to poke at it a bit before sending the other woman on her way. Then she looked at Val and Nikki as if she couldn't quite remember why they were there.

"'The Jabberwocky.' Understanding grammar without real words. Expound," she blurted out, and Nikki blinked, unprepared for the pop quiz.

"Well, the poem itself is grammatical. I mean that our brains comprehend it and can answer questions about it. What were the toves? They were slithy. Where were they? In the wabe. What were the toves doing? They were gyre-ing and gimble-ing. But the words themselves are gibberish. It's an example of the fact that, for linguistic purposes, syntax and sense don't need each other." Nikki stopped, even more embarrassed than before, feeling the beginning of a blush coming on. "Sorry again. I graduated in linguistics. My mother keeps telling me not to talk about it, in case I accidentally bore someone to death."

"No," Rachel said, stopping in front of a door. "It's interesting. I never really thought about it. What exactly do linguists do?" She put her palm up to a flat panel beside the door, and a small bar of light appeared and ran the length of her hand and back. The door popped open.

"Now, that's something I'd like to know. What exactly do you do?" asked Val with sudden verve.

"Well, broadly speaking, linguists study how the brain forms language and how language evolves in context with culture. This particular linguist, on the other hand, works for Carrie Mae."

Rachel smiled in empathy.

"It's hard to get work in your field sometimes. I was working for a forestry company as a lab assistant for two years before I started working here. And believe me, that was about two years too long."

They had entered what was either a laboratory or a rummage sale. What appeared to be ordinary household items sat among computers, delicate soldering irons, oddly shaped tools, and huge magnifying lenses. Rachel led Nikki and Val down the length of the cubicle and through another door. The room had been subdivided in a way that vaguely reminded Nikki of the shooting range at the ranch. Each cement room was shielded from the main hall by a thick piece of glass. As they passed, several people hurried out of one of the rooms.

"It's the vacuum cleaner," one of them said, bobbing excitedly up and down before Rachel.

"Oooh, wait a minute," she said to Val and Nikki. "I want to see this." Rachel took her hands out of the deep pockets of her lab coat and clapped them enthusiastically.

They all paused to watch an upright vacuum cleaner standing alone in the middle of the room. It was plugged into the wall and running. Someone was wearing an entire bomb suit and pressing buttons on the handle. After carefully pressing the last button, Bomb Suit waddled to the door and hastily exited. The vacuum continued to run for exactly forty-five seconds, and then exploded in a flurry of shrapnel. Nikki jumped back, nearly tripping over Val, but the glass between them remained in one piece.

"Not bad," Rachel said.

"We were hoping to get more flame," said Bomb Suit, taking off her helmet. The others nodded.

"Hmm, well, add some more incendiary mediums and try again." Rachel smiled at Nikki and Val, and then started, as if remembering that they were there for a purpose. "This way. Sorry for stopping, but we're working on a whole line of cleaning products and we're hoping the vacuum cleaner will be the flagship, so to speak."

"Of course," Val said calmly, and Nikki began to think that maybe the nameless techie had been entirely accurate in calling this place Wonderland. Any minute now, Rachel White would surely turn into a sheep.

"So, the two of you are off to Thailand?" Rachel asked brightly, and Val spared a bitter look in Nikki's direction.

"Word travels fast," she said.

Rachel nodded. "Jane e-mailed me a minute ago. I've set up your usual gear, Val, but what does Nikki want?" She stopped walking abruptly, and Nikki nearly ran into her.

"Sorry."

"No, my fault. It is Nikki, isn't it? I didn't mess that up?"

"Uh, yes," answered Nikki. "I mean no. I mean yes, my name is Nikki."

"Oh good," answered Rachel, and she continued on at her quick pace. "Did you know," she asked without looking backward, and clearly jumping to the next subject in her head, "that women apologize more than men?"

"Uh, no," said Nikki, looking at Val, who shrugged and shook her head.

"It's true. And women are more likely to apologize for spatial invasions or for talk offenses, i.e., when we feel we were inconvenient. Like when you bumped into me."

"I didn't mean to be a space invader," Nikki said, and tried to ignore Val's smothered laugh.

"That's exactly my point!" said Rachel triumphantly. "It was my fault, but you apologized because you felt you had imposed on my space! Interesting, no?"

"Uh, yes?" Nikki tried, and Rachel nodded encouragingly.

"So what kind of gear do you want?" she asked, changing subjects again.

"I'm not really sure," answered Nikki, glancing at Val for guidance or at least a clue. "What are my options?"

"Well, guns you'll get in country. That's just easier. But everything else we'll issue here. What kinds of activities do you think you will be engaging in?"

Nikki looked at Val again. She wasn't sure which was more strange: the question itself or the way in which it was phrased. It sounded so formal.

"Why don't we just set her up with the complete package? She can personalize next time," Val said, much to Nikki's relief.

"Great!" said Rachel brightly. She turned to Nikki. "I've got your measurements and color chart. So I'll just pull everything to your specifications, and you'll be on your way."

"Oh good," said Nikki faintly. It was hard not to like Rachel, but like the original White Queen, she did have a way of keeping a conversation off-balance.

"I'm really glad you're going for the whole rig," Rachel said as they entered the lab. She ducked into a supply closet and continued speaking, her voice echoing from the metal interior of the small room. "It's important to go out properly equipped. Val never wants to take the whole thing, and then she always comes back to borrow things."

"I always bring them back."

"Just not in the same condition," Rachel answered tartly, reappearing with a huge makeup case.

It was a box nearly two feet square and looked like something Nikki's grandmother would have owned. With folding doors and extending shelves and a multitude of tiny compartments, it was a Transformer for girls. Its pale purple exterior and a pearlescent sheen were accented by gold handles, art deco styling, and the ubiquitous Carrie Mae butterfly on the lid.

Nikki stared at it in horror. It was one of the gaudiest things she had ever seen. Never in her life had she taken that much makeup anywhere. She wasn't sure that she even owned enough makeup to fill the thing that Rachel proudly hefted onto the table.

"All right, the trick here, Nikki," Rachel said, "is not to confuse your actual product with our lab product. Although we do try to make it multipurpose, I cannot claim that all of our lab versions are up to the high standard of Carrie Mae makeup." She shook her head sadly, as if this were a personal failing.

"This is your shade of foundation, I believe," she continued, holding out a silver Carrie Mae tube with its telltale gold butterfly. Nikki nodded. "But it also happens to be a handy bit of high-grade plastic explosives that can be set off with the detonator cord concealed in the bottom of the cap." She whipped the cap apart with practiced ease and showed Nikki how to arm the foundation. "Of course, because of the chemical content, it's also fairly flammable and it doesn't taste very good. It wouldn't explode or anything," she said hastily, seeing Nikki's expression. "Plastique doesn't work that way; but you wouldn't want to get too close to any open flames."

Rachel reassembled the cap, put it back on the tube, and handed the foundation to Nikki. Nikki examined it critically. It really did look just like her regular tube of foundation, but a quick check of the label revealed that it was "EXP015-A."

"Then we have pepper spray body splash. The stun gun compact. And the tracking device earrings." The gold butterfly earrings were each about the size of a nickel.

"We didn't cover those in class," Nikki interrupted. "What do they do?"

"Oh! These are a great new innovation!" Rachel pulled out another pair to demonstrate. "Simply, bend the ear post to activate . . ." She snapped the small tine of the earring straight down. The earring made a small beep and the gemstone eyes of the butterfly flashed red. "Then just pop it into someone's pocket and track it in live time with your Carrie Mae–issue phone or this compact." She pulled out a small blush compact and pressed down on a raised butterfly icon. The mirror portion faded and became an LCD display, showing a grid pattern and a central blinking dot; the blush well flipped over and became a small panel of buttons. "The great thing is that they're a set. One earring is a tracking device, and the other is a bug. See, I've got them labeled." She flipped the earrings over, and Nikki saw that one earring had a little embossed ant on the back and the other had two squiggly lines.

"It's a track and a bug, get it?"

"Got it," Nikki said, poking at the buttons on the compact.

"The earrings have a lifespan of twelve hours, which is unfortunate, but we're working on improving the battery life in the beta version. I know, it's not that long, but it's the best we could do and still have the earrings look stylish. We did have one set that lasted longer, but nobody wanted to wear them. The review panel said they were ugly." Rachel seemed disheartened by this opinion of her work.

"Can we get a couple of those flash-bang lipsticks?" Val asked, hopping up on one of the tall counters.

"Oh, yes, that would be good. I got three new shades in yesterday." Rachel perked up again and continued on around the room, filling Nikki's arms with gear. As the pile of equipment grew larger, Nikki began to worry. She had no idea what half of it did.

"Don't worry," said Rachel, as Nikki walked away with a duffel bag and toting the enormous makeup case, "I included the manuals." It wasn't a reassuring statement.

Returning to the elevators, Nikki lugged the vast duffel and tried not to grimace at Val's dainty bag. Val had just hit the button for the lobby when Rachel came running down the hall.

"Wait! I almost forgot," she panted. Val put a hand over the door sensor and the door slid open again.

"Your cell phone," Rachel huffed, dropping the book and a cell phone into Nikki's hands. "Can't believe I nearly forgot that. Can't send you out without a company phone. It's got all the other normal stuff, and of course our extras. Unfortunately, it doesn't come in the right purple."

"Or I wouldn't use it," said Val behind Nikki.

"But the silver looks nice, don't you think?" Rachel asked, oblivious.

"Yeah, nice," answered Nikki.

"I've activated it. Here's the recharger cord, car kit, and instructions. Just push here to talk. Don't worry, the rest is in the manual." Rachel shoved the instructions and cords at Nikki as Val took her hand off the sensor.

"Now you know why we keep Rachel in the basement," Val said, as the doors closed.

"Am I going to blow myself up with this thing?" Nikki asked, holding the phone at arm's length.

"Possibly."

"That's not very reassuring."

"I strive for honesty," replied Val. "I don't usually make it, but I do try."

Gym Stones

Evening had closed into full dark and they drove through darkened streets that seemed to be full of small Hondas with underbody neon and pimped-out Caddies sporting huge stereos and bizarre hydraulics, and pulled up in front of a large, square building.

"Did you bring gym clothes?" Val asked abruptly.

"Yeah, in my bag somewhere."

"Good, let's go to the gym. I need a workout."

Nikki nodded as Val took a sudden right. They pulled up outside a dark-looking building with papered-over windows and an aura of pending abandonment. Val's idea of a gym was definitely not Nikki's idea of a gym.

Val had hopped out with her gym bag, as if it wasn't a big deal that three large men wearing wool caps and tank tops were loitering suspiciously around the entrance. The men gave Val the head jerk acknowledgment and scanned Nikki's ass like professional ass appreciators. Nikki wished she'd worn something more covering. Possibly something like a burka. Then she got pissed off. It was her ass. It was adequately covered and there was no reason why she should have to feel embarrassed. But she did anyway.

"So, um, what kind of gym is this?" she asked when they were inside the lobby.

"Kick-boxing," Val said.

"Oh."

"You know how to fight, right?"

"Uh, well, you know, we covered it in training and everything. But truthfully, I think I'm more about the gentle way." The "gentle way" was a rough translation of *judo*, but from Val's blank stare, Nikki guessed she didn't know that. Nikki had meant the remark to be a little funny, but she guessed that Val didn't know that, either.

"Right," Val said incredulously. "Well, here they're more about the 'kick you in the face' way."

"Well, that could work, too, I guess," Nikki said, feeling like an idiot and wishing Jenny or Ellen were with her.

They walked through double swinging doors and onto the main floor of the gym. The center was taken up by a full-size boxing ring; the edges of the room had been sectioned off into weights, heavy bags, and smaller rings. On the far side of the room a guy was hitting the heavy bag. At first glance he looked a little pudgy, but every blow moved the heavy bag sideways in the air. A couple of other guys were doing manly workout things with weights. Nikki watched as a skinny dude with abs like a twenty-four pack worked crunches on an incline bench. He'd been doing them since they walked in the door and he didn't show any signs of stopping.

After changing in the women's locker room that Nikki suspected had once been a broom closet, she and Val started the work-out proper. They alternated their weight sets with cardio sets of jumping rope, and by the time Val was ready to spar, Nikki was sweating profusely. She was also acutely aware of the slowly fading bumps and long purple bruise left by her dirt bike crash on the final training test. As she strapped on the shin pads and footgear, a short, stocky Hispanic man approached her.

"*Hola,* Domingo," Val said when he got closer.

"*Hola,*" he replied.

"Nikki, introduce yourself to Domingo."

"*Hola,* Domingo. *Me llamo* Nikki. *Es agradable satisfacerle.*" She was excited for a chance to practice her Spanish.

"Slow down there, babe," Domingo said. "I may look Mexican, but I was born in freaking Idaho. The only thing I do in Mexican is order food."

"Sorry," she said awkwardly, grabbing for her headgear and dropping it on the ground. She wanted to correct his use of *Mexican* versus *Spanish*, but it was his language, and she didn't want to embarrass herself more than she already had.

"S'okay," he said, picking up the headgear and handing it back to her.

Nikki threaded her ponytail through the helmet and jammed it down on her head.

"Val, I'm glad you came in," Domingo said, turning away from Nikki. "I haven't seen you in a while. I wanted to talk to you about the . . . thing."

"Everything working out OK?" Val asked.

"Yeah, more than OK. I wanted to thank you."

"Forget about it," Val answered, cutting him off. "This makes us square, right?"

"Five by five," Domingo replied with a firm nod.

"Good. I don't like leaving my markers out there," said Val, shaking his hand as if sealing a bargain.

"So," said Domingo, turning back to Nikki, his business apparently concluded, "you're going to go ten rounds with Muhammad Al-Val, huh?" Nikki paused in pulling on her hand gear. She didn't like the sound of that.

"It's just a couple of rounds for fun," she said weakly.

"Well, fun for me, anyway," Val said, shoving in her black mouthpiece and grinning. When she smiled, the black plastic gave her a creepy, toothless look. Nikki put in her own white mouth guard and gestured for Val to lead the way.

"I think I'll stick around and ref," Domingo said. Val shrugged, but Nikki was relieved.

Val tended to kick in a sharp, upward, flicking motion directly into Nikki's ribs, and when Nikki lowered her guard to protect her ribs, Val punched her in the head. Nikki tried to work to the angles and use her footwork; she threw everything she could think of, but it was as if Val could see everything Nikki was going to do from a mile away. For every point she scored, Val got two. Valerie Robinson was just better.

Domingo called points and generally controlled the speed and ferocity of the matches, which Nikki appreciated, but by round three she felt her temper rising. And then, in a sort of cosmic gold star granted for some previous lifetime's good behavior, Val skipped forward in a long, jumping front kick and Nikki slid off to the side at the last possible moment. There was a momentary tangle of limbs, and Nikki found herself in the perfect position for a hip throw. She grabbed Val by the neck and wrist and swung her down in a perfect arc. About halfway through, she decided to take the ride with her and they both landed with a thump on the mat, with Nikki on top with an unbreakable hold on Val's head and arm. Val bridged her back and tried to roll, but Nikki shifted her weight over her shoulder blades and forced Valerie back down, tightening her grip around Val's neck and arm. She hadn't dated a wrestler in high school for nothing. Val was squirming, and Nikki thought about letting go. She knew that it wouldn't be long until Val ran out of air. She didn't want to be responsible for choking out her partner on the first day. For a second Nikki wavered, and then she felt the meanspirited part of herself that always wanted to win flicker to life, and she squeezed harder. Domingo went down on the mat with them and be scrutinized the space between the floor and Val's back until it ceased to exist.

"That's it, babe," he said, slapping the floor with his palm. "You're done. Tap now before she puts you out," he advised.

The tension ran out of Val's body.

"OK, let me up." Val didn't sound pissed, but Nikki offered her a helping hand a little hesitantly.

Domingo started the next round, and Nikki ate a front kick to the gut. The air went out of her lungs like a whoopee cushion without the humor. She sat down making gasping noises.

"Lay down and stretch out your stomach," ordered Domingo.

"You OK there, kid?" Val asked, taking out her mouth guard and leaning over.

"Man, Red," said Domingo, appearing in her view. "When you get nailed like that, you just got to blitz like mad and worry about it later. You don't want them to know you don't have any air. Right?"

Nikki nodded, unable to make any other comment on the subject.

"We'll call it a night, then, shall we?" Val asked. "We want to be well rested for the flight tomorrow." She grinned and gave Nikki a padded thumbs-up.

Nikki nodded again. There was nothing else to do.

Sake Time

Nikki stripped off her gear slowly. Sweat coated the interior of the latex foam, and there was a slight pop of broken suction as she slid off the shin guards. Val pulled off her gear and dressed easily, with none of the winces or groans that Nikki was making. Nikki wanted to say something, but wasn't sure how to make conversation now that Val had kicked her ass.

"Sushi," announced Val, zipping her gear bag shut with a sound of ripping finality and walking briskly out of the locker room. Nikki yanked on her sneakers and hurried after Val, struggling to do up the button fly on her jeans and manage her awkward bundle of sweaty clothes at the same time.

"Sushi?" repeated Nikki, as they approached the car.

"For dinner."

"Sushi would be good," Nikki said cautiously.

"Great, I know just the spot. We'll get take-out and go to my place."

Val drove the Impala with her customary speed, but without

her customary cigarette. Nikki noticed that she seemed more relaxed than she had been at any time besides while shoe shopping. It seemed worthy of note that ass-kicking equaled a happy partner.

They had been driving in silence for several miles when Nikki's phone rang, startling her into a seat-bouncing hop, which caused Val to cast an amused look in her direction. Nikki fumbled on the floor for her purse, and then dug around until she found the phone. Flipping it open, she saw her mother's number on the Caller ID. With a sigh, she pushed the Talk button.

"Hey, Mom," said Nikki. She caught Val giving her a quizzical look.

"Darling, I was starting to think you had broken all of your fingers."

"Just the dialing ones," Nikki said.

"What?"

"Nothing."

"You know, you could call a bit more frequently."

"Sorry, I've been busy." Understatement of the year.

"Yes, how's the new job going?"

"Oh, you know, it has its ups and downs." She still hadn't told her mom about the "clandestine" aspects of her job, and doubted that she was ever going to.

"Are you through with training yet?"

"Yeah, kinda. I'm . . ." Nikki wasn't sure how to describe her evening so far. "I guess I'm into the orientation phase now."

"Well, what kind of stuff are you doing?"

Nell had picked a fine time to be interested in Nikki's life.

"Um." Nikki shuffled through recent events, trying to find one suitable for the public. "I'm going to a conference on women's health."

"Really? Where's that?"

"Thailand," said Nikki, without thinking.

"What?!" Nell's shriek was deafening and loud enough that even Val looked startled.

"Nicole, I don't think I'm comfortable with your going to Thailand."

"Mom, it's for work. I have to. I told you there might be travel involved."

"Do you have all your shots?"

"You don't need shots for Thailand."

"I don't know, Nikki. I don't like all this travel." Nikki sighed. Her mother wasn't comfortable with her going much of anywhere. The only Lanier who ever traveled was her father.

"It's the job, Mom. There's nothing I can do."

"Well, you call me the minute you get there."

"Sure, Mom. I'll call. Look, Mom, I've got to go. I'm with . . ." Nikki hesitated, trying to find ways to explain Valerie Robinson, and then gave up. There wasn't any way to explain Val, and she wanted her mother off the phone. She used the one line that always worked. "I'm on a date." In her mother's eyes, nothing was as important as a man.

"Nikki! Why didn't you say so? Call me later."

"OK," Nikki agreed.

"OK, bye." Nell rushed to get off the phone and Nikki let her go, feeling only slightly guilty.

"Bye," Nikki said, and hung up the phone with relief.

"Jeez, kid, you don't have mother issues or anything."

"I don't have mother issues. I have a mother," Nikki said, rubbing her temples.

"Yeah, and not a lot of backbone. Have you tried telling her to go to hell?"

"It's more trouble than it's worth, and I just don't like trouble."

"You picked just the right career for yourself, then, didn't you?" Val said. "Here's my sushi place. Wait here. Won't be a minute." Val jogged into the restaurant and returned a few minutes later with carefully bagged boxes, which she dropped neatly into Nikki's lap.

A few minutes later they pulled up in front of a small house that unexpectedly made Nikki long for Washington. The Craftsman construction of thick, square beams and geometric design looked very much like the first house her mother had rented after the move to Tacoma.

The neighborhood seemed strangely quiet after the rushing wind of a moving convertible. Val walked to the rear of the car. Opening the trunk, she tossed Nikki her backpack. Nikki managed to catch it and swung it up onto one shoulder without dropping the food.

"You're selling your house?" asked Nikki, walking past a Realtor's sign.

"Sold, actually," Val answered, glancing at the sign as if she'd forgotten it was there. "As of yesterday. I'm never home enough to take care of it. Besides it was more my ex-husband's taste than mine. High time I was moving on."

Once inside, Nikki could see that Val hadn't been kidding. Her style was modern and chic and very New York, all black leather and minimalist. Set against the comfortable, Craftsman, exceedingly West Coast house, the furniture seemed out of place. The pull of these two flavors gave the house an uncomfortable edge, as if Nikki had just walked in on a couple in the middle of an argument.

Val dropped her gym bag next to a pile of boxes, grabbed the food from Nikki, and walked into the kitchen. She dug into one of the boxes and pulled out chopsticks.

"Make yourself comfortable," she said without turning around. "Spare bedroom's down the hall. Do you want some sake?"

"Um, sure," said Nikki. She'd had sake only once before, and didn't remember it as being too bad. A little sake before bed couldn't hurt.

Nikki wandered down the hall to the back bedroom, which doubled as an office. Packing had begun in here as well. The bookshelves had been cleared of books and knickknacks. Four boxes stood by the door with GOODWILL written on them in crisp block letters. Nikki shook her head. As a longtime poor person, she knew that good money could be made selling books to used-book stores. Donating them was a waste.

Nikki sat down on the bed/couch and let her backpack slide down her arm to the floor. She felt tired and stupid and altogether unprepared for whatever lay ahead. Wearily, she kicked off her shoes and left them sitting in a jumble next to her bag. A large calico cat entered the room suspiciously. It was on the tubby side and waddled a little as it crossed the room. It patted Nikki's bag with a delicate paw and then sat down, a small roll of fur covering its hind feet. The cat was slightly cross-eyed, which gave him a Mad Hatter sort of glare.

"Don't pee in my shoes," said Nikki, but the cat only stared at her harder.

"You coming or what?" Val yelled, from down the hall.

"Coming," Nikki yelled back, and with an effort stood back up and set herself in motion. Val had laid out the sushi boxes on the coffee table and provided two plates and two sets of chopsticks. She was already settled in, sitting on the floor in front of the couch.

"So what's with all the languages?" she said, changing channels. "I thought linguists just studied languages. I didn't think they had to learn twelve of them."

"It's not twelve," said Nikki self-consciously. "My dad spoke French, and I just sort of branched out from there. And the romance languages aren't that far apart, really."

"So I hear," agreed Val, settling on *Mythbusters*, and leaning back against the couch. "So your dad spoke French. What's his deal?"

"He's Quebecois," Nikki answered, noticing, too late, that Val had steered things onto a conversational fork Nikki didn't really want to go down. "We always spoke French when I was little. Or at least he and I did. Mom wasn't into it much. She's American, but I was born in Canada, actually."

"Why'd you guys move?" asked Val, pouring a small glass of sake for Nikki and pushing it toward her.

"My folks broke up. Mom got custody; we came back here. Not a lot to it." Nikki smiled weakly and reached for the sake.

"And your dad stayed in Canada?"

Nikki shrugged. "I doubt it. He liked to travel."

"And your mom doesn't?"

"Not really. I think maybe she just worries when I travel."

"She doesn't want you to be like your dad." Val's eyes were half closed, but her gaze seemed twice as sharp for all, or maybe because of, her lazy appearance. Nikki took a gulp of sake, avoiding Val's stare.

"I guess," said Nikki with a shrug.

"You want another drink?" Val finished her own sake in one long swallow.

"Oh, no, I really don't want any more." Nikki was relieved to be away from the subject of her parents.

"Nonsense. You have to keep me company. Besides, I'm not packing my entire alcohol collection. We might as well drink it now."

"Oh, sure, of course," Nikki said.

"And try the mahimahi. It's really good."

Dinner and the sake bottle progressed. *Dirty Jobs* came on, and Nikki decided that Mike Rowe was even funnier with a half a bottle of sake in her.

"So, how did you meet Mrs. Merrivel again?" Val asked, returning from the kitchen with another bottle of sake held in an oven-mitted hand. "She didn't really just pick you out of the crowd at a recruiting meeting, did she?"

"No, it wasn't quite like that," said Nikki.

"Somehow I didn't think so. So what was it like?"

"No, I . . ." For some reason Nikki was reluctant to tell Val about Z'ev. "It was just kind of a weird coincidence. I went to lunch with a friend at this restaurant, only it turned out Mrs. Merrivel was eating there, too." Val's eyes narrowed. "And then later, at the meeting, Mrs. M recognized me from the restaurant."

"And that's when she recruited you?"

"Well, no. That was later. After the thing. Do you want to watch a movie?"

"Not really. What thing?"

"After I won the thing," said Nikki. "I don't really want another drink. I do dumb things when I drink."

"Well, then you have to have another drink," Val said with a grin. "And tell me about winning the thing."

CANADA

The Face of
Carrie Mae

Nikki opened her mouth to say something back, but found that she could manage only a small gasp. Z'ev was walking away. He had kissed her and he was walking away and she had no idea what to do.

"I hate it when they do that. How are we supposed to fight back?" said the woman in the blue suit.

Nikki shook her head, still unable to formulate words.

"You know, I'd think you were following me if you hadn't gotten here first," said the woman, easily climbing the stairs to the main door of the hotel. "Funny coincidence our being at the same hotel. You know," the woman continued when Nikki didn't contribute to the conversation, "maybe you'll think I'm rude, but I couldn't help overhearing some of your conversation."

Nikki blushed scarlet, and the older woman laughed, but it was a good-natured sound. "Not to worry. I won't say anything about bathrooms, but I was trying to figure out how long you and that young man had known each other."

"We'd just met," mumbled Nikki, blushing again.

"Ah," said the woman, nodding sagaciously. "I was wondering. That explains a lot, actually. And yet that other man thought you were married. I'm Miranda, by the way." She tucked her arm through Nikki's and led her into the lobby.

"They were business associates. There was supposed to be a girl, but she got stuck in traffic, and he didn't want to explain . . ."

"Yes, but my dear, you didn't *know* him. You must be more careful."

"I know, but . . ." Nikki trailed off again, unable to think of a decent rationale. Miranda had a sweetly understanding expression that verged on grandmotherly.

"Oh, well," said Miranda, patting Nikki's hand. "It came out all right in the end. And you were very convincing as a couple." Miranda glanced at her watch, and Nikki gasped as she caught sight of the time.

"I'm going to be late for that horrible seminar! My mother is going to kill me!"

"Are you going to the Carrie Mae speech?" Miranda's expression had sharpened into curiosity.

"Total waste of time. But my mom insists," Nikki said, making a face. "And now I'm going to be late."

"You never know, you might hear something interesting. You'll probably still be in time for the main speaker if you hurry. The ballroom's down the hall on the left," Miranda said, pointing the way.

"Thanks!" exclaimed Nikki, hurrying with tiny steps down the hall in her narrow skirt. She approached a woman sitting behind a six-foot table next to a large Carrie Mae sign awash in purple-and-silver butterflies, as the sound of applause echoed from behind the closed ballroom doors. The perky Carrie Mae lady leaped from her seat with a smile spreading over her face.

"Hey there, lady!" she exclaimed with exuberance. "Are you here to hear Mrs. Merrivel?" She seemed genuinely excited by Nikki's presence and oblivious to her use of homonyms.

"Uh, yes," Nikki replied, feeling altogether unnerved by the woman's excitement. "I was supposed to meet my mother, Nell Lanier, but I'm running late . . ." She trailed off, unable to concentrate under the high-beam glare reflecting from the Carrie Mae lady's teeth.

"Oh. Well, hopefully we saved you a seat." The woman produced a clipboard with a seating chart and began to scan it. Something about the way the woman said "we" bothered Nikki, as if she were part of some huge collective. *Resistance is futile*.

"Oh! Yes, there were two seats reserved, and it looks like your mother is already inside. I'm so glad. Please come with me." *You will be assimilated*.

Nikki nodded, following the woman into the ballroom, her thoughts scattering in the face of persistent cheeriness.

She spotted her mother's blond hair before her purple-clad escort had reached Nell's seat, and she took a deep breath, trying to prepare herself. The Carrie Mae lady indicated the empty seat on the aisle and then waved goodbye with a rigorously happy gesture before disappearing back the way she had come.

Nell looked up at Nikki and gestured emphatically to the seat. Slipping into the empty chair, she received a glare from her mother. Z'ev's kiss was still buzzing on her lips, and for a horrible moment she thought her mother could see it, pinned there on her lips like a brilliant butterfly or a scarlet letter *A*.

"You're late," her mother hissed. "You turned off your cell

phone!" The second statement was even more ferocious than the first.

"Had to, for the interview." Nikki gave an apologetic smile and made a deprecating gesture with her hand. Nell snapped her head back toward the speaker.

Nell's top was a geometric collage of bright colors and featured a deep V-neck front that introduced the world to her cleavage. Nikki always considered her mother's taste bizarre. Nell's closet looked as if someone had managed to cross-reference a hooker and the Gap. She was never entirely sure how Nell managed to leave the house each morning in anything resembling professional attire.

Nell was ignoring her now, and Nikki took the momentary respite to pull out her compact, discreetly checking her lipstick for any telltale marks or smears. Fortunately Z'ev seemed to have left her unmarred. Tucking away the compact, Nikki was surprised by a gust of laughter.

"Well, you know," the speaker was saying, "if I were going to have a diamond watch, of course, I would want earrings to match." She looked around the crowd as if to say, "Well, duh." The woman was on the plump side, with a round face to match her figure.

The crowd beamed their approval at the woman. Nikki shifted uncomfortably, trying to find a position where the ergonomically correct chair didn't press into her shoulder blades. No one else in the crowd seemed uncomfortable, and she had a sudden feeling of isolation. She felt as if she had arrived too late to a comedian's gig, well past the point when the audience has gelled and their laughter is contagious.

The plump speaker was still marching across the stage talking up the advantages of Carrie Mae. Nikki admired her ability to give such a high-energy performance in four-inch heels. Her own feet were aching from an entire day spent in heels, and she wondered if anyone would notice if she slipped them off.

"So, this is Mrs. Merrivel?" Nikki whispered to her mother. Nell shook her head. "No, she's the event organizer. Mrs. Merrivel's on next." Even as Nell spoke, the woman wound up her speech and called for a round of applause as she introduced the keynote speaker.

"Miranda Merrivel, everyone!" The woman clapped enthusiastically to get the crowd going, and Nikki's heart sank as Mrs. Miranda Merrivel, the thin, petite woman of indeterminate age in the electric blue suit, strode onto the stage.

"No wonder she knew the way to the ballroom," muttered Nikki, and then she smiled weakly at Nell's suspicious glare.

Forty-five minutes later she had a headache. The ballroom was hot, crowded, and overwhelming with the competing smell of perfumes and hair products. Mrs. Merrivel, Nikki had decided, was suffering from some sort of split-personality disorder. She had gone from being sweet and understanding in the lobby to a number-crunching supercharged saleswoman on the stage. Stage Mrs. Merrivel was Carrie Mae—the company. Stage Mrs. Merrivel needed a riding crop and an enormous American flag behind her. She was Patton in a blue suit and pumps.

At first Nikki had been interested by Mrs. Merrivel's fervor and obvious belief in the company. She had rather liked the idea of a female-powered organization, but Carrie Mae was obviously just like any other company, worse, in some ways, because the real money was not in selling makeup but in recruiting a sales group. It was a pyramid scheme dressed up in a "help women" philosophy and its own charity foundation.

An apparently spontaneous round of applause pulled Nikki back to the speech just in time for her to hear Mrs. Merrivel's concluding thoughts. Nikki suspected that one of the Carrie Mae ladies sprinkled throughout the crowd had started the ovation, but Mrs. Merrivel quieted the audience with a gentle hand as though it were genuine.

"Tonight we have a special surprise. Tonight, one lucky audience member will receive her own *free* starter kit!" The audience oohed appreciatively, and Mrs. Merrivel smiled benignly down at them. "Now, around the room you'll see several Carrie Mae ladies at various tables. Feel free to ask them any questions you might have. They are displaying product samples that you may test, and every one of these ladies can help you sign the paperwork on your own starter kit!"

"Wasn't that a wonderful speech?" the plump Carrie Mae lady cooed at the audience. "Why don't we give Mrs. Merrivel a round of applause?"

There was a thunderous burst of applause, and Mrs. Merrivel smiled again and bowed slightly. Then she slowly exited the stage waving and smiling. It was a beauty queen's triumphal walk. Nikki found herself looking for the tears and tilted crown.

"Mrs. Merrivel will be at the front booth to answer questions and sign copies of her self-help book, *Work Made Fun Gets Done*, which can be purchased for ten dollars Canadian. If you would like to enter the drawing for the starter kit, please talk to one of the ladies around the room. We'll all be happy to help."

Nikki nearly laughed out loud. There was no way she was going to enter that drawing. She was never going to work for Carrie Mae. And with that firmly decided she stood up, straightened her skirt and collected her purse from the floor, and then turned expectantly to her mother. The speech was done. It was clearly time to go.

"Wasn't she marvelous?" asked Nell with excitement.

Nikki's heart sank. She knew that look in her mother's eye.

"She was a very polished speaker," said Nikki in her most non-committal tone.

"She's a very polished person," said Nell, choosing to ignore Nikki's apathy. "I want to look at some of the booths. Be a darling and go get one of her books for me." Nell produced money from her pocketbook, and Nikki reluctantly took the bill. There really wasn't any point in fighting with her mother now. They still had to drive home.

"And make sure you get it signed," Nell demanded as Nikki trudged away.

She put herself in line for Mrs. Merrivel's book and, looking around, realized that she was the only single person in line. She felt a bit embarrassed, as if she should somehow have known to bring an extra person. She also realized that her outfit was a tad too smart for the crowd. She shouldn't have matched her shoes to her purse. The effect was too perfect, and made her feel uncomfortable amid the casual atmosphere of mothers and friends.

Nikki took refuge from her embarrassment by examining the crowd, detaching herself from it. The woman in front of her was talking animatedly in Quebec French to a woman with a sandy blond braid. The blonde was nodding in the right places, but was checking out the cleavage of a passing brunette. The first woman grabbed the blonde by the chin and kissed her on the lips.

"Pay attention to me," she said in English, and the blonde nodded obediently. Nikki was amused by this public display of affection, and mentally reclassified the blonde from friend to significant other.

They finally reached the front of the line and the crowds parted. Mrs. Merrivel was seated at a draped six-foot table behind a mound of books. She was signing them rapidly, with her beauty queen smile firmly in place.

Just as the Quebecois woman approached her turn at the front of the line, an oversize woman in a cashmere sweater, carrying an armful of purple bags, pushed her way to the front of the line and beamed vaguely at everyone.

"You don't mind, do you? I'm in a hurry." The woman gave an aggressive smile to the line without really seeing anyone in it and then turned her back to them. Ahead of Nikki, the Canadian woman began to exclaim loudly and at length in French.

"What does she want?" asked Cashmere Sweater to the line in general.

"She says she minds very much and she doesn't care how big a hurry you are in. You can wait in line like everyone else," said Nikki dryly.

"If you don't like it you can complain to the hotel staff. I'm staying here," Cashmere Sweater said, pushing past the two French Canadians and addressing Nikki.

"She said it," said Nikki, affronted, pointing to the Canadian. "I just translated."

"Oh, you think you're so special 'cause you speak French or something?" the woman demanded, poking an accusatory finger at Nikki.

Nikki found that her hands had clenched themselves into fists. She was overcome with the desire to punch the woman in her oversize nose. Just then, the Canadian woman poked Cashmere Sweater in the back. Cashmere Sweater whirled around to glare accusingly at the smaller woman.

"If you have something to say about the French language, I suggest you say it to me," the Canadian said in English.

"My girlfriend will kick your ass," the blond Canadian added, and at this comment, Cashmere Sweater's face went beet red.

"What are you? Some sort of French lesbians?"

"French-kissing lesbians," the blonde corrected. She stuck out her tongue, which was pierced, and wiggled the stud.

Cashmere Sweater looked apoplectic. For a moment Nikki thought Cashmere Sweater was going to attack the Canadians, but at the last second she collected her bags and flung herself away from the line.

"This is ridiculous," she said as she left. "I am above this."

"Well, that was just weird," said Nikki to no one in particular.

"*Très étrange,*" agreed the blonde, giving Nikki a smile.

"Ladies," Mrs. Merrivel said from the table, "if you're done baiting the wildlife, perhaps we can move the line along." The two Canadians giggled and presented their ten dollars to the Carrie Mae lady who was acting as cashier. Mrs. Merrivel signed their book with a flourish and handed it over. The girls left with a wave to Nikki, which she blushingly returned.

"Well, Nikki, how did you like the speech?" There was a distinct twinkle in Mrs. Merrivel's eye as Nikki presented her book to be signed.

"Er . . . it was very interesting. My mother really liked it."

"Oh, good. Whom shall I make this out to?" she asked, changing the subject.

"To Nell Lanier, L-A-N-I-E-R," said Nikki, and then added, "my mother."

"Does she speak French, too?"

"A little," Nikki said, glancing around the table.

"Languages must be more your thing, then? Didn't you say you graduated in linguistics?"

Nikki blushed. She hadn't thought Mrs. Merrivel had been sitting close enough at the restaurant to hear all the details of her life.

"How many languages *do* you speak?" asked Mrs. Merrivel, her pen hand hovering above the blank page.

"Four, well, five if you count Latin," Nikki said, wishing the conversation would end and Mrs. Merrivel would sign the stupid book.

"Ah, Latin. I nearly flunked that class myself, but I appreciate that someone can understand it. Personally I always think it looks like garbled Spanish."

"All the romance languages kind of look alike," agreed Nikki. "I suppose, being from California, that would be the one you'd think of first."

Mrs. Merrivel blinked and then smiled. "You're quite right. I am from California. I don't think I mentioned that, did I?"

"You use some pretty common California speech patterns," Nikki said, feeling like she'd finally managed to put the other woman on the defensive for once.

"How exciting. Just like Henry Higgins," Mrs. Merrivel said, and Nikki winced. Linguists were a little sensitive about anything *My Fair Lady* related. She glanced around, wishing that she could just get her book and leave now. Apparently the cashier agreed with Nikki, because she gave a polite cough and glanced significantly at the line of impatient people behind her.

"Well, here you are, Nikki," said Mrs. Merrivel, holding out the book. "I hope you win that starter kit." Nikki nodded awkwardly and took the book.

Exiting the book line, she found her mother deep in conversation about lipstick colors. Nikki stood waiting, while the Carrie Mae lady selling the lipsticks was arm-wrestled into accepting an expired "buy one, get one free" coupon for Nell's purchase.

"I put your name in for the starter kit drawing," Nell said to Nikki as they walked away from the booth. Nikki tripped over her own feet.

"I don't want the starter kit, Mom," she said, regaining her balance.

"Nonsense. You didn't get that job and you've got to earn a living some way. Tutoring and temping will not pay your bills forever. And you can make a real career out of this Carrie Mae thing."

"What makes you think I didn't get the job?" Nikki asked defensively.

"Because if the interview had gone well you would have told me."

Nikki writhed under the truth of the statement. "You can still look for a job, but this makeup selling stuff is a snap. I have a friend who sells candles and she always has loads of cash."

"I don't want to sell Carrie Mae," Nikki said, hearing the whining in her own voice, even though her mother ignored it. She glanced around the room, quickly calculating the odds at about three hundred to one. She could live with those odds.

She followed her mom around to booth after booth, collecting free samples and carrying Nell's purchases. The circuit of booths had almost been completed when a small gong sounded over the buzz of voices.

"All right, ladies," a cheerful Carrie Mae lady said from the stage. "It's almost time for the starter kit drawing." There was a renewed hubbub from the crowd, and the Carrie Mae lady shushed them. "If you'll all gather round, I'll have Mrs. Merrivel give the ticket drum a spin. You all have your tickets, right?"

Nell produced a small blue ticket stub and handed it to Nikki. She peered at the ticket over the mound of packages in her arms and read the number 91724. Nell's aggressively perky handwriting was scrawled across the ticket where she had filled in Nikki's name and phone number.

"Come on number 82563," Nikki prayed, picking a random number.

"That's not our number," said Nell sharply.

"Must have misread it," mumbled Nikki.

Mrs. Merrivel cranked the ticket drum and, inside their wire cage, the little blue pieces of fate whirled like snowflakes in a snow globe. Reaching into the cage, she wiggled her hand about dramatically, and Nikki felt the crowd tense. Finally Mrs. Merrivel withdrew one blue ticket and handed it to the MC.

"The winner of the complete starter kit is the holder of ticket number . . ." The MC paused dramatically. "Number 9-1." A pause, to allow a few groans. "7." A few more groans and Nikki's palm began to sweat. "2." Rising excitement from the crowd. Nikki was feeling faint. "And the last number is 4!"

Nikki stared at her ticket in disbelief.

"That's right," said the Carrie Mae lady, "Number 91724!"

Nell grabbed Nikki's hand and inspected the ticket.

"91724! That's it!" Nell shouted. "We won! We're the winners." She was dragging Nikki toward the front of the room, her hand clamped over Nikki's in a viselike grip.

"It looks like we have a winner, folks," the MC said with a giggle. "But don't let that disappoint you. We'll be giving away plenty more prizes."

Nikki and her mother were ushered onto the stage. Someone took their packages from them. There was a pause for a photograph as Nikki shook Mrs. Merrivel's hand while holding a franchise certificate.

"I look forward to hearing of your progress. Feel free to call me anytime," Mrs. Merrivel said before walking off. Nikki's eyes followed her of their own volition, watching her gliding stride with suspicion. Two effervescent Carrie Mae ladies took her place, distracting Nikki with their help. Nell hovered in the background, rubbing her hands together in delight. Nikki felt a little sick, and she had a sudden desire to be back in the peaceful sunlit restaurant, with Z'ev twirling his knife to reflect the sunshine. The moment now seemed the very essence of peace and quiet. Nikki signed some paperwork and was given a name to contact when she returned to the States. But even then she wasn't allowed to leave. Twelve women had purchased their starter kits that night: Nikki was lined up next to them and photographed until her jaw ached from smiling.

"Can we go back to the room now, Mom?" she asked, when she was finally allowed offstage. "I have a bit of a headache."

"Yes," Nell agreed, clutching the silver gray starter kit. "Let's go up to the room and look at what we've won." She led the way out of the ballroom and up the stairs.

"I wonder," said Nell. "What were the odds of your winning that drawing?"

"Lots to little, I suppose," Nikki answered.

"Stroke of luck, though, all the same," said Nell.

"Yeah, real lucky," agreed Nikki as the elevator doors opened, although her tone suggested the opposite. Nell was used to ignoring subtleties, however, and probably didn't trouble herself over this one.

THAILAND I
Going the Distance

The next thing Nikki remembered was Val kicking the couch.

"Wake up, Red. You ain't no princess and this ain't *Sleeping Beauty*. Time to go to work."

Nikki struggled upright and stared, befuddled, around the room. Sunlight streamed through the windows. A blanket had been tossed over her sometime in the night.

"Work?" she repeated, realizing she hadn't washed her makeup off the night before and regretting it.

"Right. Work," Val repeated mockingly. "Thailand, remember? We have to go rescue the girl. Don't want to be late for your first mission. Hurry up."

A far too short while later, Nikki was following Val through the sprawling warren of LAX, occasionally tripping over the carpet or her feet or nothing at all. Her head was splitting and her eyes felt as if they'd been taken out, rolled in dirt, and then put back in the sockets. She kept her sunglasses on for most of the airport process, taking them off only when the luggage screener demanded it. He'd run the glasses through the machine and quickly handed them back without any comments and with a carefully expressionless face.

They waited at a bar for their flight to board. Nikki had turned down the offer of a screwdriver so firmly that Val had laughed. Nikki grimaced, but stuck to her guns and had straight orange juice.

"Here ya go," said Val, passing Nikki an envelope full of papers.

"What's this?" she asked blearily.

"Background on our missing girl."

"Not much of a girl," said Nikki, staring blankly at the pages. "She's thirty-two."

Val was digging through her pockets, ignoring Nikki, looking for something. She had just found her cigarettes when she noticed the No Smoking signs. "Damn," she swore at the signs, and then turned her attention back to Nikki.

"Where'd you read that?" She twitched the top sheet out of Nikki's hand and scanned it.

"I didn't," said Nikki. "They showed a piece on her during training."

"Why?" Val asked, reaching for the cigarettes again, visibly struggling under the no-smoking policy.

"We were learning about the kind of causes Carrie Mae supports. Lawan is a major crusader against the sex trade. She founded a free health clinic and she works with a scholarship program for children born into brothels."

"What a saint," commented Val dryly, and switched to playing with her lighter. Nikki noticed that Val was drawing suspicious looks from the militant nonsmokers at the bar.

"They say she's dating one of the top kickboxers in the country," Nikki added, hoping that gossip would interest Val more than facts.

"Sounds good," Val said. She had noticed her audience now and her lighter fiddling became more flamboyant as she took out a cigarette and put it on the table.

"Do you always bait the wildlife?" Nikki asked, quoting from someone, but unable to remember who.

"We all have our hobbies," said Val with a grin.

"So if you could find something that irritated people without causing cancer, you'd do that instead?" Nikki asked with a laugh.

Val nodded. "Maybe."

"I think you just like causing trouble!"

"Maybe," Val agreed with an impish smile. "You should try it sometime. You might like it."

"I'll stick with my own passive-aggressive habits, thanks," Nikki said as her cell phone began to sound its familiar tune. Why she had assigned a Rolling Stones song as her mother's ring tone she never could remember. She pressed the Ignore button, hoping that her mother would take the hint and not call back. Val raised an eyebrow at her.

"My mom," said Nikki by way of explanation.

"Why don't you tell her where to get off?" asked Val.

"I can't do that. She's my mom."

"I would," Val said, leaning back in her chair.

"That's because she's not your mom. Eventually, I am going to have to speak to her again and, really, I just don't want to fight."

"What do you want?"

"What, like in an alternate universe where I have the perfect mom?"

"Yeah," agreed Val, picking up the cigarette and putting it in her mouth. The hyenas at the bar began to move. Val put the cigarette back down, and the hyenas relaxed.

"Well, I'd like her to actually be supportive, for one thing. I mean, she says she wants me to succeed, but then she does everything to get in my way."

"What do you mean?" asked Val.

Nikki tried to think of a concrete example, something that was more than just overtones and implied expectations. "Oh, like one time, in high school, I needed to lose five pounds, which I did by sticking to a diet and working out more. When I told my mom, she said, 'That's great!' and then made brownies."

Val had been taking a sip of her drink and snorted with laughter, dribbling Bloody Mary down her chin. "Not while I'm drinking, Red!" she exclaimed, grabbing for a napkin. Nikki pondered her mother and handed Val a napkin.

"I'd really like her to not judge my dates by their cars. She's so independent. I mean she owns her own home and all of her money is *her* money. You'd think she wouldn't care what my boyfriends were making. She says she just wants them to be 'good enough' for me. But really it's all about the money. There was this guy I was totally in love with, and she hated him. I swear it was because he drove a beat-up old Ford truck. But at the same time, it's like she thinks I *have* to be dating somebody. Dating a poor guy is still preferable to dating no guy. Being single just isn't an option."

"Your mother has issues," said Val. "Did she just miss the whole feminist thing or what?"

Nikki shrugged. "I guess."

"All right, what else?" Val asked. "What else would your perfect mother do?"

Nikki shook her head. Thinking about her mother just made her already splitting headache worse. She thought about Val. She was tough, independent, and divorced—a lot like Nell. But unlike her mother, Val seemed not to need Nikki to do anything but be Nikki.

"Mostly I just want to be left alone," said Nikki with a sigh.

"So, tell her. Find a nice way to say it, but tell her."

"There's a nice way to tell your mother to back off?"

"Hmmm. OK, maybe there isn't, but, really, do you want to have her calling you every day for the rest of your life?"

"It wasn't that big a deal when I was living with her."

"Well, now you're not. So you'd better do something. You have to stand up for yourself."

Nikki shrugged uncomfortably. "That's easy for you to say. She's not your mother. She may not be Perfect Mom, but she's the only family I have."

Val flipped her lighter a bit more and eyed her cigarette. Nikki watched the lighter and drank her orange juice.

"Never had any family myself. Deadbeat dad. Mom was pretty much out of the picture. Bounced around between relatives."

"I'm sorry," said Nikki, surprised by Val's revelation.

"I don't tell you this to get sympathy," Val said acerbically. "I'm just explaining. I never had much family and never really missed it. It's always been Me and Self, and generally I like it that way. Don't get me wrong—I like having somebody. You do reach a certain point in life where an empty house at the end of the day starts to look like the seventh ring of hell."

"Why don't you find someone nice and have a couple of kids, then?" suggested Nikki, interrupting Val's thought process.

"Kids? Me and kids? Together? Like at the same time? Is that really something you can picture?" Nikki smothered a smile and shrugged. "And I don't date nice people. Nice doesn't really work for me. Besides, I could already have had six husbands and how would you know?"

"No pictures around the house. No one but the company has called you. And, um, you're kind of prone to violence."

"Well, aren't you an observant little person," said Val, narrowing her eyes to slits. Then she waved a hand through the air as if dismissing Nikki's speculations. "Poor logic, though. I'm prone to violent outbursts whether I'm getting laid or not. But my point was—before I was derailed by the ludicrous idea of me procreating—that I just think it's a little weird when I run into people like you who get hung up on their families."

"Thanks so much," said Nikki dryly. "Nice to know that *I'm* the weirdo in this partnership."

A smile cracked across Val's face. "Well, it couldn't be me."

"Don't you ever get hung up on anyone?" Nikki asked. "There isn't anyone who can make you do stupid things?"

"I'm a grown-up. I can do stupid things all on my own," Val said, sternly, but there was a sparkle in her eye that belied the toughness of her attitude. "But yeah, there are one or two people who skew my decision-making skills." A faint smile hovered on her face, and for a moment it looked like she was going to say something, but then she shook her head.

"Look, all I'm trying to say is that I'm probably not the best person to listen to on the family thing. If you're happy having your mom call you whenever she feels like it, then rock on. If it works for you, then what do I know?"

"But I'm not happy about it," Nikki protested.

"Then tell her to take a long walk off a short pier."

"It's not that simple," answered Nikki, laughing.

"Yes, it is." Val flicked her lighter and watched the flame burn for a moment. At the bar the hyenas tensed, but didn't move. "I may not know about families, but I've been around the block a time or two. And ultimately, it's always that simple. That's your problem. You overcomplicate things. You have to exist right here, right now."

Hic et nunc, Nikki's brain translated gratuitously.

"You can't wait for the mythical perfect moment in the future. It won't come. See what you want and go get it. Shortest distance between two points, that's what life is all about," Val said, and Nikki frowned. She had no way of refuting Val's statement, but she couldn't quite agree with it, either. She sighed and twisted her drink glass until it tore the napkin it was resting on. Val flicked her lighter on and off, playing with the flame.

"I'm going to mess this all up," Nikki said, contemplating the soggy remains of the napkin where it clung to her glass.

"Mess what up?" asked Val, squinting at her watch.

"This," Nikki answered, gesturing carelessly around the airport bar. "The mission. Carrie Mae. Whatever. I'm going to blow it."

"You worry too much. Besides, why do you think they partner people up for the first missions? You're not alone. You've got me, and who could possibly need more than that?" Val flashed a wide, toothy grin, and Nikki chuckled.

"No, seriously, just stick with me, kid. Follow directions and everything will work out fine. You can do that, can't you?"

Nikki felt the tightness in her chest ease and she nodded, taking a drink of her orange juice to cover her embarrassment. Val flicked her lighter again and then again, until one of the hyenas by the bar made a move.

"Excuse me, madam," a man said. He was fifty-something, but very fit, and dressed in the latest in business casual. Nikki guessed that his Italian leather loafers probably cost somewhere north of six hundred dollars.

"Yes," Val purred, flicking the lighter again. The flame reflected in her eyes.

"This is a nonsmoking zone. You're really not supposed to . . ."

"Supposed to what?" Val interrupted, leaning forward and smiling. Nikki could see the predator behind the smile, but she wondered if the man could. "Don't tell me this is bothering you?" Flick, went the lighter. "It's not as if I'm actually"—flick— "smoking." Flick.

"Yes, but the latest security measures . . . you're not supposed to have a lighter at all," said the man, backpedaling a bit.

"Oh, you're worried about my safety." Val smiled and patted his hand. "That's sweet."

The man smiled back, relaxing under the onslaught of feminine charm. Nikki gulped the remainder of her orange juice. With grave deliberation, Val lit a cigarette, took a puff, and then handed it to the man.

"If you wanted a cigarette," she said loudly, standing and collecting her bag, "all you had to do was ask. But really, they're not good for you." She walked away from the table and Nikki hustled to keep up with her. At the bar, she could see a nonsmoking lynch mob starting to form.

"I think they're going to hurt him," Nikki said, looking back over her shoulder.

"I hope they do," Val said. "I hate people who think it's their job to tell me what the rules are."

They made the plane with no trouble, but once in the comforting embrace of a business-class seat, Nikki found her eyelids drooping in a southerly direction. She woke up enough to stumble through the Narita airport and onto another plane. The stewardesses changed race, but not smiles, making Nikki wonder if they simply passed the smile down from generation to generation of flight attendants.

Once in Thailand, Nikki was a step behind Valerie, as usual. Val navigated the bustling maze of the Don Muang Airport as easily as if it were her local mall. They collected their luggage, with Nikki resentfully hauling her backpack and a second bag that contained the enormous makeup case Rachel had given her. She hadn't felt confident enough to leave any of the gadgets behind, but the bulky case was messing with her packing philosophy.

Valerie led them toward the sliding double doors that opened onto a crowded sidewalk. It was nearly 10:00 P.M. local time, but the wave of velvet heat seemed to swaddle Nikki in an instant shroud. After the air-conditioned cool of the airport, the incalescence of the sidewalk pulled at her skin in a riptide of warmth. She took a deep breath as if she had just surfaced, but the heat simply swept in her open mouth and filled her lungs. Val walked on as if the torrid temperature were nonexistent.

The sidewalk was lit with the grainy tint of a freeway tunnel. Val deposited them into a medium-size line that led to a brightly lit booth.

"What are we doing?" asked Nikki, adjusting the straps of her backpack.

"Waiting for a taxi."

"We can't just take one of those?" asked Nikki, pointing at the street, which was crammed, end upon end, with taxis.

"Nah, it's some sort of unionized thing. You tell this lady in the booth where you want to go, she gives you a ticket, and you hand the ticket to the driver, who deposits you at your destination, then charges you double."

"You're kidding?"

"Yeah, you're right. Sometimes the price is really reasonable."

Nikki set down her extra bag and, still wearing her backpack, rested it on the railing that cordoned off the line, taking the weight off her shoulders. She'd never been to Asia before. Never been much of anywhere. She supposed that a taxi line wasn't all that interesting to someone who'd been there before, but she found the hubbub exciting and was having a hard time copying Val's expression of cool boredom.

They had reached the front of the line. Val told the woman in the booth the name of their hotel. The woman typed up a receipt, stamped it, and handed it to Val.

"Mandarin Hotel," the woman yelled at a driver hovering nearby. The driver nodded and helped them put their bags in the trunk of his taxi.

As they drove, Nikki noticed that many of the billboards were in English. The city seemed a vast sprawling mess, but modern enough. There was no feeling of entering some mythical, forbidden East, only another grimy twenty-first-century city. Noticing a building surrounded by scaffolding entirely constructed of bamboo, she mentally corrected her classification of the city to somewhere in the early twentieth century.

She stared out the window at the silent freeway overpass and yellow street lamps flashing by, listening to the hum of the taxi wheels on pavement. She had been on a plane for sixteen hours and her brain felt as though it might slide out her ear at any moment. High above the freeway a stark white billboard proclaimed EDEN. PARADISE FOUND. Busy watching the scenery, she was unprepared when they pulled up in front of a thoroughly modern hotel and she had to scramble after Val.

"Welcome to the Mandarin," said a bellboy in slightly accented English, as he opened the front doors with a slight bow. And for the first time Nikki felt as if she'd really and truly left home.

Delicate Elephants

Nikki woke up with the traveler's hangover. Dehydrated, confused, sweaty, and sticking to the sheets, she felt the way she did the morning after her three-day post-breakup bender in college. At fourteen hours behind, her body clock was telling her to simply crawl back in bed and stay there, but Bangkok was already bright and sunny, and bustling through its midmorning routine.

Val knocked on the door, and for once she wasn't her usual blender full of energy and cigarettes. She was carrying a cup of coffee and was already wearing her sunglasses, but her hair looked perfect as usual.

"I called Laura," she said, stifling a yawn. "She's going to meet us at Lawan's clinic."

Nikki nodded. Reaching for her suitcase, she began looking for things to make herself feel human again.

"I'm going to take a shower," said Val, waving negligently and ambling out of the room. "Knock when you're ready to go."

An hour later they walked out of their carefully chilled hotel and into the sweltering heat of a Bangkok day. Born and raised in the Northwest, Nikki had found California dry and unpleasant, like a case of morning mouth desperately in need of a cleansing glass of water, but even California hadn't prepared her for the intense omnipresent heat of Thailand. She kept moving, as if she could turn a corner and no longer be hot.

Val gave directions to a cab driver and cracked a window, preparing to light up. Nikki could tell the cabbie was irritated, and she didn't blame him. The window was the small, thin barrier against the noise and smell of the streets, and Val not only allowed all that in, but she welcomed it with a flick of her ashing cigarette.

The cab driver wound through the streets and Nikki watched the neighborhoods deteriorate from upscale business to rundown urban poor in a matter of minutes. The cabbie pulled up in front of a small cement block building. Like many buildings in Bangkok, it had a walled courtyard in front and tall front gates nearly flush with the sidewalk.

A small blue rectangle with white writing was the only indication that the building was meant for public use—the English on the sign read "Chinnawat Clinic." A guard at the gate was chasing away a gaggle of young boys as they arrived, but he let Val and Nikki in without question. Nikki couldn't help notice that he was carrying an MP9 submachine gun in the same careless manner in which someone might carry a lunch pail.

The atmosphere inside the building was one of constrained optimism. The clinic was painfully clean. Dirt and dust had been banished with a regimental exactitude, but the sparse furnishings, threadbare curtains, and sun-faded cheerful health posters featuring happy Thai couples only served to remind the viewer that times were hard.

They had barely entered the room when Laura Daniels came scuttling through an interior door to greet them.

"Oh thank goodness," she said, throwing up her hands and rushing to embrace them. "I'm so glad you're here!" She released Nikki from her hug and patted at her like a potter pushing clay into shape. "Welcome to the Chinnawat Clinic!"

She was blondish, plump, and cheerful. The wrinkles on her face were set in permanent laugh lines and her smile seemed a perpetual accessory, but Nikki thought she could detect underlying strain behind her eyes. She was dressed in simple khakis and a pink button-up shirt. Her hair had been tucked into a scarf that fluttered behind her as she moved. Nikki got the feeling that Laura thought this was dressing down.

"Thanks," said Val, dusting at her sleeve as if Laura's hug had somehow dirtied it. "Is there someplace we can go to talk?" She looked around the room, not quite resting her glance on the receptionist, who was eyeing them with a skeptical air.

"We can use Lawan's office," said Laura, beaming. "It's this way." She led them behind the desk and into a labyrinth of corridors.

"What can you tell us about Lawan?" Val asked.

"Lawan is a dedicated crusader for human rights," said Laura, proudly.

"So she didn't skip town with the contents of the till, then," Val said. Nikki knew she was joking, but she could see that Val's tone had annoyed Laura.

"We help nearly one hundred and fifty people a day, mostly women and children, and we're financed entirely through donations and volunteer efforts," said Laura. "Our patients are among the poorest in the city, and we feel that getting them medical care is only part of our mission."

"What's the other part?" Nikki asked when Val didn't respond.

"This," said Laura, throwing open a door to a wide courtyard. Children ran across the sandy ground and climbed on a plastic jungle gym. On the far wall, in big block English letters, someone had painted a quote and surrounded it with bright colors and images of flowers and trees.

PEOPLE NEVER STOP WAITING FOR THE CHANCE TO CHANGE THE THINGS THAT MAKE THEIR LIVES UNLIVABLE.

Nikki thought it was an unwieldy quote, overly long and lacking in the succinctness of a truly good line, but she appreciated the sentiment.

"Kids?" Val asked, apparently not noticing the quote.

"Those, too," agreed Laura. "Lawan was helped by my scholarship foundation. That was where we met. She was so young, but even then I could tell that she was destined for great things. We sent her to a boarding school, and it helped change the path of her life. When she came back to Thailand—and believe me, she didn't have to—she dedicated her life to offering that same chance to others. The kids come here to be in a safe place and maybe get something to eat. Without Lawan, many of them would have already been turned out in the brothels. Lawan believes in building a better future for Thailand. You can't fake belief like that. So, no, I don't think she left town with the till or any of the foundation's money."

Val half-shrugged, half-nodded, but didn't speak. Nikki looked at the building again, seeing the sparsity of decoration this time not as an indication of poverty, but as part of Lawan's spartan determination to use everything to succeed.

A tackraw ball flew through the air, interrupting Nikki's pondering. She caught it and turned it over in her hands. A bit larger than a softball, it was plastic, but made to look like interwoven strips of rattan. Tackraw was a game played like a cross between hackey sack and volleyball, and Nikki had been intrigued by it when she'd seen it in the guide book.

"Hi," said a little girl, approaching Nikki.

"Hi," Nikki said, holding out the ball. The girl giggled. With a second look, Nikki realized that the girl was probably about fourteen, but so small and pixie-like that she looked younger. She had sparkling black eyes and perfect white teeth that flashed every time she smiled, which was often.

"I'll want to see her office," Val said, and walked away with Laura.

"Play?" the girl suggested, holding up the ball.

"Sorry," said Nikki, shaking her head. The girl shrugged and kicked the ball in a lobbing arc back to the ring of waiting children. In her mind's eye, Nikki could see the life of a prostitute that Lawan had helped this little girl avoid, and she shuddered at the idea of seeing the girl painted up in garish makeup and waiting for someone to buy her soul an hour at a time. Her respect for Lawan grew even more.

She hurried after Val and Laura, and had almost caught up with them when they turned a corner. A second later she heard Laura shout out. Running around the corner, Nikki saw Laura tugging at the shoulders of a man in a white coat; he looked like one of the clinic's staff members. A second man—heavy set, Caucasian, with dark hair and a garish purple shirt—was tugging at something in the orderly's hand. Val was approaching the little group with long angry strides.

"Hey!" she yelled, and the white man's head snapped up.

He looked back at the orderly and with tremendous strength shoved the orderly backward into Laura, sending them both sprawling. The dark-haired man snatched the object he'd been struggling over out of the orderly's hands and took off running. The orderly, seeing Val and Nikki bearing down on him, scrambled to his feet and ran in the opposite direction.

"Go after him," yelled Val, pointing at the orderly. "I've got this one."

Nikki nodded as she passed and adjusted her run to a full sprint. Ahead of her, the orderly tipped over shelving, scattering supplies across Nikki's path. His footsteps echoed as he passed through a covered breezeway between buildings and then crunched out into a gravel-paved courtyard. Nikki hit the courtyard in time to see him bounce from a crate to the wall and then up and over a six-foot-tall back gate with the fluidity of an action star.

"Jeez," she muttered, scrambling after him. The street behind the clinic was busy with pedestrians, and Nikki caught only the barest glimpse of the orderly's white back as he disappeared up the street. She arrived at the street corner and looked both ways for her quarry, and then shrugged her shoulders in defeat as she saw the white jacket hanging over the edge of a stair railing.

She walked toward the front of the clinic, going the long way around the block to walk off some of her adrenaline. Up ahead of her there was a commotion and she watched as Val shoved someone into the side of a tuk-tuk as she ran by. Nikki took a step, ready to run, and then thought better of it. It was a long block and the two were already well ahead of her. There had to be a smarter way.

She ran up the block to where she'd last seen Val. Tuk-tuks were parked in the street, their drivers gathered in small groups, chatting. Nikki spotted one of the three-wheeled, open-sided vehicles with the keys still in the ignition and jumped in. Revving the engine, she tossed the tuk-tuk into Reverse and rolled out into traffic. She heard irate screaming and then a thump as the tuk-tuk's owner jumped onto the back.

Nikki rounded the corner of the block just in time to see Val's quarry taking off on a motorcycle. Val was on the sidewalk, hands on her knees, panting.

"Get in!" Nikki yelled, slowing down enough for Val to leap on.

"Your friend seems a little upset," Val said, landing in the backseat. Nikki glanced in the rearview mirror at the tuk-tuk driver, who, still screaming in Thai, was climbing in beside Val.

"Watch the road!" Val yelled, and Nikki jerked her head around in time to narrowly avoid a bus. The purple-shirted man was easily weaving through traffic on the more nimble motorcycle. Nikki pulled around the bus, gaining a little on the bike. They were in an older quarter of the city, where the streets were worryingly narrow and the human population seemed to think everything was a sidewalk. Ahead of them, the motorcycle took a hard left. But as he took the turn, a sparkling disk flew out of his pocket like a Frisbee and smashed into the wall—shattering.

"You're not going to make that turn," said Val in a carefully neutral tone, ignoring the debris from the motorcycle and focusing on more important information.

"I'm going to make the turn," Nikki said.

"You're not going to make it," said Val again, this time with a distinct note of urgency.

Nikki assessed the situation again. "You're right. I'm not going to make it. Get out."

"What?" Val yelled.

"Be my monkey," yelled Nikki, pointing out the side.

"Be your own monkey, bitch!" Val yelled back, not getting the concept.

"I need the balance. Hang out the side!" The tuk-tuk driver was spewing something, probably swear words, but was already clinging to the frame of the vehicle.

"You're not going to make it," Val yelled, climbing out of the tuk-tuk.

"I'm going to make it," muttered Nikki, as she tightened her grip on the steering wheel and took the turn. "Lean!" she screamed, as a rear wheel came off the ground.

Val and the driver were clinging to the tuk-tuk by their fingers and toes, their bodies extended as far out as possible to counterbalance the weight shift. The tuk-tuk rounded the corner on two wheels and then came down with a grinding thump, as Nikki accelerated into the straightaway. The motorcycle had slowed down for the turn, but was now speeding down the alley toward an open courtyard. They were near the river somewhere, but Nikki couldn't tell where. She had the gas pedal wedged down and grinned as she saw the distance narrowing. She could feel Val looking at her, but ignored this. The driver began to yell something again, pointing toward the end of the alleyway.

"Holy shit," Val said, pointing also.

"Holy shit," Nikki repeated, seeing the elephant walking across the mouth of the alley, its massive gray hide blotting out the sunlight. The man, showing a fearlessness Nikki had to admire, squeaked past the elephant, while Nikki slammed on the brakes and came to halt with the smell of burning rubber wafting around them. The elephant, upset by the ruckus, stamped and trumpeted, while its handlers yelled and waved sticks. One of the handlers turned to them and smacked the tuk-tuk with his stick.

"Delicate elephant!" the handler shouted.

"We could get out and run after him," Nikki offered, her fingers still clamped to the steering wheel, ignoring the yelling.

"Yeah, you go ahead and walk under the delicate elephant," Val said. "I'll wait here and see how that works out for you."

The elephant finally moved on, and Nikki edged the tuk-tuk

out into the courtyard, where the motorcycle lay abandoned in the middle. Nikki realized they were closer to the river than she had thought. The courtyard was really a wide strip of pavement before a ferryboat launch. The actual boat was obscured by a plethora of shops that spilled out into the street.

"The ferry," said Val, and Nikki nodded, already breaking into a run. They elbowed their way to the edge of the river only to see the man waving to them, his bright shirt flashing at them from the deck of a ferry as it carried him across the river.

"Damn," swore Val.

"Sorry," said Nikki.

"Sometimes life gives you elephants," Val said with a shrug.

They made their way back to the courtyard only to find the tuk-tuk driver waiting for them, cell phone in hand.

"Police!" he yelled at them.

Val opened her wallet. The driver's fingers hovered over the key pad on his phone. Val pulled out a credit card. Nikki let Val take care of the negotiating and went back to the entrance of the alley, looking for the object that had fallen out of the motorcyclist's pocket.

"Cash," she dimly heard the tuk-tuk driver say in a very firm tone of voice. There were plastic pieces scattered across the pavement. Nikki picked one up, examining it.

"But of course," agreed Val, pulling out a stack of baht. Nikki heard a click as the driver's cell phone was flipped shut instantly.

"What have you got?" Val asked, her shoes clicking on the pavement as she approached.

"A CD," said Nikki, holding up a sliver of mirrored plastic. "Self-burned. Not commercial. Useless to us now, I'm afraid."

"Too bad," said Val.

"But if it was burned off of a clinic computer, then we've still got a chance," Nikki said, and Val nodded again, slower this time.

"Who's to say it came from the clinic's computer?" Val asked. "We don't even know this is related to Lawan's disappearance."

"Of course it is!" exclaimed Nikki, looking up at her. "Because . . ."

"Because?" Val prompted.

"It has to be. I mean . . . it's so suspicious."

"Yeah," agreed Val, staring after the ferry. "Suspicious. Let's go back to the clinic. I do want to take a look at Lawan's office. You!" she shouted at the tuk-tuk driver, who was anxiously examining his vehicle. "How much to go back to the clinic?"

"No!" yelled the driver, and he started his tuk-tuk, driving off as if he thought Val would hijack it again.

"Some people have no sense of humor," Val said. "Come on, let's go get a cab."

Laura was waiting for them when they returned to the clinic, anxiously shifting from foot to foot.

"I'm so glad you're all right," she said. Her hair had been disordered in the earlier tussle. Nikki watched as the ambassador's wife began to straighten it, patting it back into place with an unconscious and practiced hand.

"Were you able to apprehend the assailant?" she asked with a polite smile, calm and order apparently having been restored.

"No. Um, sorry," said Nikki, feeling deeply embarrassed. Somehow this was even worse than being failed by Mrs. Boyer. She'd never failed an assignment where the outcome actually mattered to someone. "We lost him behind an elephant."

"Oh," Laura said, nodding, as if that explained everything.

"The orderly," said Nikki, "you know him?"

"Yes," said Laura, nodding again. "Amein. He's worked with us a long time. I don't understand why he ran."

"He ran because you yelled at him," Val said, her tone stopping just short of insulting. "Why did you yell at him?"

"He was coming out of Lawan's office. He gave something to that man. There aren't supposed to be unauthorized guests in the clinic. Something wasn't right." Laura was clearly struggling to explain what had been an instinctual reaction.

"It was suspicious behavior," Nikki said, and Laura's shoulders straightened.

"Yes, it was suspicious. That's exactly what it was. And then they ran. They wouldn't have run if they weren't doing something wrong."

"Ah yes, presumption of guilt—such a democratic ideal," said Val, brushing past Laura on her way to Lawan's office.

"We don't really have any facts yet," Nikki said, trying to strike a more conciliatory note.

"This is Thailand," said Laura. "Facts are . . ." She shrugged. "It's like my darling James says, 'Facts aren't always what they appear.' You have to trust your instincts."

"Is that what diplomacy is all about?" Nikki asked, attempting to keep Laura's attention focused on her and not on Val. Val's patience for the ambassador's wife was clearly paper lantern thin. "Following your instincts?"

"No," said Laura. "I think diplomacy is more about finding the appropriate facts to justify something you've already done."

Ahead of them, Val snorted in laughter. "Sounds about right," she said, opening the door to Lawan's office and flipping on the lights. "Now let's find some facts to justify chasing a man halfway across the city."

It was a small room—square and formed by the same concrete blocks as the rest of the clinic. The furniture was minimal. A metal-and-veneer desk and a chair faced the door, a slightly padded chair sat in front of the desk. A pile of papers covered the seat. To the right of a door was a bench with only one cushion on it and several binders where the other cushions should have been. Three middle-height bookshelves took up the left wall, piles of papers interspersed between knickknacks and a water pitcher and set of glasses. Behind the desk, two tall filing cabinets filled the space under windows that streamed sunlight onto the desk. One of the windows had been blocked out with the missing pillows from the bench.

"Has it been ransacked?" asked Nikki, looking at the mess in dismay, her hopes of an orderly search, followed by orderly clues, rapidly disappearing. She stared at the peculiar blocking of the window in confusion.

"Glare," said Val, sitting down at the desk. "On the screen," she explained, gesturing between the window and the computer screen.

"It's not usually this messy," said Laura, looking embarrassed and starting to tidy, moving piles closer together and clearing seating space. "It looks like she left in the middle of one of her projects."

"What do you mean?" asked Val, randomly opening drawers. Her quick, apparently careless movements reminded Nikki of her search of Mrs. Merrivel's desk.

"Lawan, she gets these ideas," said Laura, looking around rather hopelessly. "She's one of those people who connect things."

"Connect things?" Val repeated, tapping a cigarette on the side of her pack.

Laura sank down on the bench, arms full of papers, and stared distractedly into space.

"Lawan . . . some people," she said, starting again, "they become experts in one field. They know everything there is to know about that one thing. But Lawan knows a little bit about everything. It's like the more she learns the more she can put things together in new ways."

"What do you mean?" asked Val, lighting up, her eyes focused on Laura.

"Well," said Laura, "she figured out that recycling plants employed more women to wash bottles, so she lobbied for stricter polices on litter and incentives for building recycling plants, thus ensuring that more women would be employed in something other than the sex trade, which means fewer people with STDs, more stable family units, and more children who get education. That's the kind of thing that an outsider can't really get about Thailand. Lawan knows more about Thailand, not just because she's Thai, but because she understands all the forces that go into making up Thailand. That's what makes her so influential in politics. She knows why."

"Why what?" asked Nikki, rescuing a precariously tilted picture frame from under a leaning pile of files. The labels were in Thai, but they looked like patient records.

"Why everything," answered Laura. "If you know why someone is behaving like they do, then you know what their goal is and you can affect their behavior."

"Leverage," said Val. "She's talking about angles and leverage. Your girl Lawan knows where to apply pressure."

Laura nodded. "Only, now I'm afraid she's misjudged how much pressure to apply."

"Well, what's she been pushing for now?" Nikki asked, turning the picture frame around in her hands.

"Stronger antiterrorist measures," said Laura, shrugging.

"More cargo searches in the ports, more identity and paper checks. That kind of thing. She's been supporting a bill that's going in front of the legislature shortly."

"Maybe the government wanted to keep her quiet," suggested Val.

"It's a popular bill," said Laura with a shrug. "It hasn't been particularly controversial. Everyone wants to feel safer."

"Hmm," said Nikki, finally looking at the picture in her hand. It was of Lawan and a smiling little girl in a school uniform. The little girl had her arms around Lawan's neck, and they both appeared to be laughing at whatever the photographer was saying.

"That's Lawan's daughter, Lindawati," said Laura, noticing the direction of Nikki's gaze. "She goes to school in Canada now. After the coup in 2006, things started getting a little difficult for political activists, and Lawan was worried about her daughter's safety. She should be back soon, for vacation. Lawan was . . . is looking forward to it. I called the school when Lawan went missing. I thought she might have gone there, but they said they couldn't confirm or deny her presence."

Laura's head drooped, and she sniffed.

"Mrs. Daniels," Nikki said, not knowing what to say.

"You've just got to find her," Laura said. "Even if she missed my conference, which she never would have, there is no way on earth that she would miss being home for her daughter. Something bad has happened to her, and you've just got to find her."

"We'll find her," Nikki promised, and Val shot her a dirty look. Nikki returned it with wide eyes and a shrug. What was she supposed to say?

"Laura," Val said, sitting up and leaning her elbows on the desk, "we might not find her. We're going to try our best, but you have to face the fact that she might be dead."

"No," said Laura, in a flat refusal.

Val took a deep breath and let it out in a gusty sigh. "Well, all right then, Jenny put the kettle on, because it's going to take us a while to sift through this mess."

"I'll bring you some tea," said Laura, sitting up with a smile and bustling out of the room.

"It was a figure of speech," Val said, but it was too late. Laura was out the door already.

"Actually, it's an Appalachian folk song," said Nikki, apropos of Jenny and the kettle.

"What?" Val said, looking at her sideways. "Come on, shift your butt," she said before Nikki could respond. "Let's get started on this."

"How?" Nikki asked, looking in dismay at the mountains of paperwork.

"Piles," answered Val. "Like with like. And as soon as the major surfaces are clear, I want you to look at the computer."

It was dark by the time the cab driver dropped them off at the hotel. They trudged through the lobby and up to their rooms. Nikki was really looking forward to dinner, and a long night's sleep. Her first day as a secret agent had not been everything she hoped it would be.

Their search of Lawan's office had been a bust. The piles of papers had consisted mostly of patient files and clinic records dating back to the inception of the clinic. Her computer was half in Thai, and therefore half a mystery to Nikki. Their search of the physical premises had turned up a missing pair of Laura's earrings, a stash of chocolate kisses, and a program from a kickboxing match shoved down behind everything in the bottom drawer. In all, the room had been evidence of a very busy woman and not much else.

They had almost reached their rooms when Val's cell phone rang.

"Laura?" Val said, answering the phone. "Yeah . . . Laura, what are you doing? Saw him? Saw who? Coming out of . . . yes, following him *was* a bad idea. Going in where? No! Laura?" Val looked in irritation at the phone. "Damn," she said, looking at Nikki.

"Problem?" asked Nikki, feeling a surge of adrenaline.

"Yeah," said Val, but spoke no further as she dialed a number and put the phone to her ear. "Not answering. Stupid woman." She slapped the phone shut angrily.

"Go change your clothes," she said to Nikki. "We're going back out. Freaking amateur hour," she said, shaking her head.

Rock the Party

Nikki ran to the bathroom for a frantic grooming effort, but she still didn't feel entirely presentable by the time Val pounded on her door.

"Let's go!" Val snapped, phone pressed to her ear as she continued to walk down the hallway without waiting for Nikki. She of course had managed to throw on something that looked hot and functional at the same time.

"Here," she said, tossing Nikki her phone, "just keep hitting Redial until she answers." Nikki took the phone, hit Call, and put it to her ear. After several rings it went to voice mail.

"Hi, you've reached Laura Daniels. I'm unavailable right now, but please leave a message after the beep and I will return your call as soon as possible. If the matter is urgent, please call my assistant at . . ." She gave a phone number and signed off.

It was the most official message on a personal phone that Nikki had ever heard. She was about to comment on it, but Val was already pulling her into a cab. "The Eden," she said to the driver. "And step on it."

"Did you really just say 'step on it'?" asked Nikki.

"You have a problem with that?"

"No, I'm just glad we'll always have Paris."

"What?" said Val. "Sometimes you say the weirdest shit."

"Cliché. Detectives. Humphrey Bogart. *Casablanca*," said Nikki sheepishly, trying to explain the chain reaction of thoughts that had occurred. Val looked skeptical.

"Yeah. OK. Meanwhile, back in reality. Laura Daniels, our Idiot of the Week, spotted the orderly returning to the clinic and decided to follow him. She tracked him to a nightclub downtown, but cut out before she could give me any further details."

"Why didn't she call us?" asked Nikki.

"Because she's an idiot," Val snapped. "Keep trying to raise her on the cell phone. We'll try to find her before she gets herself killed."

"What about the orderly? What are we going to do about him?" Nikki asked.

"Nothing," replied Val. "Nothing," she repeated, cutting off Nikki's interruption. "First we make sure Laura's safe, and then, if it's the guy—and that's a big if—we can deal with him later. Got it?"

"OK," Nikki said, mostly agreeing. It was a sound line of logic, but it was boring.

The cab pulled up in a long line of cabs and various other vehicles for hire. The cabbie pointed down a street crammed with a wild assortment of ages, races, genders, and gender-benders. The bar girls strutted the streets in outfits that were revealing and, to Nikki's eye, ill-fitting. For all their vinyl and fishnet, they didn't look particularly sexy. They looked bored. The sixty-year-old men they were with looked in better spirits, or at least drunk.

"I feel like I've wandered into the dirty section of the video store," Nikki said. "These guys don't actually believe those girls like them, do they?"

"Who knows? The male ego is capable of amazing feats of self-deception. Come on, let's go find Eden."

Eden turned out to be the club with the longest line. Nikki tagged after Val, her eyes on the crowd. As usual in a crowd, she felt left out. She wasn't quite sure how to behave or where to look, so she ended up watching everyone. Watching the cues that passed between couples, the boredom of the bar girls, the fistfight that was on the point of breaking out between a naval officer and someone who was probably a marine, based on his haircut. The street was lined with shops and food stalls—purses and bright fabrics beckoned—and illuminated with Christmas lights and Japanese lanterns hanging overhead. The crush of people seemed slightly claustrophobic. Squinting through the crowd, Nikki caught sight of someone who looked oddly familiar. She caught her breath and stood up on her tiptoes, trying to get another look, but he was gone. She shook her head. She was dreaming again. After nearly six months, when was she going to forget about him? Even if by some enormous coincidence he was in Thailand, it wasn't like he was going to remember her. Rousing herself from depressing thoughts of a missed romance, she looked around for Val and saw her cutting a swath through the line. A "drop-dead" glare to the bouncer was all it took to secure her entrance.

Nikki hurried after Val, but found her way barred by a wide-armed white guy.

"Overcapacity," he muttered, and latched the velvet rope.

"You've got to show more skin than that if you want to walk in, girlfriend," said one of the girls in line. Nikki squinted again and realized that the girl wasn't actually a girl. She wondered if the guy with "her" knew that. As "she" worked a fingersnap and a y'all into the conversation Nikki decided the she-male had obviously been watching too much American TV. Nikki pondered the linguistic and cultural implications of spreading American English across the globe. Hip-hop as the great cultural unifier. Then her prom queen brain caught up with her educational brain. She had just been called not hot! Admittedly, she was wearing capris instead of a miniskirt, but her shoes were still spiky and cute. And yeah, she wasn't exactly revealing her nipples, but her tank top was still sparkly. She surveyed the American Thai guy-girl and took stock of her outfit.

It was white vinyl. Nikki wasn't down with that. She looked along the street, remembering the flash of silk dangling from the canopy of a shop. She jogged along the street, head swiveling from side to side.

"Need a dress, miss?" said a man standing in front of a shop. "We make for you—done in a day."

"I need a skirt in five minutes," said Nikki.

"Twenty minutes?" he offered.

"Really?" asked Nikki, startled.

"Short skirt?"

"OK," Nikki agreed.

"No problem," he said with a wide grin, and held open the door.

Fifteen minutes later Nikki exited the dress shop in a miniskirt and a coordinating halter top of Thai silk that precisely matched her shoes. Walking back up to Eden, she added an extra sway to her walk. No bouncer was going to put velvet ropes in front of her.

The bouncer didn't even pretend. He just pulled the rope open.

"I'm with her," said a deep voice as a heavy arm draped across her shoulders.

All six-foot-something of Z'ev was standing beside her, big as life. Big as Canada. Nikki opened her mouth to speak, but Z'ev was already tucking money into the bouncer's shirt and then they were walking into Eden. The last thing Nikki heard as the door closed was the "girl" in line.

"Now, there ya go, honey!"

"Stay here," Z'ev said, pushing Nikki into an empty space next to the bar. He disappeared into the crowd, while Nikki looked open-mouthed after him. Val walked into her line of view and handed her a drink.

"Where the hell have you been? And what happened to your clothes?"

"I . . . I got stuck. Outside. I had a wardrobe malfunction." She tried to think of a way to make a sentence out of Z'ev, but found she could think only in terms of one word or a paragraph.

"Uh, OK, well, you're in now. I'm going to go up onstage and see if I can spot any of our targets from there. You go hit the dance floor and see if you can find anyone."

"How are you going to get up onstage?"

"I'm going to sing," Val said, pointing to the stage where an Asian man was doing a fair job of "It Never Rains in Southern California" in front of a live band.

"But it's a band," Nikki protested.

"Yeah, they play, you sing. Karaoke, but better. Keep up here, Red."

"I'm trying," Nikki said plaintively. "Really."

Val laughed. "Drink your drink and go find some sucker to dance with."

"Drink. Right." Nikki took a gulp of her drink, batting away the paper umbrella that came with it.

"Right," Val agreed. "Now off I go."

Nikki took another gulp as she saw Z'ev walking toward her.

"Good, you're still here," he said with a smile. He grabbed the drink out of her hand and finished it off in one long draft.

"Yes, but what are *you* doing here?" she asked, recovering her power of speech.

"Come on," he said, sliding the empty glass onto the bar and taking her hand, leading her out onto the dance floor.

"We're not going out to dinner with a shipping magnate, are we?" asked Nikki, trying to sound casual.

"Nice to be remembered. And it was lunch," he corrected.

"I'm not likely to forget my husband," responded Nikki tartly. "And it was a late lunch at best. I didn't get back till after five."

"Before five, it had to be lunch."

"Lunch happens around noon, and that isn't the point."

"What is the point? Do you salsa?"

"Not in a long time," said Nikki with heat, as Val started to sing. Z'ev was avoiding her real question.

"Her name was Lola, she was a showgirl . . ." Val sang in a low throaty voice that suited Lola's exploits.

"So that's a yes?"

"Sort of," Nikki answered, feeling bewildered as he pushed her into a salsa step.

"That was more of a yes-or-no question," he said.

"I don't think you're allowed to bully someone just because you once shared a nonexistent marriage," Nikki snapped, starting to become irritated.

"It existed," he protested. "It just wasn't real."

"Funny," said Nikki, "the arguing feels real."

Z'ev burst out laughing and gave her an underarm spin, before she could think of something else to say.

Nikki hadn't danced this way since college, and she appreciated

Z'ev's strong lead signals; they kept her going in the right direction. She was also singularly aware of the strength of his shoulder under her left hand.

"Seriously, Nikki, what are you doing here?" he asked when they came back together.

"With yellow feathers in her hair and a dress cut down to there." Val was having a great time.

"What are you doing here?" responded Nikki, determined not to let him have things all his way.

"Asked you first," he answered. Nikki rolled her eyes. Were they really down to this already? Usually, it took at least three dates before her boyfriends reverted to grade school.

"I'm here for work," she replied.

"No kidding? So am I!" Z'ev said in mock surprise.

"Liar," she said, as he spun her around.

This entire meeting had an easy familiarity, and Nikki was secretly hoping it would end the same way as the last one. "Takes one to know one," Z'ev said.

"You know, if we're going to get all fifth grade, you'd better watch it or I'll smack you and run."

"Does that mean you like me?" Z'ev responded to the first statement, and then she saw a realization cross his face. "And you aren't Canadian!"

"I am so!" cried Nikki, slightly sensitive to her lack of true Canadian-ness. "Well, sort of. And, anyway, how would you know?"

"Canadians say 'grade five.'"

"And I thought I was the linguist in the family."

"What about the passport? You had a Canadian passport and address." His tone was sharp.

Nikki looked up, startled. "I was born in Canada," she said, stumbling over her words and feet a little. "But my mom's from Washington. We keep the PO box to deal with my *grandmere*'s estate."

There was a pause while the conversation reset itself. It hadn't occurred to her that he would be suspicious of her reappearance in his life.

"And while she tried to be a star, Tony always tended bar . . ." Val was rocking the Copa.

"So you're here in Bangkok for work. I take it you found a job?"

"Yes. Well, it sort of found me. But so far I like it."

"Oh? What do you do?" He seemed skeptical.

"Music and passion were always in fashion," Val sang. The dance floor was packed. Barry Manilow was apparently a crowd favorite.

Nikki smiled. She had a sudden memory of Cocktails class, dancing with Carmella as she asked the same question. Nikki had used nearly the same answer.

"I work for an international charity that focuses on the problems of women in the third world. I'm attending a conference here in Thailand."

Z'ev's expression hardened. "The South East Asian Women's Health Conference?" he asked suspiciously. Nikki was so startled this time that she missed the beat and stepped on his foot.

"Sorry. Yes, I'm presenting a speech on my company's efforts to aid the tsunami recovery efforts. How'd you know?" she asked, regaining the rhythm.

"It's been well publicized," he said, ignoring Valerie, Lola, and the Copacabana.

"Well, what about you? What happened to that guy we went to lunch with?"

She was about to press for more when a drunk couple stumbled into them from behind and pushed her against Z'ev. The shove was unexpected, but Z'ev reacted without hesitation. He simply tightened the arm around her waist, lifted her a few inches off the floor, and moved her out of the path of drunken destruction.

"Sorry," yelled the man over the music, and his partner giggled profusely.

"That's all right," Z'ev answered with a smile, setting Nikki down, but still holding her close. He didn't let go until the couple had moved safely off.

"Those two are a menace," Nikki said breathlessly, suddenly feeling shy.

"You're one to talk," he said, looking down at her.

"I told you I hadn't done this in a while," she said, feeling the start of a blush.

"That's not what I meant."

Nikki clapped as Lola drank herself into oblivion and Val took a bow. Z'ev was examining her critically, but after an inspection from Mrs. Boyer, Nikki thought she could handle a stare from a mere boy.

"Nikki, we should talk about Canada, but not here and not now."

"Why not now?" she demanded.

"I'm meeting someone, and I don't have time to do this all properly. Just tell me where you're staying and I'll come see you tomorrow."

"I'm not telling you anything. You're going to tell me what the heck you were doing in Canada. If you think you can dance with me and then just disappear, you've got another think coming. Whoever you're meeting can wait."

"Nikki, you don't understand. You can't be here. The guy I'm meeting is . . ."

Nikki was about to interrupt when she scanned the crowd and saw, just over Z'ev's shoulder, a familiar face lounging by the bar.

"Jirair Sarkassian," she said, suddenly realizing why Z'ev wanted her to leave. "He's here."

"Shit," said Z'ev, glancing over his shoulder. "He's early. Come on." He pushed her through the crowd and behind a pillar painted like a tree and decorated with a curving fiberglass snake. "Why'd you have to have red hair?" he complained.

"Sorry," Nikki said apologetically, and he laughed.

"Well, I like it," he said, kissing her forehead, "but it's a little easy to spot. Where are you staying?"

"The Mandarin," said Nikki, too thrown off by the kiss to be anything but honest.

"I'll come see you tomorrow at six, but right now you need to get out of here. Wait here, and I'll distract him. When he's looking the other way, you beat feet for the exit. Got it?"

"Uh, OK. Sure," she said, but he was already heading away from her, his height and bulk easily parting the crowd. Nikki glanced over her shoulder up at the stage. Val was consulting with the bandleader. No help there. Nikki looked around wildly, looking for some sort of clue as to her next move.

Jump Around

Nikki stood behind the column and sweated in her new halter top. It wasn't just the heat, which was considerable; she was paralyzed with indecision. She didn't want to mess things up for Z'ev, but she had to find Laura Daniels. She found herself wishing that Jenny or Ellen were present. Having friends along would have made this job so much simpler.

A new song started and she looked up at the stage to find Val glaring at her. Val jerked her head to the left, and Nikki turned, trying to follow her clearly meaningful glare. She was about to turn back and gesture for more explicit glaring when she saw Laura Daniels leaning over the balcony on the second floor. Nikki looked across the dance floor to where Z'ev was bullying his way through the crowd to Sarkassian. Nikki sprinted up the stairs near the stage and pushed her way through the clubgoers until she reached the ambassador's wife.

"Mrs. Daniels!" she yelled above the music. "Laura!" She reached out and grabbed the woman's arm.

Laura jumped back, alarm filling her face. "Oh!" she said, placing one hand on her ample bosom in a swooning gesture of relief. "Oh, thank goodness!"

"Mrs. Daniels, you shouldn't have come here!"

"I had to," Laura said. "I had to find out what he's doing." She pointed down to the floor below. Nikki followed the line of the accusing finger and found it pointing at a broad dark-haired man with a wide jaw, a sneering, twisted mouth, and a profoundly ugly, bright purple shirt.

"That's him, isn't it?" Laura said, pointing more firmly. "The one you chased. I followed Amein here and I saw him give a CD to that man, and then Amein left. You've just missed him."

"Shit," Nikki said, and she grabbed Mrs. Daniels's emphatically gesturing hand, hoping it wouldn't attract attention.

Nikki squinted in disbelief as the man in the purple shirt waved to attract the attention of Jirair Sarkassian. As she watched, Sarkassian joined the first man, who promptly began to shout in his ear and pull him in the direction of the stairs, pointing upward. Nikki scanned the room, looking for Z'ev, and spotted him coming off the dance floor and cutting a straight line toward the two men. She saw Ugly Shirt gesture toward Z'ev, and Sarkassian's head swiveled around, looking for the distinctive American. From her vantage point, she saw Sarkassian nod in understanding to whatever Ugly Shirt was saying, and equally clear was his quick jerk of the thumb, indicating that Ugly Shirt should leave. The strange pantomime finished as Z'ev arrived, his head turning to follow Ugly Shirt's exit. Sarkassian and Z'ev did the man hug/chest bump, and Sarkassian led him to the stairs.

"They're coming this way," gasped Laura in thrilled tones, reminding Nikki that her mission was not to investigate but to protect the woman next to her.

"Yeah, I know," said Nikki sourly.

She started to drag Mrs. Daniels in the opposite direction, expecting the back stairs by the stage to be open. After that she would just have to grab Val, and it would be just a short dash to the emergency exit. But as they approached the stairs she found their way blocked by a wall of bouncers arguing with a contingent of drunken marines. Nikki backpedaled, looking for an escape. Z'ev and his companion were nearly at the top of the stairs.

"This way," said Laura, breaking away. She apparently had not grasped that she was being rescued.

"No," Nikki said, diving after her. She dodged the crowd streaming to watch the fight on the stairs, as Laura ran straight into a room marked PRIVATE. Nikki muttered a swear word under her breath and then went in after her.

"Mrs. Daniels," Nikki hissed, gently closing the door. "We've got to get out of here. Those men can't see us." The room was decorated in brightly colored velvets. Heavy drapes muffled the reverberating bass coming from outside the room. It was all very plush, and there was a bottle of champagne chilling. One wall was a two-way mirror that looked out onto the second-floor bar. Laura Daniels had managed to find the VIP lounge.

"Call me Laura. And we have to be in here. I saw that other man come out of here earlier and I want to search it."

"What?" Nikki tried not to screech, but Laura's stupidity shocked her. "If Sarkassian came out of here, just where do you think he's heading now? They're coming back here!"

"Oh," said Laura, her face going from excited to sober as she realized the truth of Nikki's words. "I didn't think of that. What do we do?"

Nikki opened the door a fraction and peered out onto the balcony. Z'ev and Sarkassian were stopped to watch the fight, but were still standing in clear view of the door.

Keeping an eye fixed on the view outside the door, she flipped open her cell phone and thumbed a text message to Val. Then she turned her phone to Vibrate and tucked it into her waistband. It sounded as if the fight was starting to wind down, which meant she and Laura were running out of time. Nikki scanned the interior of the VIP lounge. A couch, two chairs, and a coffee table completed the furniture arrangement. No closets to hide in. No convenient back exits.

"What do we do? asked Laura, wringing her hands and looking around the room and clearly arriving at the same assessment as to the number of exits. Nikki looked through the sliver of open door again. The two men were moving toward the private room.

"We hide," said Nikki. Quickly, she pulled the couch away from the wall, threw Laura on the floor, and shoved the couch nearly back into position. "Whatever you do, don't move," she hissed. With barely a second to spare, she pulled the heavy velvet drapes away from the wall and ducked behind them herself. She tried to flatten herself against the wall and look as fabric-y as possible.

The door opened. Nikki heard the immediate hubbub of the club as well as the voices of the men as they entered.

"Look," Z'ev said, "if you're going to take these last-minute trips, I just wish you'd tell me. There's a lot of international pressure right now, and I can't protect your interests to the best of my ability if I don't know where you are."

"Jim, relax," said the voice Nikki recognized as Sarkassian's, and with a jolt she remembered that Z'ev had been using the name Jim the last time they'd met. "I appreciate your attention to detail, but you're too uptight. Bringing you out to Thailand was supposed to make you worry less!"

"I might worry less if knew what was going on with that security director of yours."

Nikki could practically hear the finger quotes around "security director."

"Are we on that subject again?" Sarkassian asked, scorn filling his voice. There was the sound of the champagne bottle being opened, followed by the distinctive splash of the foamy liquid into glasses. "Victor does his job. You do yours. Why is that so hard for the two of you?"

"Well, it's a little hard to trust a guy who disappears like a ghost every time I show up."

"He doesn't like lawyers," Sarkassian said. "And I tell him you're really nice for a lawyer, but he doesn't believe me."

"Thanks for that impassioned defense," Z'ev said. Nikki heard the couch springs creak as he flopped onto it. She winced sympathetically and hoped that Laura wouldn't get too squished. There was a rustling fabric sound, and for a moment Nikki had the paralyzing thought that Laura was being discovered.

"What's that?" asked Sarkassian.

"Someone's jacket," Z'ev responded.

"Oh, it's Victor's," said Sarkassian casually. "He was in here earlier. Here, I'll take it."

"You didn't just arrive? How long have you and Victor been here?" Z'ev asked. Nikki could hear the faint surprise in his voice as he realized that Victor and Sarkassian must have been there ahead of him.

"Victor wanted a drink; we got here just before you did. Here, I'll take the coat."

The command was more distinctively a command this time, and behind the curtain Nikki tensed.

"Sure," Z'ev said, his voice suddenly neutral as if he didn't care about the whole situation. "Where did you want . . ."

Whatever Z'ev had been about to say was cut off as the door flew open and banged against the wall.

"Oh, hey," came Val's voice. Nikki breathed a sigh of relief. Val would surely do something clever to clear the room. Smoke bombs possibly, or something else from Rachel's selection of gadgets.

"Sorry," she continued. "I thought my boyfriend was hiding out in here with some floozy. My bad." The door closed again, and behind the curtain Nikki gaped. What sort of rescue was that?

"You know," said Sarkassian thoughtfully, into the silence that followed Val's exit, "that sounds like a woman who's interested in finding a new boyfriend."

"And you're thinking of applying for the position?" Z'ev said, laughing slightly.

"Why not?" he responded. "It wouldn't hurt you to start interviewing a few possible candidates yourself. Stop you from pining over that wife of yours."

Behind the curtain, Nikki smiled.

"Who's pining?" replied Z'ev. "Unless you think that go-go dancer in Hong Kong looked like pining?"

Nikki ground her teeth.

"Then come out to the bar, we'll see if we can find something for you."

She heard the two men leave, but the door had barely shut before it opened again.

"Forgot my wallet," Z'ev said. "I'll be right there."

The door shut again, and Nikki, peering carefully through the curtains, saw Z'ev cross the room with quick strides and, with rapid fingers, begin searching Victor's jacket. She saw him look out the two-way mirror into the bar and grunt in dissatisfaction, as he carefully returned the jacket to its former position. He was reaching for the door when it opened of its own accord. Nikki yanked her covering curtains back into place as she heard Sarkassian speak.

"Are you coming?"

"Yeah, right behind you," said Z'ev as the door shut again.

Nikki counted to ten after the door closed behind them and then slid out from behind the velvet curtain with exaggerated care.

"Laura," she whispered, hurrying to the couch and tugging it away from the wall. "Laura, are you all right?"

The ambassador's wife responded with a deep groan.

"I'm not as slender as I used to be," she said, sitting up. "That was not pleasant. And I'm pretty sure there are some undergarments under there, and Lord knows where they were before they got there."

"Well, with undergarments it's a pretty easy guess, actually," Nikki said, leaving Laura to stare through the two-way mirror. Outside the window, she saw Sarkassian sliding onto the barstool next to Val. Val did look good sitting there, with her black hair swinging at a provocative angle against her cheek and her lips caressing a maraschino cherry. Nikki could see why Sarkassian would be interested. What she was more worried about was that Z'ev still hadn't moved far enough away from the VIP lounge for her comfort. She and Laura would be spotted the second they left the room.

"Watch him," she told Laura, indicating Z'ev, who was ordering a drink from a waitress as she began to ransack the pockets of Victor's jacket. "If he comes back this way, tell me."

The pockets were mostly empty. A few receipts, a Pai Gow domino, and a cell phone were all they contained. Nikki stared at the phone—the model looked familiar—and it reminded her of something she'd read in her cell phone manual on the plane ride over. There was a trick she thought she could use here.

"What're you going to do?" Laura asked, trying to talk over her shoulder without taking her eyes off Z'ev.

"I'm going pull out the battery and SIM card," Nikki said, reciting steps one and two.

"What's a SIM card?" asked Laura helplessly.

"Watch the window," ordered Nikki, as she popped out the SIM card and then found the narrow slot in the side of her phone and plugged it in. A green download bar began to chug across her screen.

"What are you doing?" asked Laura.

"Well, theoretically I'm uploading all the info on his phone into mine. And when we're done . . ." The phone dinged and indicated that it was now safe to remove the SIM card. Nikki replaced the phone in Victor's pocket and tucked her own phone back into the waistband of her skirt.

"He's going to the bar," whispered Laura.

"Great," Nikki said, grabbing Laura by the arm. "Time to go."

Moving quickly, she dragged Laura into the hallway and down the stairs. She pushed her way through the crowd and into the street, expecting the cool thrill of night air, but feeling instead only the sticky grittiness of a Bangkok night. At a loss as to what to do next, she was relieved when her own phone vibrated with an insistent buzz against her hipbone.

"Yeah," barked Nikki, flipping it open.

"So my meeting is running longer than I thought it would," Val said.

"What?"

"I won't be able to meet you for dinner like we planned," said Val, and Nikki sensed the slightly gritted teeth at the end of the sentence. She sighed. It was a clear sign she was being dumb again.

"You should just go back to the hotel," continued Val, "and I'll meet you later."

"I don't think that's a good idea," Nikki objected. "You shouldn't be in there without backup."

"Trust me," said Val. "I have everything under control. I'll meet you later." And then she hung up. Nikki stared at the phone in fury, wondering if she should call back.

"What do we do now?" asked Laura.

"We take you home," Nikki said, "and I wait for Val to report." She didn't like this plan, but she tried to sound as if she were behind it one hundred percent. She couldn't show anything less than a united front to an outsider.

"Well, all right," said Laura, getting into a taxi. "If you think it's the best plan. I'm so glad you're here! I would have messed this all up without you. But it turned out just great!"

"Uh, yeah . . ." said Nikki with a backward glance at the club. It felt wrong to leave her partner alone inside, but what else was she supposed to do? "Just great."

The After Party

Nikki quietly shut the door of her hotel room. She had left Laura with assurances that she would call with any updates or information. Laura had been reluctant to leave the matter there. With crossed fingers and a guilty conscience, Nikki had claimed to be a professional and that Laura should trust her to do her job. Surprisingly, Laura seemed to buy it and had gone inside. After that, Nikki had spent the cab ride back to her hotel trying to make sense of the events of the evening, but without much luck.

She dropped her purse, overstuffed with her original ensemble, on the bed and walked to the window, stripping off her heels as she went. The city of Bangkok glimmered beneath her window like a Lite-Brite. She adjusted the air-conditioning and washed off her makeup, then sat on the bed and opened her phone. But several minutes of poking the buttons produced no results. She couldn't find the information she had theoretically downloaded from Victor's phone.

With an angry sigh, she paced the length of the room. She felt useless, confused, and worried. Val wasn't with her. Z'ev was in town. And she'd already botched her first attempt at using Carrie Mae technology. Sighing, she kicked at her luggage. Half a step later she was back at her luggage and digging out the Carrie May–issue computer.

Nikki looked in dismay at the tangled octopus of cords and computer. Setup should have been a simple procedure, but faced with the dusty bits that Val had simply jammed in the computer bag, it looked more complicated. After a frustrating five minutes, the computer was at last plugged in and humming with electricity. She deftly logged on to the Carrie Mae website and sat staring at the blinking prompt. With a sigh for her ineptitude, she grumpily clicked on the Do You Need Assistance? tab.

"Yes, I really think I do," she muttered at the screen. The computer scanned for the webcam and then directed her, through a series of universal pictograms, to place the headset on her head. Nikki jammed the headset on and clicked the Ready button.

"Just a moment, NICOLE LANIER, while we page your case worker."

Nikki knew that it was a simple computer program that filled her name into the correct field for the pop-up button, but she couldn't help feeling a little bit less alone. Someone knew she was out here. She had been recognized by the greater computer world of Carrie Mae. She belonged. A few moments later, Jane appeared on the screen, her three-cornered face delineated by Bettie Page bangs and red lipstick that Nell would have approved of.

"Hey, Nikki! Did you find Lawan?" Jane's perky nature was at odds with her rebel wardrobe, but right in line with Carrie Mae culture.

"No, I . . ." Nikki said. She didn't think she could explain the entire of chain of events, so she just skipped to the end. "I think

I used the Download feature on my phone to upload someone's SIM card, but now I can't find it. Did I totally mess it up?"

"I doubt it," said Jane reassuringly. "Let me look." There was a flurry of typing, and then Jane nodded. "You just e-mailed it to yourself. It's the default setting. If you shut the phone without selecting an alternative, that's what happens. Do you want me to sort through it for you and give you a report?"

"Can you?" asked Nikki, feeling guilty about passing her work to someone else.

"I'm your technical support," Jane said. "It's what I do!"

"Oh," said Nikki. "Well, thanks."

"No problem," said Jane cheerfully. "What else can I help you with?"

"Uh, well . . ." She didn't really want to confess her ineptitude to a relative stranger like Jane, even if she seemed nice. And she really didn't want to discuss Z'ev with Mrs. Merrivel. It would be just too embarrassing. What she needed was a friend.

"I need to talk to someone, but I don't know where they are or how to reach them."

"I can find anyone," said Jane confidently. "Who am I calling?"

"My friends Jenny or Ellen from the academy," Nikki said, and Jane's face sort of wrinkled up.

"We're not really supposed to connect agents to agents," she said, her fingers poised over the keyboard. "It could compromise all of your missions."

"Yeah, I know," said Nikki, "but they already know about parts of this one and I need their advice."

"I'm not supposed to," repeated Jane, looking apologetic.

"But you could if you wanted to?" Nikki pressed. "Please, Jane. Please, please. I really need their help. I can't do this by myself. And besides, like I said, they already know about this mission. It wouldn't be putting them at risk any more than they already are."

Jane stood up briefly, looking over the wall of her cubicle, then sat back down.

"I really can't do that," she said, holding up a tablet of writing paper on which she had written NAMES?

"You really can't contact Jenny Baxter or Ellen Marson?" asked Nikki, catching on. "You can't help at all?"

"No, I really can't help," said Jane flatly, her fingers flying over the keyboard. There was a ding, and Jane smiled. She scribbled briefly on the notepad again and then held it up to the camera.

LUCKY. ELLEN ONLINE. JUST A MINUTE. THEY WON'T BEER. TURNING OFF RECORDING NOW.

"They won't beer?" Nikki read. Jane looked confused, then looked at her sign. Nikki could hear her scribbling on the paper and then she held up the sign again. BEER had been clarified heavily with a marker to read HEAR.

"Oh, right," said Nikki. "Sorry."

A second window opened on her screen, and Ellen appeared.

"Nikki?" Ellen said, squinting at her screen. "I don't think we're supposed to be doing this. Are you OK?"

"No!" Nikki burst out. "No, I'm not OK! I'm in Thailand and he's back!"

"Who's back? You've never been to Thailand. How can you be back in Thailand?"

"Not me! Z'ev. And that Sarkassian guy," she added as an afterthought.

"Ooh!" exclaimed Ellen, clapping her hands. "You really liked him! Is he as cute as you remembered?"

"Yes!" Nikki wailed. "It's a disaster!"

"What's a disaster?" asked Jenny, appearing on-screen. "I just got the page. Who are you? Who's she?" she said, looking at Jane and then back at Nikki.

"I'm Jane."

"She's my case worker," explained Nikki.

"You remember that guy from Canada?" said Ellen, ignoring both of them and diving straight into the topic at hand. "The one who picked Nikki up at a bar by proposing to her and took her to lunch with the mysterious foreign jerk-off where they had to pretend to be married?"

"Jerk-off?" repeated Jenny. "I must be rubbing off on you, but never mind. What about him?"

"He's back!" Ellen said happily. "Well, they're both in Thailand. So, not really back, but they're there. Together, you know."

"Yay!" exclaimed Jenny. "We liked him and he was funny. Well, this is good, right?" They both looked at Nikki, who was shaking her head. There was a crunch as Jane bit into a handful of popcorn.

"Don't mind me," she said. "I want to find out about Canada. Nikki's life sounds more interesting than mine. I can't even get picked up at a regular bar. Let alone proposed to. So the guy is a good thing?"

"It's not good," said Nikki. "It's a disaster. I think they've done something bad. Or at least their friend might have. I don't know what to do."

"Wait," Jenny said. "I'm lost. How did you get to Thailand in the first place?"

"I got partnered with Valerie Robinson. And Mrs. Merrivel's friend is the wife of the ambassador to Thailand, and *her* friend is Lawan Chinnawat, who is missing. So Val and I came to find her."

"Nikki's life is definitely more interesting than mine," said Jane.

"So where does the guy come in?" said Ellen. "And what was his name again? Something funny."

"Z'ev," Nikki said. "But he's still pretending to be Jim Webster."

"How old is he?" asked Jane, typing on her computer.

"I don't know. Thirty-something?" answered Nikki.

"He's a lawyer," Ellen said in Jane's direction. "Specializing in international shipping."

"Uh-huh," said Jane.

"And that Sarkassian guy is still with him," continued Nikki. "Only now Z'ev is working for him. So I think maybe we're still supposed to be married or something. But there's this other guy, Victor, who we saw getting a handoff from the orderly at Lawan's clinic. And we chased him, but then we lost him behind the elephant."

"Hmm . . ." said Jane. "You said you were pretending to be married to this guy?"

"Yeah," said Nikki. "I was Kim Webster."

"Well, then apparently you got divorced three months ago."

"What?" said the other three women at the same time.

"Check your screens. You'll see a lovely picture of Nikki and our handsome bachelor from an engagement announcement in a Vancouver paper. Also, there's a wedding certificate, and a divorce decree."

"That's the head shot from my passport picture!" Nikki shrieked.

"Photoshop is great," said Jenny.

"Not great! I look like I'm on crack!"

"He looks good, though," said Jenny.

"It's not that bad," Ellen said. "You just look a little vacant."

"A little . . . that was majorly harsh, Ellen," said Nikki.

"Sorry, dear, but passport pictures are never meant to pass for a wedding photo."

"I can't believe he divorced you without alimony. What a bastard," said Jenny.

"Actually," Jane said, "I think you're all missing the bigger picture. You can't just fake a Canadian wedding or divorce on a whim. This guy is soooo clearly not who he's pretending to be. Did you say he had another name?"

"Z'ev," said Nikki. "He said he was named after his grandfather and that Jim was his middle name."

"Makes me wonder about that Sarkassian fellow," said Ellen.

"Good point," Jenny agreed. "Look him up, too, Jane."

"Sure, what's his name?"

"Jirair Sarkassian," said Nikki. "He said he was in shipping. Armenian. Seemed bitter about it."

Jane typed, and the girls waited. Eventually Jane shook her head.

"This is going to take longer. I'm dealing with a lot more databases and a lot fewer details."

"Well, let's get some details," said Ellen. "What exactly happened tonight, Nikki? And where's Mrs. Robinson?"

"With them," said Nikki. Briefly she sketched an outline of the day for Jane and the girls.

"That all sounds extremely suspicious," Ellen said when she was done.

"I know!" agreed Nikki.

"And I don't like this Victor guy at all," Jenny said.

"I know!" said Nikki.

"But Z'ev sounds kind of hot," said Jane.

"I know," Nikki said with a sigh.

"But what is Val thinking, running off without you?" Ellen demanded. "You're supposed to be a team."

"I know," repeated Nikki, shifting uncomfortably in her chair, "but someone had to distract them and someone had to take Laura home. It just worked out that way."

"But really, she should have left right after you, and then you all should have regrouped outside the club and left together," Jenny said.

"Oh," said Nikki. "I didn't think of that. Yeah, you're probably right. I wish you guys were here. I totally forget everything I know when I'm standing next to Val. She just sounds so certain all the time."

"Well, just stay calm and you'll make it through," said Ellen. "You can do it."

"Yeah," said Jenny. "You're our fearless leader. You can do anything!"

"Right, sure," Nikki said, rolling her eyes. "Outright lies about my abilities aside, what am I supposed to tell Val?"

"About what?" asked Jenny, her brows furrowing.

"About Z'ev and Canada!" Nikki exclaimed. "What have we been talking about for the last hour?"

"Jeez, Jenny, keep up here," said Jane, crunching through another handful of popcorn.

"Don't make me come over there," said Jenny, and Jane grinned. "Sorry," Jenny continued. "I just didn't realize Val didn't know. Personally, I say don't tell her anything."

"You have to tell her," Ellen said. "His behavior sounded suspicious when you first told us about it, and now I'm even more convinced. It affects the mission, and Val should know."

"Hell, no," said Jenny. "If she tells Val, then Val might pull her out of the mission."

"Well, what if she tells Val, but skimps on the details," suggested Jane. "Just be all, 'I went to lunch with this guy and the other guy assumed we were married.' Spin it like Nikki has this contact that they should pursue."

"Well, that could work, I guess," agreed Jenny grudgingly, then she looked over her shoulder and ducked a little. "Uh . . . time to go. Love you guys. Don't die!"

"Love you, too," Nikki said, startled by the proclamation, but feeling good about it. Jenny's screen went dark, and Nikki looked back at Ellen.

"I'd better go, too," said Ellen, looking thoughtful. "Jane, I'll be around the computer a lot this week. Can you keep me updated?"

"I . . ." Jane looked uncomfortable, but shrugged. "Sure, what the hell?"

"Be careful, Nikki," Ellen said. "Call if you need help. I still say tell Val."

"I will," agreed Nikki. Ellen disappeared and Nikki was left staring at Jane.

"Good friends," Jane said. "I'll keep looking into these guys. It'd help if you got pictures of Sarkassian and the Victor guy."

"I'll see what I can do. In the meantime, I guess I'll just wait for Val to come back." Jane nodded. "Have you ever worked for her before?" Nikki asked. "Is she always like this?"

"Pretty much," said Jane with a shrug. "She just likes to do things her own way."

"Yeah," said Nikki. "Seems like."

There was a knock on the door as Nikki hung up on Jane. And Nikki took a deep breath as she went to the door. They said confession was good for the soul, but she wasn't looking forward to this.

Gun Shopping

The morning's mission of procuring guns had seemed exciting and exotic, and Nikki entered the hotel lobby riding a small wave of adrenaline, which Val had squashed immediately by entering a very prosaic cab and proceeding to ignore her. Being ignored by a grumpy partner in a cab that smelled slightly of poultry was not at all the adventure Nikki had hoped for. And more than that, it gave her too much opportunity to make the confession she had somehow managed to avoid the night before. Nikki rationalized in her head that she'd barely had time to get a word in before Val had gone to her own room and so therefore it was not her fault, but the other half of her wasn't buying the rationalization at all.

Nikki sat in the cab, scratched at the bead of sweat that was slowly forming on the inside of her arm, and stole sidelong glances at Val. Val sat on the other side of the cab and watched the traffic through the glass. The street was packed with an endless stretch of vehicles. People on bikes jockeyed for position among scooters, motorcycles, tuk-tuks, cars, and trucks.

"Er," said Nikki, which she knew was not a strong beginning, but it was better than silence.

"Yes?" said Val, sighing, as if talking to Nikki made her tired.

"There's something I should probably tell you." Val grunted in a way that Nikki interpreted as an entreaty for her to continue. "Um . . . you know those guys? From last night?"

Val actually turned her face in Nikki's direction, and Nikki stared into the vortex of Val's black sunglasses. They seemed to swallow her reflection like a black hole.

"Yes?" said Val again, her voice flat.

"I've met them before," said Nikki, forging ahead, intending to follow Ellen's advice and tell the whole truth.

Val continued to stare at her.

"In Canada," said Nikki, and abruptly chickened out. "I was at a bar and that lawyer guy was trying to pick me up and then the other guy came in and assumed we were married, and Jim said that if I played along I'd get a free lunch out of it. He said it was important because it was kind of an interview for him."

"I see," Val said slowly. "Why you didn't tell me about this before?"

"I didn't know it was pertinent," said Nikki. Val didn't sound mad, but Nikki was never very certain of Val's emotions. "I mean, he was just this guy at a bar and it's not like I ever saw him again. I mean, till now."

"Hmm," said Val.

"But there was one odd thing," Nikki said, creeping up to the truth, hoping to attack it from the rear. "The lawyer, when he was trying to pick me up, he used a different name. Different from the one he used with the Sarkassian guy."

Val frowned. "What did he say it was?"

"Z'ev," said Nikki, feeling slightly guilty, as if she were telling the wrong person a secret. Which was silly.

"I always thought that was odd," she continued, "but now that we know he's connected with the Victor guy, well, it's downright suspicious."

Val opened her mouth as if to speak, but then shut it again and turned again to look out the window, her lips twisting and her fingers drumming as if in concentrated thought.

"You said this was in Canada? That wasn't the trip where you won the starter kit, was it?" asked Val.

"That was later," said Nikki, waving her hand to put it in the past. "They weren't related or anything." Were they?

"Right," said Val, fiddling with her lighter the way she did when she was trying to put her thoughts together.

The cab crossed out of the tourist area and into the scrambling warren of buildings, street vendors, and shops. The car's pace became slower as the streets became narrower and the pedestrian traffic thicker. They drove past a cluster of monks in orange robes and sunglasses. Nikki wished she'd brought her camera.

"What did he say last night when you saw him?" Val asked abruptly.

"He asked to see me so that he could 'explain.'" This was where things got sticky. Last night Nikki's version of events had been very brief, and while she could gloss over Canada, she knew Val would be irritated that she hadn't been fully honest about last night. "And I figured we needed to find out about these guys anyway, so I told him I was staying at the Mandarin and agreed to see him."

"And you couldn't have told me this last night?" Val snapped.

"Well, you sort of rushed in and out," Nikki said weakly. "I told you about the phone and what they said in the room and everything."

"Right. Yeah, the cell phone. You mentioned that. Jane's working on that?" Val fiddled with her lighter a bit more.

"Yeah, she said she'd have information soon. But don't you think we should find out who they are? And who Jim Webster really is? And what their connection to Lawan is?" Nikki asked hopefully.

Val flipped the lighter through her fingers and didn't look at Nikki. The cab was slowing, as if it was searching for their destination.

"I already know him after all, and he's agreed to talk to me. It seems worth pursuing."

Val finally looked at Nikki and nodded as if reaching a decision. "Yeah, I think we should. It is suspicious. We should find out everything we can about this lawyer. You can't trust a guy like that. He could be very dangerous."

"I don't know," protested Nikki. "He never made any threats or anything. I mean, he lied, but . . ."

"The dangerous ones don't make threats. Besides, everyone knows you can't trust lawyers."

Nikki laughed weakly as the cab pulled to a stop in front of a store with grimy windows displaying undusted carvings of Thai elephants.

"Is this the place?" asked Nikki, looking doubtfully at the display, as Val paid the cab driver. "It looks kind of shady."

"What, you expect to buy guns at the local gun emporium?" Val was looking around the area as if expecting to see someone.

"I suppose," Nikki said, and pushed the shop door open hesitantly. Hanging bells jangled against the doorframe as she entered. The shop was cluttered with carvings and furniture. Nothing looked organized and the place had the musty smell of disuse.

"Kovit," called Val, stepping in behind her, but no one answered.

"Kovit!" Val called again, impatiently this time. "Shit," she swore when no one answered, and Nikki felt a prickle of nervousness run across the skin on the nape of her neck.

"Is something wrong?" Nikki asked.

"Eh? No. Look . . . just stay here for a minute," said Val, and she walked toward a bead-curtained doorway behind the sales counter. The curtain made clicking noises that sounded extra loud against the silence.

Nikki walked up and down the aisles of woodcarvings, passing Buddhas, boddhisatvas, and topless princesses with their sweet smiles and heavy-lidded eyes.

Nikki's phone began to ring with the repetitive sound of her mother's ring tone. She fumbled in her purse, anxious to turn off the racket, but the phone slipped from her fingers and clattered to the floor. She bent over to pick it up and was surprised by a soft popping noise and a sudden rain of splinters as the head of a statue in front of her exploded.

Nikki yelped and scrambled in an army crawl down the aisle, diving under a table as two more carvings sustained bullet damage. She heard the footsteps before she saw him. He was dressed in black, a black gun and silencer held easily in his hand. Her view of his face was obscured by a table's edges. All she could see was the red patch with an *R* sewn to the arm of his jacket. Nikki tried to quiet her breathing, which was coming in ragged gasps, and look for an escape. But all she could think was that, somewhere, her mother had clearly hit Redial without leaving a message because the phone was ringing again.

The man was getting closer. Nikki crawled away. She ducked behind a life-size statue of a baby elephant, risking a look at her attacker through its legs. They were in the animal section now. Behind the man a life-size gazelle thing with twisted horns seemed ready to attack on her behalf and a monkey squatted, covering its eyes. She was prepared to bet that somewhere two other monkeys were covering their mouths and ears, respectively.

There was a clicking noise and her attacker turned away from her. Nikki recognized the noise. It was the sound of Val coming back through the bead curtain. Instantly, Nikki launched herself. She wasn't about to let her partner get shot. The man saw her coming and swung back toward her, but there was an ear-shattering report and the man's arm and shoulder sprang up as if jerked by a rope. Unable to stop herself, Nikki hit him low. There was a tangle of limbs as both of them struggled for his gun. At last, Nikki wrenched it from him and kicked it away. The man flailed and then fell crashing through the monkey and onto the pronged horns of the gazelle statue.

Nikki stared in horror as the man plucked at the wooden horn poking out of his chest. She was dimly aware that Val was standing beside her now, a gun in her hand.

The man looked from the horn to them, his face an uncomprehending mask of surprise. "But why?" he said, and then stopped breathing.

Nikki gasped, choking on her own tears, and Val slipped an arm around her shoulders, hugging her briefly.

"You killed him," said a new voice.

"Shit happens," Val said, turning to the newcomer and letting go of Nikki.

"Yes, but does it have to happen here, Mrs. Robinson?" he asked, sounding peeved.

Nikki tore her eyes away from the body and looked at the newcomer. He was Thai, thin, with a very round head. He took a cigarette from behind his ear and put it in his mouth.

"So you want that gun or what?" he asked.

"Yeah, it'll do," Val said.

"The body will cost you extra. Extra, yeah?"

"Yeah, Kovit, extra," she agreed, and the man nodded, apparently satisfied.

"You need anything else?" he asked.

"A backup piece, maybe a Walther PPK," said Val with a shrug.

Nikki tried to pretend she wasn't shocked. There was a dead man in front of her, and neither Val nor the shopkeeper appeared disturbed by it.

"Sure, sure, we can do that," said Kovit, nodding. "I'm running a great deal on some Uzis right now, any interest? How about some grenades?"

Val shook her head. "Just the sidearms."

"All right, no problem, no problem. So the Glock for you, and I think I'm out of the Walthers just now, so how about a Smith & Wesson 38?"

"It's got to be small. I want it in an ankle holster."

"Sure, sure. Snub nose. No problem. You want holsters also?" Val nodded, and he made some more notes in Thai on a receipt pad. "Anything for your friend?" They both looked at Nikki. She felt frozen under the weight of their combined gaze.

"Uh, a .45? Colt 1911, if I can." Nikki blurted out the first gun that came to her mind. The reliable performance and stopping power of the 1911 had made it a favorite of armed forces around the world since World War I, but Nikki had liked it in practice because the slim grip made it easier for her smaller hands to control. It was amazing to her that she could focus on these small details while still wanting to throw up.

"You bet, you bet," answered Kovit, nodding. "The 1911. Plus shoulder holster?" He looked at Val, ignoring Nikki. Val nodded again. "Will you be needing ammo?"

"Yeah," agreed Val." And spare clips."

Kovit nodded and disappeared into the back of the shop.

"He's dead," said Nikki, pointing at the body. "I'd be dead right now if it weren't for you. He was going to kill me, and you shot him. And then there was the falling . . ."

"Yeah," Val said. "I wish that hadn't happened."

"What do we do?" asked Nikki.

Val shrugged. "Kovit will take care of it."

Kovit returned, and Val inspected the guns, handing Nikki the .45. It seemed a huge weight in her hands. Nikki collected her now beeping phone and purse from the floor and tucked the gun into it—hammer carefully down. During moments of emotional stress it was important to adhere to safety procedures—Mrs. Boyer's voice echoed in her mind.

"Thanks for your time, Kovit," Val said, and pushed Nikki toward the door.

Kovit waved as he pinched out his cigarette and tucked it behind his ear again.

They were four blocks away before Nikki began to have rational thoughts.

"We should have searched the body for clues," she said.

Val nodded.

"Why was he trying to kill me?"

Val shrugged.

"And how did he know we were there to try to kill us?"

Val shrugged again.

"Haven't you got anything to say?" demanded Nikki.

"The lawyer," said Val. "I think we need to find out about the lawyer."

Weapons of Choice

Valerie shoved herself into a cab, and Nikki mimicked her movements, looking back over her shoulder. But what was she looking for? Her nervous glances simply took in the busy street and bustling people.

"All right," said Val, finishing her "international English" discussion with the cab driver—which mostly involved a lot of pointing at a map. "Let's talk about this thing."

Nikki nodded. She wanted to cry, but knew that was unacceptable. Instead, she found her breath coming in short gasps as if she couldn't get enough air. She could feel her heartbeat in her fingertips, like the fluttering wings of a hummingbird.

"So you tell the lawyer where you're staying, and the next thing you've got is someone following us and trying to kill you."

"Following us . . ." Nikki was taken aback. "No . . ."

"Yes," Val contradicted.

"But I think that guy was already there," said Nikki. She couldn't remember why she thought that. "I didn't hear him come in," she said quickly, knowing that her time to speak was quickly running out. Her breath was evening out. The panic was starting to ebb, but she didn't feel any better about it.

"He probably slipped in the back," Val said dismissively.

"How could he have known we were there?" asked Nikki, still not quite following Val's rapid words.

"That's what I'm saying!" exclaimed Val, as if they'd already covered that ground. "I know *I* didn't tell anyone where we were going, so someone must have followed us. And since your boyfriend, the lawyer, is the only one who knows where we're staying, I'm going to go with him as a prime suspect."

"I didn't see anyone following us," said Nikki doubtfully.

Val rolled her eyes. "You weren't exactly looking, were you now?" Nikki bit her lip and said nothing, knowing that this was true. She hadn't been really careful about checking for tails.

"So you were right," continued Val. "We need to investigate the lawyer."

"I think"—Nikki tried to marshal her thoughts, but they kept straying away—"I think we need to check out other guys, too. The purple shirt guy, Victor, and Sarkassian. You spent some time with Sarkassian. What did you think? Did he say anything suspicious?"

"Suspicious, double entendre, whatever. Look, Sarkassian's out of your league, kid. Leave him to me."

"OK," Nikki agreed readily. "But don't you think we should check them out?"

"Yeah, sure. We will," said Val, although there was something less than reassuring about her tone. "But we need to stay focused on our mission. Lawan is our first priority."

Nikki nodded. That was true.

"We need to search her apartment before we worry about Sarkassian."

Nikki scratched the back of her neck, pushing tendrils of hair out of the way. Searching Lawan's apartment had been second on the list of duties for the day, but Nikki felt that somehow a mysterious gunman and his death should dislodge the day's to-do list.

"OK," she agreed reluctantly, picturing a repeat of the hours spent at Lawan's office, but on a larger scale.

Lawan's apartment was in a shabby turn-of-the-century building with clear British influences and a very sturdy iron gate. Val punched in the code from the numbers that Laura had scrawled on the back of a business card and they entered a quiet courtyard with a slightly rusty swing set in the corner. The interior of the house was clean and nearly spartan in its lack of clutter. The two exceptions were the little girl's bedroom and Lawan's home office.

The girl's bedroom was an explosion of pink and purple. No surface seemed to have escaped being treated with paint or ruffles. Even the mosquito netting over the bed had been dyed purple. The office was just as cluttered, but clearly not through intentional design. Magazines, newspapers, and piles of computer printouts, were scattered everywhere. But pictures of Lawan and her daughter covered the walls.

"Check this out," Nikki said, picking up an award nearly buried beneath the clutter. "I saw her get this, in the documentary they showed in training. She rescued some Russian women who'd been sold into prostitution. She got an award."

Val shrugged.

"You don't think that's cool?" asked Nikki.

"It won't do any good," said Val impatiently, poking at a pile until it toppled over onto the floor.

"What do you mean?"

"Rescuing people . . . it doesn't do any good."

"But you've rescued lots of people," protested Nikki. "Those five women doctors in Afghanistan."

"One," said Val, holding up a finger. "Just one. The rest have died or thrown themselves into some fresh mess. And the only reason the one who's left hasn't done anything to get herself killed is because she's too busy dying of cancer. You can't really save anyone, Red. The best you can hope for is to save yourself."

"No," protested Nikki. "You saved people."

"I'll search the rest of the house," Val said with a shake of her head. "You start in here."

Nikki eyed her partner in dismay as she walked away. Then she looked back at the disaster of the office and groaned. With a sigh, she crossed the threshold and set to work.

An hour later, Val reappeared with lunch and then went away again. Two hours after that, she poked her head in the doorway once more.

"When is your boyfriend coming over?"

Nikki stared up at Valerie, lost for a moment as to whom she was talking about. "He's not my boyfriend," she said, at last aligning her thinking with Val's.

"Boyfriend, lawyer, whatever," Val said with a shrug.

"He said six," answered Nikki, checking her watch. It was a quarter after four.

"And what'd you say?" asked Val.

"I don't think I had time to say anything," Nikki replied.

"There's always time," said Val. "You've got to start asserting yourself."

"I'll work on that," Nikki agreed halfheartedly. Her mother frequently gave these kinds of pep talks, and she didn't mean them, either.

Val walked to the window and stared out at the dusty narrow

alley behind the house. Above them the bass thump of a stereo drifted down from a neighbor's apartment.

"We should go," said Val. Nikki had gone back to reading and it took her a moment to register the words. "You need to be getting ready for your date."

Nikki shook her head. "I think this is more important. It's a bunch of stuff on Rival Shipping. Lawan had piles of it. Google searches. Financials. Articles from the English-language Bangkok paper. Gobs of stuff. On a hunch, I called Jane. She hasn't had time to look over the stuff I downloaded, but she could tell me that Victor's phone was being paid for by Rival Shipping."

"OK," Val said with a shrug.

"They're a shipping company."

"I gathered that from the name."

"Mostly container ships to the U.S.," continued Nikki, trying to maintain her line of thought.

"Yeah?" said Val, looking bored.

"Well, didn't Laura say that Lawan's most recent project was antiterrorist measures in the port? Searching cargo containers, stuff like that?" Val yawned, and Nikki clenched her jaw in frustration. "It also has an interesting logo," she said, holding up a printout of a circle containing a serif letter R with a line through it. "Look familiar?"

"Not especially," Val said.

"The guy in the antique shop, the one who tried to kill me, this was on his jacket."

"Well, we've already established that Victor and the lawyer work for the same place. So I can't say I'm surprised. Now, really, shouldn't we be going?"

Nikki glanced at the clock. It was a quarter after five.

"Yeah, we should. Did you find anything in the rest of the

place?" Nikki shuffled all of her pages into a bunch before looking at Val, who was looking at the stack of papers.

"Nah," she said. "Nothing worthwhile. Come on, let's go."

"I need another shower," said Nikki, as they rode the elevator up to their room. She hadn't noticed before, but now, in the harsh light of halogen, the streaks of dust, grime, and what she really hoped wasn't a blood spatter were painfully apparent.

"Traffic will do that to you," Val agreed, and Nikki wanted to say that she hadn't been thinking about traffic, but she let it go.

In the shower, Nikki scrubbed her hair and tried to bully the events of the day into a linear story, where one thing led to another. She felt that if she could just get a reason for everything, put a label on it, and put it into the correct box, she'd be able to figure everything out. But she was troubled by Val's theory on Z'ev. She knew Val was the more experienced agent. And her reasoning about Z'ev sounded logical. But she couldn't quite bring herself to believe it. He just hadn't seemed like . . . well, he hadn't seemed like he wanted to kill her.

She thought back over the night at the club. He had been abrupt and slightly suspicious, but he hadn't seemed threatening. In fact, he had seemed far more suspicious of Victor—what with the searching of Victor's coat and all. And he had been such a good dancer. Nikki stopped herself before her thinking got muddled by emotions. She needed to concentrate on evidence.

After her shower, Nikki laid her clothes out on the bed and looked at her shoe selection. She glanced at herself in the mirror and had a sudden flashback to the hotel in Canada, when she had tried on interview outfits. She could almost hear her mother humming in the bathroom. She felt like a Virginia Slims ad. She'd come a long way, baby. Thinking of cigarettes reminded her of

Val, and she wrapped her towel more tightly around herself and dashed next door.

"Come help me pick out an outfit," she demanded when Val opened the door.

"Wear what you've got on right now."

"I'm wearing a towel!"

"It'll knock him dead."

"I'm not looking to knock him dead. I'm looking to . . . well, I don't know what I'm looking to do, but I know I'm going to be doing it in underwear."

"That's an option," suggested Val, and Nikki glared. "OK, fine," she said, and they trooped back to Nikki's room, where Val surveyed the clothing laid out on the bed.

"Go with the green shirt, the khaki capris, and the wedge sandals," she said without hesitation. "The shoes will give you height, so you can look him in the eye; the pants show off your ass, and the shirt is a good color without flashing any cleavage. Sexy without looking like you're being sexy for him."

Nikki nodded. "I'll wear some big earrings and put my hair in a ponytail."

"Spunky and functional," Valerie agreed. "OK, we good?"

Nikki nodded and Val walked to the door. She was about to leave, but she paused, with one hand on the doorknob. "And you should wear a thong. Those pants are low cut; it will show if you bend a bit."

"The whole point of a thong is to be discreet," Nikki said sternly. "It's not supposed to show. No matter what the pop stars say."

"Well, you've got to even the odds somehow. Use the weapons you've got." Nikki threw a shoe at her. "And don't forget your gun," Val added, ducking out of the room.

After Val left, Nikki guiltily picked out a green thong that matched her shirt and put on the rest of her clothes. Thongs were not an unfamiliar item in her lingerie drawer. Visible panty lines were an evil in the Lanier household, second only to polyester track suits, but she felt it was wrong to wear one solely for display and distraction.

Nikki was applying the last stages of her makeup when someone knocked on the door. She checked her first instinct to answer the door and looked through the peephole. It was Z'ev, standing with apparent impatience in the hallway.

Nikki practiced her smile once, took a deep breath, and opened the door.

"Hi," she said with perk. "Come on in. I just have to finish putting on my face."

"You took it off somewhere?" he asked dryly, shutting the door behind him. Nikki suppressed a sarcastic reply and laughed instead.

"It's something my mother always says. I suppose that's a good reason to stop saying it." She pretended to be indecisive about her earrings, and then bent over her jewelry bag on the chair, allowing the thong to show. Her back was to him and she couldn't see his reaction, but when she stood up he quickly became absorbed in the ceiling, so she knew he'd definitely noticed.

"Jeez," he said, taking his eyes off the ceiling and noticing her makeup case. "Got enough makeup?"

"It's for work," she said.

"My sister would be in heaven."

"You have sisters?" she asked, closing the lid to the case firmly and lugging the behemoth into the bathroom.

"Just the one," he answered, wandering over to the window and peering out through the sheer curtains. "What about you? Any siblings?" he asked, flipping the ball back into her court.

"No. At least, not that I know of," she added, considering that her father had been gone long enough to have given her a few brothers or sisters she didn't know about.

"Hmm" was his only reply. He was examining the desk now, staring at a half-written postcard to her mother.

"So, are you going to explain the whole Canada thing or not?" Nikki asked bluntly, stabbing an earring through her lobe and watching Z'ev in the mirror. He was fidgeting with a pen from the desk and at last pulled out the desk chair and sat down.

"My name isn't Jim Webster."

"We established that in Vancouver," interrupted Nikki. "It's Z'ev."

"Yeah, it is Z'ev. Z'ev Coralles." He paused again, and Nikki felt some sort of reply was in order.

She leaned against the dresser and glared at him. "I said at the time you were a big fat liar."

"No, I'm not," Z'ev protested. Nikki raised an eyebrow. "Look, when I met you . . ." He trailed off with a frown.

"Don't tell me the horse-faced sister story again," said Nikki disbelievingly, and she watched him grin.

"I never said she was horse-faced. She's just really . . . *strident* I guess would be a good word." Nikki kept her face skeptical. "The thing you have to understand about Sarkassian is that, well, first of all, he's Armenian and a bit of a traditionalist about a few things."

"Marriage being one of them?"

"His sister's happiness being one of them," corrected Z'ev. "She pretty much gets what she wants. I just thought it would avoid any potential social snafus if I were conveniently unavailable. I never thought he'd actually want to meet my wife. Simple really."

"Uh-huh. Why didn't you use your real name?" Nikki pressed.

He sighed, rolling the pen back and forth on the desk with one hand.

"I use it for business. I found Z'ev Coralles was a little too ethnic for some firms."

"Hmm," said Nikki. "That's stupid."

"I can't account for the prejudices of others," Z'ev said with a shrug.

"Isn't he suspicious that I'm not here with you in Thailand?" asked Nikki for the fun of watching him squirm. His story didn't quite match the things she'd overheard in the VIP room.

"I . . . well, I told him you didn't want to go to Thailand and that we split up."

"You ended our marriage? Just like that?" asked Nikki, pretending to tear up. "You couldn't have even tried counseling?" And if he was so worried about the sister, why had he gotten "divorced"? She thought about pointing out that hole, but didn't.

He laughed. "Well," he said, "we could try reconciling over dinner."

"I don't know," Nikki said, applying the finishing touches to her eyeliner. "My mother always said to never date a divorced man. They have baggage."

"Speaking of baggage," he said, kicking at her luggage. "Tell me about this new job?"

"It's with the Carrie Mae Foundation," she said, letting him change the subject.

"Like those makeup people?"

"Yup, those makeup people."

"So what do you do?"

"I'm supposed to travel around to various conferences, representing Carrie Mae, and liaise with people and try to get them to help with the various foundation projects. It's kind of exciting, really. Outside of a trip to Paris in high school, I've never gotten to travel much."

"Pretty cool," agreed Z'ev. "So," he said, standing and stretching, which reminded Nikki of how big he actually was. "Does that mean you can put dinner on the expense account?"

"No," Nikki said with a laugh. "I don't think anyone's going to believe that you're a useful source of information on women's health."

"Shoot. Guess I'll have to put it on mine. I'll call it informational networking."

"Lawyers," said Nikki. "You can think of a way to write off anything."

"Of course," Z'ev said. "It's our chance to be creative."

Nikki grabbed her purse and ducked into the bathroom to arm herself. Sorting through the Borg cube of makeup, she selected the stun gun compact that Rachel had included, but she refused to bring the gun. She knew what Val had said, but it didn't fit in her purse, with all the other crap she'd stuffed in there. And honestly, she didn't think Z'ev rated a gun.

"How do you feel about Muay Thai?" he asked, opening the door for her.

"Kickboxing?"

"That's the stuff."

"It's interesting?" said Nikki, trying the opinion on for size. Girls just didn't go around telling boys that for the last three months Friday night had been Girls' Fight Night at the dorm. It would seem unfeminine. Maybe if she explained about the facials . . .

I Predict a Riot

"So we were standing here, with a guard standing in front and one just behind." He leaned forward, pulling their water glasses into formation to demonstrate. "And he says to the border guard, 'If I wanted to smuggle drugs in, do you really think I would leave it in my bag?'"

Nikki covered her eyes with one hand, laughing from under it.

"I know," Z'ev said, reaching up and pulling her hand down. "I thought we were destined for the rubber hose room. Let that be a lesson, college roommates are not to be trusted." His hand was warm, and Nikki felt a tingle run up her arm as his thumb caressed over her knuckle.

"Then he says, 'No, I'd put it in the dog food, like the couple in front of us did.' And then they went out, and twenty minutes later they came back and we were free to go. I don't think I've been closer to a body cavity search in my life." Nikki laughed again. "Man, that kid was nervy. Crazy, of course, but nerves of steel."

"Crazy sounds about accurate," agreed Nikki, deciding that

whoever invented holding hands was a genius. The longer dinner had gone on, the more she became convinced that Z'ev was exactly what he said he was—a lawyer with an odd heritage that worked against him, being employed by some rather suspicious characters. He'd clearly left some things out earlier, but people got themselves in hard-to-explain situations. She was living proof. But his every response matched his body language, and all the tells that she'd been trained to watch for simply reinforced the words that came out of his mouth. He was being honest and he liked her. She'd never thought about using her Carrie Mae–instilled skills to assist in dating, but she was finding them helpful. She knew he liked her, and she was just about to do something impetuous, like lean in and kiss him, when his phone rang.

Z'ev pulled his hand away and leaned back in his chair. But Nikki felt the withdrawal was more than just distance; his face changed as well. An expression of cool detachment dropped over him. The conversation was brief, consisting mostly of grunts and affirmations, but Nikki could see that dinner was over. He was already waving to the maitre d', handing him his credit card.

"I have to go," he said, tucking his wallet back into his breast pocket.

"I thought you had the evening off?" Nikki said, feeling slightly hurt.

"I did. Something's come up."

"Oh."

"Do you need cash to get back to the hotel?"

"No!" she snapped, feeling offended, but unable to name the reason why.

"Sorry, Nikki," he said. "But I've really got to go. Sometimes my job doesn't really allow for a personal life." He looked genuinely sorry for a moment, but then he walked out.

"Well, that didn't end well. Where's he going?" asked Val, dropping into Z'ev's seat. Nikki stared at her in surprise.

"You're following me?"

"Well, yeah. You didn't really think I was just going to send a newbie out on her own, did you? Now, what'd you learn? Other than how to make googly eyes?"

"He went to the University of Arizona," said Nikki, knowing it was extremely weak.

"Ah, the Devil Dogs," said Val.

"Devil Dogs are Marines. You're thinking of the Sun Devils, which is Arizona State. He went to the University of Arizona, and they're Wildcats."

"At least I didn't waste a whole dinner to find that out, and at least my dates don't walk out on me."

"I don't think he is up to anything," Nikki said defensively. "I think he's just a lawyer working with some weird guys. If he's doing anything, it's trying to figure out what that Victor and Sarkassian are up to."

"Uh-huh. Yeah, right. Wake up and smell the curry, kid. He's not just a lawyer."

"Yes, he is," said Nikki, throwing down her napkin and reaching a sudden decision. "And I'll prove it to you." She hurried to the front of the restaurant where Z'ev's cab was just pulling away. She waved to a tuk-tuk and leaned in to negotiate.

"No!" yelled the driver, pointing at her in recognition.

"Hi, again," Nikki said, recognizing the tuk-tuk driver from the elephant incident.

"What're you going to do, kid?" Valerie asked, following her out of the restaurant. "Yell, 'Follow that cab,' and get into a wild chase across the city?" She made "wild chase" sound quaint.

"No!" the tuk-tuk driver repeated, hugging the steering wheel and glaring at Val.

"Maybe," said Nikki. "What do you care? You wanted me to find out about him. So I'll find out about him."

"Determined to prove me wrong?" Val smirked in amusement, which only infuriated Nikki more.

"Yes," she answered, which would have flunked her if she were still being graded on witty repartee. She turned back to the tuk-tuk, but the driver hugged the wheel more fiercely.

"OK, OK, you drive, but I want to follow him." She pointed at Z'ev's quickly disappearing cab. The driver looked suspiciously at the cab, but didn't release the steering wheel. "Umm . . ." Nikki mentally rifled through the phrase book, trying to remember something useful. She couldn't believe she was actually going to do this. Why did Val always have to be one step ahead of her? *"Thaim laung ta-xi caun naun."* (Follow that cab.)

The driver screwed up his face in concentration, either considering her Thai or her request, then he jerked a thumb at the backseat.

"Keep in contact, Red," Val said as Nikki jumped into the tuk-tuk. "Try not to do anything too stupid."

The driver revved his engine and zoomed into traffic with a reckless abandon that sent Nikki spilling backward into her seat. She clutched the metal railing and hoped Z'ev wouldn't notice her driver's exuberance. She glanced back at Val, who was leaning against the awning post. Nikki waved, but Val was already turning away.

Nikki bit her lip and turned back to concentrate on her driver's efforts. She hoped Val wasn't mad at her.

Z'ev's cab pulled up in front of a square, unassuming building about the size of a high-school gym, and Nikki's driver pulled up a few cars back. Nikki squinted at the busy scene in front of her, uncertain of what Z'ev was doing.

"Muay Thai!" exclaimed her driver, pointing at the building and the myriad vendors and tourists outside. "Thai boxing!" He mimed punching, and Nikki nodded.

So Z'ev was going to the fights after all. Now, why couldn't she have come along? Nikki thought about calling Val, but Z'ev was on the move again, his tall, muscular frame clearly visible as he strode through the milling crowd.

"Tickets?" asked Nikki, pointing after Z'ev.

The driver's face lit up. Flipping off the engine, and carefully taking the keys with him, he hopped out of the tuk-tuk, beckoning Nikki to follow. He led her to a crowded plaza and pointed to where Z'ev was preparing to buy tickets. As with anywhere else in Bangkok, the building was crammed with people; it vibrated with a humming, raw energy. Z'ev was talking to a pretty girl in a traditional Thai costume. Nikki slipped her driver a tip, and with a wink, he gave her a thumbs-up before waving farewell.

Nikki hesitated before moving in on Z'ev, remembering Val's parting words. She felt a strong urge to ignore Val's command, but eventually she chose caution over her pride and quickly thumbed her location in a text to Val. She was certain that Z'ev was just a lawyer, but something bad could still happen.

"One ticket?" asked the pretty Thai girl. She held a roll of stickers in one hand.

"Make that two," said Nikki, linking her arm through Z'ev's. "He's with me." She handed the girl a wad of baht, and she deftly made change and slapped a sticker on each of them.

"This way," the girl said, leading them into the mezzanine.

"You're not supposed to be here," Z'ev said, his voice dangerously quiet.

"And yet I am," countered Nikki. "You said you would take me to the fights—I expect to go to the fights. Nobody ditches me in the middle of a date." She tossed her hair as the doors opened and another girl in a Thai silk outfit gestured for them to follow her. Nikki set the pace, knowing that Z'ev would have no choice but to follow. They were led past rows of folding chairs to the very front row; it was only a few feet from the ring. A band was playing softly; the soft tap of drums and whistle of a flute echoed through the hall.

"I'm meeting someone, Nikki. You cannot be here. You have to go *now*." Z'ev was wearing what might have passed for a smile from a distance, but Nikki knew it was really just a baring of teeth. He was genuinely angry. She hadn't expected him to be this mad. Could Val have been right about him?

"Z'ev," she said placatingly, laying a hand on his arm. "Whoever you're meeting . . ." She paused, trying to frame a logical reason for him to let her stay. "Wouldn't it be better to look like you had a date? There aren't a lot of other single fight-goers here tonight."

She watched as he looked around the room, taking in the crowd of couples, friends, and tour groups. He was hesitating. A couple walked in front of them, led to seats just down the aisle. The woman was complaining about going to something so boring and violent.

"You didn't have to come," the man snapped.

"And let you be here by yourself?" she snapped back. "With all the hookers? I don't think so!"

"Look, you do your business, and I'll just sit here and look pretty." Nikki pasted on her best Carrie Mae smile. He had hesitated too long; she knew she had him.

"Don't do that," he said, leaning away from her.

"What?" she asked, tilting her head and adding a cheerful lilt to the end of the question.

"That smile scares me," he said. "Makes me start wondering if you've been invaded by the Body Snatchers."

Nikki laughed, cracking the smile into a thousand pieces, as the first boxers entered the ring, while the referee stood, arms folded, in the center of the ring. Both fighters bowed to their respective corners and began a slow, solemn dance. The referee made no movement, but looked endlessly bored by the proceedings.

"All right," Z'ev said, "you stay, but the second I say go, you go. And if I have to get up and leave, then you just stay put and wait for me to get back."

"Do they always do that?" she asked, ignoring him and watching the fighters.

"Yes, it's to show respect to the trainer and pull luck and power into themselves," Z'ev answered. "Now, do we have a deal?"

"Yeah, sure," Nikki agreed, feeling a guilty ping for what she was 90 percent certain would turn out to be a lie. "Can we get a program?"

For a moment she thought Z'ev was going to argue, but with a sigh he gave in.

"Sure, why not?" he asked, waving a vendor over and purchasing a program. He handed the program to Nikki, who smiled and impulsively kissed him on the cheek.

"Thanks! I'm sure this will be helpful," she said brightly, pretending that she wasn't nervous about his reaction. She flipped open her program, intending to bury herself in it, only to find that it was all in Thai.

Resolutely, she studied the program intently, determined to find something of value. The interior pages were filled with grainy photos of fighters and looping Thai script. The center spread was devoted to the main fight of the evening: two tough-looking men, one sporting a scar through his left eyebrow, and the other a shock of black hair that stood straight up. Z'ev leaned over her shoulder, examining the program as well. Nikki could feel the warmth of his breath on her neck and the strength of his leg pressed against hers.

"Well," she said when she felt that someone had to say something before the moment got awkward, "I can't understand a word of it, but the pictures are good, and I think this is where they say who's favored in the betting."

"Yeah, it's here in this column," agreed Z'ev, pointing to an inset box on the page. "That means that the guy in the green trunks is favored this match."

They both looked back up to the ring to see if the odds would be accurate. The opening ritual had ended, and the fighters were now squaring off.

The ring was in the center of the room. Two sides had been filled with rows of folding chairs and the other two had concrete riser seating. One section had been cordoned off with a chain-link fence, and activity inside this area was fierce. Nikki decided it was the betting pool.

The fight proper had begun now, and the music switched to an up-tempo beat. Both fighters were small and wiry. They wore red and green trunks that to Western eyes looked as if they were on backward. Nikki knew it was nothing more than the fact that the Thai put writing across the front, instead of the butt of the shorts, but she couldn't shake the feeling. The movements of the fight were quick and brutal, both fighters battering away with knees and elbows. The din of the stadium increased to a fevered pitch as the music and fight sped up. The fighters were rocking in blows now, with the sharp, stinging smack of flesh on flesh.

"Red Trunks is going to win," predicted Nikki, drawing a strange look from Z'ev.

"Green's got the reach," he disagreed. "And he's the favored man."

"But Red has the kicks," Nikki said, just as Red Trunks sent a roundhouse kick whistling in and landed it across Green's temple. Green staggered backward and sat down, sprawling gracelessly upon the canvas. The ref called the fight, briefly raising Red's arm in the air. The Green team hustled their fighter back up the ramp in a wheelchair.

"Yeesh," said Nikki, "they didn't even stop to wake him up—poor guy was seeing stars."

"He's still seeing stars," Z'ev answered. "But they don't waste time on seeing if you're OK. They've got to get the next fight going. If you lose, it's the Wheelchair of Defeat for you."

"That's not funny," she said mid-chuckle.

"How'd you know he was going to lose?" Z'ev asked, distracting her.

"Oh, you know," replied Nikki vaguely.

"No, I don't," he said, smiling, but insistent.

"I was a cheerleader in junior high and high school. You go to enough sporting events, you get good at picking the better athlete." That was true as far as it went.

"What'd you cheer for? Football, I'll bet."

"Why football?" asked Nikki, puzzled.

"You knew that the U of A were the Wildcats. Plus, football always got the varsity cheerleaders. All the popular girls were on varsity. Simple equation, really."

Was there a trace of bitterness there? She squinted at him. His analysis of her, while accurate, had revealed something about him—something he hadn't intended to share.

"What makes you think I was popular?" she asked, challenging his rationale.

"Your underwear matches your shirt."

Nikki blushed.

"So I'm color coordinated, that doesn't mean I was popular," she said primly. Z'ev was trying to hold back his smile, and Nikki laughed in spite of herself.

"Yes, it does. To be popular, you have to know how to dress. I bet you dated the quarterback."

"Ha. No, I didn't." He looked skeptical. "All right, so I did date the captain of the baseball team for a bit, but it's not the same thing." Z'ev gave a small chuckle. "So I take it you didn't play football?" she asked, choosing to ignore his laughter.

"No, my brother did," he answered, shifting uncomfortably as if she'd asked something far more personal. "He was a regular all-American hero." His tone was an odd mixture of pride and sarcasm.

Nikki was about to ask him about his high-school career when the next fight began. The sound of the band increased, and they had to shout a bit over the din of the arena.

The arena was underlit and the atmosphere was muggy and heavy with cigarette smoke and incense. Nikki knew that for proper femininity she ought to be deploring the violence or covering her eyes, but the best she could manage was to duck when sweat flew her way. Z'ev didn't seem to notice, and in between fights, Nikki found that she was leaning comfortably into his shoulder, and the arm on the back of her chair seemed suspiciously close to being around her.

"The title fight's up next," Z'ev said, as two fighters marched into the ring. Scar Face and Electro Hair jostled past each other on the narrow ramp down to the ring. The audience was on their feet and cheering.

"Would you like a program, sir?" said an usher who had suddenly appeared beside Z'ev.

"No thanks," Nikki said, looking up at the usher. "We already have one."

"This is a special program," said the usher, shoving the program at Z'ev. Nikki took another look at the usher and noticed that his white jacket was ill fitting—short around the wrists, tight in the biceps—and that his knuckles had the callused, scabbed look of a fighter.

Z'ev accepted the program with a nod, and the usher walked on. Nikki frowned as Z'ev began to flip through the pages. Looking around for the usher, she saw him hurrying up the ramp toward the fighters' entrance. The title fighters were entering the ring– beginning their dance.

"I have to go now," said Z'ev. "This is the part where you wait here until I come back?" He clearly had intended that to be a statement, but it came out as a question.

"Yes, all right," she said, smiling, because she didn't mean it. Val couldn't be right about him, she would prove it.

As Z'ev hurried up the aisle, his tall figure easy to spot among the shorter Thais, Nikki heard her cell phone buzz. Digging blindly into her bag, she tried to keep one eye on the usher, who was now departing into the fighters' area, and one eye on the rapidly disappearing Z'ev.

"Hey," Nikki said, picking up the phone, expecting it to be Val.

"Nikki, it's Jane. I've deciphered a lot of the info you sent me from that SIM card. We're still tracking down numbers and so forth, but we've come across something fairly disturbing that I think you should see. It's a picture we found on Victor's phone."

A particularly resounding smack sent Scar Face to the floor, and for a moment Nikki stared directly into his face, with only a few feet separating them. The shock of eye contact made her focus on the fight.

"Jane, I'm a little busy at the moment. Can you tell all this to Val?"

"She's not answering her phone. I'll hang up, but I just wanted to warn you before I sent the picture."

"Yeah, OK, send it my way," said Nikki, looking for either Z'ev or the mysterious usher, but they were gone. She hung up the phone and threw it back into her purse. She had scooted to the edge of her seat, but was stalled temporarily, uncertain of her next move. Why wouldn't Val answer the phone? She brushed the thought aside and tried to focus on Z'ev, ignoring the faint alarm bell in the back of her mind.

Scar Face had regained his feet and bounced back into action. Scar Boy, in her opinion, should have been spanking Electro Hair, but apparently he was having an off night because he was slow to reach for an opening and the lighter Electro Hair was walking all over him.

"So," said Victor, suddenly sliding into the seat next to hers. "Who will be winning this one?" His dark hair was slicked back above his broad forehead and crooked nose, which gave him the air of having just slithered out of a swamp. An impression not helped any by his faux alligator skin button-up shirt with orange embroidered detailing. Nikki froze in position.

"The guy with the scar," she said, hoping she sounded conversational and cool. "If he gets his act together."

"Not going to happen," answered Victor smugly.

She glanced around, hoping Z'ev would come back.

"I think maybe I should go," she said, starting to stand.

"I think you should stay with me," said Victor, grabbing her wrist and yanking her back into the seat. "Where is he?"

"Where's who?" asked Nikki, playing dumb.

"Don't lie to me," he said, his grip on her wrist tightening to a painful level. "Where's Jim? I know he's here somewhere. Tell me where he is."

"I don't know what you're talking about," Nikki said, trying to regain control of her mind. She had trained for this. There were things she was supposed to do. There was a checklist. Step one: assess threat level. OK, yup, Victor seemed a danger to her physical self and to the mission. Step two: formulate escape plan. Uh . . .

"You think I didn't see the two of you at the club last night? He's up to something, and I think you're going to tell me what it is. Aren't you, pretty girl?"

He shook her arm, jerking her whole body back and forth, and for the first time Nikki looked him in the eye. She'd had enough.

Step three: execute plan with the full force necessary.

Riot, Part Deux

From the fighters' entrance a noise erupted. Nikki and Victor both looked up to see a man dressed in a short-sleeve yellow button-up shirt and brown polyester slacks come running down the aisle toward the ring. He was dripping blood from a cut over his eyebrow. He reached the ring and grabbed for one of the fighters, shouting something in Thai. The entire arena burst into shouts and yells. From the betting section came an immediate flurry of paper and screams. The entire arena seemed to be stampeding for the ring.

Seizing the opportunity, Nikki snapped her arm out of Victor's grasp and hit him in the face with the nearest thing to hand—her purse. She knew it was a girlie move, but her purse did pack a significant heft, and he jerked back in surprise and pain. Dodging away, she made it to the aisle and began to battle her way toward the exit. She glanced over her shoulder, checking to see if Victor was following, but he was being pushed toward the ring and away from her. Arriving in the front hallway, breathless and skidding on spilled drinks, she looked around for an escape.

"Nikki!" Z'ev was bullying his way through the crowd by his sheer height, and seemed to be dragging someone along in the wake behind him.

"Victor!" she yelled, pointing back the way she had come. Z'ev frowned, reached behind him, and pushed the someone out in front of him, bringing Nikki face to furious face with Lawan Chinnawat.

She was a small woman—slender and just over five feet tall. She wore her black hair in a no-nonsense shoulder-length bob and blunt-edged bangs. If it weren't for her determined and angry expression, her perfect cupid's bow mouth and almond eyes might have looked sweet. Instead, she looked as though she might start breaking things momentarily.

"In here," ordered Z'ev, shoving both women at a door.

"We can't go in there," Nikki protested, digging in her heels. "It's the men's room."

"So? You've been in there before," said Z'ev, recalling the Canada incident and what Nikki thought was a very inopportune moment, and pushing them through the door.

"Who the hell are you?" demanded Lawan, turning to Nikki.

"My name's Nikki Lanier," Nikki said, speaking quickly. "I work for Carrie Mae. Laura Daniels sent me to help."

"Sent you to help? You call this helping?" She gestured angrily around at the men's room. Nikki's phone rang out of the depths of her purse, but she ignored it.

"I didn't start the riot!" snapped Nikki.

"You are leading them right to me!" yelled Lawan.

There was a shuddering thump on the outside of the men's room door. Nikki's phone blared insistently, and there was another crash on the bathroom door.

"I think," said Nikki, breathing deeply. "I think it would be better if you went in here." She indicated a stall.

"I'm not hiding in a stall," Lawan said flatly.

"Well, unless you have Tony Jaa skills that I don't know about," Nikki said, pushing Lawan in and shoving her purse at the angry woman, "I really think you should." She reached into her purse, extracted the stun gun, and pulled the stall door shut, just as the bathroom door broke off its hinges, sending Z'ev and Victor sprawling across the floor. Closely following them were two equally burly men. Victor was the kind of man who traveled with a pack.

"Get her!" yelled Victor, pointing at Nikki. Whatever he had been going to say next was cut off as Z'ev threw him into a stall. The two goons were clearly torn between helping their boss and following instructions.

"Your move, fellas," Nikki said, palming the stun gun and hoping she didn't sound as scared as she was. The two men split up, one going after Z'ev and the other reaching for Nikki. He was surprisingly fast, but she was ready for him. She faded left and kicked him in the stomach. He grunted and spun around after her. Dimly she was aware that there was suddenly a great quantity of water spraying in the air and her phone was still beeping. The goon closed the distance, reaching for her neck, but he never got that far as she slid the stun gun out and up into the soft spot under his jaw. The man dropped, hitting the floor with a smack that made her wince.

She looked up to see how Z'ev was doing. The bathroom was covered in water from a spraying pipe that had been wrenched from the wall. Z'ev was in the process of giving the second goon a swirlie. Victor was shaking his head, staying upright only through the aid of a urinal. Just as Z'ev stood back from the unconscious man, Victor recovered from his stupor, lunged forward, gripped Z'ev in a bear hug, and heaved him into the air. Z'ev cracked his head backward into the man's face, then threw his body weight onto Victor's grip. Victor, surprised by pain and slippery from the spraying water, let Z'ev loose. Z'ev landed firmly on his feet and sent the man stumbling back with an elbow to the chest. As Victor skidded backward in her direction, Nikki took advantage of the moment and jabbed the stun gun into the base of his skull. Victor made a high-pitched grunting noise and hit the floor, where he lay twitching.

Lawan came out of the stall, dropping Nikki's purse. When she saw Victor's body, her face contorted with rage, and she began kicking the prone man and screaming in Thai.

"Whoa," said Nikki.

"Hey," Z'ev said, his tone sharp and commanding. When Lawan didn't respond, he grasped her under the armpits and lifted her away from Victor, her legs still flailing.

"What goes on here?" asked a voice, and they all turned to find the room was suddenly filled with Thai boxers. Nikki recognized the one in front as the "usher" who'd given Z'ev the program. "Are you all right?" His question was clearly directed toward Lawan.

Z'ev put Lawan down, but she continued to yell angrily in Thai, pointing at Victor and then at Z'ev. At one point she even gestured toward Nikki, and Nikki tensed. None of the kickboxers was big, but they looked as if they'd been carved out of teak. They might only have weighed a buck twenty apiece, but Nikki was willing to bet that it was a buck twenty that bought a whole lot of pain. If this was going to be a fight, she was thinking she maybe should have brought her gun. The kickboxers made a move toward Victor.

"I can't let you take him," said Z'ev, stepping between Victor and the kickboxers.

"If you're not going to help," said Lawan, "then stay out of my way."

"I'm trying to help," Z'ev said, "but I have to do it my way. We need him."

"That doesn't help Lindawati," said Lawan.

"I'm doing my best," Z'ev said.

"Not good enough, government man," said Lawan, turning on her heel and storming around Victor's prone body and out of the room. The kickboxers went after her, leaving Nikki and Z'ev under the steady drizzle of the burst water pipe.

"They tore your suit jacket," Nikki said, picking up her purse and slipping the stun gun into it. She was certain there were more pertinent things to say, but it was the only thing that came to mind.

Z'ev glanced at the place where the pocket had been ripped from his jacket. "Yeah, they did," he said, straightening up. He turned to the mirror and wiped the blood off his lip with the casual air of someone performing a routine task. "Come on," he said, opening the door for her. "We're getting wet." He followed her out into the hallway. The sound of crashing seats and angry voices still came from the arena.

Picking up a janitor's broom, placed to the side of the hall like a piece of flotsam, he shoved it through the handle on the door, locking Victor inside. Then he flung his torn and bloody jacket casually over his shoulder so that none of the damage showed.

"What happened out here?" Z'ev asked as a few people ran by.

"I'm not sure," Nikki answered. "There was some sort of upset about the fight."

"Yeah?" he said, putting one hand on her shoulder and steering her out of the arena. She could tell that he wasn't really listening.

"Can I borrow your phone?" he asked, as they left the building.

The walkways were crowded with knots of chattering fight fans. Lawan and her kickboxers were nowhere to be seen.

"Um . . . yeah," answered Nikki, delving into her purse again, pushing aside the stun gun, her sunglasses, compact, and lipstick she was hoping was of the nonexplosive variety, before pulling out her cell phone.

"That button and dial," said Nikki, pointing out the call buttons. "But not those two! I haven't read far enough in the manual to figure out what they do yet," she explained hastily. She didn't want to mention that she was worried that he would push them and accidentally blow something up. He took the phone with one hand, but his eyes remained fixated on her purse.

"Think you've got enough crap in there?" He started to dial without looking, still staring. "And how do you fit it all in there? It's not like it's a big purse."

Before Nikki could respond, someone answered Z'ev's call and he walked a few steps off the path. Nikki stayed where she was, trying to process all that had just happened, but it was hard to concentrate over the sound of the phrase "government man" ringing in her ears. That could mean only one thing: Val had been right. Z'ev wasn't who he said he was. Nikki was suddenly very hurt and then very, very angry. Who did he think he was? Did he really think he could just go jerking her around like that? And who cared what she put in her purse? It was her purse. And no, she wasn't just going to stay put and wait until he came to claim her. She spotted a couple of tourists who had also been inside at the time of the fight and approached them.

"Hey, do you guys know what happened in there?" she asked, smiling.

"Took us a while to figure it out," one of the men said, his accent distinctly Australian.

"We had to ask one of the ring judges," said the other, also Australian.

"Turns out the fight was fixed. One of the trainers found out and they tried to stop him from telling, but he escaped."

"I knew he shouldn't have been losing!" Nikki exclaimed. The two Australians looked startled.

"You'll have to excuse my wife," said Z'ev, coming up behind her, the phone still pressed to his ear. "She does like the fights." He draped an arm across her shoulders, and the two Australians laughed as if he had made an actual joke. He nodded to the two men and walked away, effectively forcing Nikki to go with him. Nikki smiled for the strangers, seething silently.

As they walked away, she heard one of the Australians mutter, "Lucky bastard," which only reinforced her anger. Z'ev was lucky—lucky she didn't kick his ass.

"Yeah, OK, got it," Z'ev said, speaking into the phone. Stress made his consonants harder and more American than usual. "I'll get back as soon as I can. No, it's a call on the other line. Yeah, bye." He punched the Off button and without asking Nikki, answered the waiting call.

"Nikki's phone," he said. Startled, Nikki reached for the phone, but he leaned away from her outstretched hand. Nikki felt a slosh of panic. It had to be Val on the phone, and she was going to get so reamed for this. She held out her hand more emphatically, but Z'ev just grinned.

"Uh, yes, ma'am," he said, as his face made a dramatic change to serious and he handed her the phone. "It's your mother," he said with one hand over the speaker.

Nikki shook her head, backing away from the phone. He held it out with more conviction.

"Nikki?" Her mother's tiny voice could be heard echoing from the phone. With a sigh, Nikki took the phone from his hand and put it to her ear.

"Hey, Mom."

"Nikki? Who was that?"

"Oh, you know, just someone I met." She didn't want to talk about Z'ev while he was standing there.

"And you're letting him answer your phone? I don't really think that's wise. What if he goes through your phone book and copies down all your information and steals your identity?"

"He couldn't fit into my dresses," answered Nikki. Z'ev gave her a strange look.

"What? That is not what stealing your identity means, Nikki. Why do you say such ridiculous things?"

"I lent him my phone to call someone. You were on the other line."

"Oh. Well, I suppose that's all right then." There was a pause, while her mother regrouped for the next attack. "Is he good-looking?" Nikki gave Z'ev the once-over and Z'ev met her stare with a bland smile.

"Some people think so."

"Hmm. He had a nice voice. Is he nice?"

"Sometimes," Nikki answered.

"What does he do? He isn't a native, I hope?"

"He *says* he's a lawyer," answered Nikki, and saw Z'ev wince at her stress on his lie.

"Oooh, that could be good."

"I think it's more complicated than that."

"Well, still, he sounds promising: I won't keep you. But you said you'd call and you didn't call. I worry, you know."

"Yeah, sorry. But I've been really busy, and I wasn't sure of the time difference. I didn't want to wake you up."

"Don't be silly. As if I'd be mad at you for waking me up." Nikki considered pointing out that her entire childhood indicated otherwise, but she thought better of it.

"OK, I'll call you later then." Nikki hoped Nell would take the hint and hang up.

"Bye, sweetie."

"Bye, Mom." Nikki pushed the Off button and took a deep breath, releasing it slowly. "So," she said, turning to Z'ev, "Are we going to have another one of those conversations where you explain why something bizarre is perfectly reasonable?"

"Like your relationship with your mother?"

"My relationship with my mother is not bizarre," she snapped. "Besides, I'm trying to get over my mother issues. Now what about those guys in the bathroom?"

"It's taken care of," he said.

"What about Lawan?"

"How do you know about her?" he demanded sharply.

"My company donates to her foundation. She's one of the people I'm supposed to talk to here. She's the keynote speaker of the conference! Now, what was she doing with you?"

"You know we aren't really married," he snapped. "I don't have to answer your questions. Why are you worried about her, anyway? I don't think this kind of thing is your job."

"Carrie Mae helps women," Nikki said. "It is my job."

"Carrie Mae sells makeup," he said harshly.

"Hey! There is nothing wrong with selling makeup. Each Carrie Mae consultant is her own boss and earns her own money, on her own time. That kind of flexibility and extra income can really help families." She paused, realizing that she was giving the wrong impression. "And I only did it once. And besides, it's not like the experience was scar-free."

"You got scars from selling makeup?"

"I didn't say they were my scars," replied Nikki, avoiding eye contact, trying to figure out where she'd lost track of the conversation. "My point is that the Carrie Mae Foundation helps women, so it is my job to help Lawan. How do you know her? Why did she call you?"

"We're not having this conversation," he said, cutting her off and looking around while making shushing noises with his free hand.

The sound of police sirens could be heard in the distance, and Z'ev pulled on her arm, trying to make her move. "This conversation is bad for both of us. We are not having it."

"No," Nikki said, resisting. "Why don't you just tell me the truth?" He walked a step away and then came back, towering over her. Nikki held her breath, frightened for a moment, and then angry that he could do that to her.

"Nikki," he said, stepping away, as if sensing her sudden change in mood, "this is really not something you want to be involved in, and I'm not someone you want to be involved with. Let's just leave it at that."

He took her arm again and walked away, increasing the length of his stride, forcing Nikki to break into a trot to keep up. He slowed down to a walk again as they came out onto a sidewalk, putting his arm around her waist, attempting to blend in with the other strolling couples. But Nikki's spine remained poker straight and she knew that anyone who looked closely would notice the distance between them.

"What about you?" he whispered in her ear, which might have been romantic under different circumstances. "Do you always pack a stun gun?"

"Yes," countered Nikki, as if he were crazy for asking. *When in doubt, pretend you're the normal one.* "Particularly when I go on dates with suspicious 'government' men."

She could tell he was mad by the way he clenched his jaw, but as he opened his mouth to say more, a tuk-tuk pulled up to the curb. Z'ev leaned in to bargain with the driver, but Nikki recognized him immediately.

"Hey!" said the driver, smiling and pointing at Z'ev.

"Hey," Nikki replied, and climbed in without negotiating a price. "Mandarin Hotel."

The driver made a questioning sound and pointed at Z'ev.

"Meh," said Nikki, and she shrugged.

"Oh," he said, clicking his tongue in a *c'est la vie* manner as he started the engine.

"Hey," Z'ev said, quickly climbing in before the tuk-tuk could pull away. "I take it you've met before?" he asked, looking suspiciously between her and the driver.

"You could say that," Nikki said. "Just don't ask to drive."

"What?"

"Nothing."

The driver's presence forestalled any further conversation. They reached the hotel safely, and the doorman ushered them into the lobby. Nikki shivered as they walked into the wall of air-conditioning.

"I'll walk you to your door," Z'ev said as they got on the elevator. Nikki didn't reply.

"You shouldn't have been there tonight," Z'ev said, turning to her as soon as the doors closed, his voice harsh. Nikki didn't reply. "I told you I had to leave. Why'd you follow me?"

"I thought you were ditching me," said Nikki. This wasn't a conversation she wanted to have. She wanted time to think. "I don't like being ditched."

"I told you it was work related."

"Yeah, just exactly what kind of work do you do?" she demanded. He couldn't be angry at her; she was already mad at him.

"You know I'm a lawyer," he said, but his eyes wouldn't meet hers.

"Yeah. Right," she said. "The kind of lawyer who meets with a woman who's been missing for two weeks and gets in a fight with someone he's supposedly working with. And speaking of fighting . . . I've met lawyers before, Z'ev. They couldn't fight their way out of a paper bag, much less rip a pipe off the wall, beat someone with it, and then stick that someone's head through a toilet. And you said that 'we' needed Victor. Who's 'we'? And if you were working for the same place as Victor, why didn't Lawan go after you like she did Victor? It doesn't add up."

"Nikki, you don't get to be pissed," he said, clearly frustrated. "You barged into someplace you didn't belong."

"Trust me, Z'ev, I can be pissed if I want to. It's a free country." She paused to take a mental rundown of the Thai government. Yes, it was a free country, mostly. "And besides, I didn't barge in. You invited me when you asked me to marry you."

"Well, now I'm uninviting you." He was growling through the sentence, trying to maintain a grip on his temper.

"Oh, that's right," Nikki said bitterly. "We're divorced."

The elevator door opened and Nikki marched briskly out, tugging on the key card in her purse. The more she thought about the evening, the madder she became. The card slipped through her fingers, and Z'ev picked it up.

"Nikki," he said, holding out the card. She snatched the card out of his hand and slammed it into the door slot. "I didn't mean it to sound like that. It's just . . . it's just not safe to be around me. Would you just listen?"

"To what? Your lame explanations? You're a government agent. Why don't you just admit it?"

"Nikki!" he said sharply, and looked in both directions down the hallway. "Nikki," he said again, lowering his voice, "I have a job to do and you are putting it and a lot of other people in jeopardy. Do you understand?"

"Oh, I understand," she said, refusing to be quieted. "I understand just fine. You're a liar. I said it in Canada and I'm saying it now—liar. I'll tell you what, Z'ev, next time you need to be hauled out of a bathroom, call someone else. I've got better things to do with my time."

On that final note, she slammed the door shut in his face and leaned against it, breathing hard. In the following silence, she heard her phone beep sadly, indicating a missed call.

Universal Truth

Nikki threw her purse at the bed and spun around to look through the peephole. Through the fish-eye perspective, she saw Z'ev raise his hand as if to knock on the door, drop it again, and then shake his head before walking back toward the elevators. She counted to ten and then opened the door. The elevator doors were firmly closed and Z'ev was nowhere in sight.

Nikki marched out into the hall and across to Val's door. She gave it a hearty knock and waited, composing her speech to Val. It was going to be a towering tirade of a wronged woman, but after standing in the hallway shifting from foot to foot she realized that not only had Val not answered the door, she hadn't even heard the telltale rustle of movement from within the room.

Nikki felt a shiver of oncoming fear, like the first wavelet caressing the beach before a tidal wave. She knocked again—harder this time, but the answer remained the same. Down the hall another door popped open and a man's head appeared, annoyance scrawled across his face like graffiti. She gave an apologetic smile and retreated to her room.

Where was Val? They had been attacked at the gun shop. What if after she had left Val at the restaurant there had been an *incident?* What if by leaving Val to chase the myth of a trustworthy man she'd left her partner vulnerable? What had she been thinking?

Nikki sat down on the bed and put her head in her hands, breathing deeply. There had to be an explanation. Val was following Nikki and hadn't gotten back yet. Val had gone to talk to Laura Daniels. Val was tracking some as-yet-undiscovered clue. She could think of a few more, but her phone kept beeping repetitively, putting sonic periods in the mid-sentence of every thought she had. She wanted to sit down to take a breather, call a time-out, have some time to think. Instead, she reached into her purse, fumbling through the layers. The phone beeped again, and she hurried faster. She dropped her purse, scattering items on the floor. She ignored them, concentrating on the one task of making the phone *be quiet.* Flipping open the phone, she expected to see a message from Val, and instead saw one unread message from Jane.

Belatedly remembering her brief conversation with Jane earlier in the evening, she opened the message and waited for the image to fully open on her screen. She glanced around the room before looking back at her phone, then wished she hadn't.

The image, even on the phone's little screen, was disturbing. A little girl of about nine or ten stared back at her from the tiny square—hands and feet bound and tied to a chair, her mouth gagged, but clearly screaming. The whole image made Nikki's guts churn.

She hit the Call Back button and dialed Jane.

"What the hell did you send me?" she demanded when Jane picked up.

"I told you. It's the picture from Victor's phone," Jane said, sounding impatient.

Nikki was afraid. All her mother's warnings about what happened to little girls who went outside alone or went somewhere after dark or just plain left the house seemed to have reared up in the darkest part of her mind.

"That's it? Just the picture? There's nothing to explain it?" Nikki barked into the phone, knowing that she was yelling at Jane for something that was not Jane's fault.

"There's the date and the number he sent it to. It was to a cell-phone account that's been closed out. We're working on figuring out who used to pay the bill."

"What about the date?"

"Two weeks ago. Same time frame as Lawan's disappearance."

Nikki rubbed her head. It was turning out to be a long day.

"All right, well, you're cross-referencing all of Lawan's known numbers or companies against Victor's phone, right?"

"I . . . uh . . . yeah . . . I'm working on that," Jane said.

Nikki could hear her typing in the background. "You haven't done that yet, have you?" she asked tiredly.

"I'm only one person," said Jane patiently. "And you're not my only case. It got bumped to the bottom of the priority list."

"Well, bump it back up," snapped Nikki. "A little girl's life might be at stake."

"I'm on it," Jane said, sounding hurt.

"I'm sorry, Jane," Nikki said. "It's been a long day, and to top it all off, I'm not sure where Val is."

"You're not the only one," said Jane. "Dr. Hastings put in like three 'request to calls,' and Val's ignored every single one of them."

"Is that normal?" Nikki asked, trying to fight the urge to curl up into a ball.

"For Val? If it's insensitive and inconvenient, it's par for the course."

"Jane," said Nikki, sinking down onto the floor and leaning against the door. "The number of things I'm certain about in this situation is limited. Victor's a bad guy, but I don't know what he's up to. Or rather, has been up to, since I think he just got taken off the playing field. Lawan doesn't seem to be missing, so much as intentionally absent. Lawan and Z'ev may be working together, but I don't know why. Z'ev clearly isn't who he says he is. I'm pretty sure he's some sort of government agent, but he's not about to tell me the truth. Sarkassian is a mystery. And now there's a little girl in trouble, and my partner is in the wind. I need fewer question marks, OK? I can't do this without help."

"I'm sorry, Nikki," Jane said, sounding distressed. "I know I'm not being the best informational specialist I could be, but Dr. Hastings keeps piling extra work on me. She knows I'm working with you and Val, but it's like she wants me to work twenty-four hours straight. At this rate, I'm going to miss something crucial, I just know it. But I will do better. I promise."

"Get Jenny and Ellen to help," suggested Nikki. "They might have a few minutes to spare you, and they know the situation. Dr. Hastings doesn't have to know."

"I . . . I might ask." Jane sounded depressed, and Nikki guessed that if she was willing to ask for help, then the workload must be significant. "Meanwhile, did you and Val get the map I sent? I collated Victor's most-called numbers and marked them on a map of Bangkok. I e-mailed it this afternoon."

"No," Nikki said. "I'll look now."

Scrambling over to the desk, she turned on the computer. As

she waited for it to boot up, she distinctly heard a click on the phone line and a sigh from Jane.

"That's Dr. Hastings paging me again," said Jane. "Can I call you back?"

"Yeah, sure," agreed Nikki. "I'll log in to the website. You can get me through there."

"Cool," Jane said, and hung up.

Nikki pulled up Jane's e-mail. Numbers, contact list, calendar appointments, etc.—all had been collated into neat columns that Nikki's tired eyes blurred over. Jane had also marked a map of Bangkok with Victor's most frequently called numbers, but as she commented in a dry footnote, all locations were subject to inaccuracy due to Thailand's high cell phone usage. Addresses were only good for billing; on-site confirmation would be required.

Nothing about the e-mail seemed particularly urgent. Victor called a warehouse owned by Rival Shipping most frequently. Second most frequent was Sarkassian's number. An unspecified business in the poorer part of town and a strip club downtown completed the list of most-called numbers.

The next e-mail from Jane contained the picture, and Nikki reluctantly opened it up to view it on a big screen. Once it was bigger, she could see something that she had missed the first time. Staring at the picture, she was convinced that she'd seen the little girl before—in pictures all over Lawan's home and office. It was Lawan's daughter.

Nikki leaned her forehead onto her hand. She felt hot and sticky, but immediately got goose bumps when the air-conditioning kicked on, and she shivered. She felt ill, then wondered if she should take a trip to Lawan's clinic. Her head snapped up and she pulled up Jane's e-mail again. Then she ran to her bag, pushing clothes out of the way in an attempt to find the sheaf of papers Val had given her on Lawan. Moments later she was comparing the business address on Jane's e-mail to the printed one in Lawan's dossier. There it was, plain as day. The third most-called number on Victor's phone was Lawan's clinic.

She brought up the phone log and looked at the dates on Victor's phone calls to the clinic. The calls went back at least six months and continued after Lawan's disappearance, so it couldn't have been about the kidnapping. If Victor had been talking to Lawan, it had been for another purpose.

"But why? She hated him." Nikki spoke out loud, and the sound of her own voice startled her in the quiet of the room. Thoughtfully, she reached for the phone and dialed Val. Moments later she was listening to Val's voice mail message. Frowning, she dialed again, this time trying for Laura Daniels.

"Have you found her?" was Laura's immediate response—not even a hello.

"Not exactly," said Nikki, "but I need to know about the clinic."

"What about it?" asked Laura, her voice sinking, and Nikki could picture her shoulders sagging downward.

"Do they carry a lot of drugs or anything that someone might want?"

"No," Laura said firmly. "They carry a very limited supply of drugs. Drugs are such a problem already that it's really a struggle to keep people clean. Why?"

"I saw Lawan tonight," said Nikki, still trying to sort through her own thoughts.

"You did?!" Laura's voice rose to a startling pitch, and Nikki jerked the phone away from her ear. "Is she all right?"

"Yeah, I think she's been hiding out with her boyfriend, a Muay Thai fighter."

"Saman? I called him," Laura said, sounding hurt. "He said he hadn't seen her."

"I also saw the guy from the clinic and the night club—Victor—and she definitely is not a fan of Victor's, so I'm wondering why her clinic is the third most-called number in his phone."

"Well, you wouldn't call the clinic if you wanted to talk to her," Laura said defensively, and Nikki realized that her question could have been interpreted as accusatory. "You'd call her cell phone. She's in and out too much to get her at the clinic."

"Sorry, of course," Nikki said, backpedaling. "But he is calling the clinic, so who's he talking to?"

There was silence on the other end of the line as Laura considered. "What's the actual number?" she asked.

Nikki gave it to her.

"That's Patient Records," Laura said. "The clinic has two numbers—one for the public, one for doctors or pharmacies calling in for prescription confirmation or patient records."

"Patient records?" Nikki repeated. "Like the ones Lawan had all over her office?"

"Yes," Laura said, slowly as if thinking, "she did."

"I don't get it. What's the connection?" mused Nikki. "What could Victor possibly want at the clinic, let alone in Patient Records?"

"I don't know," Laura said.

"Tell me about Lawan's daughter," Nikki said, realizing that Laura was going to be horrified if told about the picture on Victor's phone. She would have to handle this tactfully.

"Lindawati," said Laura. "She's absolutely darling. And so smart. She's supposed to be coming back for summer vacation soon. I called the school when Lawan disappeared, to make sure they didn't release her, though. I didn't want her coming back to all this. They wouldn't let me talk to her. They said it was against their security protocols." Laura sounded bitter. "I've been working the network trying to find someone with an in at the school. I'm so afraid that the end of term will roll around and Lindawati will be stuck there with no explanation."

"The network?" repeated Nikki.

"The people who can afford to attend boarding schools are a rather limited social group. I just have to find someone who's got leverage there who owes me a favor."

"You make it sound like the mob," Nikki said, and Laura laughed, but Nikki wasn't listening. She was thinking about Lindawati, who was clearly no longer at the school. Somehow Victor had gotten past the school's security. She replayed the scene in the bathroom, ignoring Laura. "That doesn't help Lindawati," Lawan had said. Victor had kidnapped Lindawati to use against Lawan, but why? Lawan had been investigating Rival Shipping in her office at home. She'd been poring over patient records at work.

"Nikki?" said Laura. "Are you still there?"

"The orderly," Nikki said, following her thoughts. "I forgot about the orderly."

"What?" asked Laura, nonplussed.

"Victor's been calling the clinic, and we saw the orderly hand him a disk. So he must have been talking to the orderly. Meanwhile, Lawan was investigating Rival Shipping because of her support for increased security measures at the port. She must have found out about whatever he and the orderly were up to—found the connection between Rival and the clinic—and they kidnapped Lindawati to keep Lawan quiet."

"What?!" Laura screeched, and Nikki grimaced. "That's impossible! Why didn't you tell me? I called the school. They said she was fine. We have to call the police immediately!"

"If Lawan thought the police could help, I think she would

have called them by now," said Nikki, and she heard Laura sigh in exasperation.

"I can't take this! Rival Shipping, you said? Why, I have a good mind to march down there and demand an explanation."

"Laura, that is a very bad idea," said Nikki, wishing she'd kept her mouth shut. "You have to leave this to the professionals." She was thinking of Z'ev and his mysterious government agency—it had to be the CIA.

"You're right," said Laura, clearly struggling under this command; her breathing was still labored. "I'm sure you and Val will find them and everything will be all right, but I'm so worried about Lawan. And God, poor Lindawati . . ." There was a stifled sob at the end. Nikki gulped, realizing that Laura was relying on her to be the professional.

"But what is it that they don't want Lawan to reveal?" asked Laura, sniffling into the phone. Nikki grimaced at the noise. "What could a shipping company want with a free health clinic?"

"I don't know," Nikki said, "but we'll find out, I promise. We'll find Lawan. It will all be all right." She tried to sound as if she believed it herself.

"I just wish there was something more I could do. I could go to the clinic and look at the patient records?"

"No, I don't think it's necessary," Nikki said quickly. The last thing she needed was one more person in danger.

Laura said goodbye and promised Nikki she would wait by the phone.

There was a mirror behind the desk, and as she hung up the phone, Nikki took in her reflection. Her eye makeup was smudged from the water in the bathroom. Her hair had decided that the humidity was unacceptable and was sending out tendrils as if seeking escape. The room was a disaster area: shoes scattered across the floor, her purse leaking onto the floor, clothes spreading like a slow lava creep from her backpack. Nothing was where it was supposed to be. She remembered the way Z'ev had looked at her purse in disbelief, and she sighed.

Her purse was a just a smaller picture of her suitcase. Her suitcase was just a miniature of the room. Her room was just a snapshot of how she lived her life. It was all the same: she jammed things in and then couldn't find them later, and all the things she could find were never the things she wanted. The universal truth that a woman was her purse hit her with an impact that left her ego stinging; it was something she wished she didn't know.

The instant messenger sound dinged, interrupting her misery.

I DON'T SUPPOSE VAL HAS APPEARED? Jane typed.

NO, Nikki typed.

DR. HASTINGS IS GOING TO LEAVE PERMANENT BITE MARKS ON MY A$$—GOT TO FIND VAL QUICK.

IS SOMETHING WRONG? Nikki typed.

DON'T KNOW, Jane replied, BUT DR. H HAS GOT A BUG UP HER BUM ABOUT SOMETHING. IT DOES SORT OF SEEM LIKE SOMETHING'S UP. NOT THAT ANYONE IS GOING TO TELL ME.

DOES SHE WANT TO TALK TO ME? offered Nikki.

I DON'T THINK SO, Jane replied. ACTUALLY, I GET THE FEELING THAT SHE DOESN'T WANT ME TALKING TO YOU AT ALL. SHE JUST WANTS VAL.

I NEED YOU TO WORK ON THE STUFF FROM VICTOR, typed Nikki. I THINK THERE'S A CONNECTION BETWEEN LAWAN'S CLINIC AND RIVAL SHIPPING. I THINK LAWAN FOUND OUT ABOUT IT AND THEY KIDNAPPED HER DAUGHTER—THE GIRL IN THE PHOTO. I NEED TO KNOW WHAT THE CONNECTION IS.

I HEAR YOU, BUT DR. H JUST DUMPED A CASE REVIEW ON ME AND TOLD ME IT WAS TOP PRIORITY.

At the desk Nikki fumed, drumming her fingers against the glossy wood.

FIND ME VAL, AND MAYBE I CAN GET BACK TO YOUR STUFF, typed Jane. Maybe? Nikki could practically hear the hopeful tone in Jane's written message.

I DON'T KNOW WHERE SHE IS, typed Nikki. She didn't want to tell Jane what she was really afraid of—that Val was either still mad at her, or that Nikki had left her vulnerable to an attack.

WELL, NOT TO BE FLIP, BUT YOU ARE A TOP-OF-HER-CLASS CARRIE MAE AGENT, AREN'T YOU? was Jane's response. FIND HER!

Nikki sighed. It wasn't that easy. Val was never that easy.

I'LL TRY, she typed, and got a smiley face and an abrupt TTYL back, before Jane's IM icon disappeared.

Party Like It's 1999 . . . Again

Without much hope, Nikki crossed the hall and banged on Val's door again. When no one responded to her repeated knocking, she went back to her room. If Val wouldn't open the door, she would have to open it herself. Rooting through the gadget box, she found the digital lock pick/eye shadow compact and went back across the hall. Moments later she slid into Val's room and flipped on the light. She wasn't sure what she had expected to find, but it hadn't been a perfectly ordinary room.

She toured the room, dragging her fingertips across the smooth fabrics in Val's closet. There was an empty hanger in the middle of a row of four dresses. The makeup was organized with rigid military precision. The clothes she'd worn earlier in the day had been tossed negligently across the bed, which seemed out of character. Perhaps it indicated some sort of time constraint? Perhaps she had dressed in a hurry? Her favorite pair of black stilettos

were present, but a pair of very expensive Manolos were conspicuously absent.

"She wasn't wearing any of that at the restaurant," Nikki muttered to herself, picking up the clothes from the bed and shaking
them out. A cell phone slipped from the jacket pocket and hit the
floor. Nikki picked it up and stared at the butterfly logo. Val had
left her Carrie Mae phone behind. Either she'd been in an unbelievable hurry or she'd done it on purpose. Neither explanation
was particularly satisfactory. Nikki thumbed through the menu
and hit the most recently called number.

"Mandarin Limo Service," a voice said.

"This is Mrs. Robinson," she said.

"Ah, Mrs. Robinson." The voice was polite and slightly eager.
"Did you change your mind about pick-up service?"

"Pick-up service?" Nikki repeated, stalling. "Uh, yes. That
would be good. Could you repeat the address?"

"Certainly!" the woman chimed, sounding relieved. "The
address was . . ."

Nikki snatched a pen from the desk and scrawled the number
and her best guess at the street name on the hotel stationery.

"Thanks," she said, and hung up the phone. What the hell was
Val up to?

Returning to her own room, she tiptoed to the bathroom and
peered in. The cube was waiting for her, she knew, the lid flung
open in a Grendel-like leer. Rachel had packed it with an infinite
variety of gadgets, and sooner or later she was going to have to
use one of them. Sighing, she approached the case and pressed a
button, then jumped back as a series of shelves telescoped out.

Letting the tiers and drawers sprawl out like octopus arms, she
surveyed her resources. Next to the official Carrie Mae equipment, she placed the Colt 1911. The black metal finish looked

extra threatening next to the graceful lines of the silver, gold, and purple Carrie Mae equipment. Peering into the depths, Nikki began to explore her options.

"Ooh," she said, lifting the lid on a small compartment. "Earrings." She remembered Rachel's pride in creating earrings that acted as a tracking device or bug and still looked cute. Picking up the earrings, she got closer to the kit—might as well see everything. Peering into the depths of the makeup kit she saw something made of a shiny, slick-looking fabric. Reaching in, she felt the unexpected weight of Kevlar, but holding up the garment, she saw it was no ordinary bulletproof vest.

"The Anastasia," she read from the label, and held up the bustier in front of her. It was hard to tell if the corset was designed for under- or outerwear, but it looked like it was her size. She pulled it on and took a walk to the mirror.

"Nice," she said, eyeballing her cleavage in the mirror. Rachel had done a masterful job on this one—it definitely enhanced her assets.

Returning to the box, she poked into another compartment. Small bottles of nail polish stood in neat ranks. The shelf below held lipsticks and a stack of compacts. Nikki sifted through the entire case and pulled out everything that looked useful. It was probably overkill, but she didn't want to be caught without the appropriate gadget.

From the bottom of the case, she pulled out the equipment manuals that Rachel had left for her. One cover read *Eye Shadow, and What You NEED to Know About It*, the other said *Choosing the Right Foundation for You*. Flipping through the pages, she tried to spot some useful nugget of information.

"How to construct a silencer from found objects and the contents of your Carrie Mae kit," read Nikki, stopping at one chapter title. Her eyes slid over the edge of the book and down the long drop to where the .45 was lying in wait.

In training, she had tried to picture herself shooting someone, but the thought had sent shivers through vertebra after vertebra until she shook herself like a dog after a swim just to get the feeling out. But now she was sitting pondering her next move. And that next move might very well involve guns.

Val had gone out dressed to kill in Manolos and a dress. That spoke of some sort of party or date, so Nikki should probably dress the same. But on the other hand, it could mean that she would be at a disadvantage should there be trouble.

She put on foundation and applied waterproof mascara, thinking of Mrs. Boyer. There were two types of missions: infiltration and assault. If Val was doing infiltration, then that left it to Nikki to do the assault. She didn't need party clothes; she needed sneaky clothes and comfortable shoes. That sounded right. Maybe . . . she chewed her lip and wondered if she needed a contingency plan.

Ignoring her doubts, she began to compile her assault wear. Proudly she pulled out the pair of sneakers that Val had bought her. Black and comfy, with breathable mesh, they were the perfect shoes for Thailand. The Anastasia, a black shirt, and black pants completed the look. She packed her gear bag and adjusted the strap so that it fit snugly against her back. She had packed the interior of the bag with regimented care, determined to fight the universal truth currently being spelled out by her purse and prove that she could be more like Val.

The address from the chauffeur service led her to a house. The house, unlike most others in Bangkok, had managed to retain a large parcel of land surrounding it, partly due to the fact that it was situated high up on a hill. From down in the street, Nikki could see that the first floor was lit up like the Fourth of July, and explosions of laughter and music shot forth into the night and rolled down the hill.

Nikki paid the cab driver and waited until he'd pulled away before scaling the wall and dropping down into the lush garden. There was a security system in place, and it took a great deal of dodging and weaving to avoid both the living security guards and the cameras stationed throughout the garden. Her bag of Rachel's tricks came in handy, and eventually she found herself sitting below a wide veranda watching the party from the dark. She could see the partygoers walking to and fro. One woman threw her head back and laughed, the pitch rising in intensity like a hyena. The dresses were both low and high, and the suits were all hand-tailored. Nikki knew she was not going to fit in dressed as she was.

She hung her head; she'd been afraid of this. Her perfect theory of infiltration and assault clothing was not working out. It was time to go to contingency plan Λ. Pulling off her black shirt, she revealed the cleavage-enhancing Anastasia and jammed a pair of Carrie Mae butterflies in her ears. Then she slid on a necklace that she was pretty sure was the detonator to the explosive lipstick, pulled a handful of water out of the birdbath, and slicked back her hair, wished she were wearing heels. She knew that even with the bustier she still didn't look appropriately slutted out. Black pants were a universal fashion, but the flat-soled sneakers were a dead giveaway.

She walked confidently into the house and straight into the bathroom, where she upgraded her makeup, slathering on a layer of lipstick and smoky eye shadow.

"Don't get close to an open flame," she muttered to herself, drawing a strange look from one of the women in the bathroom. "Too much hairspray," she said, and the woman nodded, but moved subtly away from her.

Coming out of the bathroom, she converted her bag to the 'stylish purse' option and went to find Val. Three propositions and a glass of champagne later, she finally spotted her. She was with Sarkassian, holding court in the main foyer. The sight of the Armenian made Nikki shiver—she really hoped Val knew what she was doing.

Sarkassian had his arm around Val's waist, and she had hers draped over his shoulder. Occasionally, he would steal a kiss during a pause in the conversation. He looked crisp in a white button-up and dark slacks. Val's silk dress clung in all the right places; the black fabric accentuated the pale luminosity of her skin. There was a band playing, and she heard Sarkassian jokingly call for Val's favorite song.

"'You Got a Fast Car,'" he announced, and Val smacked him on the shoulder playfully.

The band leader paused, clearly offering to play it, but Val waved him off.

"He's joking," she said, her voice carrying across the room. "He knows I hate that song."

Nikki shrugged. She'd always kind of liked Tracy Chapman. She thought about sending Val a note, but hesitated. Val seemed in control of the situation, and Nikki wanted to find out a little more about Sarkassian—maybe even find where they were keeping Lindawati. With Val occupying Sarkassian's attention, it might be the perfect time for a little search-and-rescue. Of course, there was a guard on the stairs; she'd spotted him earlier, a thug in a monkey suit, with an ill-concealed gun under his jacket. He had grimaced and flashed a Heckler & Koch MP7 personal defense weapon. Nikki's brain had run down the stats on a small-size assault rifle, but none of the numbers was going to help her get past the guard. She walked slowly toward him, racking her mind for a plan.

"I'm telling you," said a young man coming into the hallway from the other end. "My series on modern beauty has more to do with the harsh juxtaposition of softness against the cruel realities of the current era. The nudity is not gratuitous. The two of you should pose for me." He wore all black, had a girl on each arm—a blonde and a brunette—and a camera slung around his neck like an extra penis. Nikki wondered if he'd left his beret at home; he seemed like an unbelievable cliché of an art photographer.

"Hey," she said, approaching, "aren't you that photographer that does the modern beauty series?"

"Why, yes," said the photographer, graciously extending a hand. "I am."

"That's so fantastic," Nikki said, her Carrie Mae smile on full. "You know, I was looking at this security guard"—she gestured to the man by the stairs—"and I was reminded of one of your photos. You know, the one with the . . ." She left the sentence dangling, hoping he would fill it in.

"Oh yeah," he said, "the one with the soldiers during the coup."

"It's too bad you don't have any models here," she said. "It would be a good photo."

"We can model," exclaimed one of the photographer's companions.

"Uh, well," the photographer said, taken off-guard.

"Oh yeah, totally," said Nikki, nodding. "They're hot."

"Awesome," shrieked the blonde, and she ran to drape herself over the security guard.

"I don't think . . ." began the security guard, trying to disentangle himself.

"Don't think," commanded the photographer, already snapping photos, "just keep doing what you're doing. Baby, try to get the gun in there more."

"Here," Nikki said, grabbing the brunette and putting her into the picture as well.

"Yeah," the photographer said, "all three of you. Freaking *Witches of Eastwick*. I love it!"

Nikki stayed for three more frames and then crept up the stairs when the security guard had his face buried in the blonde's bosom.

The rooms upstairs were immaculate, and Nikki was slightly disturbed by the lack of clutter. It was as if Sarkassian lived in a hotel all the time. And there was also something about the upscale, vaguely Zen urban decor that reminded her of Val's house, although she couldn't quite say why. Perhaps it was the hard lines of the metal modern furniture juxtaposed with the ornate but serene Thai antiques.

Nikki walked slowly down the hall, listening carefully. The third door was slightly ajar and she could see the luminescent glow of a computer screen from inside. Ducking low, she tried to get a glimpse into the room from floor level. The room appeared empty, but she stayed low and slithered in carefully anyway.

It was a strange office. She had expected the room to be something like Sarkassian's wardrobe—expensive, hand-crafted, with European details. Once inside, she realized that she had been very mistaken. The office was much more reflective of the actual man than his wardrobe. The floor was a hard, dark slate tile with dark grout. One wall was a bank of louvered cabinets. She opened them and found the shelves filled with books and ledgers, a plug-in for the laptop, various bits of computer accessories, and one long cupboard, meant to be a closet. The desk was a smooth sheet of glass on what looked like a pair of ancient wooden sawhorses, and was occupied only by a small basketful of desk equipment, a laptop, and Sarkassian's Sidekick. There were two chairs in the room, both black leather with metal frames. Overhead, a ceiling fan moved the air in lazy chunks. In all, it was an empty, rather echoing place, full of hard angles and no unnecessary pieces.

Sitting down at the computer, Nikki pressed the Space bar, and the screen saver stopped moving, hanging in place for an instant before changing to a log-in panel. She chewed her lip. She had no idea what Sarkassian's user name and password were. She thought back to the computer classes in training. User names were most likely to be a variation of initials and names, with first initial and full last name being the most common. She typed JSarkassian into the User Name field, then hit the tab for the password. There was a rattling buzz and Nikki nearly jumped out of her skin. Sitting next to the computer, Sarkassian's Sidekick vibrated, clattering against the top of the desk. Seeing the Sidekick sparked Nikki's memory, and she confidently began to type in the letters she had seen Sarkassian feed into the phone so many months ago in Canada.

"H-i-c. Latin for *here*. E-t, meaning *and*. N-u-n-c. *Now*. She typed the last *c* on *nunc* and confidently hit Return. She'd puzzled over Sarkassian's password. Latin was unusual enough, but she wondered what *hic et nunc* meant to him.

The log-in screen disappeared and revealed the desktop. The desktop was as spartan as the office. No files labeled "Super Top Secret" or "Dastardly Plan—Option A" had been conveniently left out. Figuring that she could spend at least an hour poking around the hard drive and still not find anything, she headed directly for the e-mail.

"Corey100!@hotmail.com" had a long string of messages sitting in the inbox, and Nikki clicked on the most recent one. "Corey" didn't exactly sound like the name of a hardened Mafioso. It sounded more like an escapee from New Kids on the Block. Nikki found herself wondering just what kind of dirt Sarkassian could really be up to with a Corey.

THIRTY SOUNDS LIKE A PERFECT NUMBER. I TRUST YOU ON THE QUALITY; YOU ALWAYS SELECT THE HEALTHIEST STOCK. I'LL WIRE YOU THE AGREED-UPON PRICE. HALF NOW, HALF IN CASH ON DELIVERY. I TRUST VICTOR WILL BE THERE AS USUAL?

Puzzled, Nikki was about to click the previous e-mail and find out what "stock" meant when she heard shouting from the direction of the stairs. She quit the e-mail program and ran to the door, preparing to make a dash into one of the bedrooms or the bathroom. Peering out, she saw that Sarkassian was already halfway up the stairs. Behind him stomped two heavyset men and the orderly from the clinic. The orderly looked as if he were marching into the den of a lion. They were all clearly heading for the office, and with no options left, Nikki hopped into the closet.

"Shut the door," Sarkassian ordered, dropping into the desk chair and slamming shut the computer that Nikki had left on.

Peering through the slats in the closet, she could see the orderly standing nervously in front of the desk. One of the goons leaned against the door, the other lounged nonchalantly in the second seat.

"Where is Victor?" asked Sarkassian, straightening the basket of desk equipment to a precise ninety-degree angle.

"I don't know," said the orderly.

"Amein," Sarkassian said, "he went to talk to you. He suspected you knew something about Lawan. Afterward, he was supposed to call me with your answers. He hasn't called me."

"He came to see me," admitted Amein, "but I told him I couldn't help him. I was let go. They fired me. I don't know anything."

"Uh-huh." Sarkassian didn't appear to be listening. "Amein, I understand that being Thai, you might have some sense of affiliation with Lawan." Amein began to shake his head and opened his mouth to speak, but Sarkassian raised his hand, forestalling any comment. "I understand that, but I just don't care. You were paid money to give us information and to do it quietly. Instead, we got some damn political activist hounding our every move. Now I have to go out of my way to shut her up. That's expensive."

"I didn't tell her," protested Amein. Nikki could see a bead of sweat trickling down the side of his face. "I swear."

"Then you manage to expose Victor to the wife of the U.S. ambassador and a certain element that I would prefer not to get involved with. Now I've got to deal with that. And that's expensive, too. You are costing me money, Amein. I don't like things that cost me money."

"I didn't know that Mrs. Daniels was going to be there that day. How was I supposed to know?" Amein's eyes darted back and forth between the guard in the chair and Sarkassian, looking for some sympathy. Neither gave any.

"Let us return to my real problem: Victor went to see you, and he did not come back."

"He got a call," Amein said. "He asked me about Lawan, but I don't know anything, and then he got a call. He left."

"Uh-huh. And who was this phone call from?"

"I don't know. How can I know?"

There was the barest flicker of a glance from Sarkassian to the man in the chair. The man in the chair lashed out suddenly with his foot, kicking Amein in the leg, buckling the knee.

Amein screamed and fell to the floor, clutching his knee.

"I have other informants, Amein," said Sarkassian, remaining at his desk. "You were seen." The man in the chair got up and rolled his neck around, making the vertebrae pop.

"Seen? Seen where?" Amein wriggled on his back, away from the man.

"You were seen talking to Lawan. What did you tell her?"

"I didn't tell her anything!" Amein gasped.

"But you did talk to her," Sarkassian said.

"No! No. Why would I do that?"

"There could be several reasons," said Sarkassian, cocking his head to one side. "Personally, I think that it's because she paid you a large amount of money."

"No. No, she didn't." Amein shook his head, but even from the closet Nikki heard the slight hiccup in his voice. He was lying.

There was the flicker of a glance again and the big man lashed out with his foot again, crunching it down onto Amein's ribs. Amein lay gasping and making burbling noises. Inside the closet, Nikki put her hand over her mouth, stopping the shout that threatened to burst forth. She wanted to jump out of the closet and stop them.

"There's just no honor among thieves anymore," said the stomper, shaking his head. "We paid you first." There was another kick, and Amein began to cry.

"Thieves have no honor," Sarkassian said. "It's an oxymoron." He paused as if considering the broader truths of the world, and then shook his head, refocusing on Amein. "I expect as much, really, and in other circumstances I might be able to use this duplicity to my advantage. But in this case, you have information I need. I don't have time to play cat-and-mouse. I need to know where Victor is."

"I don't know!" said Amein, and his statement was followed up by another kick. "I don't know!" he screamed. And this time Stomper hit Amein in the face.

"Shhh," Stomper said. "We don't want to disturb the party guests."

In the closet, Nikki began to cry, tears running down her face. She covered her mouth with her hand, holding back any sound.

"Sorry, Mr. Sarkassian," Stomper said, holding up Amein's unconscious and bleeding head. "I hit him too hard."

"I think you bounced him off the floor," said the man by the door. "It's a hard floor."

Sarkassian uttered a profound sigh. "Get rid of him," he said.

"Get *rid* of him, get rid of him?" Stomper asked, making a finger gun by his temple and pulling the trigger. Sarkassian rolled his eyes.

"Get rid of him. Go down the back stairs. Dump the body in the river. And find Victor. I'm going to the warehouse." Sarkassian stalked from the room.

"I just like to be clear," Stomper said with a shrug.

"I know," the man by the door said. "But you know the boss, he gets short-tempered when he's worried."

"And when he's happy. And when he's sad," Stomper said, hefting Amein over his shoulder and following Sarkassian from the room. "And when he's had a bad meal. And when . . ."

THAILAND XII
Before

Nikki let out her breath in a ragged gasp and wiped the tears from her face. She had never felt so powerless in her life. How could she have just sat there and let them do that to Amein? Along with her guilt, there was the adrenalized rush of relief that it hadn't been her. She opened the closet door and stood up. Her legs felt shaky, but with a determined sniff she went after Amein.

Once in the hallway, she headed for the last door. The others had opened onto rooms. It was the only door she hadn't tried; it had to be the back stairs. She pulled open the door to stairs, felt for the wall. It was dark as pitch, and she wasn't at all sure where the floor was. Stairs presented themselves, and she hurried down them, her footfalls making a rhythmic thump that sounded too loud in her ears. A dusty beam of cold light streaming through a window above the door showed her she had reached the end of the stairs. She had one hand on the door handle and one hand on her 1911 when she heard the sound of an engine turning over and the creak of a gate being opened.

Nikki yanked open the door and looked around. It was a wide cobblestone area linked to a multicar garage. Expensive cars glimmered in the moonlight. But the car with Amein was already pulling through the gate and out to the street. She had to go after him. And she had to get Val away from Sarkassian. Torn, she hesitated, and as she hesitated, there was a surge of light and noise from the main house. She whirled in time to see the door to the stairs click shut. She grabbed the handle and pulled, but it had automatically locked.

She sprinted into the garage—the only cover available. For a moment she considered hiding in one of the cars and then decided that, with her luck, that would probably be just the car Sarkassian picked. Instead, she took shelter behind a workbench and tool chest. She had barely hidden herself when the lights flicked on.

"I don't know why we have to go right now," said Val, and Nikki's heart sped up. "I was having a good time." Thinking of Val alone with Sarkassian made her sweat. Sarkassian was a cold-blooded killer. There was no telling what he would do next.

"Business first" was Sarkassian's blunt reply.

"Isn't this a Leopard Roadster?" Val asked. Nikki could just see her around the corner of the toolbox, running her fingers along the edge of the convertible in front of Nikki.

"Yes," Sarkassian said casually, but Nikki heard a slight tinge of pride.

"Are you sure it's not a knockoff, like everything else in Asia?" asked Val teasingly.

"They only made twenty-five of them. They're all numbered. It is very rare and very expensive."

"Yes," Val said, lounging against the Leopard with an unspoken sexiness that Nikki envied. "But it's Polish."

"Funny," Sarkassian said, leaning in as if he were going to kiss her. Instead, he opened the car door under her bracing hand. The result was a slightly ungraceful change in Val's position. Val gave him a warning look that would have frozen Nikki, but Sarkassian just smiled, his eyes crinkling in unvoiced laughter.

"Get in," he said, opening the door wide for her. His smile made it more of an invitation than a command.

As Sarkassian rounded the front of the car, Nikki realized two things. The first—Val was much better at being undercover than she was. The second—Val was leaving with a man who had just ordered the death of Amein. There was no choice now. Amein was beyond her reach, but Val was right here. She had to choose rescuing her partner over rescuing Amein. Thinking quickly, she yanked out an earring, snapped the post down—as per Rachel's instructions—and heard the activating beep. The tracker was on. As the convertible rumbled into life, Nikki tossed the earring in an underhand arc that dropped it into the backseat of the roadster.

Sarkassian pulled out into the courtyard and then up to the gate that opened automatically. Hurrying, Nikki ran out after them, trying to keep to the shrubbery and shadows, but still make it to the gate before it closed. Breathing hard, she dove through the gate and sprinted for the tree line at the edge of the property. She heard a shout from the guard at the gate, but she was already dropping down into the neighbor's yard. By the time he looked over the fence into the neighbor's yard, she was already gone.

Panting, she continued running, trying to reach a busy intersection where she could hail a cab. She needed transportation. She could not leave Val alone out there with Sarkassian. She finally found a main street, but taxis whizzed by without stopping.

Reaching into her bag, she pulled out her shirt and what appeared to be a small blush compact and pressed down on the raised butterfly icon, just as Rachel had shown her. The mirror portion faded and became an LCD display, showing a grid pattern and a central blinking dot. The blush well flipped over and became a small panel of buttons. She punched a few of the function keys and hoped she wasn't inadvertently starting World War III. GPS coordinates appeared, and the map began to fill in. All she needed now was a cab.

She pulled her shirt on and walked to the corner, raising her hand and waving wildly at a taxi as it drove past. It didn't even slow down. She spent what felt like an eternity walking and waving before a tuk-tuk finally slowed down and pulled up to the curb. By that time, the blinking green dot had stopped moving on her screen.

"Hi," Nikki said, leaning in, and then stopped when she recognized the tuk-tuk driver. Was he following her? Bangkok was a big city. She could not just keep bumping into him by accident. Similar thoughts appeared to be going through the tuk-tuk driver's mind because they spent a long moment staring into each other's eyes, like gunfighters waiting for the final tick of a clock.

Nikki gave in first. "I need to go here," she said, holding up the compact.

"GPS," he said, taking the compact from her and examining the screen carefully.

"Yes," Nikki agreed. "Go there." And she pointed emphatically at the dot.

He looked doubtful. "No driving," he said. Nikki nodded. "No boy?" She shook her head, assuming he meant Z'ev, and the driver shrugged. "OK." He handed the compact back and revved the engine. Nikki climbed into the backseat and prayed that he knew where he was going. She didn't have time to waste on a wild goose chase.

She spent the drive crafting a careful text message to Jane. In the end, FOUND VAL. POSSIBLE TROUBLE. CONTACT AGAIN SOON was what went out, but it didn't seem to have the immediacy that she wanted to convey. On the other hand, she was hoping it didn't make her sound like the freaked-out wreck she was, either.

The driver pulled up at the end of a very dark street and looked around nervously. The river was in front of them and warehouses loomed around them. He pointed down the pier, where a warehouse showed a few lights in the windows. Nikki reached into her bag and pulled out binoculars. Through them, she recognized the Leopard Roadster sitting behind a chain-link fence patrolled by armed guards.

She tried not to sweat in her all-black clothes. It was the Carrie Mae–approved breaking-and-entering outfit, but she sensed that it hadn't occurred to Rachel to test the high-tech fabrics in the sweltering heat of a Bangkok night. She peered through the binoculars and tried to ignore the bead of sweat rolling down the inside of her upper arm.

She scanned the roofline and then the waterline. With a sigh, she realized that the most convenient access point really would be from the waterside. It was a depressing thought. It meant that she was going to have to get wet.

"OK," she said, handing some cash to the driver. "Thanks."

The driver made a questioning noise and pointed at the warehouse.

"Yeah, I'm going in there," Nikki said. "My friend is in trouble. I have to go get her."

He cocked his head to one side, frowning. Clearly he thought she was crazy. She wished she could explain the whole thing to him. She thought about asking him to wait, but all of that was silly. Even without the language barrier and the fact that she wasn't supposed to reveal Carrie Mae to anyone, it was her fight. She couldn't expect anyone else to take an interest.

"Thanks," she said again, and walked away.

As she walked, she extracted various bits of gear from her bag and put them on. Hood and mask, gloves and booties, knife strapped to her belt. She knew she looked like a ninja frogman, but she felt like a cream puff.

The plunge into the Chao Phraya River wasn't as bad as she was expecting. The water was warm, but the occasional bump into the unidentified floating object caused her to bite her tongue in an attempt to suppress girlie squeals of disgust. She tried to tell herself that Michelle Yeoh wouldn't freak out over icky things in water, but it didn't help much. Her webbed Kevlar gloves made scaling the pilings easier, but she felt a barnacle cut through the leg of her pants all the same. The blood mingled with the water, running off her in ticklish trickles.

From the pilings it was a scramble over the edge of the dock and a game of hide-and-seek as she worked her way closer to the building without being spotted by the guards and then up a stack of cargo containers to peer through the high windows.

She pressed herself against the wall of the warehouse and tried to breathe quietly. Below her a security guard walked with the dull, thudding pace of someone who expected a boring night. Nikki felt a thrill of exhilaration as she realized that he was totally unaware of her. She waited until he had passed, and then wiggled her way closer to the window.

The inside was dimly lit, but she could clearly see that the warehouse had been divided into two stories. The lower was full of large containers and boxes, and the upper had been extended loft style only partway across the length of the warehouse. Nikki noticed with a sense of dread the ominous sign of a row of cargo containers being lined up on the floor. The doors were open, and workers appeared to be bolting metal frame bunk beds into each container. The stairs upward had been blocked off with a gate locked with a keypad. Anyone wanting to go upstairs would have to know the correct code. Her interest piqued, she climbed higher, working to get a better view of the second floor. Finally she had climbed high enough to stare through a grimy window into the upper story.

Row upon row of narrow cots filled the space, and on each cot rested a woman. Some not even women—girls barely old enough to claim puberty sat on those cots as well. Nikki felt her stomach drop. She looked back down to the main floor and counted up the beds and containers. Her head swiveled back to the loft. There were far more women than beds for those containers. They were planning on packing them in like sardines—probably only the strongest would survive. With the sudden clarity of a cartoon light bulb going off over her head, she realized what Sarkassian and Victor wanted with the patient records at Lawan's clinic.

These women were the healthiest stock. They had been vetted by a doctor, after all. Sarkassian had taken the patient records and then taken the women. And now he was going to sell them like human cattle. They would become slaves and prostitutes.

In horror, Nikki saw that Lindawati was in the nearest corner of the warehouse. The little girl sat with her arms wrapped around her knees, rocking back and forth. A chain led from her ankle to a pipe next to the cot. Nikki sat back down below the window and put her head between her knees, her mind racing. She felt like throwing up. She tried to examine her options and think clearly. She hadn't brought nearly enough weaponry to get all the girls out by herself. She needed the police. Possibly the

National Guard. She didn't care who. She just wanted it to stop. She needed Val.

Climbing down the boxes, she slithered into the shadows, heading for the front of the building. She'd seen a small prefab shed in there. Men had been wandering in and coming out with clipboards and paperwork. And Sarkassian's car was there. Surely, that's where she would find Val. She would know what to do. She would save them.

She found Val leaning against the office shed and exhaling a lungful of smoke in curling waves.

"Val!" Nikki hissed.

Val's eyes swiveled, but her head remained in position. "What are you doing here?" she whispered back.

"I figured it out," Nikki said. "We've got to get out of here!"

Val yawned, stretched, and walked away from the hut and toward the corner of the warehouse. Nikki followed her path, but kept to the shadows. When she turned the corner, Nikki stepped out into view.

"We have to get out of here," she reiterated. "We've got to get backup and come back here with the police or something."

"Get it through your head," said Val. "For us, there is no police."

"Well, we need some sort of help. We have to get them out of here."

"Slow down, Red. What's going on? What happened with the lawyer?"

"Forget the lawyer. You were right about him."

"I told you so," Val said automatically. "Now, how was I right? What's he up to?"

"Probably the same thing we are," answered Nikki. Val was still walking, aiming toward the edge of the pier. "He's government," Nikki continued, "probably CIA. He's probably investigating Sarkassian."

"Investigating Sarkassian for what?" Val's eyes looked like black slits in her face.

"I figured it out," Nikki said excitedly. "They've been bribing Amein to give them patient records from Lawan's clinic. They go through the records and select the healthiest girls and then they sell them and ship them overseas in cargo containers. The girls have to be healthy to survive the journey and they have to be poor enough to go to Lawan's clinic, otherwise someone would miss them. Lawan found out. She must have been about to go public, because they kidnapped her daughter to keep her from talking. Her daughter is upstairs in the warehouse along with the rest of the girls. We have to get them out of there!" Nikki finished her summation breathlessly. Val had stopped walking and was staring at her. The stare went on long enough that Nikki started to fidget.

Val finally pulled her gaze away and looked out at the river. "The Chao Phraya looks beautiful this time of night," she said.

Nikki turned to see what was beautiful, but saw nothing but the lights from the other side. "Sure," she said flippantly, her mood rebounding now that she had Val to back her up. "You can't see the water." She fiddled with the straps of her bag, cinching it down tighter on her back. Val's mood was throwing her off.

Val sighed. It was a sad sigh, as if Nikki had said something incredibly disappointing.

"You're funny, kid. You really are. I even kind of like you."

"Don't sound so thrilled about it," Nikki said, still staring at the lights on the other side. She wondered what stories were behind those lights.

"I'm not," said Val. "It would be a whole lot easier to kill you if I didn't like you."

Nikki turned around laughing, then stopped, staring at Val in disbelief. She recognized the gun—the silencer was new—but the sight didn't make any sense.

"Sorry, Red," Val said. Nikki looked left and right, for the guards. Val wouldn't point a gun at her. But they were alone, and Val's hand seemed perfectly steady. Nikki tried to decipher the look on Val's face, but couldn't.

"Why?" she managed to stutter out. "We're partners."

"Come on," said Val, looking angry. "Don't pretend you're not spying on me for Mrs. Merrivel. You don't really expect me to believe that we got paired together by accident or that you just happened to have met Jirair in Canada." She laughed—a barking, unpleasant sound. "I was nearly free and clear. I'd sold the house. Most of my money had been transferred to the Swiss bank account. No one suspected anything. All I had to do was disappear, and Jirair and I could have been sailing to Bali with no one the wiser. And then you came along, all wide eyes and innocence. I might almost have believed it, except for the Canada story—but that's what made you perfect, wasn't it? You already knew what was going on. She just needed you to put the nail in my coffin. Mrs. Merrivel must have thought you were manna from heaven."

"I don't know what you're talking about," said Nikki, enunciating every word as clearly as she could, as if her life depended on the transparency of language. She backed away from Val, one step at a time. She knew it was foolish. Val wasn't going to shoot her. Not really. But she backed up another step anyway. She knew the river was close behind her. "I am not spying on you. Mrs. Merrivel just assigned me to you."

Val shook her head. "Well, then she just signed your death warrant. At least you know who to blame."

There was an odd popping sound and Nikki felt a burning pain in her side. The gun popped again and Nikki felt the second impact in her torso. She took one more step and realized she was out of ground, out of time, and out of luck.

Down the Rabbit Hole

It was Orion's Belt that told Nikki she was alive. She had opened her eyes, or at least thought she had. But everything was darkness. Everything was the same temperature as she was. She couldn't tell where her body left off and something else, anything else, began. There didn't seem to be any sound, and when she opened her eyes she couldn't remember the feeling of movement, and so she wondered if she was alive. And then, through the clouds and pollution, she'd seen the dim outline of Orion, forever shooting at an unknown foe.

She opened her mouth and immediately swallowed a lungful of water. She coughed, her body contorting itself around the cough, and immediately gasped in pain. A shock wave of agony radiated out from her torso, manifesting itself as fireworks before her eyes and spreading out in rippling waves to the rest of her body. Freezing under the pain, she started to sink under the water again—she could feel it crawl up her nose. Her limbs began to move then, in an uncoordinated dog paddle fueled by panic. She tried to suppress her coughing, both to stop the pain that it caused and because of the realization that somewhere out there in the darkness, Val waited with a gun.

Taking a deep breath, she tried to figure out what to do. She needed a plan. Mrs. Boyer always said that the first step toward creating a plan was to assess the current situation: where was she, what was her condition, what were her assets? She didn't know where she was; everything was dark. She couldn't tell if she was bleeding or not; everything was warm and wet. Panic was rising in her. Panic and fear. She felt herself beginning to slip into the place where there was no thought, only instinct, and that made her all the more afraid.

"Assets!" she commanded her brain, and her voice was a frog's harsh croak in the blackness. Her only asset was her buoyant waterproof gear bag.

Realizing that her gear bag was really the thing keeping her afloat, and not her frantic paddling, she began to breathe a little more regularly. Painfully, she wormed out of the straps and pulled the bag around to the front of her. Wrapping her arms around it, she began to breathe a little easier.

The second step in creating a plan was to identify the problems. Problem one—she didn't know which direction to swim. Problem two—she honestly didn't know if she was bleeding. She'd been shot. There were two spinning worm holes of pain in her chest, but she was breathing. Which meant that she might pass out from blood loss at any second or she might be fine. Problem three—even if she did manage to live, she didn't know what she was going to do about Val.

The third thing wasn't really a problem, because she was probably going to die, and then Val would be someone else's issue, so she could just ignore that one. And she couldn't control the second problem, so she might as well act like she was fine. Which left the first problem—which way to swim? She tried to look in a circle, but from her vantage point everything looked black. She could feel the panic starting to seep back in.

Inside the bag, her cell phone began to ring. Even muffled by the fabric, she could tell it was her mother's ringtone, and long years of conditioning made the bumping rhythm of "Sympathy for the Devil" hard to ignore. It was her mother after all. She had to answer. And more than that, the idea of speaking to her mother made her eyes well up with tears. She wanted to talk to her—now, when she didn't know what to do. Her mother might not be able to fix the situation, and would probably just nag her into some sort of rash, rebellious activity, but at least her voice would be familiar.

Nikki pondered this and stared into the darkness. She'd managed not to answer many of her mother's phone calls while she'd been in Bangkok. She hadn't meant to; she'd just been busy. But the one time she actually wouldn't have minded hearing the familiar tone of her mother's voice, she couldn't answer the phone without deflating her only asset.

The river pushed against her in laughing little waves, and she glared at it angrily. It seemed to be mocking her pain. But it pushed against her all the same, pushing in one steady direction.

Gingerly, Nikki paddled the water and tried to picture the map of Bangkok in her head. The river bent and twisted, but mostly flowed north to south. She'd entered from the right bank, which made it the eastern side. So if the water was pushing against her left side . . . She bobbed around until it was. Then she was pointing east.

She kicked once and felt the responding fireworks of pain, which left her gasping and lightheaded.

"Can't stay here," she said out loud. She knew it was true, but staying there felt so much easier. "Change is hard," she quoted Mrs. Boyer to herself. "You must maintain momentum." She had thought Mrs. Boyer meant big changes—losing weight, becoming tougher, taking charge. She hadn't thought it meant little changes like moving her legs up and down.

Slowly kicking, feeling every muscle and where it connected to her stomach, she began to make progress. It was a long journey. Things bumped into her. She could feel fish occasionally nibbling at her fingers—she hoped they were fish, anyway. And after what seemed like an eternity, she thought she could make out a pier. Lower jetties ran out from the shore. Moored boats bobbed in profile. Nikki tried to identify Sarkassian's warehouse, but couldn't. None of the landmarks looked the same. Even the pier looked different. Nikki realized, as she approached a floating dock, that everything looked different, because it was different. She had come up on an entirely different pier from the one she'd started from.

Laughing slightly at her own stupidity, and in relief that she didn't have to confront Val immediately, she reached the edge of the dock and tried to pull herself up. Her arms shook, her body screamed in pain, and for a very long moment she thought she wouldn't make it, but at the last second she found a reserve of strength and pulled herself over the edge and onto the dock. She lay there a long time, feeling the rolling motion of the dock underneath her. Inside the bag her phone rang again.

"Please allow me to introduce myself . . ."

She tried to ignore it, but even the sound of her mother's ringtone nagged her to some sort of action. Slowly, carefully, centimeter by centimeter, she pulled up her shirt and felt for the spot where the pain was coming from. She put her hand down to her chest and felt the stiff fabric of the Anastasia. Remembering the Kevlar bustier encouraged her and she felt farther. There were two holes in the bustier—one in her side and one in her chest, the edges frayed and torn—and when she pulled her fingers away there was still the faint smell of river water and cordite.

It smelled sharp and burnt like shame. Nikki wanted to curl around herself and hide. She had failed. How could she not have known that Val would betray her? Of course, Val never really liked her. Why would she? Nikki was stupid and gullible.

"I should have gone after Amein," she said out loud, and tears leaked out of her eyes. His death was on her head, too.

Her phone rang again and with a sigh she opened the bag and took it out—giving in to the strident tones. Giving in to her mother again, adding another trivial failure to the mountainous pile.

"Hi, Mom," she said, putting the phone to her ear. Her voice sounded funny, but she couldn't say why.

"You answered, so I know your fingers aren't broken."

Nikki looked carefully at her fingers. Her nails were torn. She needed a manicure. And was that blood? That was going to hurt. Eventually.

"I think you're right," Nikki said. "They just look icky." She sounded a million miles away from her own voice.

"Would it kill you to call me? You know I worry." Her mother was ignoring her again. That was probably good.

"Yes, sorry," Nikki said, following the usual scripted answers. She felt disconnected from everything.

"Well, just be careful. You're so naïve. Maybe it's my fault for sheltering you too much, but I'm just afraid everyone will take advantage of you."

"Yes," Nikki said, twitching as her memory put Val's face in front of her eyes. "You're probably right."

"Are you all right, Nikki?" asked her mother sharply. "You

sound tired. You're not getting sick, are you? Maybe you should come home. It's all right if this job isn't working out. You can find another one."

"Yeah, maybe," said Nikki.

"Nikki!" said Nell, her voice shrill. "What's wrong? What did you do?"

"I didn't do anything," said Nikki. That at least was true enough. Why had she just stood there? "I just . . . it was one of the other women at work."

Talking was starting to hurt and other things were starting to wake up now. Her legs were clamoring for their fair share of the pain load. The breeze tickled a gash in her pants, creeping in to disturb the blood that seeped down her leg. Looking down the length of her body she saw that one shoe was missing.

Val wasn't going to be happy about that. She had bought her those shoes. Nikki reached up to rub her temple, but immediately dropped her arm again when it set off ripples of pain along her rib cage.

"Nikki, what did you do?" demanded Nell suspiciously.

"Nothing, Mom," Nikki replied, trying to keep the pain and tears out of her voice.

"Nikki . . . ," said her mother in the warning tone that promised untold retribution if Nikki even thought about lying.

"It's Val. She walked out on me. And the company. She . . . left everything for a guy who's a total dirtbag." She couldn't keep the tremor out of her voice, but she hoped her mom didn't hear it.

"Well, when a woman is in love," said Nell philosophically, "she thinks she can change—"

"Yeah, yeah, a man is a home improvement project. It's dumb." Nikki's pain flashed over into bitterness, and carefully she reached up to wipe tears out of her eyes.

"I was going to say," Nell said, irritation frosting her tone, "that a woman in love thinks she can change herself to suit him. She thinks she can make herself not care about the unchangeable bits of him. But you can't. You're always going to care."

Nikki didn't answer, aware, even in her aching state, that they were treading over very delicate emotional ground—cavernous pits of anger and bitterness were likely to open beneath her feet at any moment.

"The joke is," mused Nell, "that women do want to change a man. His clothes and whatever, superficial stuff, and really, all of that's for his own good. But it's women who change, trying to match themselves to what he wants. They try and try, but it's a mistake. You should never try to be what you're not."

"I shouldn't try to be what I'm not," repeated Nikki, hearing the death knell of her Carrie Mae career in those words. "Maybe I should come home."

"Don't be ridiculous," Nell said sharply. "You were in training only last week, and now you've been given a plum assignment. This career may not be perfect for you, but clearly they think very highly of you. You can come home after you get the job done."

"I don't know," Nikki said. Breathing was getting easier. She took a shallow breath, then another.

"Well, I do," said Nell, her usual demanding tone returning. "Now, what are you going to do about this Val woman?"

"I'm not sure," Nikki said, still at a loss.

"You should just do your little conference thingie on your own. You'll look like a hero, and everyone will know she dropped the ball and you won't have to say a thing."

"Yeah," Nikki said, trying to remember what cover story she had given her mother and what conference she was talking about.

"That's what *I* would do," said Nell. "I would just do it myself."

"It's not that easy," Nikki said.

"Get over it," her mother said crisply.

"I . . . ," Nikki said. "OK."

"Good. Now what I really called to tell you about was my week from hell with Mr. Van Der Meer. You remember me telling you about him? He's Dutch and has wandering hands. Which fortunately I know how to deal with, but poor Cissy, at the office . . . did I tell you we hired a new girl?"

"I have to go now, Mom," said Nikki.

"No, I'm telling you about Cissy. She wears false eyelashes and giant silver hoops . . ."

"I'll call you when I get back to the States. Talk to you soon, love you, bye." She hung up the phone, ignoring the irritated bleatings of "Nikki! Nikki!" and let it fall onto the dock, where it landed with an echoing thump. It was the sound of a hollow victory. She'd just hung up on her mother. Well, maybe not that hollow. She felt a slight tingle of warmth that spread up her arm from the cell phone.

"You're going to have to move," she told herself.

"But it will be hard," she replied.

"It's already hard," she argued back. She got no reply to that one, and decided to consider the matter settled.

"Stupid momentum," she muttered as she rolled over onto her hands and knees and began the painful, slow process of getting to her feet.

Staggering up the dock, she took stock of where she was. It was nowhere she knew. But looking along the shoreline, she guessed that she had drifted around a short bend in the river, and the fastest way to get back to anywhere was a long walk in the generally forward direction.

She had gone only a few steps when a headlight swept into view, pinning her in its glare. She raised her hand against the light, but knew that she was toast, history, done for. Instead of the sound of a gun or Val's angry voice, she heard a voluble stream of Thai.

"Bad men!" her tuk-tuk driver said, emerging from the vehicle. He grasped her by the arm and pushed her toward the back of the cab. "I look for you! Bad men!"

"Bad men!" he said again, and Nikki nodded her agreement. "Stupid girl!" he said, shaking his finger at her.

Nikki nodded again. "Stupid girl," she agreed. And he frowned, as he helped her into the tuk-tuk.

"You don't have to help me," she said plaintively, but not wanting him to stop, as he drove toward her hotel.

"Must help," he said, eyeing her in the rearview mirror, and then turning back to look at her as he paused at a red light. "Karma."

Nikki wondered what he'd done in a past life that could possibly have merited her. The night air of Bangkok flowed over her. It carried a hot, torpid smell of a city at rest, layered with car exhaust and the scent of fresh jasmine that tried to remind everyone of the sweetness of life, but could never quite compete with the cacophony that was Bangkok.

Her cell phone rang. Nikki eyeballed it suspiciously, not recognizing the phone number.

"Yeah?" said Nikki.

"Nikki, it's Jane."

"Jane?"

"I don't have a lot of time, but I need to tell you."

"Tell me what?"

"Don't call in."

"What?" Nikki was confused.

"Don't call in. Don't e-mail. Dr. Hastings is going to call you back to California."

"I don't understand."

"I don't, either. I think it's political. I talked to Mrs. Merrivel, and I'm . . . Yes! I'll be right there!" Jane was bellowing at someone else, but Nikki's head jerked back at the noise. "I have to go now. Don't call in. I'll contact you in twelve hours."

"Twelve hours? Jane . . ." But the line had already gone dead. "Shit," said Nikki, staring at her phone.

After Shot

They pulled up to the front of the hotel, and Nikki exited slowly, wincing at every movement.

"Thank you," she said to the tuk-tuk driver. She wanted to say more, but a language barrier and pain stopped her attempts to utter anything but the most basic of emotions. The driver smiled and shrugged, and Nikki shook her head.

"Why did you come looking for me?" she asked, not really expecting an answer.

"We must embrace the road," he said, gesturing out before him to indicate the path before them all. "Just not too hard," he added, and poked at one of her bruises. Nikki smiled painfully, and he drove off with a wave. She thought about not going inside, but realized that Val thought she was dead. The hotel was probably, the safest place to be.

Once inside her room, she stripped off her clothes, trying to keep what little momentum she had left, and examined the damage.

Her right hip had a raw gouge and a bruise that radiated out from it in a yellowish puffiness. Her back was laced with scrapes and scratches, and her legs also had their share of scrapes. But her rib cage showed the real damage, with three quarter-size welts that were already starting to spread and turn purple.

Nikki limped to the bathroom, waiting until the steam began to rise before stepping into the shower and pulling the curtain closed. Leaning against the cool tile, she felt each cut and scratch send up a painful wail as the water hit it. After a few minutes everything had settled back down again, and she began to take comfort in the steam.

The heat of the shower finally began to seem oppressive and her fingers were beginning to prune. She held out for a few more minutes, breathing in the warm, damp air and enjoying the torturous heat for the sake of the fact that the air-conditioned room would now seem cold.

She dried herself and applied Band-Aids on a need and reach basis. After spending a futile five minutes trying to reach a spot on her back, she reclassified it as "can't reach" and gave up. She delicately fastened on a sports bra and pulled on sweats. The sweats were junkable, but she didn't have any shirts she could afford to get blood spots on.

She was about to choose her least favorite shirt when she heard the sound of footsteps in the hallway and the click of Val's door being unlocked. She froze for a moment and then ran to her makeup kit. Pulling out the handgun and electronic lock pick, she went out to the hall. Through a crack under the door she saw lights go on in Val's room and a shadow pass back and forth. She quietly unlocked the door, put her hand on the knob, and took a deep breath.

Throwing open the door, she dove into the room, shoulder-rolled, and came up with a perfect target on the occupant of the room—who happened to be a small Japanese man. He held up his hands, his eyes wide. Nikki looked around the room in confusion. She could see none of Val's belongings.

"Very sorry," she said, getting up and lowering the gun. She took a glance in the bathroom, hoping to see a bevy of gold butterflies, but found only men's shaving products. "Wrong room." She smiled awkwardly and backed toward the door. The man hadn't moved. His hands were still up. Nikki reached for the door with one hand and waved goodbye with the other, realizing too late that she was waving with the gun hand.

"Very sorry," she muttered again, and jumped out of the room, slamming his door shut. After a moment she heard the lock click shut on his side. She walked quickly back to her room and shut the door.

"Well, that was embarrassing," she said to herself. Val must have cleaned out her room while Nikki was pulling herself out of the river. Nikki leaned against the door and thought about going down to the bar and getting blind, stinking drunk. It was a good plan. For one thing, it had clear, actionable steps. Pour shot, drink, repeat. Everything else seemed out of her capability. She couldn't even begin to list the problems she had right now, let alone form a plan for how to solve them.

She had just made up her mind to go with getting drunk when there was a knock on the door behind her head. She flinched and then took a firmer grip on her gun.

She opened the door and put the .45 in Lawan's face. Lawan didn't move.

"What?" Nikki said.

Lawan stared her down, ignoring the gun. "I came to ask for help," she said at last.

Nikki felt the bruises on her rib cage and the cuts on her back with a searing clarity. She couldn't even help herself. "You may wish to reconsider that," she said, lowering the gun.

"I hope not," said Lawan, brushing past her. "Because I need you."

"What are you talking about?" Nikki asked, shutting the door.

"I thought I could take Sarkassian on my own, but . . . he's got my daughter and I'm not any closer than I was two weeks ago. Laura called me. She said you found out about how Sarkassian's been using the clinic. I went to meet her at the clinic tonight—it was on fire."

"Laura . . ." Nikki said, picturing the worst.

"She wasn't inside. She got everyone out in time. But it's just the latest . . ." Lawan paused, clearly trying to maintain control. "He's going to take everything from me. I can't let him do that. Laura said you could help. I'm hoping she's right."

"Why'd you disappear?" Nikki asked, stalling and looking for a few answers.

"I thought that if they couldn't find me, they couldn't threaten me, and they'd have to wait until I turned up to make demands. Only, I guess they've learned from their mistakes. While I was talking to Laura, a child rode up on a bike and gave me a cell phone. Sarkassian says no waiting. A straight trade. Me for her."

"Wait, back up," said Nikki. "Just what the hell happened to you?"

"Bangkok happened," said Lawan with a shrug.

"Don't give me that crap," said Nikki harshly. "Don't shovel that 'it's a big city, mysterious East, you're a foreigner, you wouldn't understand' line of horse pucky because I'm not buying it! What happened? You were investigating the port, weren't you? Because of the antiterrorist bill."

Lawan made an impatient gesture that ended as she sank down onto the bed, her shoulders slumping in defeat. "That's where it started. I didn't give a crap about terrorists. I mean, sure, crack down on them, but really . . . it's about slavery. Women and children are being sold into slavery and shipped out through the ports. The problem has only gotten worse since the tsunami—so many children lost parents and support systems. They are even more vulnerable now than they used to be. I figured if they passed the anti-terrorist bill that they'd catch more slavers. Two-for-one special, as it were." She gave a hollow laugh. "So I was looking into it. Trying to find the biggest offenders and the most efficient ways of catching them. I didn't expect to catch one selling people out of *my clinic*." Her eyes sparkled in anger, her fist thumping on the bed.

"What happened after you found out?" Nikki sat down beside Lawan, wanting to hug her, but not brave enough to actually reach out.

"I tried to stop it. I couldn't wait for the police. I had to save the girls now. And that's when they took my daughter."

"How'd they get her?" Nikki asked.

"Airport. They tried to get me, but I fought them off. Then they took Lindawati."

"Laura said she called Lindawati's school after you disappeared, but the school wouldn't confirm that you'd been there."

Lawan nodded. "I pay them a lot of money not to answer questions from inquiring strangers, but, yes, I went to get her. With Sarkassian's international contacts I couldn't trust that he wouldn't be able to get to her. I was taking her to Saman's relatives, up in the hills. Once up there, I knew she'd be safe. But we never made it that far. Ever since then, I've been moving around the city, never in one place for more than twenty-four hours. I thought I could figure out a way to take him down, but he's got too many people and too much money. I can't trust the police. And now he's offering a trade—her for me. I have to risk it for my daughter's sake."

"He's not going to let either of you live," said Nikki.

"I know that," Lawan said. "That's why I'm here. You're my last hope. Laura says you help women in trouble—that you can't be bribed or bought or scared off."

Nikki stared into the mirror above the desk. Her skin, always pale, had taken on a greenish cast and her eyes looked shadowed and frightened. Her hair formed a sort of golden-red nimbus around her face. She looked like a candle flame and she felt just as easy to extinguish—as if all anyone had to do was blow hard enough and she'd dissipate like smoke.

"I . . . ," she began. What could she do? She was alone. She had already failed. Her phone rang. Numbly, she reached for it.

"Hi," Jenny said. "Guess where we are?"

"What?" Nikki couldn't form a coherent thought. "Guess, what?"

"Nikki? Nikki, are you all right?" Jenny sounded irritated, like she always did when she was worried.

"No," Nikki said flatly.

"Where are you?" Jenny demanded. "We just landed here. We'll come and get you."

"Who's we?" Nikki asked, trying to keep up. "Where's here?"

"Ellen and me. In Bangkok. We came to help. Where are you?"

Nikki took a deep breath and felt her lungs expand with relief. Things were going to be OK. She wasn't alone.

"I'm at the hotel. What'd you bring with you?"

"Just the basic equipment," answered Jenny.

"Guns," said Nikki. "You need guns, and I wouldn't mind having a helicopter."

"I can get you a helicopter," Lawan said.

"What time is the exchange?" Nikki asked, looking at Lawan.

"Ten," she answered.

Nikki checked her watch. There was less than three hours to go.

"What's the location?"

"They're going to call a half hour ahead of time and let me know."

Nikki nodded. That was smart of them.

"Nikki?" Jenny's plaintive voice sounded from the phone.

"Forget the hotel," said Nikki. "We don't have time." She gave directions to Jenny and hung up the phone. "Were you serious about the helicopter?" she asked Lawan.

"Yeah, it's just a little commuter chopper, but it's a helicopter. My friend uses it for tours and to chauffeur rich people around."

"How does he feel about maybe getting shot at?"

Lawan looked thoughtful. "Probably OK. Some of his clients are drug dealers."

"Great," said Nikki. "Then we've got a chance."

Second Gear, Hang on Tight

It had taken a few minutes to get dressed and get Lawan committed to the plan. And a couple more minutes to convince Lawan to lend her a motorcycle, but eventually Nikki found herself staring through dirty windows at elephants, with their perennial layers of dust, at the antiques store where she and Val had purchased the guns.

She slipped down the back alley to survey the back of the shop. It wasn't any cleaner, but it did at least have the appearance of use. Using a conveniently placed drainpipe, she climbed up onto the second-story balcony of the neighboring building and then onto the roof. There was a small roof garden and a few sun-bleached wooden chairs. Nikki took out her gun and tried the handle of the flimsy door that led to the inside of the shop. It was locked, which surprised but didn't deter her.

Her phone rang, buzzing in her pocket.

"Hey, Ellen," she said, flipping it open.

"We're here," said Ellen. "I think. Elephants in the window, right?"

"That's the place. I'm going in through the back. Give me . . ." She checked her watch and eyeballed the door. "One minute twenty and come in the front."

"Got it," said Ellen. "Starting the clock now."

"Yup," agreed Nikki, and she hung up.

A firm stomp from Nikki's foot ended the door's resistance. No one came running, so she continued her journey down the stairs.

The stairway from the roof was a narrow, dark place with low ceilings. She crept out of the stairway and into a second story filled with large wooden crates. A quick peek in the crates revealed stack after stack of guns, in all shapes and sizes. A foldaway cot and small electric range burner, along with various other living items, told her that this floor was used for more than storage.

She ignored it all and opened the door to the first floor. Downstairs she could hear Kovit yelling loudly into his phone. He switched frequently from Thai to English, and it was difficult to follow the conversation. He hung up the phone and threw it across the room.

"Jeez, Kovit, that's no way to treat the hardware," Nikki said, strolling down the stairs, her gun leveled at his chest. He spun around and swallowed hard. He made a sort of jerking motion toward the desk, but Nikki beat him to it and then cracked him across the face as he ran toward her. She removed his gun from the drawer and leaned against the desk, trying to look cool. Her free hand was beginning to shake, so she stuffed it into her pants pocket. She'd never questioned anyone before.

"What do you want?" asked Kovit, wiping blood out of his eyes.

"Mrs. Robinson," Nikki said.

Kovit laughed. "Do you know who her boyfriend is? Do you know who my main supplier is?"

"Jirair Sarkassian," said Nikki. "I want him, too."

"And Victor, too, I suppose," Kovit said bitterly.

"Nope, he's taken care of."

"I suppose you've got him tucked away somewhere, while Sarkassian scours the city?" He was slowly edging toward the door to his showroom. She wondered if he thought she was too stupid to notice. There was a wide filing cabinet by the door, and she guessed there was a gun hidden in that general area.

"Not exactly, but let's just say Victor is out of the way. Why don't you give me Sarkassian and Val, and we'll make it a clean sweep?"

"Well, aren't you smart?" he said bitterly.

"Smarter than you," she said, as he dove for the door.

There was the sharp smacking sound of fist on flesh, and Jenny dragged Kovit back into the room.

"Hi," said Jenny.

"Hey," Nikki said.

"There's more of you?" Kovit sounded furious.

"There's a whole freaking army, sweet pea," Jenny said, patting him on the side of the face with a soft slapping sound.

"Hi, honey," Ellen said, coming in. "What do you need us to do?"

"Clean him out," Nikki said. "The guns are upstairs. Take whatever you need."

"What?" yelled Kovit, lunging forward. Jenny yanked him back by his hair. "You can't do that. That's my merchandise."

"Not anymore," Nikki said. Ellen marched upstairs, taking a couple of duffel bags with her.

"Mrs. Robinson is going to kill you," he said sullenly.

"She already tried that," said Nikki, ignoring Jenny's startled look. "It didn't take. But wouldn't you like her to have a second try?"

"Yes," he said, squirming under the pressure of Jenny's hand.

"Then tell me where they're meeting this morning," said Nikki reasonably.

"I don't know," he answered, watching her with angry eyes.

"But you know people," Nikki pointed out. "You can find out."

"They'll kill me," he said.

"Hell, son," Jenny said. "I'm going to kill you way before they do."

Kovit looked from Jenny to Nikki as if trying to assess how serious they were.

"She's probably serious," said Nikki. "But let me put it to you this way . . . if you're so sure they're going to win, then what's it hurt to send us to them? And if we win, then they can't kill you, can they?"

"She's right," Jenny said, pulling his head back to look him in the eye. "It's a win-win situation for you."

"I found lots of good stuff," Ellen said, lugging the first duffel bag down the stairs. "Did you know he has a whole crate full of the old-school Dragunovs?"

"Yeah, yeah," Kovit said, "there's been a glut in the market since the Soviet Union fell and Russia upgraded the stocks. Take as many as you want."

"No, thanks," Ellen said cheerfully. "I took one of the H&K PSG1s."

"What? No! Do you know how much I can get for that? Put it back!"

"No," Nikki said. "She's going to take that one and whatever else she wants, and you're going to tell us where the meeting is this morning because you want us to leave."

Kovit glared at her.

"If you don't think she can get a truck here in twenty minutes to take *all* of your merchandise, you are sorely mistaken, my friend," said Jenny, beaming at him.

"I need a phone," he said. "I have to make some calls."

"Sure," said Nikki, flipping open her phone, "but let's put it on Speaker."

Twenty minutes later, they had a location.

"Yeah, sure," said Kovit's contact. "Everyone knows it's going down over at Ratchadamnoen and Atsadang. Sarkassian owns a building there. I think he wants to remodel anyway, so no biggie if shit goes down, right?"

"Right, right," Kovit said. "Thanks, Racha."

"Yah," said Racha, and he hung up.

"Ratchadamnoen and Atsadang," Kovit said. "Just before the bridge on the north side. You leave now? Yes?"

"Sure, sure," Nikki said, imitating his speech pattern and yanking his phone line out of the wall. "After we tie you up." She tossed the cord to Jenny. Jenny went immediately to work trussing him up like a calf at a rodeo.

"What was my time?" she asked, stepping back and throwing up her hands.

"I wasn't timing," Nikki said.

"Oh shoot," said Jenny.

"You're going to pay for this," Kovit yelled.

"Nope," Jenny said, shoving a shop rag in his mouth. "I don't really think I am."

The girls walked out of the shop, with Jenny and Ellen each carrying a duffel bag full of weaponry. They had left a cab waiting for them

Nikki paused, looking at her friends.

"How are you guys even here?" she burst out, and Jenny laughed, running to hug her.

"Mrs. Merrivel sent us," Ellen said, hugging Nikki, too.

"I thought we were being recalled?" asked Nikki, mystified.

"That's Dr. Hastings," Ellen said. "There's some sort of situation going down back at headquarters, I think over you and Val, but Mrs. Merrivel was pretty tight-lipped. She just said she thought you'd need us. She didn't exactly tell us to go, but she made it pretty clear."

"And she left her planner open on her desk," said Jenny. "It had your name and an address for the Mandarin Hotel."

"So we figured we'd better come," Ellen said.

"I'm really glad you did," said Nikki gratefully.

"Well, good," said Jenny. "I'd hate to spend that long on a plane and not be needed."

Nikki laughed and hugged her again.

"Enough with the hugs," said Jenny, looking embarrassed. "We've got to go save people, right?"

"Right," agreed Nikki. "You gave the address to the cabbie?" she said to Jenny. "I'll see you there?"

"With bells on!" Jenny said with a wink, getting into the cab behind Ellen.

Nikki headed back to her motorcycle and couldn't help but let it squeal a little around the first corner. Things were definitely looking up.

The northeastern corner of Lumpini Park was an intersection of three busy roads that merged into one road that ran across one of the few bridges that spanned the Chao Phraya River. At the intersection of all these roads was a small triangle of paved land. Nikki stood in this spot and swiveled this way and that, trying to figure out what she wanted to do. Around her, early-morning tourists and Thais streamed by, all intent on their own business.

Ratchadamnoen, one of the roads Kovit had mentioned, curved a little to meet up with the bridge road. In the other direction, Nikki had an unobstructed view of the roadway straight down to the large Democracy Monument.

She spotted Sarkassian's building. It was a rundown hotel with the bottom windows boarded up and real estate posters on the front. The only real signs of life were that the plywood had been pulled off the door.

"What do you think?" she asked as Jenny and Ellen got out of the cab.

"I'm going to want to see the interior layout," said Jenny.

"I want to be up high," Ellen said, and Nikki nodded, pointing to a building directly across the wide street from the rundown hotel.

"Will that do?"

"Should," said Ellen. "You're going to try to find Z'ev? You sure about that?"

"I told Val he was CIA. If I'm right, Val and Sarkassian are planning on cleaning house. He's as much at risk as Lawan, and it's my fault."

"All right, then," Ellen said. "See you when I see you." She hefted her bag a little higher on her shoulder and set off across the street.

"What about you, Jenny?" asked Nikki.

"I think I want a few things out of my luggage," she said. She emerged from the trunk a moment later, duffel bag much fuller.

"You haven't got much time; they'll probably be here soon," Nikki said, checking her watch.

Jenny nodded. "They will if Val's running it by the Carrie Mae handbook," commented Jenny. "Get to the location early and be waiting—that's the way to do it."

"What do you think we're doing?" Nikki asked, and Jenny almost laughed in response. "You going to be all right?" asked Nikki, feeling suddenly worried.

"Yeah, sure," Jenny said, putting on her sunglasses. "You going to be able to get our luggage back to the hotel?"

"Since arriving in Thailand," Nikki said, "I've learned that motorcycles can carry a great deal."

Jenny shrugged and went to pay off the cabbie while Nikki bungee-corded their luggage to her borrowed bike. She waved as she pointed the bike back in the direction of the hotel. Jenny raised her hand in salute.

Lawan was waiting for her at the hotel, pacing a track in the carpet.

"My team's in position," said Nikki, as soon as the bellboy had dropped off Jenny and Ellen's luggage. "Any luck with calling Jim?"

"Yeah," Lawan said, throwing the phone down on the bed. "He says he can't help!"

"He really said no?" Nikki felt surprised and disappointed. She hadn't expected that from Z'ev.

"I think he would, but I get the feeling it's not his decision. Do we really need him?"

"No," Nikki said, and felt a rebellious counter to that thought in her heart, "but I would like to know where they are. Keep Jim and whoever he's working for out of the way, if nothing else."

"Someplace with their heads up their asses. That's where they are," said Lawan bitterly.

Nikki laughed.

"I've got to introduce you to Jenny. I think you'd like each other."

Lawan's only response was a grunt.

"Nine ten," Nikki said, checking her watch. "Twenty minutes until they call you with a location?" Lawan nodded, and Nikki nodded, feeling a surge of nervous energy.

"OK, let's get you ready," she said, taking a deep breath, steadying herself.

She dug into Jenny and Ellen's bags, pleased to see that Rachel had pressed the Borg cube of makeup on each of them. Soon the contents were scattered across her bed as Nikki pulled out everything she thought she needed. Jenny's Anastasia was not built for Lawan, but a few bits of duct tape later it was strapped into place.

"You sure this thing is going to work?" Lawan asked.

"Yes," said Nikki firmly. "It's, uh . . . been tested. All right, next thing: charm bracelet. Pull the grenade charm and throw it down."

"There's a grenade charm?" Lawan said skeptically. "Doesn't anyone think that's weird?"

"Of course it's weird," said Nikki, "but who actually looks at a woman's charm bracelet? Now, when it breaks there will be a thick white smoke, and that is your opportunity to use the mini-perfume. Just spray it directly into someone's face, preferably into the eyes or nose, and do not, I repeat, do not get any on yourself. The knock-out gas works in less than three seconds, so make sure you're standing upwind."

"Tell me again what you're going to be doing while I'm standing upwind?" Lawan asked.

"I'll be . . . well, hopefully, I'll be taking care of any surprises that crop up."

"You mean the Valerie woman you told me about?" Lawan asked.

Nikki nodded. "Your job is to get yourself out of trouble while my team covers us."

"Uh-huh." Lawan sounded unconvinced. A few minutes later her cell phone rang. Nikki held her breath as Lawan replied in monosyllables.

"Ratchadamnoen and Atsadang," she said at last.

Nikki breathed out. "Yeah, I know the place. Yeah, I'll be there."

"OK," Lawan said, hanging up. "Thirty minutes, starting now."

Nikki looked at her watch and thought about Z'ev.

"I wonder," said Lawan. "If I just hit Redial, would Sarkassian answer?"

"Why would you do that?" Nikki asked, still thinking her own thoughts.

"To tell him I'm going to kill him," said Lawan.

Paint It Black

Nikki stared at the hotel. Jenny and Ellen had confirmed that everything was in place. Sarkassian, Val, and the little girl—all the players were inside. Along with half an army of Sarkassian's friends. They were all waiting for Lawan to arrive. Jenny had left an entry point for her. As she hauled herself up bamboo scaffolding half a block down the street and climbed from building to building, Nikki thought about seriously having to redefine "entry point" for Jenny—predefine it to something easier. Finally she was sitting next to Jenny on the roof and staring down at the interior of the old hotel through an enormous skylight.

The hotel was built on a courtyard floor plan, with a wide shaft rising up through the middle of the building. The open area had at some point been covered with a skylight and looking through the grimy glass, Nikki could see, four stories below her, Lindawati looking scared but defiant and hugging a grimy teddy bear. Sarkassian lounged by the bar, and Val was nowhere in sight.

"Where's Val?" asked Nikki, scanning the crowd below her.

"Don't know," Jenny said. "She scampered away after they got inside."

"That's not good," muttered Nikki.

"Too bad you can't get your boyfriend to come help," Jenny said.

"He's not my boyfriend," Nikki said automatically. "We don't really want the CIA involved, do we? Plus I think his boss is being a dickhead."

"It's a common problem," said Jenny with a shrug, her eyes trained on the street below. "They'd probably just get in the way anyway."

"But the extra firepower would have been nice," said Nikki, matching her stare. The seconds ticked by with infinite slowness.

"She's late," said Jenny, stating the obvious.

"Oh hell," said Nikki as a car pulled up and two people got out.

"What?" Jenny hissed, maintaining her position by the skylight.

"It's her boyfriend. She brought her freaking boyfriend."

"Oh hell," Jenny said. "What are you going to do now?"

"Stick to the plan," said Nikki, crawling back to the skylight. "There's nothing else to do."

Below, the door opened, and Lawan and Saman entered hand in hand. Lindawati yelled something and tried to run toward her mother, but one of the guards brutally shoved her back. The pair were patted down and then pointed at Sarkassian.

"I'm not getting any audio," Nikki hissed. And Jenny made shushing noises as she fiddled with the equipment.

". . . not get away with this, Sarkassian," Lawan said, the audio cutting in. "The Thai people will no longer accept this sort of degradation and abuse from outside influences."

"Oh for..." Sarkassian slammed his hand down on the bar, making dust motes jump. "Wake up! Thailand is clinging to democracy by its fingernails. It's a playground for the rich and the corrupt of Europe and America. You keep trying to make things better for these poor people... it's pointless. Thailand doesn't care. America doesn't care. No one cares. Why don't you just give up?"

"Because she's better than you," Lindawati said. Sarkassian's reaction was quick and brutal. And even without the listening equipment, Nikki could hear the impact of his slap as it echoed off the walls. The little girl was spun around and thrown to the ground by the impact. She sobbed, and Lawan went white. Even the thugs around the room looked surprised.

"What?" asked Sarkassian, spreading his hands and looking around. "I'm the bad guy."

"Oh crap," Jenny said. "We've got company."

"Company?" repeated Nikki, looking back at Jenny, who pointed back down the skylight.

The front doors banged open, and Z'ev and Victor walked into the room.

"What the... did we post fliers or something?" Nikki demanded. "Does everyone know where this secret meeting is?"

Jenny shrugged and shook her head.

"Victor?" Sarkassian said, clearly startled.

"He got picked up on a raid of his favorite Pai-Gow club," Z'ev said, sounding smug. "Couldn't buy his way out, since he'd lost all his money. I had to go haul him out of a jail cell."

"Fucking licensing division of the police ran a crackdown," Victor said, but there was something nervous in his voice.

"Any booze?" Z'ev asked, wandering around behind the bar.

"Interesting," Sarkassian said, ignoring Z'ev and eyeing Victor carefully. "And what are you doing here?"

"We went back to the house. Everyone says you've been looking for us. Where are we supposed to go?" Victor said.

"Well, I have to admit that I didn't expect you to actually show up," Sarkassian said. "I mean what with Jim being with the CIA, I rather thought you'd be in prison by now."

Behind the bar, Z'ev froze. There was the small click of multiple weapons being cocked and pointed at him.

"But now here you *both* are. That's unexpected."

"I brought him to you," Victor said. "I had to warn you." He was sweating.

"I'm very disappointed in you, Victor," said Sarkassian, taking a gun out from under his jacket and setting it on the bar.

"What are you doing, Jirair?" said Victor. "I brought him to you. We kill him and we get out of town."

"Get out of town? With you?"

"Yeah," said Victor eagerly. "We get the cash. Set up somewhere else. Cambodia, maybe."

"And how am I supposed to trust a man who agreed to wear a wire?" Sarkassian asked, reaching into Victor's alligator shirt and pulling out a microphone.

"I had to," Victor said, backing up, but his voice was still strong. "To get out. I bring them to you." He had backpedaled until he was standing next to one of the goons. His next move was lightning fast—he back-slammed a fist to the goon's face and then grabbed at the man's gun. But it wasn't fast enough. Sarkassian fired four times, and Victor sagged to the ground, falling face-first onto the floor.

"Jenny," Nikki said. "Any sign of Z'ev's CIA buddies?" Some part of her mind noted that her voice sounded strangely empty.

"Negative," answered Jenny in the same curiously flat tone.

"What are you doing, Jirair?" Z'ev asked.

"Don't! Don't open your mouth," commanded Sarkassian. "This is your fault! You brought the CIA. Everything was just fine, and now you come in here and make a mess. I don't like mess." The last words came out in a threatening hiss.

"So, what are you going to do about it?" Z'ev asked, looking as cool as ever. As if Sarkassian and a gun weren't mere feet away.

"You want to know what I'm going to do? I'm going to kill you."

"I figured that," Z'ev said, with a shrug. "But it's not like that will make the problem go away." He was casually walking the length of the bar. Sarkassian tracked him with his gun, but apparently Z'ev's bravado pleased him, because he laughed.

"I'm going to clean up the mess. Wipe the slate clean. Scorched-earth policy, you might call it."

"What about the women?" Lawan demanded.

"What women?" Sarkassian replied with an evil glint in his eye. "I told you—I'm cleaning up the mess. When I'm done, there won't be anything left."

Lawan made a furious yelp, and Sarkassian laughed. His cronies followed suit. Saman put out a hand, restraining Lawan.

"Maybe I should show the little girl what her mother used to do for a living," one of the men said wolfishly—Nikki recognized Amein's killer from the night before. At the time she had called him Stomper, and it appeared his bullying ways had not changed because he prodded Lawan in the back with his gun. "Remind her what women are good for."

Lawan appeared to flinch and move aside, but the movement only covered Saman's spinning roundhouse. But instead of a kick, he pulled it up short and put his knee right into the man's chest.

"Here we go," Nikki said.

"Yeehaw," Jenny said, and broke the glass.

The man went down gasping, and Lawan tossed the smoke grenade as the glass from the skylight rained down and everyone scattered. But as the thick white smoke went up, Nikki saw a muzzle flash from a gun on the third floor, and Lawan jerked backward.

"Ellen, we've got a shooter on the third floor," Nikki yelled, as Jenny threw herself off the roof and into the courtyard. "Could be Val," she added. "I don't have a visual on her."

"Gotcha," Ellen said, but Nikki barely heard her. She was concentrating on the humming of Jenny's rope. She had a job to do and she couldn't afford to get it wrong.

Jenny hit the floor, grabbed Lindawati, and Nikki hit the Recall button, laying down cover fire as the two rose through the air. Once they were over halfway up, Nikki launched herself off into space, firing at the shooter on the third floor. She thought she ought to be able to hear more gunfire, but she could only see the flash of muzzles. It was if she'd gone deaf and things were moving in slow motion.

She hit the bottom floor and everything sped back up. She disconnected herself from the rope and looked around for Lawan. She caught sight of Z'ev chasing Sarkassian up the back stairs to the second floor. Lawan had found a gun and was firing at the retreating backs of several men as they ran after Sarkassian and Z'ev. Stomper and Saman had crashed through a wall and into the lobby. Nikki took another look around for Val, but still didn't see her.

"Come on," she yelled, and grabbed Lawan by the arm. She could hear the high-powered rounds from Ellen's rifle singing through the upper floors. There was a small explosion as someone hit a booby trap that Jenny had set up before the meeting. Nikki dragged Lawan out to the front of the hotel just in time to see Saman put a flying elbow into Stomper's chin. The bigger man staggered and went down as if he'd been hit with a load of cement, and he didn't get back up again. Might never get up again, Nikki thought, looking at his face. Amein, at least, might rest a little easier for that.

Saman looked up, and Nikki shoved Lawan at him.

"Get her out of here," she yelled, pointing at the door.

"Where are you going?" Lawan yelled, as Saman pulled her away.

"I'm going to help Z'ev," Nikki yelled back, but Lawan shook her head, not understanding. Nikki pushed her at the door and then turned and ran for the stairs.

Taking them two at time, the blood pounding in her ears, she sprinted up the back stairs, her breath coming in gasps. She rounded the bend and headed for the second floor. Cautiously opening the door from the hall, she slithered out onto the carpet next to an upright piano.

She could just make out Z'ev behind one of the large pillars. Directly in front of her, she saw the body of one of Sarkassian's men. He lay in a pool of his own blood. Nikki was grateful that she couldn't see his face as she picked up his gun. Two men were firing at Z'ev from behind another pillar farther down the length of the balcony. As Nikki watched, Z'ev's gun ran out of ammo. The two men began to sneak forward, firing at Z'ev's column. Nikki fired her .45, mostly at random, and ran forward, aiming for the marginal cover of a huge potted fern.

"Z'ev!" she yelled, throwing him the MP5, as she dove behind the enormous pot. Z'ev caught it with a look of surprise, but used it without hesitation, spraying bullets at the pair of Sarkassian's men. One went down. The second man, checked in his tracks, took cover behind a pillar. Z'ev used that momentary advantage to run forward, shooting with steady kachunka-chunka-chunka.

Nikki's heart was in her mouth. There was no way Z'ev's ammunition was going to hold out. And it didn't. There was a click, and Z'ev was empty. The man behind the pillar jumped out with a triumphant look on his face, but Z'ev didn't hesitate and continued on at a sprint, barreling into him and busting him across the face with his now-empty gun. The man had time to register one look of utter surprise before crashing to the floor.

"Nikki!" Z'ev yelled. "Move it."

Nikki ran forward to join him.

"Gee, honey," said Z'ev, holding up the MP5 before dropping it on the floor and picking up the unconscious man's weapon. "You give the best gifts."

"Well, you're easy to shop for," she answered, breathing hard.

"Where'd you come from?" he asked, collecting the clips as well.

"I came with Lawan," she lied. Mentally, she crossed out *lied* and inserted *simplified the truth*. "And I heard gunfire, so I figured you were involved." It was sort of true.

"Most people run *away* from gunfire," he commented, peering around the pillar.

"Oh. Well. No one ever said I was bright, did they?" It was weak, but it was the best she could come up with at the moment. She'd never been in a gun battle before. She was just glad Mr. Bamoko couldn't hear her. Her witty repartee was kind of sucking.

"OK" Z'ev said, turning around to look at her. "I'm going to cover you. Go out the way you came in. My people will handle it."

"I don't see them here," she responded.

"They are on the way," he yelled back, as a hail of gunfire smacked into their pillar. The sound of bullets cut off conversation for a moment, as both of them tried to squeeze into as small an area as possible.

"People are shooting at me!" she yelped in a small pause between bullets. She hadn't had time to process it before, but now that she'd gotten Lawan out of the building and theoretically completed her mission, she was having time to think. She felt shocked; she'd practiced for it, but it hadn't seemed like a real possibility. And she couldn't believe that people really wanted to hurt her. It was a terrible time for reality to be setting in.

"Yes!" Z'ev agreed, firing and ducking back behind their pillar.

"I was a cheerleader, goddamn it!" Nikki muttered, and took a firmer grip on her gun. She slid around the corner and fired a few shots before yanking herself back. "People don't shoot at cheerleaders. I mean, stab them in the back, sure, but nobody shoots at cheerleaders! How did I even end up here?" Nikki talked to herself while she was reloading. She knew she was being irrational, but she couldn't help it. People were shooting at her.

"I don't know," Z'ev answered, changing clips himself and interrupting her monologue. "How *did* you end up here?"

"I'll tell you how I ended up here," she responded, slamming the clip into her gun. "Grades. I should have flunked math like all the other girls. You get good grades and pretty soon you're going to college and then you're picking some retarded subject like linguistics and then you're working for Carrie Mae and getting shot at by modern-day slave traders. I should have married Billy Hollis, the captain of the baseball team, and popped out six or seven kids like Caitlin Barcourt!"

"Yes," Z'ev said, standing up and kissing her on the mouth. "But then you wouldn't be having this much fun."

Victor's men returned fire, and as Nikki ducked behind the pillar again, she caught sight of several men running toward the stairs on the first floor. Any second now they would burst through the door behind them. She was about to point this out to Z'ev, but he seemed busy with the guys in front of them. She looked back toward the stairs, the fern, and the upright piano.

"Cover me!" she yelled to Z'ev, and ran toward the stairs. Z'ev, startled, but acting quickly, obeyed.

Nikki raced back to the stairwell door and wedged it open. Then she ran to the piano and put her shoulder against it. She could hear the sound of heavy boots on the stairs. Beads of sweat stood out on her forehead. Her biceps felt as though they were straining against a brick wall. With a Herculean effort, she gave a final shove and felt the small, rusty wheels give way and begin to move. She steered the piano through the door and worked up to a jogging speed.

Momentum was on her side as the piano raced toward the edge of the first stair. She could see the men rounding the corner, pointing at her, and shouting. With a final shove, the piano took its swan song, barreling down the stairwell toward four men with horrified expressions. Nikki had been so intent on pushing that when gravity took over, she nearly toppled after the piano. She teetered for a moment, watching as the men below her reversed direction or were run over. As the piano hit the bend in the stairs, it bounced twice and wedged itself in, inextricably blocking the stairway.

Nikki had just balanced herself and was admiring her handiwork when one of the survivors fired at her through a small triangle of space available to him. Startled, Nikki threw herself against the wall and returned fire. She wasn't sure if she'd hit him or not because another of Jenny's booby traps went off, shaking the building and sending a shower of plaster down on her head.

Slowly Nikki slid back out onto the second-floor balcony. Z'ev was nowhere in sight. Above her, she heard the sound of gunfire. The fight had apparently moved to the upper floors.

Running across the floor and up the front stairs, she gained the third floor and looked around. Z'ev had picked off most of Sarkassian's army one at a time and now the fight had come down to just the two of them. Sarkassian was lanky and had a longer reach, but Z'ev compensated for the lost inches in weight. Nikki watched for a second, undecided about helping. She rather thought this was something Z'ev had been wanting to do for a while.

As she watched, a figure stepped out of one of the rooms. She was dressed all in black and carried a rifle. Her black hair swung in a perfect arc around her head. Nikki wasn't aware of it, but she must have made some noise, because Val glanced over her shoulder, a cigarette dangling from her lips. When she saw Nikki, her mouth curved upward in a sly smile, before turning back and taking aim at Z'ev.

Nikki yelled something, but she couldn't remember what, and ran forward, slamming into Val in a full-body tackle. Val spun slightly, the bullet going astray, and they both tumbled into the room Val had just come out of.

"I never should have bought you shoes," Val said, standing over Nikki. "You feed a stray once and it follows you home."

Nikki tried to stand up, not bothering to reply, but Val kicked her in the chest. Nikki sat down hard on her butt, rolling to her back.

"Why is it that whenever a woman finds a good thing, some other bitch has to come along and ruin it?" Val's voice was grim. Nikki shook her head, trying to get the sparkles to clear out. "Just never know when to leave well enough alone, do you, Red?"

Nikki squinted up at Val. The day was proving to be a bright one. Val was standing between Nikki and the window. Her shape was reduced to a looming black shadow.

"What about you?" snarled Nikki, getting slowly to her feet. "Being a Carrie Mae agent wasn't enough?"

"Sure, kid," Val said, pacing slightly, waiting for Nikki to regain her composure. Clearly not concerned about Nikki as an actual threat. "Yeah, sure, my life's just great. I'm forty-two. I have a mortgage and an incontinent cat. I work for a company that pays half what the CIA does and expects me to take it on the chin because it's good for women. I've got a shoulder that doesn't rotate all the way because that's where I got shot, and the older I get the more likely it is that there will be more bullets in my future. Now, maybe when you're twenty-five that sounds like fun, but when you get to be my age, it pretty much sucks." She made a wide gesture, spreading her hands away from her body, and Nikki took the opportunity. She lunged forward, aiming for a tackle. Val had been expecting a punch, not a full-on assault, and only partially evaded it, managing to turn her hip, but they tumbled to the ground in a sprawling mess.

"What about all those women?" said Nikki, pulling Val into a headlock. "The ones who were going to suffocate or freeze to death inside those cargo containers, who Sarkassian was going to burn? What about Lawan?"

"Who cares?" Val grunted and slammed her elbow into Nikki's rib cage right on top of one of the bruises left from the gunshot to the Anastasia. Nikki gasped in sudden pain. Val shrugged her off in a hip throw and tried to lunge away from her. Nikki recovered, spinning, and in fury charged after. Speed was with her, but balance was not, and they both tumbled through the window and out onto the roof.

They both went sliding down the roof before bouncing off an awning below them. Nikki landed in a selection of silk skirts, but Val fell onto a table of meditation balls. The silvery orbs bounced out of their boxes, chiming merrily into the street.

Black SUVs were pulling up to the front of the building. Men in suits were running into the building. Nikki figured that they must be Z'ev's cavalry, but she didn't have time to worry about it because Val rolled off the table and ran out into the street, flagging down a motorcycle messenger on a junker sport bike. Without giving him time to react, she gave him a tremendous shove, sending him sprawling onto the pavement. She picked up his bike and left the messenger cursing in the street. Nikki ran for her own bike, parked just around the corner, and burned rubber as she peeled out after Val.

She wove through the traffic, twisting the throttle past the enjoyment level, intent on keeping sight of Val. There was a moment of panic as she tried to pull her gun out of her waistband and felt the bike dip to the side. She wasn't really skilled enough for this, but the gun came free and the bike righted itself. Nikki edged closer to Val and pointed her gun at the other bike, trying to get a clear shot. The wind whipped into her face, blurring her eyes with tears and snapping her hair back and forth with stinging impact. She shook her head to clear her eyes and pulled closer to Val's bike. They were nearly to the bridge.

As they drove onto the bridge, Nikki fired a shot at Val's bike's rear tire. Val applied the brakes and, unprepared, Nikki sped past, swerving to get around her without crashing. She hit the brakes and risked a look over her shoulder, just in time to see Val's black bike jerk sideways and go down in a skid. Nikki looked forward again and found she was quickly closing in on the back of a truck jam-packed with construction workers. She squeezed the brakes tighter and felt the rear end slide as she watched the tailgate of the truck get closer.

"Shit, shit, shit, shit," she prayed, as the construction workers hastily tried to raise the tailgate. She slid to a stop, millimeters from the bumper and face-to-face with a man in the back of the truck. Nikki let her breath out in one long stream, and carefully released her death grip on the brakes. The construction worker echoed her movements, peeling his white knuckles off the tailgate. Then he pointed behind her.

Nikki looked back and saw Val running toward her. She stepped off the bike in time to receive a diving tackle that threw them both into traffic. Nikki hit the pavement and heard the squeal of brakes around them. She took the momentum of Val's tackle and continued the roll, flipping Val over and landing on her chest. Val shoved upward at Nikki's jaw with an open-handed strike that made Nikki's teeth click together and her head reel back. The sudden shock loosened Nikki's grip, and Val wriggled free. Around them, cars were stopped, their drivers honking and yelling, but above the noise Nikki felt the steady rhythm of air being pushed out of the way—a helicopter was coming. Nikki ducked a punch and kneed Val in the stomach. Val elbowed her in the ear, and Nikki stepped back.

"You are so full of shit," Nikki yelled. "You are doing this for your boyfriend!"

"I'm doing this for me," screamed Val, and punched her. Nikki staggered under the blow, but swung back and added a front kick straight up the middle. She planted her foot on Val's chest and shoved. This time it was Val who moved.

She had no idea where her gun was. They had traversed the width of the bridge now, and Val leaned against the railing that separated them from the long drop to the muddy, brown river below.

"I tried to tell you," said Val, "you can't save them." Nikki opened her mouth to argue, but Val cut her off. "There's no point. You can't save any of them."

"I hung up on my mother," said Nikki. "People can change."

And just for a moment, she thought she saw the real Val. The thumping blades of the helicopter were close now, and Nikki glanced over her shoulder. The helicopter was holding steady at road level, with Ellen leaning in its open door. Her gray hair fluttered in the wind. As Nikki watched, Ellen picked up a rifle and aimed it at Val.

"Val," screamed Nikki, one hand flying out, following her instinct to warn her. She stopped in mid-gesture. Val, as poised as ever, had found Nikki's gun and was pointing it directly at her. Time seemed to stretch out for an eternity, and Nikki could only notice the striking depth of Val's brown eyes. She didn't hear the gunshot, but she saw Val jerk and fall over the railing. Nikki ran forward, catching her hand as it slipped from the edge of the bridge.

"Val!" yelled Nikki. Val's hand was sliding from her grasp; it was wet with blood. Nikki leaned farther over the railing, feeling a precarious shift in balance. Val looked up, her naturally pale face even paler. Behind her, Nikki heard the helicopter settling onto the bridge.

"I take it back, Nikki."

"What? Val, hold on!" Nikki wished Val would focus on the problem at hand.

"I take it back. I'm not sorry I bought you shoes."

"I lost those shoes! It doesn't matter! None of it matters!" Nikki was screaming now. "Just hold on to my hand!"

Val looked down at the water. Nikki heard the pounding of feet behind her. Val looked up into Nikki's face and smiled. Then she let go.

"Val!" Nikki screamed as her friend tumbled into the turgid water of the Chao Phraya.

A moment later Ellen was standing at the railing, looking critically into the water. Jenny was only a step behind her, gun drawn. Nikki looked at Ellen in disbelief. She had no idea what to say or do.

"Come on, let's go," Ellen said.

Nikki shook her head. Her eyes were glued to the water. "She might not be dead."

"It was a solid, center-mass hit, and there's blood spatter," she said, pointing to the railing. "And the cops are coming. Even if she isn't, we're out of time."

Nikki stared at Ellen, unwilling to accept reality.

"Nikki, come on. We have to go. The cops are coming." She pointed to the edge of the bridge, where the traffic jam had stopped the police cars and SUVs.

Nikki shook her head again.

"Nikki, we've gotta go," Jenny said, touching her lightly on the shoulder. Nikki flinched. "Nikki," Jenny said, and took a firmer grip on her arm. "Come on." She pulled Nikki toward the helicopter. "Are you OK?" Jenny asked as the helicopter began to lift away from the bridge.

Nikki shook her head, not trusting herself to speak. She felt sick to her stomach. The helicopter rose and pivoted along a steep arc over the long line of black SUVs. Nikki turned her head away. She didn't want to see Thailand anymore.

Cleanup Crew

Nikki sat next to Ellen and tried not to shift in her chair. Between her bruises, cuts, and lack of sleep, she was finding it difficult to concentrate on Lawan's speech. It seemed to be going well. The other conference delegates were nodding along, and Lawan was impassioned, but Nikki had reached the point of weariness where she couldn't track the words.

"You got this?" Nikki asked, leaning toward Ellen.

"Sure, sweetie. What's up?"

"I just need to stretch my legs a bit," Nikki whispered, before ducking out of the conference hall. She reached the front lobby, where booths had been set up and a sparse crowd still milled around. She found a pillar and leaned against it.

"Nikki?" said Laura, sounding confused.

Nikki looked around the pillar and saw Laura Daniels standing in front of the doors, her head swiveling this way and that.

"Over here," Nikki said, stepping out to be seen.

Laura smiled radiantly. She was dressed in a powder blue suit of dupioni silk that offset her blond hair and blue eyes. She looked, Nikki thought, exactly how an ambassador's wife should look.

"Nikki, I have to go back in, but I wanted to take a minute to thank you for everything you've done."

"No," Nikki said, feeling uncomfortable, as usual, with praise. "I didn't really do anything."

"Didn't do anything? Nikki, it's not just Lawan and Lindawati you helped. Every woman in that warehouse owes her life to you."

"What about next time?" Nikki asked, voicing Val's doubts. "What if some other scumbag comes along and tries to do the same thing?"

"We can't predict that," said Laura, shaking her head. "But what matters is that today they were saved. Today you made a difference. Today we are all at this conference standing up for the rights of women. Maybe all of those girls in the warehouse won't go on to live happily ever after, but they got the opportunity to do so because of you. That's what life is—an opportunity and a gift. You risked yours to help others, and I appreciate it."

Laura stepped forward and embraced Nikki in a breathtaking hug and then, covering sniffs of tears, dashed back into the conference room. Nikki leaned back against the pillar and shook her head in astonishment. She felt as if she were thinking through a cotton ball. Taking off her dark sunglasses, she rubbed one eye tiredly and then carefully felt around the edges of her Val-induced black eye. That one was going to hurt for a while.

"Nice black eye," said a gravelly voice.

"It goes so well with yours," Nikki said, looking up at Z'ev and slipping her glasses back on.

"Mine isn't as puffy," he replied, pulling her glasses back down her nose with one finger and scrutinizing her face.

"True," she conceded, then reached up to turn his head for a better view, "but at least mine didn't require stitches."

"You know," he said, looking around the convention center lobby, "I didn't think I'd actually find you here."

"I came here for the conference," she said.

"You kept saying that," he said musingly. "I just didn't believe you."

"What did you think I was doing here, then?" Nikki said.

"I thought you were a foreign agent working on breaking the smuggling ring," he said with a shrug.

"A foreign agent who works for a cosmetics company? That's just silly," said Nikki, forcing a laugh.

"I didn't think you were actually working for a cosmetics company," he protested. "I thought that was just a cover!"

"But now you believe me?" asked Nikki, relieved but still nervous.

"My . . . uh . . . friends did a background check." He looked a little embarrassed.

"And did your 'uh . . . friends' arrest Sarkassian and get those girls out of the warehouse?"

"Yeah, they did. They're running into a little trouble with the encryption system on his computer, but they'll get it figured out. It's not like they have to have it done right here and now."

"I'm glad to hear it," Nikki said.

"You know, even if you are really a Carrie Mae girl, there are still a few things that could use explanation," he said. "What were you even doing there?"

"I came with Lawan," she said, extemporizing. "I'd been working with Laura Daniels, and she said Lawan needed help. When she told me about her daughter I had to do what I could. I suppose it was stupid to think we could do it ourselves, but I couldn't let Lawan go by herself."

"Yeah, do me a favor and next time . . ." He stopped and shook his head. "You know what? Just promise me that there won't be a next time."

"How can I do that?" Nikki asked, flipping her hair a little, as much as her sore neck would let her. "'Helping women everywhere'—it's not just a company slogan."

"You are trouble," he said. "I should have seen that the first time I met you."

"Oh, you mean when you asked me to marry you? Seems to me that I wouldn't have been in this mess if it weren't for you."

"And good grades in math," he recalled. "You really should have married Billy Hollis and popped out six or seven kids."

"I didn't think you were listening to that," she said, blushing.

"I listen to everything you say," he answered.

"Right, I forgot," she said, laughing.

"I don't suppose you're going to be in Thailand much longer?" he asked.

"I fly out tonight," she said. "I don't suppose you'll be Stateside anytime soon? Maybe go on a sort of vacation or something?"

"You mean like an extended period of time where we could use our real names and not get in any fights?"

"And no one would shoot at us," Nikki added. "And there wouldn't be any riots. And we could go on a real date. And nobody has to lie . . ."

"Yeah, no," he said, cutting her off. "My company doesn't really believe in vacation time. I mean, theoretically it exists, but no one's ever seen it."

"Shoot," said Nikki, trying to keep things lighthearted, but unable to manage more than a weak smile.

"Ah, what the hell," said Z'ev, and kissed her.

She knew that she should have been uncomfortable. He had put his arm around her waist, and her ribs were bruised and possibly cracked and her back was laced with cuts and road rash, but she didn't feel any of it. She couldn't even feel her feet. It was as if all sensation were wrapped up in his lips.

"Right," Nikki said, stepping away and bumping into the pole behind her.

"Exactly," he agreed, shaking his head slightly.

"Um," she said, looking over his shoulder. "I think your friends are here. Why are your friends here?"

"For Lawan," he said, turning to glance at the three out-of-place men in suits. "We need her testimony."

"Right," Nikki said again. There was the sound of thunderous applause from behind the doors to the auditorium. "That's your cue," she said.

"Time to go back to work. "Goodbye, wife."

The doors sprang open and Lawan walked out, surrounded by throngs of conference delegates all trying to talk to her at once.

"He is cute," said Ellen, appearing beside Nikki.

"Too cute," granted Nikki, pushing her glasses farther up her nose and folding her arms across her chest.

"Too bad it couldn't work out. Sometimes I guess all you get is the moment."

"Just the here and now," Nikki agreed, and then stopped and slapped her forehead with her open palm. "Ah, son of a . . ."

"What?" Ellen asked, looking concerned.

"Here and now," Nikki repeated to Ellen's blank expression. "Oh, never mind. Here, lend me a pen."

Taking Ellen's pen and a brochure from a nearby booth, Nikki wrote HIC ET NUNC on the piece of paper in bold letters. Then she began to force her way through the crowd toward Z'ev.

"Hey," she yelled, tugging on his sleeve. He made a questioning face, and she shoved the paper at him.

"What's this?" he asked.

"Sarkassian's password," she said.

"How do you know?" he asked, raising his voice above the chattering voices of the conference-goers.

"I saw it in Canada," she began, then stopped as a woman pushed between them. "It's Latin. It means 'here and now.'" Another woman bumped her from behind and Nikki stopped again. The story was just too long. "I'm a linguist," she said, grabbing him by the lapel and kissing him. "It's what I do." Then she let go and let the crowd push them apart.

So Fancy Free

"Hey there, little lady," Mr. Merrivel said as Nikki stepped out of customs.

Nikki smiled involuntarily. "Mr. Merrivel! What are you doing here?"

She had left Jenny and Ellen in Thailand to return to their original assignments and hadn't expected to see another friendly face until Dr. Hastings fired her.

"What am I doing here?" Mr. M looked puzzled by the question. "I came to pick you up, of course."

"You didn't have to pick me up." Nikki was moved by his thoughtfulness.

"Well, I heard you had a bit of a rough time at your convention. Nice shiner," he said, pointing at her purple and yellow "black" eye. Nikki blushed and quickly put on her sunglasses. "I figured maybe you wouldn't want to take a taxi."

"No, not really," said Nikki, smiling again. "About the taxi, I mean." She wondered a little at his ability to say things like "convention" with a straight face. She shouldered her bag and winced as it hit a sore spot. Mr. M took it away with a slight smile and together they walked in comfortable silence to the car.

"How'd it go, by the way?" he asked, when he had tucked her into the car and they were cruising down the highway.

"I think I kind of blew it," she said.

"Don't be so hard on yourself."

"Well, my partner was a double agent, Lawan wasn't missing—she had the situation pretty well figured out—and I managed to get almost killed. Oh, and I also managed to blow the CIA guy's cover. Not really such a good first outing. I'm pretty sure Dr. Hastings is going to fire me."

Mr. Merrivel laughed. "But you got it figured out eventually."

"Yeah, eventually. But first I messed it all up."

"Nikki, I'm pretty sure that if you'd messed it all up you'd be dead."

"Mph," snorted Nikki, and she stared glumly at the passing scenery.

"I heard you got the bad guy, though," Mr. M said brightly.

"Z'ev got him," Nikki said. "I just threw a piano down the stairs."

"Who's Z'ev?"

"The CIA agent," Nikki mumbled, blushing slightly.

"Oh ho! Now we're getting to the good stuff. Is he—dang it— what did that girl on the TV call them the other day? Oh yeah. Is he a hottie?"

Nikki laughed. "He is kind of hot, yes. And please don't say 'hottie.' It's just not you."

"You don't think I can pull off 'hottie'? Hmm, probably true. Very well, but will the young man be calling at some point?"

"I don't see how," Nikki said, falling once more into gloom. "He's working in Thailand, and I'm here mostly. And," she added reflectively, "it's probably better considering the kind of work we do. I mean, how long could I pull off the 'I just happened to be passing by' routine?"

"But did you give him your phone number?"

"I . . . no," Nikki said, suddenly stricken by that horrible realization.

"Well, if he's any sort of decent CIA agent, he'll find you."

"I don't think so, Mr. M." Nikki sighed.

"We'll see," said Mr. M with a confidence that Nikki couldn't help feeling was entirely misplaced. "They wanted to see you as soon as you got in," he said, changing the subject. "So I'm taking you directly to the office."

"OK," Nikki said. "I guess it is better to get fired right away."

"Nikki, they are not going to fire you," Mr. M said with exasperation.

"Dr. Hastings does not seem like the kind of person to let circumventing her authority and ignoring her commands go by without comment," said Nikki.

"It's not over until the fat lady sings," said Mr. Merrivel. "Now stop being a Gloomy Gus and find me some good tunes on the radio."

Nikki fiddled with the radio settings until she found the oldies station. Soon they were wondering if you were lonesome tonight, giving Elvis cheerful accompaniment. As they pulled up to the front of the sparkling Carrie Mae offices, Nikki felt the good mood that Mr. M had spun dissipate, even as the wheels stopped turning.

"Leave your bag here," Mr. Merrivel said as she opened the door. "I'll bring it back to the house, and you can stay with me and Mrs. M until you find a place of your own."

"You really don't have to," began Nikki, but he waved her silent.

"You're not getting fired, and you'll need a place to stay."

Nikki looked into Mr. Merrivel's cheerful but determined face and gave in. It was hard to argue with that kind of kindness.

She squared her shoulders and marched into the lobby. It had the same sparkling, just-bleached appearance as the last time. But this time she noticed that a sense of calm presided over the atmosphere. Certainly the place was busy, but it was a beehive sort of busy, a well-organized swirl of happy workers. Nikki felt a swell of envy. She would have liked to have been a part of this hive.

She pushed the button for an elevator and the doors slid open almost immediately, revealing Rachel White. Her frizzy blond hair was being held in place with pencils.

"You used the Anastasia?" asked Rachel excitedly. "How did it work?"

"Well, I'm still here," Nikki said, without enthusiasm.

"You were shot? From what kind of distance? The report was less than specific."

"I don't know, about twenty feet," Nikki estimated impatiently.

"It's a new construction process. Was there bruising?"

"I'll send you pictures," said Nikki sourly.

"Really? That would be great!"

"Uh-huh," Nikki said, edging into the elevator.

"Are you on your way up?"

"They want to see me," she answered glumly.

"Yeah, she's interviewing everyone," Rachel said, stepping out of the elevator. "I'll let you get up there. Have fun!" Rachel waved cheerfully as the doors closed.

Left alone in the empty elevator, Nikki felt a moment of panic as she tried to remember what to do next. Eventually she pushed the button for the top floor, and when the elevator stopped she picked up the phone and uttered the password for the week. Jane had e-mailed it to her before she left Thailand and Nikki had puzzled over it all the way to her Narita connection. In the end she'd found a bookstore in the airport and bought a copy of *Alice in Wonderland*.

> *Don't let him know she liked them best,*
> *For this must ever be*
> *A secret kept from all the rest,*
> *Between yourself and me.*

It was an obscure quote, and much like Alice, Nikki would have given a sixpence to have it explained to her. She was still pondering it when the doors opened. Jane was waiting for her.

She clapped her hands together and bounced up and down excitedly. "Nikki!" she squeaked, rushing forward to hug her. Nikki returned the hug somewhat awkwardly, feeling small scabs crack and bruises protest. "It's so good to see you. I'm so glad you're not dead!"

"Me, too," Nikki agreed fervently.

"Come on into the conference room." Jane began to speed-walk through the corridors. Nikki followed at a trot. "You know, if I'd known about Val being a double agent and everything I would have told you, right?"

"Uh, sure," Nikki agreed.

"Oh, and he's CIA, by the way."

"What?" Nikki asked, trying to keep up.

"The guy! You know, your boyfriend? I know you probably figured it out anyway, but I finally broke his cover story while you were on the plane home. He's definitely CIA."

"I kind of figured," Nikki said. "And he's not my boyfriend," she added halfheartedly.

"And if I'd known Dr. Hastings had figured it out, I would have told you first thing, if I could have," Jane said, switching topics as she turned a corner.

"Yeah. Of course," Nikki agreed, not knowing what else to say and puzzled by Jane's comment.

"I did the best I could by sending Ellen and Jenny to Mrs. Merrivel." Jane seemed anxious to clear things up, but she was only making Nikki more confused.

"Wait, Jane," Nikki said, following her into a book-lined conference room. "What happened while I was in Thailand?"

"Dr. Hastings was found to have been in dereliction of duty and was relieved of her position," said Mrs. Merrivel, looking up from the documents spread out in front of her on the conference table. She tucked her papers into a folder as Nikki entered.

"Mrs. Merrivel warned her about Val, but Dr. Hastings tried to cover it up instead of acting on it. That's why she kept piling work on me. She didn't want me to delve too closely into Val's case."

"She was hoping that Val would return of her own accord. Clearly that faith was misplaced," Mrs. Merrivel said coolly.

"And then Mrs. M had to come in and put the smack down," Jane said, triumphantly miming a WWF-class elbow.

"Well, let's just say I'm running the West Coast branch at the moment," Mrs. Merrivel said, smiling in bemusement at Jane's antics.

"Oh," Nikki said, unable to think of anything else. "That's good?"

"I like to think so," Mrs. Merrivel said. "Now, dear, why don't you take a seat? You're looking a little bit worse for wear."

"I came straight from the airport," Nikki said.

"Ick. Just driving by the airport makes me want a facial," Jane said. Nikki and Mrs. M stared at Jane, who blushed. "Well, not that I do, but honestly that place puts ten years on your skin—the fumes, the horrible lighting, and the recycled air . . ."

"True," agreed Mrs. Merrivel, and Nikki nodded. There was another pause while everyone tried to figure out how to get the conversation back to where it had been.

"I spoke to Laura this morning," said Mrs. M. "She spoke very highly of your efforts in Bangkok."

"She did?" Nikki asked, sounding dubious. "That was, uh, very nice of her."

"I take it you don't think your trip to Thailand was very successful?" Mrs. M asked, jogging her stack of papers with a firm thwack against the tabletop.

"It could have gone better," answered Nikki.

"You weren't instrumental in helping the Thai government apprehend Jirair Sarkassian?"

"Well, yeah, I mean I guess the piano is an instrument." Mrs. M smiled, and Nikki continued. "But I didn't bring in Val."

"Nikki, it isn't as though we could have brought Val to trial. And we certainly couldn't have allowed her to fall into the hands of any other intelligence agencies. She was a traitor and a threat to our organization."

Nikki swallowed hard, realizing what Mrs. Merrivel meant. "Even if I'd captured her, you would have killed her?"

"Yes. It's not something we're proud of, but it's a necessity."

"Well, I'm sure that makes Val feel all better," said Nikki bitterly.

"If Val had cared at all, she wouldn't have betrayed us in the first place. It's unfortunate, really. She was such a good agent, and now we'll have to remove her name from the 'Consultants of Note' plaque." Mrs. Merrivel shook her head sadly, but there was a cement hardness to her tone that made Nikki doubt her sincerity.

"But what's done is done," Mrs. Merrivel continued. "And I'm glad it's done. We will discuss matters after your reports and debriefing are concluded, but initial reports indicate that you did fairly well on your first assignment. At this time we would like to discuss further options with Carrie Mae."

Nikki nodded hesitantly, not sure what this was leading up to, but fearful that she'd end up back on the real front lines—selling lipsticks that had no explosive properties whatsoever. She just wasn't sure she was tough enough for that.

"Now, as you know, usually after the first assignment, agents are asked to join the company on either a full-time or a per-contract basis. We would like you to join full time. I'm thinking I would like to put you in charge of a new quick-response team I'm forming. Would you be interested in something like that?"

"I guess so," said Nikki. As usual when dealing with Mrs. Merrivel, her brain felt fuzzy.

"Excellent," Mrs. Merrivel said. She produced a contract from a folder. "This is simply an extension of your first contract, and all you have to do is sign at the bottom."

She offered Nikki an elegant black-and-gold pen. Nikki took the pen, but looked around the room instead of at the contract. Mrs. M was wearing a cream pantsuit with rubies, and Jane was wearing one of her plaid skirts, but had dignified the occasion by wearing heels instead of boots. Nikki, in her black T-shirt and jeans, was underdressed, sporting a black eye and a bad mood. Just as she was starting to feel the first pangs of inferiority, she had a sudden flashback to the evening she'd spent in jail. She remembered the brusque lawyer and the advice she had offered.

"Don't sign anything without reading it, and always ask for more than is being offered."

"Just on principle," she said, remembering.

"I beg your pardon?" Mrs. Merrivel asked with a polite smile, but a questioning lift to her eyebrow.

And then Nikki knew why Val had always smoked at Mrs. Merrivel's house. She didn't like being a little cog in a big machine. Val wanted to be remembered, even if it was badly. She liked to stand out. Nikki never stood out. At least she had never felt as though she did.

The sun was streaming in golden bars across the table, and as Nikki watched the dust motes dance, she had an epiphany. Her chin came up.

"Seventy-five thousand," she said, sitting back in her chair.

"I beg your pardon?" Mrs. Merrivel repeated, sounding more like Nikki's mother every minute.

"Seventy-five thousand a year, plus full medical and dental. I don't want co-pays. I don't want to split anything. I want you to cover everything from a facelift to a bullet through my skull. I want an insurance policy on my life, made out to the beneficiary of my choosing, for one million dollars, and I don't want to pay for an apartment while I'm living in this stupid state."

Mrs. Merrivel opened her mouth to speak, but Nikki thought of another demand.

"And I want Valerie Robinson's name left on the 'Consultants of Note' plaque as long as I'm alive."

For the first time in Nikki's speech Mrs. Merrivel smiled.

"Fifty thousand, medical and dental, plus the insurance policy. But you pay for your own apartment and Valerie's name goes."

"Sixty-five," Nikki countered. "And the name stays."

"That's more than double what we're offering you. Do you really think you're worth it?" Mrs. M asked with some asperity.

"Yes, I do," Nikki said, staring her in the eye. "You only ever gave me half the information I needed, and I not only figured it out, I lived."

"Sixty-thousand and Valerie stays on the plaque. That's my final offer."

Nikki stared at Mrs. M and tried to measure just how far she could push the matter. Mrs. M's smile was hard and there was a glint in her eye that told Nikki this was as far as she was going to go today. Nikki held out her hand. Mrs. Merrivel shook it with a smile, and for the second time that day, it seemed genuine.

"I assume John asked you to stay with us while you're looking for a place?"

The change of mood and topic was dramatic, and it threw Nikki off-balance.

"Uh, yes. I hope that's OK?"

"Of course. We're always glad to have you. I'll have Legal make the changes and bring the contract home tonight." Mrs. Merrivel stood up. Nikki and Jane followed suit. "You know, I knew you'd fit in perfectly here." She had the air of a baker pulling a perfect cake from the oven.

"I guess it's a good thing I won the starter kit then," Nikki said with a smile, thinking of the strange twist of fate that had brought her to this point.

"No. It's a good thing that I rigged the drawing. Jane will get you agent profiles and help you with team selection. Just give me your list of selections for approval when you're done." Mrs. Merrivel beamed at Nikki and Jane and then walked briskly from the room.

Nikki watched her leave and then turned around to look at Jane in bewilderment. Jane was grinning like the Cheshire Cat.

"Pick me, pick me," she said, bouncing up and down.

"For what, Jane? What did I just agree to?"

"You agreed to be a team leader, which is, like, a huge opportunity. She asked you to put together the team, so that means you get to pick everyone. This is so great! I get to be your analyst, don't I? Please, please."

"Yeah, sure, of course." Nikki was still reeling. "I knew she fixed it. I don't know how she did it, but I knew it. I knew I couldn't have been that unlucky!"

"Awesome," said Jane, ignoring Nikki's rambling. "We will pick the best team. This is going to be awesome!"

"Awesome," repeated Nikki, feeling lightheaded.

The Morning After

Mr. Merrivel helped Nikki angle the heavy box full of coffee table parts up the stairs and into her new apartment. They dropped it flat onto the floor, probably irritating the downstairs neighbors.

Nikki flopped onto the couch. "Thanks, Mr. M."

"Whew," he said. "Didn't think we were going to get it in here for a sec."

"You should have been here when they moved the couch in. I've never been a hire-movers kind of person, but I have to admit they were worth it."

Mr. M nodded. "It's one of the perks of having money. It makes it easier to get things done when you're by yourself. You know," he said, looking out the window and changing the subject. "I gotta say that's one heck of a car you got for yourself."

"It's . . . it *was* Val's. I figured she'd want someone who cared about it to have it."

"I doubt it. I expect she'd want to drop it off a cliff before someone else got to play with her stuff."

Nikki grinned. "I thought of that, too. And it still seemed like a good idea."

"What'd you do with her cat?"

"Gave it to Jane," answered Nikki with a guilty smile. Mr. M laughed. "You want a soda pop?" Nikki asked, going to the fridge.

"Sure, if you've got diet-something."

"Diet root beer?" she suggested, standing in the cold blast of the refrigerator. "You know I still cannot believe that apartments here don't come with refrigerators. I nearly had a heart attack when I saw how much they cost."

"There are apartments that come with refrigerators?" Mr. M asked, accepting a root beer and sitting down at the kitchen table.

"In Washington there are!"

"Huh. Must make it easy to move."

Nikki nodded and looked with some pride around her first very own apartment. It had taken two weeks to find it, and she had practically wiped out her bank account furnishing it, but it looked good. And there were bigger and better paychecks to come.

Thinking of paychecks reminded her of her new job, and she frowned. "You've hired people before, haven't you, Mr. M?" she asked, sitting down.

"And fired," he answered.

"How do you decide who's the best person to hire? I have to put together a team, but everyone looks really qualified. I don't know what I'm doing."

"Nikki," said Mr. M in exasperation. "You said that before you went to Thailand, and look how that turned out."

"It could have gone better," she said honestly.

"Sure, things can always go better, but you figured it out, didn't you? You persevered and trusted your instincts, and things came together. Be more confident!"

Nikki laughed. "That's why I like you, Mr. M. You're like my very own pep coach."

"Everyone needs a little pepping up now and again. And if you want actual advice about hiring, well, I find that the best way to hire people is face-to-face. A piece of paper can't tell you what you need to know about a person."

Nikki nodded.

"OK, sweetie, I'm off to do the golfing thing." He kissed the top of her head and ambled toward the front door. Nikki followed after him and waved goodbye from the front stoop. The phone was ringing as she shut the door, and she ran to answer it.

"Hello?"

"Nikki, what is this nonsense you just sent me?" Her mother's voice sounded crisply across the phone line.

"Just some stuff from Thailand, Mom," Nikki said with a sigh. "I told you I was going there for a conference. I thought you would like some souvenirs. There's some Thai silk and some pearls underneath the pictures and carvings."

"I don't think you should be spending that much money on souvenirs."

"They're really cheap in Thailand, Mom. And I just got a raise."

"A raise?" asked Nell skeptically. "You've only been with them a couple of months!"

"I did a pretty good job at the conference," Nikki said, taking the phone into the living room and lying down on the couch.

"Huh," said Nell. Nikki felt like laughing. Her entire life she had been under constant assault from her mother to better herself. Her post-collegiate life had been one barbed comment after another about her being a jobless slacker. Without that staple of conversation her mother was speechless.

"So, who are you dating?"

Nikki really did laugh. "Mom! I just got back from Thailand. I've barely had time to find an apartment. I don't have time to meet anyone new."

"Anyone new? So you broke up with the lawyer?"

"The lawyer?" Nikki repeated in confusion.

"That man with the nice voice."

"Oh, right, the lawyer." Somehow *lawyer* was not the term that sprang to mind when she thought of Z'ev.

"Will you be seeing him again?"

"He works in other countries, Mom. It wouldn't really work out."

"Well, you're not getting any younger, Nikki. I was married and had a child by the time I was your age."

"You had a child? Do I know her?" Nikki asked incredulously.

"Don't be strange, Nikki. You know what I mean."

Nikki could hear some rustling in the background.

"These elephants are kind of cute." Nikki congratulated herself on sending the elephants instead of the dragon-faced mask. "Oh! I just found the pearls. These are pretty!"

"I'm glad you like them, Mom. I wanted to get something you'd like."

"Well, I'll wear them to the office tomorrow."

There was a silence between the two of them as neither one could think of another time when they had been so in complete agreement. It was uncharted territory; they had sailed completely off the edge.

"Well, I should go," Nell said with verve. "I don't want to run up the phone bill."

"Yeah, sure. I won't keep you."

"Nikki . . ." There was a pause, and Nikki felt a moment of

panic. She had never heard her mother sound so uncertain. "I'm really glad you're doing well."

"Thanks, Mom." It was all Nikki could do to stutter out the words.

"But you know that it's all right to fail. You can always come home again."

Nikki sighed and thought about arguing. "Well, that's good to know, Mom. Bye."

"Bye."

Nikki hung up the phone and grinned. If her mother ever gave an unqualified compliment they would both keel over from the shock.

She looked around the apartment. Life was good. She had friends, money, a job, a really cool car, an apartment, and she had actually been praised by her mother. Why, then, did she feel this little empty spot? She rubbed her head. She knew why, and she knew who would fit perfectly into that spot. But he was in Thailand, and she wasn't going to think about him. It wouldn't do any good.

LOS ANGELES III
Discovering America

Nikki stepped off the elevator and into the lobby, feeling the urge to skip, but maintaining her grown-up facade. It had been a good day at work. Mrs. M had approved her final team list, a list that included Jenny and Ellen, who would soon be returning from their missions, and then she could begin team training sessions. She had several new ideas for the team. She'd been reading non-stop about tactics and training, and she couldn't wait to put some of her theories into practice.

She felt she had a right to the self-confident swagger she was strutting at the moment. She was beginning to feel as if she really belonged here. She shared her sense of well-being by smiling at the security guard as she passed the information desk. She instantly regretted the bold move when the guard called her name.

"Miss Lanier!"

Nikki turned with an inquiring expression, masking her sudden spasm of doubt. *Miss Lanier, you're wanted in the principal's office.*

"I was just about to call upstairs. There was a gentleman here looking for you," the guard said, looking concerned.

"Gentleman?" Nikki repeated, frowning.

"He was cute and had a really deep voice," said the information girl with a smile.

"We told him we couldn't let him upstairs or confirm that you were here," the security guard said repressively.

"But he left a note," the information girl added with a giggle.

Nikki took the note, which read I'LL BE AT THE BAR ACROSS THE STREET. Z. Nikki had the giggly, dizzy, elated feeling she used to get as a child when she'd whirl around as fast as she could until she fell down.

"I watched," said the information girl helpfully. "He went into the Lion and Unicorn."

"Thanks," Nikki said.

"Is there a problem?" asked the security guard. "Should I notify anyone upstairs?"

"No, I don't think so," Nikki said, shaking her head. She tucked the note into her purse and walked across the street.

The Lion and Unicorn was owned by a retired Carrie Mae consultant. It had a large wooden shield over the door showing a lion and unicorn fighting for a crown. The bar drew a high percentage of Carrie Mae employees and was usually busy during the lunch hour and after quitting time, but at three in the afternoon it was fairly quiet.

Nikki stood in the doorway, letting her eyes adjust to the gloom. Z'ev was sitting at the bar staring skeptically at a woman next to him. She was laughing loudly and had her hand on his thigh. Nikki walked toward them, her shoes making the usual warning clatter, but neither one of them noticed.

"Would you mind taking your hands off my husband?" demanded Nikki when she was standing behind them. The woman froze and narrowed her eyes at Nikki. Nikki stared back.

"Should have told me you brought the wife," she muttered, and flounced away from the bar.

"Now, what did you do that for? She was really nice," Z'ev said sarcastically.

"With our luck," Nikki said, taking the barstool next to his, "she'd turn out to be an Armenian gun smuggler."

"You have a point," conceded Z'ev, sipping his drink and watching her in the mirror behind the bar.

"So what are you doing in California?" asked Nikki, getting to the point.

"You know that guy who thought the world was round? And everyone told him it was flat and then he sailed around the world and proved it really was round?"

"Magellan?"

"No! The famous guy."

"You mean Columbus?"

"Yeah, that's the guy."

"What about him?"

"Well, I guess you could say I'm the Columbus of vacation time. I'm currently proving that it exists."

"Vacation time?" repeated Nikki incredulously. "Since when?"

"Since Monday. I would have been here sooner, but it took me two days to find you."

"You are seriously telling me that you are on vacation."

"Yes."

"For how long?"

"Two weeks."

"Two weeks with no bullets, bombs, or fistfights?"

"Not unless they're aimed at you," Z'ev said seriously.

Nikki ignored this comment and considered the prospect of two weeks with Z'ev. "So, you're going to be here for two weeks? That means we could go out to dinner and I could probably see you every day."

"Probably," Z'ev agreed, taking another sip of his drink.

"That would be so weird. It would almost be like having a boyfriend or something."

Z'ev's reserve cracked at that point and he laughed. "Or something. Hey, if I'm getting demoted to boyfriend, can we do stuff?"

"Do stuff?" Nikki asked, raising an eyebrow. Just what did he mean by that?

"Yeah, like Disneyland. I've never been, and everyone says that Pirates of the Caribbean is really great. And I kind of want to see the Chinese theater and all those sidewalk stars."

"Disneyland, Hollywood, sure. What about surfing?" asked Nikki with a laugh.

"Yeah, surfing. That'd be good, too."

Nikki found that she was grinning at Z'ev and he was grinning back. He took some cash out of his pocket and tossed it on the bar. "Come on," he said, standing up. "The world's not getting any rounder."

Nikki stood up, and when she did he reached for her and pulled her into a kiss.

"Nikki!" yelled Jane, bursting into the bar. Nikki groaned and buried her head in Z'ev's shoulder.

"Go away, Jane," she said, not moving her head.

Jane hopped from foot to foot in agitation. "There's a problem. A kind of big problem."

"Yeah?" Nikki said, finally looking at Jane.

But Jane had noticed Z'ev. "Oh golly, you're him, aren't you? You aren't supposed to be here."

Z'ev looked questioningly at Nikki, who shrugged.

"What kind of problem, Jane?"

"There's a, uh, package that's gone, uh, missing."

"Missing?" Nikki repeated, wondering what the hell Jane was babbling about.

"Missing," Jane answered. "Mrs. M says to come quick." Nikki looked back at Z'ev. He returned her gaze and shrugged. It was up to her.

Nikki tried to assess how likely it was that Mrs. Merrivel would fire her.

"Tell her I'm on vacation," said Nikki with a laugh, and she kissed her boyfriend.

Acknowledgments

Like Nikki, I am surrounded by amazing women who have supported and inspired me. Their efforts have not only shaped this novel, but myself as well. My aunt Linda inspired me to actually do something serious with my writing. Heather, Michal, and Michelle, who, when I confessed my brilliant idea for a book about the militant wing of a certain home-sales cosmetics giant, laughed at me, made up the Carrie Mae salute (chest thump, mascara twirl), but never ceased to encourage me. Juel's wit, assistance, and sage advice came always just at the right time. Theresa has been my champion in the battlefield of publishing. And Jennae. I could probably write an epic poem about the ways Jennae has helped me, but suffice it to say she has been my comforting shoulder to lean on, my true editor, and my friend for over a decade. Without these women, *Bulletproof Mascara* would not have made it from my head to the page or from my computer to print, and I cannot acknowledge or thank them enough, but for what it's worth—my undying thanks and love to all of you.